AN **OFFICER** AND A **GENTLEMAN'S** DAUGHTER

FILM AND TELEVISION PROJECTS BY DOUGLAS DAY STEWART

The Boy in the Plastic Bubble
STARRING JOHN TRAVOLTA
ABC MOVIE 1979
NOMINATED FOR AN EMMY FOR BEST WRITING
NOMINATED FOR A WRITERS GUILD AWARD FOR BEST WRITING

The Blue Lagoon
STARRING BROOKE SHIELDS
COLUMBIA PICTURES 1980

An Officer And A Gentleman
STARRING RICHARD GERE, DEBRA WINGER AND LOUIS GOSSETT JR.
PARAMOUNT PICTURES 1982
NOMINATED FOR ACADEMY AWARD FOR BEST ORIGINAL SCREENPLAY

Thief of Hearts
PARAMOUNT PICTURES 1984 (WRITTEN AND DIRECTED)

Listen to Me
COLUMBIA PICTURES 1986 (WRITTEN AND DIRECTED)

A – The Scarlet Letter
CINERGI PICTURES 1995

THEATRICAL PROJECTS BY DOUGLAS DAY STEWART

An Officer and a Gentleman – The Musical
TAKARAZAKA PRODUCTION 2010
SYDNEY, AUSTRALIA PRODUCTION 2012
UK TOUR 2018
US TOUR 2021-22
NEW UK TOUR 2024

AN **OFFICER** AND A **GENTLEMAN'S** **DAUGHTER**

ACADEMY AWARD–NOMINATED SCREENWRITER
DOUGLAS DAY STEWART

BLACKSTONE PUBLISHING

Copyright © 2024 by Douglas Day Stewart
Published in 2024 by Blackstone Publishing
Cover and book design by Alenka Vdovič Linaschke

All rights reserved. This book or any portion
thereof may not be reproduced or used in any manner
whatsoever without the express written permission
of the publisher except for the use of brief quotations
in a book review.

The characters and events in this book are fictitious.
Any similarity to real persons, living or dead, is coincidental
and not intended by the author.

Printed in the United States of America

First edition: 2024
ISBN 979-8-212-24464-0
Fiction / War & Military

Version 1

Blackstone Publishing
31 Mistletoe Rd.
Ashland, OR 97520

www.BlackstonePublishing.com

I dedicate this love story to the love of my life,
my beautiful Judith Ann Gersten Stewart,
who taught me the secret of trust,
and without whom I could never have evolved
into the writer I always hoped to be.

ONE

★★★

AMERICA'S FAVORITE SON

WASHINGTON, D.C.

May 30, 2008

Zack watched his bag loop a second rotation around the baggage carousel. Nothing in that large gray Navy-issue duffel but a reminder of his years of loneliness. A cramped captain's stateroom as squadron commander aboard a succession of aircraft carriers cruising the Mediterranean Sea. Endless hours at the gunwales of the floating cities, mourning his wife and missing their daughter.

Fortunately, the days were punctuated by merciful minutes of supercharged revenge, conducting aerial sorties with his squadron against the Taliban, which had sheltered Bin Laden and his fellow 9/11 plotters. With every kill, he was waging a personal war. The 9/11 attack, coming less than a month after Paula's tragic death, hit America's Favorite Son harder than most. His home had been attacked, then his homeland, causing him to conflate the two events. A victim of childhood abuse, his mind worked that way. From boyhood, it had been him against life, and life had dealt a near-death blow to him with the loss of his wife, and with his daughter's decision to deal with her grief by retreating into herself.

He fought back with smart bombs and Vulcan strafing guns. This dark passion for payback kept him alive. But revenge was a chemical that got into your blood and changed you. The warm tones of life, marriage, family, and love had retreated into caves of distant memory. But now he was home. Not for a visit. To stay. And he was even angrier than when he left. Where would he channel that anger now that his days of combat were over? The answer was obvious. Put an end to his war and form a family again with his fellow survivor, his favorite person in the world—his strong, precocious daughter, Shannon. But that wouldn't be easy. Paula's death had changed all that, and the six years that followed had opened a gap between them he never thought possible. Shannon had not picked up any of his calls in nearly a month.

His first hint of trouble came earlier in the year when her first poor grades caught up with him on the *USS Abraham Lincoln*, steaming in convoy with its sister ships in the Med. On their weekly call, he confronted her about it. "I'm trying to have some fun for a change, Dad," she explained. He wasn't sure what she meant. She was twenty-two, so it could be anything from drinking to having sex.

Later in the month, Zack received orders to come home to Oceana to head up the Fleet Replacement Squadron. At first, he was bitter that the Navy was retiring him from war. He knew with certainty that, at fifty-eight, he retained most of his skills in aerial combat and that the wisdom he had accumulated made up for anything he might have lost to age. He was still the only pilot in military history who had never lost a dogfight in a war or in war exercises. Luckily, the Navy had thrown him a bone. He would be the oldest man on record to be teaching in the cockpit of a military airplane.

After months of stewing about it, he finally resigned himself to leaving war behind and found hope that his orders might bring his beloved daughter back into his life. According to a plan that had been in place since she was eight years old, after graduating from college, Shannon would apply to Officer Candidate School, and two years later, if all went well, she would apply to the Fleet Replacement Squadron for jet training. This would put them together as head instructor and student. His hopes for his own future now rested on that happening.

Zack watched his bag move slowly toward him once again on the conveyor belt. An attractive middle-aged woman wearing a straw hat smiled and nodded at him as she waited for her luggage. Even at his age, Zack cut a fine figure in his dress whites. His unusually thick hair was now white, but he still had the piercing hazel eyes and compact physique that were his trademark as a young officer. The woman asked, "Were you away long?"

"Five years."

"Oh. Well, thank you." She was flirting. Zack smiled. Snatching his duffel, he tipped his officer's cap and walked out. The woman watched him appreciatively. There was a slight hitch in his stride that made him even more interesting. Here was a man who had lived life.

The white Lincoln Town Car that greeted him outside the airport to take him to the Pentagon held an important shine. Having missed his scheduled military flight from Kabul to Frankfort, Zack had been forced to take a commercial flight into DC to be on time for his own honorarium. He considered himself lucky that the Pentagon had sent a driver. In November of 2002, when he went back to the battlefield, the war on terrorism had still been a hot-button topic, but after watching their government spend a billion dollars a month for six years, it was something that most people now wanted to forget. By 2008, the world had moved on. Nine-eleven had become an annoyance, a thing that meant long lines at airport security. But Zack couldn't move on. He was stuck in 2001.

Settling into the back seat, he positioned the air conditioning vent toward his face and closed his eyes. An arctic breeze formed a mask around his face. It was the first time, in a long time, that his skin had felt cold and calm. In the Arabian Sea, an aircraft carrier was a nuclear furnace, and even the air-conditioned cockpit of a Super Hornet at 30,000 feet couldn't provide the relief he was getting now.

A short time later, a stout woman in a gray business suit, with a security badge and clipboard, greeted Zack at the Pentagon's front checkpoint, then shepherded him up an elevator and into a large, ornate banquet room with wall-to-wall beige carpeting and twenty blue chairs in eight neat rows facing a stage. Behind the podium, six flags representing the six branches of the military made a colorful backdrop. Zack noted each one with respect: Army, Marine Corps, Navy, Air Force, Coast Guard, Air National Guard.

To the right of the entrance was a banquet table with a few simple platters of finger foods and a cake. Mayo chuckled to himself. The Pentagon had substituted a low-key medal ceremony for the lavish ticker-tape parades that had sent the first wave to war. After all the years spent dedicating himself to a mission to eliminate Al-Qaeda, all he got on his return were cold vegetables and a store-bought sheet cake.

"Mission Accomplished!" The cake read in blue cursive, decorated with white frosting and red stars. And just like that, the last five years of his life became reduced to something to slice into, break apart, and chase down with a cup of coffee. The painful truth was that their mission had failed. After America had abandoned Iraq, Al-Qaeda was refashioning itself as ISIS, and the threat of terrorism to the world had escalated dramatically.

A small group of men and women in dress officer uniforms had assembled around the buffet table, eyeing the food, not knowing if they should serve themselves before or after the ceremony.

"Looks like a birthday party," observed a young male Marine lieutenant with a buzzcut.

"I was expecting something . . . bigger," added a Navy lieutenant commander in his midthirties.

A female Air Force lieutenant dryly observed, "I've seen more people than this in my parents' living room at Christmas."

"Couldn't they turn up the air a little in here?" questioned an Army Green Beret major in his early forties, wearing aviator sunglasses. "It's hotter in here than Zabul," he groused, wiping his brow.

"Poor baby," said an Army captain about the same age. "You were in the mountains, Major. Try to rack out with moon dust choking your lungs day and night."

A Marine Corps captain with a ruddy face said, "Try running bomb patrol on Chicken Street in full gear. I've seen fucking lizards melt."

"Shit," they all said in unison.

Zack studied the group of officers, many of whom were a good two decades younger than he was. He was the only one in the group adorned with so many combat medals, the only one with a serious collection of wrinkles.

He turned suddenly to the Marine wearing the sunglasses and casually inquired, "Were you at FOB Abu Ghraib, Major?"

The proud officer glanced at the man who had addressed him. "First Battalion, Fourth Infantry Regiment."

"Heard it was summer camp up there," Zack jousted.

"Til it was a bloodbath," the younger officer retorted testily. "Couple of Super Hornets bailed us out, thank the fucking Lord, or I wouldn't be here today."

"One of those FA/18s was me," Zack offered with a wink.

The officer took off his sunglasses, his eyes widening as he put the pieces together. "Captain Mayo?" he sputtered. Zack was a legend, nicknamed "American's Favorite Son" after his heroics during the Gulf War. His five "kills" in aerial combat against Iraqi pilots had earned him widespread recognition as the first "Ace" since Vietnam.

Just then, two officers Zack's age entered and waved to him from the door. The short one with the trim mustache and dark eyes was Captain Emiliano Della-Serra. The tall Black man with the shoulders of a bear was Captain Louis Perryman. The three had met thirty-five years ago in Officer Candidate School, the year the Vietnam War ended, and had worked together as a unit for most of their careers. Zack was the pilot, and Emiliano and Louis were his skilled maintenance and operations officers. Over the decades, they had saved each other's asses more times than they could count, in war and in the most personal of ways: marriage, divorce, death of a child, death of a wife.

Leaving the idle chatter of the young officers, Mayo joined his friends. "Jesus Christ, where have you been? I'm babysitting kindergartners over there."

"Their first awards ceremony, how precious . . ." chuckled Della-Serra.

"And probably our last," said Perryman in his gravelly Texas drawl. He bellied up to the table and casually made himself a plate of food, not much caring if he should wait or not.

Two young women in Marine Corps uniforms began to lay out

medals on a table near the dais that faced the chairs, and Della-Serra commented in a sarcastic voice, "Sorry, boys and girls, no key to the 'Admiral's Club,' but how about a five-dollar medal?" His friends chuckled grimly. This promised to be a hard day for the veteran warriors.

"You could have, at least, warned us you'd be MIA on that flight, boss," said Perryman.

"You kidding? I loved that place so much I didn't want to leave," Mayo lied glibly. His friends laughed. Nobody ever used the word "love" in conjunction with duty in the Middle East. The truth was, the morning of that flight, he had just blanked out. He woke up on a golf course mid-putt.

His friends saw through his bravura. People who live together in combat know each other better than any mate could hope to. They knew their boss was fighting re-entry with the same urgency as he had fought to join them a year after the Twin Towers fell. They were all war junkies, but Zack led the pack in that regard.

"Honorees, welcome to the Pentagon," intoned a voice thick with an Alabama accent over the public address system. Secretary of the Navy, SECNAV, Topper Daniels, a short, overweight civilian with dyed-red hair that revealed a botched hair transplant, stood at the dais, flanked by two admirals with braided shoulder boards. Some civilians and service personnel from the building had joined the small crowd, but the turnout remained sparse.

The twenty officers from the first wave of assault after 9/11, sixteen men, four women, were called forward and pinned with medals recognizing their individual accomplishments. SECNAV called Zack's name last. He had joined the war effort a year late, but this was the main event, and everyone knew it. A best-selling biography about him entitled *One Man's War* had been published in 1982 and had been widely read in the military community.

"Finally," Daniels said with an unctuous smile that didn't match his flinty eyes, "Captain Mayo."

Zack got up from his chair and went to the podium with all the excitement of someone walking to his own execution. The two men took each other in with a sense of history. They were the exact same age, but Zack had weathered the years better. There was a weakness to SECNAV's plump features that suggested an over-privileged life. His hands and fingers were soft and doughy, his wedding ring so tight on his finger that it threatened to cut off the flow of blood to the rest of his body.

"America salutes you for your patriotism, sir," said Topper Daniels in his oily twang.

Zack wanted to laugh, even though nothing about this man standing so close to him was funny. Topper Daniels had been Zach's self-appointed adversary for his entire career. Their rift had begun as young men at OCS when Zack laughed at Topper for not fighting back against Foley in the martial arts ring. It reached a boiling point when Zack easily passed the dreaded Dilbert Dunker and Topper panicked and failed. To Zack's eyes, Topper had been a misfit for this program from the start, and he cheered when he dropped on request.

By itself, this was not enough to warrant over three decades of enmity between the two men. Topper came from a line of famous aviators and had been expected to achieve glories like they had. Instead, he had "bilged out" of OCS and did not serve in the military, rising to power as a civilian in the Department of the Navy until he held the top position, Secretary of the Navy. In the meantime, Zack became the military hero Topper was supposed to have been. Zack knew that it had been Topper's vote that had knocked him and his friends, Perryman and Della-Serra, out of the admiral's club.

"It is my honor, sir, to welcome you home," droned SECNAV ingenuously. There wasn't anything heartfelt about the words coming out of his mouth, and he and Zack both knew it. They were doing their dance. Topper saluted and Zack dutifully returned the salute.

"Thank you, Mr. Secretary," he managed through clenched teeth. He felt an awkward energy every time he spoke to this man.

"Today, it is my supreme honor to award you with the Air Medal with Combat Valor," intoned Topper, reaching for the last of the medals on the table and clearly enjoying the moment too much. He had won their war, and they both knew it.

Zack's chiseled jaw tightened as he was pinned. This was a death sentence. It was akin to the gold watch ceremony dreaded by every working man or woman. It signaled that the end of the road was near. After a two-year tour as head instructor of Fleet Replacement, Zack would be out the door. As a civilian with the State Department, Topper had no such age limits and would be in power for years to come. The shorter man's rodent eyes blazed with personal triumph.

"As a tribute to your continued excellence in Naval Aviation, it is my privilege to inform you that you will be the oldest pilot in Naval history to be teaching in the cockpit. Enjoy this last lap, sir. You have certainly earned it."

Zack respectfully saluted Daniels again before he stormed off the small stage, past the cake, and out the door. Perryman and Della-Serra exchanged looks of concern.

As Zack entered a long corridor, he could feel his heart pounding in his chest like knuckles banging on a door. He stopped suddenly and turned to face a wall adorned with historical photos in alabaster frames. He felt like putting a fist through the wall. The whole event was a set-up to embarrass him. He had been the poster boy for the Navy, the most decorated pilot of all time. But Topper Daniels had just made him feel as expendable as a gallon of Haze Gray paint.

"Rough day?" a familiar female voice said from behind him. It was smooth and gentle. He held his hands to the wall, processing the voice—one from his past, so close to his soul. He turned slowly toward the woman, and their eyes connected immediately. She moved in closer. Both of their faces softened into smiles.

"Mayonnaise," she said. She wore working whites with the shoulder boards of a vice admiral.

"See-gar," Zack whispered. He quickly corrected, "Vice Admiral Seegar." Casey had recently been elevated to that high office. This made her the highest-ranking woman in the armed services. As Navy Chief of Staff, she was directly under Topper Daniels in the chain of command.

"One of us has to deal with the ogre in the room," she answered, glancing toward the banquet room where SECNAV was pumping some admiral's hand solicitously. They had both been there the day Topper had failed the Dilbert Dunker and "bilged out" of OCS. Casey's good fortune was that she was a woman and had not alienated the complex young man.

"You look good, Zack," she said at last. Her eyes were bright, her shoulders strong, her short-cropped hair now revealing wisps of gray. She was a vibrant woman, and she could tell he thought so. They had enjoyed a subtle chemistry that preceded Paula by several weeks, and they both remembered those nascent feelings all these years later.

After their casual flirtations during the first three weeks at OCS, when they were confined to base, Casey was looking forward to dancing with Zack at the formal naval ball that would launch their first weekend of freedom. Growing up under a domineering father, she had had little experience with men, and she found herself drawn in a primal way to this handsome loner from the wrong side of the tracks.

She would always remember the night of that ball in a bittersweet way. Zack entered with their classmate Sid Worley. After three weeks in work khakis, his hair shorn to a stubble in the "Poopie" way, as the candidates were referred to in those first three weeks, Zack was a poster in his dress whites. The band was playing "Tie a Yellow Ribbon Round the Ole Oak Tree." As Casey watched helplessly, the two young men were introduced to two local girls, brunette Paula Pokrifki and her blonde friend, Lynette Pomeroy, and the rest was history.

Casey had carried a secret crush for her old classmate throughout her life. At least, in the beginning, it was a secret. As dynamic women of their time, she and Paula became good friends over the years. One day, over a champagne lunch in a popular DC restaurant near the Capitol building, Casey confessed her feelings for her friend's husband. Paula wasn't surprised, and when she told Zack, he just laughed. He was not stupid. He had always felt a special energy from Casey.

Casey took out a pen and wrote something on a piece of paper. "My new private numbers," she explained, "if you ever want to talk."

Zack took the paper. He noticed that she had labeled the first number "HOME IN DC" and the second "LAKE HOUSE."

"How are the fish biting?" he asked pointedly.

"I'm a fish-catching machine," she boasted. He recalled that she had said the same thing five years earlier at her lake house when he had visited to congratulate her on becoming a rear admiral, the only one of their original group to reach that goal. Their eyes remained joined for a long moment. That trip would always evoke difficult memories for the two friends.

"The old gang is proud of you, Case," said Zack sincerely. "The highest-ranking woman in the military." Then he added, "I told you you'd do it."

"You told me," she echoed warmly. Then her tone became more serious. "You were over there a long time, Zack. Why so long?"

Zack shook his head as if trying to make sense of it himself. "I never expected to stay so many years. It gets in your system. You think one more kill will do it. Then it's the one after that. You've been there. War's funny. In the moment, it becomes your everything, but it has no magic on a sunny day."

Casey smiled. "You're a poet now? I wonder what Paula would say about this new you." The moment she said the words, she cringed.

Zack stared back in physical pain. She was the only friend he had allowed to see his grief in any way. This had happened during that fishing trip. He trusted his male friends with his life, but not in matters of the heart. "My God, Casey, I miss her more today than when it happened," he confided. "I thought, if I stayed away long enough, that it would get better. But it didn't."

"It will," she soothed. "You and Shannie will be back together soon. I know she's excited. We spoke a few weeks ago."

Zack's brow creased with concern. "How did she sound? I haven't been able to reach her for a month."

Casey seemed to have a lot she wanted to say, but at that moment, an aide dashed up and whispered something in her ear. The aide ran off, and Casey turned back to Zack apologetically.

"I have a fire to put out," she explained. Then she said, "Shannie's struggling just like you, Zack. This change will be good for both of you." Smiling her Midwest cheerleader smile, she walked away.

Zack clenched his jaw and studied her slender frame as she rounded the corner out of sight. In so many ways, she and Paula were alike. It was no wonder they had become best friends. He made a mental note to call Casey in a few weeks, maybe meet her in the city for dinner. A congratulatory dinner. Nothing more. Nothing had changed since that lake trip. He still saw everything through a lens called "Paula."

Back at the hotel room, Zack stared at his duffel for a long moment before opening it. The sight of its contents made him recoil as if they gave off a putrescent odor. There was, in fact, no smell. And the contents of the bag could not be more orderly. They told the story of a man whose life had been reduced to what he could fit in a canvas container. On top of his clothing was his framed photo of "The Core Three" that accompanied him everywhere. It was taken on a family trip to Rehoboth Beach, Delaware, shortly before Paula's death. Three whackos, clowning their asses off outside a street fair. He had asked a stranger to take it.

He decided not to bother unpacking and went to the bar to have a drink.

The hotel bar was modern. Smooth jazz played softly in the background. Zack put his "cover," as they called the gold-braided hats, on the counter and sat down, favoring his bad hip. He ordered a whiskey and shot it straight back before ordering another.

An attractive woman in her late thirties sat next to him and ordered a cosmo. She was dark-haired and petite and reminded him of Paula. In her tailored black Ralph Lauren pantsuit, it was obvious she worked out. Paula had also been a fitness freak.

"Going to an official occasion?" she asked, taking in his dress whites and all the combat ribbons, including the new one.

"Just came from one," he said with a grin that took twenty years off his age. "I needed a drink to reset my clock."

"You're a Navy officer, right?" She took in his wings. "A pilot?"

"Yep. Temporarily," he said, taking a thoughtful sip from his drink. "I'm on my last assignment." He hoped she would say something about how young he looked to be on the cusp of retirement, but her mind was in another place.

"My boyfriend died overseas," she offered out of nowhere. It often started like that for Zack. He was a symbol of something, just as she was a symbol of something. The young woman served up a slightly off-center smile. It wasn't Paula's captivating, amused, sly grin, but it was an approximation.

"You're married?" she asked, eyeing his wedding ring.

"Was. She died." He removed the ring and put it in his jacket pocket.

"You didn't have to do that," she said.

Zack wasn't sure why he had taken off his ring. He was lonely, but he already knew the outcome if he tried to take her to his room. The first sign of his "little problem" came nearly a year after Paula's death. Subsequent efforts with strangers like this girl had netted the same results. He was the very definition of a one-woman man.

"Are you staying in this hotel?" she asked in a way that made her intentions even clearer.

"Yes," he replied. He drained the last of his glass. It was time to make his own intentions known. "I'm sorry if I misled you," he began. "It's been a rough day, and I was looking for some company. Thank you." He put down cash to pay for their drinks and rose from his stool.

The woman was disappointed, but she was a sensitive person who could relate to the pain in this older man's eyes. "Get some rest, Captain," she said warmly.

Zack returned to his room. He stripped out of his dress uniform and hung it neatly in the closet. He set an alarm on his phone before crawling into bed and turning off his light. He thought of calling his daughter again. But he was secretly a little hurt by her failure to return his recent calls.

He decided to surprise her as he had done when she was in eighth grade. After a long absence, he had shown up in his dress whites and carried her out of her classroom in his arms, just as he had carried her mother out of that factory. Paula had accused him of "recycling." That moment of old-school chivalry had worked miracles. Maybe it would do the same now.

TWO

★ ★ ★

AN OFFICER'S DAUGHTER

UNIVERSITY OF VIRGINIA

June 1, 2008

Things started to look familiar as the lush green campus came into view at 5,000 feet. Shannon Mayo knew what she was doing was reckless. There had to be some cardinal rule on the books forbidding it, but she didn't care. She just wished she had the audience that mattered. But her father was in Iraq bombing the shit out of Al-Qaeda.

Fuck it, she decided. It would be worth it anyway.

She touched the cool, smooth surface of the dials on the control panel of the little four-seater Cessna 172. Four glass dials to the left, four dials to the right of the yoke. Clock in the middle. Her father had taught her how to fly when she was fourteen, and every year she had met the requirements of her license. The clock read 1300 hours EST. It was graduation day, and she planned to go out with a bang.

Shannon had her mother's looks, brown hair that fell into chocolate drops past her shoulders, eyes that smiled when she spoke. She had inherited her father's strong jaw and proud chin, his compact, athletic frame. Her eyes were a color of blue you seldom saw. The result was that she was frighteningly beautiful in a way that made her intimidating to both women and men.

To detract from the unfair power her beauty gave her, she had foresworn makeup and boasted piercings in her nose, ears, and lip. As a twenty-two-year-old woman entering her prime, it was getting harder and harder to hide her breathtaking beauty, but that didn't stop her from trying.

The tattoo proudly displayed on the left side of her neck was another departure from her mother's more traditional appearance. It was a way to distract the viewer, to throw up smoke and mirrors to hide her painfully sensitive interior. The tat consisted of the initials "PPM", woven together in an angry gallic cursive, and contained by a halo of fire employing every color in the tattooist's pallet. She had gotten it a year ago as a tribute to her mother.

A dip caused her belly to rise. She never got over that sensation, no matter how many hours she had clocked behind the stick. "You guys okay?" she inquired of her friends. Her three passengers tittered. A bunch of rebellious eccentrics usually swimming in a fog of pot smoke, the girls were bright-eyed in the tight cabin. Today they were a brat pack of activists fighting against the constructs of traditional higher educational systems, or, at least, that's what they'd told themselves. They had been planning this mission since the start of the school year and knew that they would be front-page news the next morning. Shannon glanced over her shoulder, careful not to knock off her mortarboard cap in the tight quarters. The two girls in the back held laundry baskets filled with water balloons.

Shannon had awakened that morning with a sense of dread about the future. It had been the plan forever that she would follow college by attending Officer Candidate School, with the goal of going on to jet training. But after a year on the party trail, the prospect of entering a military world was forbidding.

She wished she could share her conflict with her roommate, Annie, the lanky, all knees and elbows girl seated up front with her, but she hadn't shared her secrets with anybody since her mother died. Nobody really knew her. She was that girl with the too-blue eyes. She was where the party was.

Annie lit a joint and passed it to Shannon, who took a big hit before passing it to the girls in the back. "Here we go," announced Shannon, banking the small plane sharply to the left. Maybe too sharply. She adjusted quickly, earning her a relieved smile from Annie, whose mousy brown hair boasted streaks of bright purple that matched her graduation gown.

"Big day, huh?" asked Annie. "Tomorrow, we have to become grownups." Annie was the smartest of the bunch next to Shannon. She had a quirky attractiveness, and she loved to party.

"Or not," replied Shannon, and they shared a naughty laugh. "Buckle your seatbelts, girls," she instructed as she began her descent. The sudden dip caught them all by surprise again.

"Oh, fuck!" exhaled Annie.

Shannon glanced over as Annie's purple-streaked hair caught the sunlight in a way that sent forces into motion. Sudden bursts of light or sound were usually the culprits, but anything could do it. A line of dialogue in a movie. A lyric from a song. The smell of something burning. Shannon tried not to close her eyes because she knew, if she did, she would be in the middle of one of her "day-mares" as she called the panic attacks that had assaulted her since her mother's death, terrifying episodes where she was literally transported into her mother's shoes as she burned alive.

"Fucking A!" She heard Kimmy laugh shrilly behind her. "I can't believe we're really doing this." Her words yanked Shannon out of her day-mare and refocused her on the plan.

"Don't get chickenshit on me now," she warned. Flying closer to the target, they could make it out now, a banner over the outdoor proscenium proclaimed: CONGRATULATIONS, CLASS OF 2008!

"Happy graduation, ladies," Shannon declared. "Let's do this." As she descended on the gathering below, she pushed open her side window to get ready. The drill of the twin engines was jarringly loud. The girls in the back excitedly handed out water balloons, opened their windows, and positioned themselves for a shot.

"Get lower!" yelled Michelle whose toplessness under her graduation gown was exposed by the wind. "I want to make sure I hit my mom's new boyfriend, Rick."

As her friends searched for family members, Shannon barely took notice. She hadn't spoken to her father in over a month. Thirty feet off the ground, they could make out faces. It was a safe height to drop their missiles. Shannon tossed the first balloon and shouted, "Bombs away!"

"Bombs away! Bombs away!" They released their balloons in a flurry, and they splattered around the guests, disrupting the ceremony.

Wild laughter exploded in the cockpit.

Then Shannon's face drained of color as she saw the figure below. In his dress whites, her father stood out like a klieg light. His head was turned up. He was frowning.

"Oh, fuck," she muttered. What came next was totally unplanned. Her too-blue eyes hardening with a terrifying resolve, she came out of her dive and flew toward a bell tower with a wide oval opening at the top.

Realizing her intent, her three friends began a chorus of objections.

"Shannon, no!" shouted Kimmy.

"Don't do it!" screamed Michelle.

"It's too small!" Annie wailed. As Shannon's best friend and roommate, they had shared some wild adventures, but this was outright crazy.

"Only one way to find out," Shannon said. After all the years holding it inside, here was her chance to make a statement. A fuck-you to the fickle finger of fate that had rocked her life, the choking self-doubt that came in the same package, the heart-shrinking loneliness she had suffered with a party girl smile for too long.

And she had the audience she wanted: her father.

The opening in the bell tower was thirty-seven feet, two inches. She knew the exact dimensions because the tower was a subject of extreme pride on campus, and freshmen were required to know all the details about its history and dimensions. More than a few times over the past four years, she had imagined what it would be like to fly through that narrow opening. And now she was doing it.

She quickly did the math. Knowing the dimensions of her rented craft, she had a margin of thirteen inches. *Piece of cake.* Her friends watched with eyes that grew larger and larger as the small plane flew through the opening, coming scant inches from clipping off a wing and spiraling to its doom. Insane laughter filled the cockpit, and Shannon let out a defiant cry that came from some cavern within her.

"Yaaaaaa!!"

Despite their euphoria, her three passengers reacted to Shannon's primal cry by meeting eyes in shared awareness of how close they had come to death and how little they really knew their leader. There was madness in those sapphire eyes that went beyond college hijinks.

On the ground with the rest of the family and guests, Zack was not surprised. Shannon had been a handful since she was born, always taking risks she shouldn't take, her spirit untamable, but he'd never seen her take a chance like this. He had attempted some wild things in his life, but he had never risked a margin so tight. He knew, in that moment, that his daughter was welcoming him home from war with a one-finger salute.

The thrill of Shannon's accomplishment was short-lived. A police helicopter summoned by campus police appeared beside the small plane like a bloated walrus, a uniformed officer in the bay with a bullhorn to his lips. "State Police," bellowed the officer. "Land immediately! You are under arrest!"

"Shit," moaned Shannon. "Toss everything," she ordered her shaken crew. "Do it!" she screamed when no one moved. As she made a wide loop toward the airport, the police chopper close behind, the girls dumped a few joints, a small vial of pills, and the remaining water balloons.

As the Cessna touched down at the small commercial airfield where Shannon had rented the aircraft, the four girls were met by just about the entire Charlottesville police department and a half-dozen state troopers, with weapons extensive enough to take on a cartel. When they stepped out of the airplane in their gowns and high-tops, there was a moment of comical confusion among the army waiting for them.

The Charlottesville police station was newer on the inside than Shannon had expected. Her friends were guided to separate rooms to be questioned while she was booked immediately and put in a cell.

She pushed down her fear. She was good at that. The past six years had made her an expert. She had known, when she decided to fly through that bell tower, that it would kick up waves. That had been her plan. She had spent the past year as Icarus, and the next chapter would be a collision with the sun. Unless something changed.

The sunlight that came from down the hall slowly disappeared. The thought of spending the night in jail didn't worry her. What worried her was that her father would bail her out like all the other times and her cry for help would go unheard. She wondered if her friends were back in the dorm, laughing their heads off.

"Mayo," a police officer's voice broke the silence. The cell door opened, and she recognized the officer as the one who had handcuffed her at the airport. He had been gentle with her and seemed decent.

"Shannon Mayo, you're out," he drawled in a smooth Virginia accent. His face glowed like a fan who'd just met his favorite entertainer. "Your father's a great man," he stammered. "He gave me his autograph for my little boy." Shannon could not count the times she had heard words like this.

He'd saved her again. She was doomed.

Zack stood outside the police station, still in his dress whites. To Shannon's eyes, he wore the same disappointed look he'd had the last time she'd pulled one of these stunts. Midway through her sophomore year of college, she had been charged with smoking pot in her dorm. Zack had lectured her bluntly about drugs, then, in his usual fashion, got the crime expunged from her record. This incident was far worse, and they both knew it.

"My God, Shannon," he erupted. "You were inches from killing yourself and your friends."

"If you're going to berate me for a stupid little prank, then don't bother driving me home," she said defensively.

He said nothing. He hadn't seen her since a brief trip in the spring. Seeing her this close for the first time in several months, he was stunned by the amount of weight she had lost. With the sun low in the sky, the air was cooler, and the tank top and cutoffs underneath her graduation gown weren't enough to keep her warm.

Zack handed her his crisp white military suitcoat, and she wrapped it around her slender shoulders. The warmth and smell of his clothing were comforting, and she took a moment to breathe him in. Then she saw that his eyes were trained on her neck.

"What the hell is that?" he asked disgustedly.

All the warmth she had felt dissolved in an instant. She had designed the bold tattoo herself. She'd hid it at Christmas under a parade of turtlenecks. On his spring trip, she had refused to go to the beach with him for fear of his seeing it. Now it was right there in his face.

"You have a tattoo as well," she remarked in their give-and-take way. This was how they'd talked in their halcyon years, as sidekicks, pals, running mates.

Their eyes came together. He knew the initials were Paula's. He understood the symbolism of the halo of fire. It dawned on him, in that moment, that, while he had spent five years fighting an unwinnable war, she had been jousting with windmills of her own. He wanted to put his arms around her, but he stopped himself. Something in her demeanor wasn't inviting it. Six years stood between them like an unscalable wall. That clock had started with Paula's death.

Zack opened the passenger door of his perfectly maintained black 2008 Corvette Stingray, and she got in. Shannon put her hands in the pockets of his coat and was surprised when she felt what she thought was a ring. While her father went to the driver's door, she took it out and studied it. It was her father's wedding ring. The gold still held its shine. She wondered if he had taken it off for a liaison and had forgotten to put it back on in his hurry to make his morning flight. Not wanting to know the truth, she slid it back inside and said nothing.

They drove in silence along the streets of Charlottesville. When he made the turn toward Route 29 going south, she said, "Dad, my dorm's the other way."

"I'm taking you home. You can come back to pack up the rest of your belongings in a few days."

Shannon's original plan had been to party for a week straight with her friends, but she was exhausted after her adventure, and the thought of being home sounded nice, especially since her dorm room was pretty much all boxed up. She closed her eyes and slept through the three-hour ride to Oceana Beach.

Shannon sleepily followed her father into the two-story Moorish home her parents had purchased when her mother's income began soaring in 1998. Before that, the family had lived in officer housing on the base. Shannon collapsed onto her bed, the only bed she'd ever really loved to sleep in.

When she eventually woke up, the sun was high in the sky. She looked at the clock, and to her surprise, it was almost noon the next day. She was sick to her stomach, her mouth was dry, and there was a slight tremor in her hands. On the kitchen counter was a note from her father saying he'd gone to the PX to get groceries and would be home to fix her lunch.

Shannon held her body against the counter, trying to steady herself. She was dizzy. Her throat felt like sandpaper. She went to the small powder room off the kitchen. Everything was the same. Same pictures, same hand towels, same bar soap. Nothing had changed. *Please, please, please,* she thought. She opened the medicine cabinet, hoping she would find something to calm her prickly edge. There was nothing but a small vile of sample cologne and a jumbo bottle of Tums.

"Dammit," she said. Then, looking more carefully behind the Tums, she spotted the familiar orange label, a bottle of prescription medication her father took for his hip and back pain. She pulled it out and smiled like she had just been reunited with an old friend.

"Hello, Cotton. Fuck yeah," she whispered. Turning on the faucet, she popped a couple of pills in her mouth, then bent down, her mouth hitting the cool stream of water.

Shannon's involvement with opioids had begun at the end of her junior year, when she was prescribed OxyContin for a torn rotator cuff that she had suffered while leading her tennis team to a state championship. The drug had crept up on her like a subway pickpocket. That summer, her best nights were with Oxy.

But after that, her senior year was a train wreck. Her grades fell. She quit tennis and student government. She hardly thought about her dream to fly jets. She told herself she was finally mourning her mother, but in truth, she was hiding even deeper from the pain and guilt she associated with that horrific, life-altering day.

When she walked out of the bathroom, she was already starting to feel better. She went to the liquor cabinet and stared at the contents.

When Zack arrived home, she was sitting in a stiff-backed dining room chair in the living room in shorts and a tee that read "University of Virginia Tennis," a glass of clear liquid in her hand. In the afternoon light from a garden window, Zack could see that her face was pinched with worries too profound for someone her age.

"How're you doing?" he asked with some concern.

"How does it look like I'm doing?" she complained. "Finals nearly killed me." She took a swallow from her glass and saw him staring. "What're you looking at?"

"Nothing," Zack assured her. Casey Segar's words returned to him like a clap of thunder. *Shannie's struggling just like you, Zack. Your return home will be good for both of you.* "What's in that glass, sweetheart?" he asked casually.

"Water."

"Let me taste it."

"No."

He took it from her, spilling some on his hand. "Jesus Christ, Shannon, this is vodka." He put the glass down on a table, his mind turning in dark ways. At Christmas, she had drunk a lot of wine.

"Were you drinking in that plane yesterday?"

"No. Of course not." She didn't mention the pot.

"Do you know why you're not still locked up back in Charlottesville?" he demanded.

"Your buddy from Afghanistan?" she answered flippantly. There was always a buddy from Afghanistan. "I heard you gave out autographs." Her knee began to pump up and down with a life of its own. He remembered that it had pumped like this at Christmas.

"They found the pills one of you tossed. Opioids." He let the words sit out there in the silence, hoping to hear some denial.

Her knee pumped harder.

"Were they yours, Shannon?" Nothing. Her jaw was locked tightly, and her knee kept doing its thing. "I asked you a question, Shannon."

"Why are you always on my case about something?" she demanded irritably.

"Maybe that's the problem," he snapped. "I've never been on your case about anything. That was Mom's job."

"Everyone in college does drugs, Dad," announced his daughter. "Kids snort it off their desks between classes."

Zack saw fear in her eyes, and Shannon saw fear in his.

Her knee was a telegraph key. It was telling a story.

"What's going on, baby?" he asked softly. When she didn't answer, he glanced in the direction of the bathroom. She had left the door open, and he could see the familiar vial she had left on the sink. He marched into the bathroom and shook the bottle. It was empty. "Those are my back meds," he exhaled. "Jesus Christ, Shannie, are you high right now?"

She faced him with her cobalt eyes. She wanted this moment of truth. She had engineered it and craved it more than the rush of drugs. She was so tired from her year of excess that her soul hurt. She wanted to come home.

"Daddy, I'm scared," she whispered, her lower lip quivering like a child's.

Zack felt like crying. She hadn't called him daddy in years. This was the first time since Paula's death that she had opened up to him. Shannon began to sob, and he rushed to her and held her tightly in his arms. "Easy, baby, easy," he soothed. "We'll beat this like everything else."

Shannon wanted to give in to his embrace. She wanted to melt into him and be a kid again. But things were too complicated. Her eyes found a photo of her mother on the wall. In her mind, Paula seemed to be judging her harshly for her lack of character. Wrenching free from her father's embrace, she picked up her empty glass, and threw it at the picture, hitting it squarely, glass shattering everywhere.

"Shannon!" yelled a stunned Zack, staring in horror at the battered photo and the shards of glass that now divided him and his daughter. If one still frame could capture the unspoken volumes of the past six years, this was it. Two people, who had been closer than thieves, didn't know each other anymore.

Shannon bolted from the room. In the garage, she found her black 2001 Harley Super Glide under a tarp. It had been her sweet sixteen birthday present. Next to her tennis rackets on a wall, she found a helmet with flames adorning the sides, and she put it on. She opened the garage door and prayed, "Please start, please start." And to her surprise, it did.

Zack was waiting for her on the street, his arms raised. "Don't go. We need to deal with this together."

Shannon swerved to a stop short of hitting him. "How do you propose we do that?" she shouted. "We haven't faced anything together in years."

"Whose fault is that?" he challenged. "You shut the door on me when Mom died."

Shannon struggled to contain her emotions. "I've told you a million times. I was just dealing with it the only way I knew how," she insisted.

"How do you plan on handling this?" he demanded. "You're strung out on drugs, Shannie. You need to enter a facility where they specialize in these things."

"A facility?" she sputtered. "I can quit any time I want. Everything can be like we planned."

"Baby, I don't think you understand," he interjected. "With drugs on your record, the Navy won't consider you for OCS."

Shannon stared back at her father like she'd just been slapped. Her fingers tightened on the accelerator, and the engine bellowed like an angry elephant.

"Don't go, Shannie," pleaded Zack. "I mean what I said. We'll take this on together."

Shannon fishtailed away in a report of burning rubber. Hitting the open road, she cranked back on the throttle and, in no time, was doing a hundred miles per hour. With no chance of Officer Candidate School in her immediate future, her road was clear. She was on her way to Virginia Beach to party.

THREE

★★★

FLEET REPLACEMENT SQUADRON

OCEANA BEACH, VIRGINIA

Two Years Later — December 2010

"Big day, Lieutenant Saunders. You ready?" Zack spoke calmly into his oxygen mask. The call sign printed in black on the back of his bright white flight helmet was MAYONNAISE, the nickname given to him in OCS by his drill instructor and later bestowed on him as a call sign in advanced jet training where he flew the A-4 Skyhawk.

"Feeling good, sir," replied Saunders, the cocky top candidate in the outgoing class. "Odds at the O Club are two-to-one I take you down today, sir."

"Really? You got skin in the game, too?" asked Zack.

"Five hundred big ones, sir," replied Saunders, his voice brimming with the unshakeable confidence of youth.

Their two FA/18s faced each other a mile and a half apart in the "Working Area," fifteen miles off the coast of Virginia. Zack had cut his teeth on Tomcats, but he had flown the FA/18 since it became the new workhorse fighter jet on January 7, 1983, and he always found its cockpit as confining as a tomb. Instruments, panels, and gauges blinked around him like a galaxy of stars and planets. He was at the controls of a flying computer, the most techno-savvy plane in history.

His eyes, blazing bright, matched the color and intensity of the turbulent green sea below.

Today was a good day for a bad dog fight, Zack decided. He and his star student had been jawing about this showdown since the start of classes a year ago. "Are you a student of history, son?" Zack inquired casually as he reviewed his radar attack display and selected his AIM–9X Sidewinder heat-seeking missile. Since this was an exercise, the missile would stay on its rails, and the kill would be determined by mathematical data.

"Yes, sir," answered Saunders. "You've never lost a dog fight. But this is my day, sir. I'm putting my name up on that board."

"Too much of that Red Bull will get you killed," warned Zack as he finished his personal checklist. Making sure his mic was off, he coughed hard several times. His throat often got dry before a dogfight, whether it was war or training. It was nothing, but Zack couldn't risk showing any signs of weakness, not at his age, not in his position, not with this eager kid. It was a rule he had learned only too well as a kid on the streets of Olongapo. An injured wolf never shows its limp.

"Turning in left to left," announced Zack, signaling his intention to pass his opponent left wing to left wing.

"Turning in left to left," echoed Saunders.

With that, both pilots accelerated through a barrier and went to "afterburner," the powerful explosion of pure energy that was needed for taking off and for fighting another plane. At over a thousand miles an hour, it took no time at all to erase that mile and a half. At the very instant they passed, left wing to left wing, five hundred feet apart, Zack announced, "Fight's on."

"Fight's on," chimed Saunders. The two planes began to go at each other's asses. Basic Fighter Maneuvering (BFM) was its official name, but the way it looked and sounded when two planes went at each other full throttle, all teeth and tail, twisting and pouncing, was more animal than machine.

Training rules dictated that the two combatants maintain a separation of five hundred feet between planes, but in combat, there were no such rules. In 2005, Zack had collided in midair with an Iraqi opponent, losing part of a wing, but survived to watch his opponent crash into the desert floor.

Zack was responsible for keeping his students alive during training. But it was keeping them alive during combat that preoccupied his mind in this final chapter of his career. As he had feared, ISIS was emerging in Syria and the threat to American armed forces was at a new high.

———

Because of this threat, Zack had driven the students in this class so ruthlessly that he had earned their whispered acknowledgment as "instructor from hell." He tested his charges in ways that suggested he didn't give a shit, when, in truth, he cared about them more than their mothers and fathers.

"*Bobong tanga-tanga!*" swore Zack as he sought position to deliver his simulated missile. It was Tagalog for "stupid piece of shit." Part of Zack's charismatic persona was that he made a habit of spicing his training dialogue with the worst swear words he had learned growing up in the Philippines. His students knew it was a trick to throw them off their game, yet it worked most of the time.

"Trying to mess me up again with that Filipino talk, sir?" asked Lieutenant J. G. Saunders. "It won't work, old man," he crowed, expertly somersaulting over his instructor's head before Zack could get off a shot.

Old man. Zack winced but let out a convincing laugh. In a dogfight, trash talk was commonplace, and normal rules of military etiquette didn't apply. He was impressed with the psychology behind his opponent's comment. Identify a pilot's weaknesses and go for the jugular. But to Zack's unerring eye, Saunders had revealed a disturbing weakness during training that the other instructors hadn't noticed. Behind the boy's masculine bravura, Zack smelled a coward, and he planned to teach him a special lesson today.

The seven surviving students from Saunders's class and the ten incoming members of the new class listened to their trash talk in the TCTS (Tactical Combat Training System) building on the east corner of the base and observed the fight in graphic detail on an armada of sophisticated monitors.

Captain Louis Perryman watched from the door. It had been two years since Shannon had driven off on her Harley and disappeared off the face of the earth, and the changes in his best friend had been profound. There was a darkness in Mayo, a street edge that reminded Perryman of the man he had met thirty-five years ago in Officer Candidate School. Perryman had personally never given up on the hope that Shannon would show up, but he knew that Zack had been forced to slam the door on hope.

Zack suddenly passed his younger opponent's jet at only three hundred feet. Saunders half-jumped in his harness as he saw how close Zack had come. "Holy shit!" he grunted.

"Got your attention, Big Spendah?" demanded Zack in a sarcastic drawl.

Saunders gathered himself. Zack had been riding his ass all year. It was time to turn all that around. "Two can play that game, sir," he replied, veering to within two hundred feet of Zack's right wing on the next merge.

They were now so close that Zack could see that his opponent's visor was up and his face was flushed with adrenaline. He knew this was, by far, the closest the young man had ever come to another plane in a high-aspect dogfight.

"Pull into me!" goaded Zack. "Keep the pull!"

The student shook his head. "Negative! Negative!"

Zack closed to a hundred feet or roughly the distance of six pickup trucks parked bumper to bumper. "Feeling the heat, Lieutenant?" Zack teased. There was something deeply unsettling in the calm intensity of his voice. It was common knowledge that people were changed by war and personal loss. The graduating class had been conjecturing that this had happened to their legendary leader after the death of his wife and the disappearance and presumed death of his daughter.

"Knock it off! Knock it off! Training rules!" said Saunders, raw fear in his voice. In theory, when anyone said the "K" word, the fight was instantly over, but Zack had other plans.

"How much do you want this?" demanded Zack. "Follow me up if you've got the balls," he taunted, rocketing his Super Hornet straight up at seven g's.

The student reluctantly followed. As the g's mounted, Saunders blinked repeatedly, struggling to maintain consciousness. He knew this was not training. This bordered on combat.

At twenty-seven thousand feet, Zack pirouetted, and they were snarling at each other's asses again. Zack closed to fifty feet, and his younger opponent's eyes widened in sheer disbelief. They were only a few car lengths apart. *It was like being in the same room.*

Zack picked up the taunt again. "Pull into me," he ordered. "Keep the fucking pull." At this close range, Zack's eyes revealed that unhinged element the students were coming to fear.

Perryman snatched up a headset in TCTS. It was rare for a maintenance officer to inject himself into the equation like this, and the students from both classes shared concerned looks. "Captain Mayo, you heard him. Knock it the fuck off," ordered Perryman.

Zack showed no signs of hearing his best friend. "Make the fucking kill!" he bellowed sternly. "Or I will!" He was testing the boy's mettle. Zack was offering his opponent the chance to execute the kill, but he had to overcome his fear to do it.

"We're too close! Knock it off! Knock it off!" bleated the younger man.

Zack had had enough. He changed his weapon selection from "Missile" to "Gun." "*Putangina mo!*" he cried like a deranged warrior, swooping into place behind the student's exhaust. As with the missile, no actual bullets were loaded into his M61 Vulcan Cannon. If they were, 6,000 rounds of ammunition would have been unleashed per minute.

"Trigger down! Pippers on tracking," declared Zack triumphantly. "I just rock-raped you, Lieutenant." In a dogfight, there were two kinds of kills. Killing with your missile was like shooting fish in a barrel. Shooting down an enemy with the Vulcan Cannon was the "Old West" style known as rock-rape.

"Son of a bitch!" yelped Saunders. Panicking, he attempted a defensive break turn to avoid the shot, but the g's mounted too fast, and he passed out.

Suddenly his jet was hurtling toward blue water like a meteor.

Zack watched dispassionately. He knew that there was a vague middle ground between consciousness and unconsciousness. He had floated in that void himself on many occasions. Pilots test the boundaries of g-forces on a regular basis, and it was not uncommon to experience brief stretches of unconsciousness. He coughed hard again, the only indication that he was feeling emotion.

He barely raised his voice as he said, "Cut the crap, Lieutenant. The enemy doesn't give a fuck if you take a nap. Saves them ammunition if the ocean does their job."

Nothing from Saunders. Blue sea was a hungry mouth. Whitecaps were sharp teeth.

"Wake up or die, Saunders. It's a simple choice. Personally, I don't give a shit." His voice held no trace of human emotion. But he got the result he wanted.

The younger man's body convulsed wildly as he came back into consciousness, his hands flailing, his mouth puckering like a fish. Seeing the water fill his view, Saunders sat upright like someone had goosed him. "Oh, shit!" he exclaimed and yanked back hard on his stick to resume altitude.

"Good job," commended Zack. "Now who's feeling old?"

"Jesus Christ," mumbled the student. "Holy fucking Christ." He had died and been reborn. It would take time to wrap his head around that. One day, the lesson would save his life.

Zack knew there would be hell to pay for his behavior. Incidents like this quickly traveled up the chain of command, and his old "buddy" Topper Daniels was still the Secretary of the Navy. The two men had not crossed paths since the medal ceremony at the Pentagon two years ago, but Zack could always feel his enemy breathing down his neck.

"What the fuck was that all about?" Perryman asked a short time later as Zack's boots touched the tarmac.

Zack's eyes were still ablaze from the dogfight. "Am I the only one who knows how ill-prepared that hotshot is for war?"

"Our job is to train them to fly our plane. War comes later," his friend reminded him.

"I don't see it that way," countered Zack. "Al-Qaeda—ISIS—whatever those bastards call themselves now has never been stronger. They won't stop until they've dragged us back into the fifth century." His eyes still contained their earlier fever.

"Boss, I'm worried about you," interjected the taller man, deep concern in his gray eyes.

"Me?" Zack protested. "I'm flying better than ever. Let those fuckers at the Pentagon find out what a mistake they made." He had recently received notification that his third and final bid to join the admiral's club had been rejected. Perryman and Della-Serra had received similar letters.

"You were inches away from killing yourself and that kid, Zack. Fucking inches," rumbled Perryman, unafraid to go face to face with this man, even though Zack was technically his superior. "Do I need to remind you that the Navy can still hurt us?" He continued, "You don't want to give SECNAV the pleasure of yanking your pension, do you?"

"Fuck him!" spat Zack disgustedly. "He's been going after me my whole career."

"He has a new reason to do it this time," observed his wise friend.

Zack was well aware that Topper's son, Taylor, was in the incoming class. He had broken all of Zack's records in basic and advanced flight. The handsome young man was a favorite with the tabloids. He fronted a band with a song on the charts, and there were rumors that he nurtured presidential ambitions.

"He'll earn his place like everyone else," vowed Zack. As he started toward maintenance, he faltered slightly and was forced to hold onto Perryman's shoulder for support. The two friends exchanged a look. That dogfight had taken more out of Zack than he realized. He shook his head to clear away the spin and let go of Perryman; then, they resumed their journey. When they reached the giant hangar, Zack walked inside alone, doing his best to hide his limp. Perryman watched him with troubled eyes.

In his quarters above the maintenance hangar, Zack peeled off the rest of his g-suit. He was assaulted by his own odor. He knew that smell. He had first encountered it as a boy forced to survive on the streets of Olongapo, in the Philippine Islands. As a pilot, he had smelled it every time he made a kill or delivered a smart bomb into the bowels of the enemy. It was the odor of death. To teach a grim lesson, he had nearly killed that boy, and himself. Death always came with a smell, even if no one actually died.

He finally emerged from the shower and studied himself in the mirror as he toweled off, a mix of admiration and disgust. He had been David; now, he was Bacchus. He still had his abs, but they were covered in a thin layer of fat. He was still strong in his upper body, but his shoulders had a slope to them, as though bent by the weight of tragedy.

Zack opened a wall safe that he used primarily for important documents and removed a safety deposit box. In a manner suggesting a religious ritual, he opened the lid and took in the items recovered from Paula's body after her death. Every object showed some element of fire damage. He picked up her blackened wedding ring and stared at it a moment before putting it back. He removed her singed phone-wallet. Inside the crusty leather case were three photos that had somehow gone untouched by the fire.

He removed the first one. It was a shot Paula's Aunt Bunny had taken of Zack and Paula when he carried her out of that paper bag factory. In a gesture of her own worth, Paula had put Zack's officer cap on her head. The sunlight streamed in from outside like a life force, drawing them forward to an exciting new life.

Zack's mouth curled into a warm smile as he remembered their first stop at a justice of the peace in Seattle who pronounced them man and wife. Then they drove on Zack's Triumph 750 to Beeville, Texas, where Zack would begin primary flight training, stopping along the way in motels that they "christened" by making love so often they lost count. The Vietnam War was finally over. Richard Nixon had been the first American president in history to resign. Glen Campbell's "Rhinestone Cowboy" played on every station.

The three days and three nights on the road provided their first real chance to discuss what each wanted from the future. It was not surprising, after knowing each other only thirteen weeks, that they would find themselves on different pages.

"I want a family. I want it right away," announced Zack. After climbing the ladder to officer status, he wanted the big prize that had eluded him all his life. A real home. A family. Paula had other ideas.

"I want to go to college," she declared. "I want to be like you. I want to make a difference in the world."

Zack was not unmoved. He knew he owed her a great debt for helping him get to his finish line. She had been there for him when he was ready to throw it all away. "I'll make you a deal," he suggested reasonably. "Let's have a baby and spend the next ten years making a difference in our child's life. After that, it's your turn, if you still want it."

When Paula didn't argue or try to negotiate the terms, Zack was not surprised. Paula had been raised in a conservative, blue-collar home, which her stepfather, a plumber, ruled with an iron fist. It was only natural that she would endorse her husband's plan. That was the norm of the time. School could wait. And he had made a promise.

Ten years. Then it was her turn.

Zack put the photo back in the wallet and took out the second photo. In it, he and a groggy Paula held their baby daughter in their arms after her birth. It was June 20, 1985. They were in a theater watching *Prizzi's Honor*, when Paula's water broke, and they had to rush to the hospital. It had taken ten years for Paula to bring a child to term. She was now thirty-two and Zack was thirty-five. Shannon Pokrifki Mayo was a striking child with cobalt eyes and her parents' intelligence and silly humor.

At one point during the difficult delivery, an exhausted Paula believed she wouldn't make it. After all the failed pregnancies, she was convinced she was doomed not to bear a child. But Zack had been her stalwart partner, reminding her over and over, "Don't forget, we're going to win." After that day, the words became a catchphrase between them whenever one or the other was feeling overwhelmed by life. It was their safety net. *Don't forget, we're going to win.*

A lot had happened for women's rights in the past decade, but Paula's dream to make a difference in the world was still on the shelf. To her credit, she worked out daily and looked barely older than when she met Zack. Motherhood proved to be an exciting new challenge, and she took it on with all the energy she gave to everything she did. Her child wanted for nothing. She sent her daughter to school with elaborate lunches that always contained some secret message of love. She nurtured her frequent bruises and slights. With Zack engaged in overseas conflict, she worked especially hard to fill the gap. As time passed, Zack never brought up the ten-year deal, but he knew Paula was still counting.

Zack was overwhelmed by the feelings that accompanied his daughter's birth. It was nothing short of a journey into the miraculous. Nothing had ever been this important to him. His own flesh and blood. Because of Paula being unconscious for the C-section, Zack's was the first face Shannon encountered after the delivering doctor's. To her father's eye, Shannon was the most beautiful daughter in history.

"Hello, Miss Shannigan," were his first words to her. Her cobalt eyes glowed as she responded to his deep voice. He had been talking to her through the wall of her mother's stomach since she was conceived. He sang to her. He hummed to her. He motorboated her. He played his guitar for her. He did his character voices. And now he could do all those things face-to-face.

The third and final photo was a black-and-white close-up of a young man in Navy officer dress whites, on the day of his commissioning. He was handsome, with thick dark hair and alert eyes. Paula had carried it around since she had found it in her mother's drawer as a child. The man was her real father, Tom Hollingsworth. Zack knew she had obsessed over him all her life. More than once, she had lamented never meeting him. She had grown up, instead, with a stepfather who had never welcomed her into his home.

Putting the wallet back in the box, Zack picked up a St. Christopher's medallion on a chain and slowly brought it to his lips. Protected from the fire in that sacred hollow between her breasts, the medal tasted salty, the accumulation of nine years of his tears. He knew the medallion had been a gift from her mother when Paula turned ten, and sometimes he imagined he was tasting Paula's tears as a child alongside his own.

Zack returned the box of treasures to the safe. Losing Paula had been a nearly life-ending blow for him. Accepting Shannon's presumed death six years later had proven beyond his powers as a man. He could not forgive himself for how he had handled their last time together. She had come to him for help, and he had allowed her to drive away.

After she left on that fateful day, he made some urgent calls and learned she was staying at Annie's parents' house in Norfolk. When he got no answers to his calls, he made the twenty-seven-minute drive to investigate, but there was no one home. He left a message in the mailbox asking her to call, but she never did. Then one day, he got a call from Annie alerting him that Shannon had not come home for three days. A few days earlier, he had read about a party boat fire in international waters off Norfolk that killed all twenty-eight passengers and four crew members aboard. Annie didn't remember Shannon saying anything about a party boat outing, but she had to admit it sounded like Shannon's kind of hang.

Zack would learn that one body, the last to be found, could not be identified because of the damage it had suffered from being attacked by a shark, then submerged for so long. Zack drove to the Norfolk morgue to see for himself. He was not alone in that bright lab. Six other parents in search of answers were also there. Zack would never forget the sight of that formless lump of gristle, gnawed on by a shark, then left submerged for days. *Was it Shannie?*

Still, he held out hope. He became a student of the opioid crisis that was suddenly challenging the country. The problem had started with the over-prescription of OxyContin, but it had exacerbated in the past year when a synthetic opioid called Fentanyl hit the market. Rumored to be a hundred times more powerful than heroin or Oxy, it was manufactured in China, then sent in raw form to the Mexican cartels where it was "finished." He read that young people were buying it online as easily as the latest pop song and were dropping like flies.

Zack woke up each morning and googled "opioid deaths," experiencing a dark rush of adrenaline every time, knowing with certainty that he would see Shannie's name. When he didn't, it would take hours to come down from that unwanted high. A few months ago, he had received a call from the FBI alerting him that the body of a girl Shannon's age had turned up on a beach in Bermuda, only to call him a few days later to inform him it was not his daughter. This heart-crushing routine had been his life sentence since she'd disappeared.

After receiving his retirement orders, he did something he'd sworn never to do and entered weekly therapy with a Navy psychologist to deal with his ever-present grief and his impending retirement. It was what Paula would have suggested. Commander Eric Mann was a few years younger than Zack, but he understood the military mind better than anyone Zack had ever met.

The psychologist was a wiry-fit man with long hair who reminded Zack of an aging John Lennon. In addition to his nonregulation haircut, he wore garish Hawaiian shirts, instead of a commander's uniform. The Navy obviously considered him too much of an asset to question his fashion and grooming choices.

In their weekly sessions, Zack began an inquiry into his own past, in hopes it would provide answers about what he'd done wrong in the raising of his complex daughter. Zack had never taken recreational drugs of any kind, but Eric reminded him that there were all forms of drugs that people enslaved themselves to. *Fame. Money. Sex. Revenge. War.* Zack knew that he had been at war all his life. Living with a suicidal mother had been war. That state home and the streets of Olongapo had been war. For twenty-two years, he had been a fighter pilot at war.

"War is a drug that leaves its minions addicted to hate," counseled Eric. "It fills your system. It replaces your life force. Sitting at home in front of their TV sets, normal people never see any of this," he explained. "Men and women like you, our warriors, see it for them. That takes its toll. That's why war is a drug that few ever beat."

Week after week, Zack lamented to his therapist about not being man enough to stop his wife from going to Atlanta and not stopping his daughter from driving off after she'd finally been vulnerable with him. Eric finally called him on it. "Manliness seems to be a big theme with you."

"Isn't it with you?" Zack shot back testily.

"Yes, but it's not the same," said Eric. "You treat it like some kind of religion."

"And how do you treat it?" challenged Zack.

"Like a song we each sing in our own way," Eric answered. "That we line up perfectly in one camp or the other is the biggest bullshit that society has sold us."

"What the hell does any of this have to do with me?" asked Zack impatiently.

"As long as you blame your concept of manhood for your mistakes, you won't be able to see where the real fault lies."

"And where's that?" asked Zack imploringly. He was desperate for answers.

Eric shrugged. Most psychologists deferred from giving direct advice on the belief that change must come from the patient, but Eric had his own direct way. "That answer seems to be buried in whatever happened the day your wife died."

Zack just nodded. Everything in his life was buried in the morass of that day.

Eric studied him with compassion. "How many showers so far today?" Zack's penchant for long, hot showers had become a running joke with them. Eric knew it dated back to nights on the street when Zack was young, waiting for a signal that he could come home. It was symbolic. If he could stay under that hot spray long enough, maybe it would wash away his pain.

"Just this morning," answered Zack. "And right after lunch," he added sheepishly. They shared a friendly laugh.

"Maybe it's time for you to begin a series of letting go's," suggested Eric.

"Like what?" asked Zack in alarm.

"Maybe start by not going online," he suggested, "and stop obsessing on that photo." He was referring to that lump of someone's remains that Zack kept at the ready to torture himself.

Zack took his advice. He weaned himself from googling "opioid deaths" and deleted that ugly photo. He sold the old house so that he wouldn't go into Shannon's room and sit there for hours holding her teddy bears and tennis trophies as if they contained her DNA. On

Shannon's twenty-fifth birthday, he asked his friends not to mention her name or inquire about how the search was going.

Today, he had to admit that all the letting-go's weren't working. He missed his daughter in ways that felt literally fatal. His aerial battle had been the latest proof that his mental health was faltering. He hadn't cared one way or the other if he had lived or died teaching his student to survive.

———

"Attention on deck!" shouted a student, and the new class came to attention in a smart line near a stage in a large briefing space fitted with theater chairs. They all wore flight suits bearing the rank of Lieutenant Junior Grade. They had started as Ensigns, but eighteen months of school had added up fast.

Zack and his three class advisors entered the room in their working uniforms. Perryman had sent word to Zack that he was attending to a priority matter and would meet the class later. Zack had questioned that news because Perryman prided himself on always being at his side to welcome a new class.

"At ease and welcome," Zack began. "I'm Captain Mayo. You'll meet Captain Perryman, your maintenance officer, a little later. This is both Captain Perryman's and my last class, so treat us relics with due respect."

Guarded laughter from the class. They all knew this was the great Mayonnaise Mayo's last class, and they were honored to be in it. It was something they would tell their children and grandchildren. But after witnessing his near-fatal dogfight with the superstar from the previous class, there was a nervous energy in the room.

Zack did not invite them to sit down, although that was the general practice predating his arrival as head instructor. Since taking over, he had begun to channel his old drill instructor from OCS, the fearsome Foley. Keeping them standing gave Zack the "eyeball edge" he wanted.

Give them a hint of madness to keep them guessing. It was all an act, or was it?

"We know why most of you are here," said Zack, grinning menacingly as he paced their ranks, his eyes probing into their most secret places. "Ten and out and a plush paycheck from Delta Airlines. But a lot can happen in ten years. Your character will be tested in ten years. Three of you will be dead in ten years. Let me be clear. There can be no secret in your heart if you want to fly my plane."

The students knew this was the famous Mayonnaise Mayo's mantra. In the book based on his life, he had revealed to his biographer that he had come up with this worldview following the suicide death of his friend in OCS who had carried a fatal secret in his heart. Sid Worley's secret was that he was chasing his father's love by trying to replace his dead brother. When a local girl rejected his offer of marriage, the troubled Okie took his own life.

Zack stopped in front of Taylor Daniels, twenty-five, handsome, auburn hair, conflicted brown eyes. At five-ten, Zack found himself looking up at the young man who had to be, at least, six-two. "Class, we have genuine Naval blueblood among us today," he announced. "Lieutenant JG Taylor Daniels, son of the current Secretary of the Navy."

Taylor smiled easily, exposing perfect teeth. "No pressure, right? I blow it here, and my old man feeds my balls to his piranhas." His remark drew a ripple of laughter from the class. Regardless of their pipeline into the Fleet Replacement Squadron, they all knew Taylor was the son of the Secretary of the Navy.

"It doesn't surprise me your old man keeps piranhas," Zack intoned humorlessly. The memory of that embarrassing medal ceremony in Washington returned to him like a bad smell. It was hard to find any resemblance between the short, pompous man who failed OCS and this tall young man who had shattered all records in advanced flight once held by Zack. Taylor had inherited his father's auburn-red hair, but his was not dyed, and it was as thick as a redwood forest.

"He warned me you two have a history, sir," Taylor said, enjoying the attention the moment was providing him. Zack sensed that he was one of those people who did everything well but needed others to know it. He reasoned that you don't grow up under a father like Topper Daniels and not pay the price for it.

Consulting a file, Zack said, "I hear you're a pop singer in your spare time. Why jets if you could be the next Mick Jagger?"

"Any reason I can't do both, sir?" asked Taylor good-naturedly.

"Life happens fast for a fighter pilot," Zack answered sagely. "There can be no secret in your heart if you want to fly my plane." There it was again, his mantra. Before he was finished, it would belong to all of them, and they, in turn, would teach it to generations to come.

He moved on to a tall girl with Chinese features and short blond hair. She wore clunky spectacles that magnified her blue, almond-shaped eyes. "Lieutenant Junior Grade Sidney Lee," he read from his clipboard. "Father and three brothers in the black shoe Navy. Why jets? Trying to one-up the boys back home?"

"Why not, sir?" replied Sidney with a grin. "A woman can do anything a man can do."

"The Navy must agree," responded Zack affably. "This class has the highest number of female candidates in history." His eyes washed over the group, falling on two female candidates, one short and athletic, the other tall and curvy, before seizing on the slender young woman at the end who had been mostly hidden from his view until now.

Time stopped. He forgot to breathe. Zack consulted his roster and saw the name "Lieutenant Junior Grade Shannon Castellano." He had seen this name before in the paperwork and never suspected a thing. He saw the students and instructors staring at them in shock as their kinship registered. Zack wanted to laugh, and he wanted to cry.

"Shannon??" he stammered. Little remained of the party girl who had run away on her motorcycle. She was now a twenty-five-year-old woman in the best shape of her life. The piercings were gone and even the little holes had disappeared. Her angry tattoo was hidden under her flight suit. Her dark hair was cut in a severe crewcut. Her too-blue eyes felt electrically charged.

"Surprise," she said, remembering to add, "sir."

FOUR

★★★

ASHES OF A DOG

NORFOLK, VIRGINIA

Two years prior — Summer 2008

The four college friends had pooled their resources to keep the party going through the summer at Annie's parents' house in Norfolk. Annie, Michelle, and Kimmy all had bank accounts they could draw on, but "military brat" Shannon sold drugs to pay for her ride. Looking like she did, it was an easy job. It was in her role as a tan and sexy dealer in a snow-white Azzedine Alaïa micro-mini and bra top that she happened to be three miles out to sea that night on a party boat named the *Durban Poison*.

The summer had been one long, endless party, and she was tired. With fall coming, change was in the air once again. Her roommates were bailing on youth to take jobs in their parents' businesses. With her dream to fly jets off the table, and no plan to replace it, she had no idea what the future held.

In her year of addiction, Shannon had witnessed a dark side of life. Drugs seemed to transform the world into predators and prey. Girls and boys routinely traded their bodies for the chance to get high. As a dealer, she was able to bypass that hardship, paying for her drugs the old American way, through commerce. But this didn't free her from the dance with death that druggies play routinely. She had watched the thrashing final seconds of the life of a friend who'd overdosed on Fentanyl. It was not lost on her that she had been next in line for a hit. Fellow druggies often lauded a drug by saying, "It's so good you can drop on it." *As in die.* Living in that kind of mindset will change you.

Tonight, she had sold the last of her supply and was leaning against the gunwale on the starboard side, contemplating the future. Adhering to her routine to not party while she worked, she was probably the straightest one on board. Her bluer-than-blue eyes took in the drug-fueled revelry around her. In international waters, all bets were off, and this was a bobbing, floating, listing, undulating Sodom and Gomorrah. Katy Perry's "I Kissed a Girl" bombarded her ears. People were flagrantly making out. Lighters and matches burst into flame fore and aft as partyers chased the dragon or lit cigarettes and opium-laced joints.

It came out of nowhere, as it always did for her. Someone ignited a Zippo a few feet away from her face, and the sudden appearance of the blue-and-red flame jettisoned her brain into her mother's body at the very instant of her death. Shannon was burning alive.

This time, fantasy and reality did a strange dance. The lighted Zippo fell out of its owner's hand, landing on cushions that burst into flame like gossamer kindling. With great will, Shannon forced herself out of her day-mare. The music was so loud that it muffled the screams filling the air. Panic reigned. The captain, a tattooed and pierced hipster wearing a cowboy hat with blinking lights, was so stoned that his efforts to fight the fire with an extinguisher drew wild laughter from onlookers.

Shannon watched the flames leap like an imp of perversion around the party boat. It was her day-mare coming to life. A flaming American flag fell on a young couple, turning them into a ball of fire. An effort to launch a lifeboat was an effort in futility. The music pounded like thunder on a loop. Most patrons aboard the doomed *Durban Poison* stared at the flames like they wore virtual reality headsets.

Shannon heard her father's voice as though he had miraculously appeared beside her.

The difference between the living and the dead is fractional. Move! Move!

Shannon threw a leg over the gunwale and jumped. She pierced the cold water and wanted to stay there. When she surfaced for air, she saw the boat explode into flames. Someone cried out, "Shark! Shark!" A moment later, there was a horrible scream. A few passengers leaped desperately into the water before the boat disintegrated in a sudden conflagration and quickly sank.

Guiding on a familiar landmark, the outline of ships at anchor off Norfolk Naval Base, Shannon swam for a public beach just north of the facility. For several minutes, she heard the cries of other swimmers, noting the change in tone when they knew they were drowning. There was a terrified scream of "Shark! Shark!" Then a horrible scream. Shannon expected to be its next victim. She imagined its teeth severing her feet as she kicked. Finally, she heard only the lonely slap of her weak arms on the water. She was grateful for her father's harsh lessons in the cold base pool. He was a tyrant who suffered no weaknesses, no childish tantrums. *Keep swimming. Keep moving. I'm not here. This is all you.*

Eventually, a merciful wave rolled her close enough to dry sand that she could crawl the rest of the way to safety. Tears came in a deluge, along with hacking and retching. Fate had dealt her a gigantic favor. She had hit rock bottom at twenty-three and miraculously survived.

When she got to Annie's house, her roommates were not there. While packing up her things, she saw a television report that all crew and passengers of the *USS Durban Poison* had perished. As stoned as the captain and crew were when they left the harbor, it was no surprise that there had been a miscount.

I'm off the radar. It's a blank slate. It's all up to me now.

She had heard of a rehab facility in San Miguel de Allende, Mexico, where the addicts' names were anonymous and they paid for their treatment by picking oranges. Nestled in the jungle thirty miles to the south of the cobblestoned colonial town, Granada Retreat was founded in the AA tradition but was wrapped in a warm blanket of hippy mysticism due to its founder, "Monkey" Millstein. A boy who had gone there had told her, "This is a spiritual place. You come away different."

Shannon wanted to do more than quit drugs. She wanted to come away different.

With her limited savings, Shannon bought a roundtrip ticket to

Guadalajara, Mexico. In severe withdrawal, she shook like an epileptic for the two-hour bus ride to San Miguel de Allende. A kind woman put her shawl over Shannon to keep her warm. It smelled like roasted peanuts.

The rehab was a spartan adobe maze of classrooms and living quarters, nestled in a deep jungle. For the first ten days after reporting, she never left her bed in the women's dorm, unless it was to go into the bathroom to relieve herself or throw up. Getting clean would prove to be one of the hardest challenges she would face in her young life. But she had come to the right place to begin that journey.

Finally, she was well enough to join her fellow addicts in the large dining room. The food was vegetarian and generous. After dinner there was a family council outside in a jungle clearing around a fire, where the addicts passed a geode the size of a baseball and "shared." Whenever the heavy stone changed hands, it caught the firelight, sending out stabs of color. The addicts were from all over the world. They were of every race and age. Firelight warmed their hopeful faces into a family.

"We have someone new joining us tonight," resonated a deep Bronx baritone at the far end of the circle her first night around the fire. This was her introduction to Monkey Millstein, a fifty-something New Yorker with a wide nose and curly white hair. "Welcome, Chelsea," he boomed in a voice that pierced the night air with authority.

"Welcome, Chelsea," chanted the addicts, using the name she had given when she arrived at the facility.

Shannon was rail thin after her battle with drugs and terrified to begin this journey. For the past year and a quarter, drugs had been her source of love. In their absence, she felt a loneliness that was staggering. "Glad to be here," she said quietly.

Millstein smiled warmly, a wise round face in the fire glow. "We're a family, Chelsea. A real family. We are your true friends here." His accent was so thick Shannon wanted to laugh. Monkey Millstein was a hippy Mel Brooks.

She did not share that night, but she briefly spoke the following night. She had resolved to be friendly without revealing anything that might help her father find her and rescue her again. She had a big personal makeover to do before that could happen. She needed to know how she had gotten to this low point in her life, so she could avoid it ever happening again. In the six years since her mother's death, she had done everything to avoid this personal journey. Gaming. Super-student. Drugs and alcohol. Now she was determined to do the hard work she had been putting off for so long.

All day she picked oranges in the hot sun and thought about her life. In the fireside councils, she spoke often and openly, sparing no secrets, but always speaking in a code that left out any mention of details that could identify her to her fellow addicts and alert her father to her whereabouts. Digging relentlessly into her memories, she realized that she was a contradiction: the pretty, intelligent, athletic girl who could do anything, and the "inner Shannon" who had doubted her own worth all her life. She told the council how conflicting it had been to be accorded so much power as a child because of her appearance. Instead of emboldening her, it did the opposite; it made her question herself.

What did I do to deserve this? Is that all I am, a pretty face?

She shared about growing up the only child of one national hero, and then two. In her cover story, her father was a much-lauded police detective, and her mother was a fashion leader. *How can I ever live up?* She spoke about being a mommy's girl for ten years, with a father who was always on a case, then the sudden turnabout when her father took over as her principal parent and her mother became the one missing in action. One night, with the geode pulsing in her hand like a human heart, she spoke about her mother's death. No details that would give her identity away. Just the suddenness of it. Of being there to witness it. Of having some role in it.

One evening, Monkey Millstein asked each of the addicts what they saw in their future. When it was Shannon's turn, she answered in the sarcastic tone she had resorted to since her fall from grace. "What future?" she mocked, making a comic face. Jets had been her future. But that was off the table, and nothing had flowered in its wake.

"The future does not belong to the past," lectured their charismatic leader. "It belongs to the present. I was addicted to heroin. I spent five years in prison for dealing drugs. But today I am doing what I always dreamed of doing. You can do the same."

"This is different," said Shannon with a leaden finality. "I'm talking about breaking the law," she said. She cautioned herself to stay in code. "They won't allow me to follow my father into police work if they find out I did drugs. I could go to prison if I tried."

Shannon had a very strong sense of right and wrong. When her father had said she could forget about her dream of flying, she didn't question it for a moment. Imagine if the Navy found out that she had dealt drugs to pay for her ride. "An Addict and a Dealer" didn't chime with "An Officer and a Gentleman."

"Man has his many rules and laws, but our first allegiance is to God and then to ourselves. If you can work it out with God, then I personally believe you're good to go." Mickey's eyes danced merrily. It was not hard to imagine what he had been like on drugs.

"I don't think God thinks too much of me lately," she answered. Shannon was surprised by her own choice of words. She seldom gave God a thought. God was her mother's thing.

A few weeks into her stay, Shannon relapsed. A newly arrived addict who called herself Dewey had brought a supply of cocaine with her. It was a trick that dealers often resorted to. What better market than a bunch of druggies in rehab? Monkey was quick to ferret out the fox in the henhouse and send her packing.

"Who has a confession to make tonight?" he asked that night at the family counsel, his gentle eyes slowly sweeping the group around the fire. He had a good idea who the offenders were, but he wanted them to come forward on their own.

Shannon held out her hand for the speaking piece, and it made its way to her. She felt terrible about her failure, but she played it for laughs. "I fucked up," she said, then added, grinning, "It was the worst shit I've ever had." Her fellow addicts laughed, the ones who had relapsed the loudest. Dewey's coke had been laced with so much baby powder that it burned the nostrils like kerosene.

Millstein was not amused. He had been worried about Chelsea's commitment since she joined their family councils. Her dark vision of herself made him wonder about her recovery. "This isn't funny, Chelsea," he growled. "This is life or death stuff here. How are you going to make sure this doesn't happen again?"

Shannon felt everyone's eyes on her. This time her acting skills deserted her. She spat out the words, "I can't promise anything. I know it will happen again. That's just who I am."

The geode suddenly slipped from her grip and landed in the sand in front of her with a dull plop. Seconds passed before she collapsed in sobs. Millstein rose from his place and approached her. Kneeling at her side, he pulled a small jar from his pocket and opened it to show her and the others the dark ashes inside.

"These are the ashes of a dog," he explained. "A dog is the embodiment of pure, unconditional love. A dog always forgives." He put a sprinkle of ashes on the back of his hand and leaned closer to her, smiling comfortingly. "Breathe in normally," he advised.

Spellbound, Shannon watched him gently blow the ashes into her face. She breathed in a tang of bitterness and swallowed it back like cough medicine from a foreign country.

"How do you feel?" asked Monkey.

"I feel a little light-headed, but I feel good," she conceded. It was true. She felt a wave of wellness wash over her. It was the exact opposite of drugs. It came with a clear head. It was like a slap to the face, a good one, a wake-up call.

"This dog is with you now," he explained, "forgiving you."

That night, as she lay in her bunk in the women's dormitory, Shannon began to nurture the idea of resurrecting her dream to follow her father into naval aviation. This had been the grand plan all her life until her mother's death. As a child, she had watched him perform his aerial magic with wide-eyed wonder. By the time she turned ten, he was giving her flying lessons in a rented Cessna. At twelve, he gave her the controls for the first time, and at thirteen, he put her to the test. Flying over the ocean on the Virginia coastline, Shannon was at the wheel when Zack suddenly gave out a grunt of pain and clutched his chest.

"What's wrong, Daddy?" She implored, terrified.

"Heart attack," he grunted before slumping unconscious in his seat.

"Don't play around, Daddy! I'm scared!" she cried. He didn't move. "Stop it, Daddy! It's not funny!"

Again, there was no reply. It wasn't until after she had successfully landed that her father announced that it had been an act. She flew at him with fists flying.

"I hate you! I hate you!" she shouted.

"I know," he replied softly. "But, one day, you'll love me for it."

On her fourteenth birthday, she announced at dinner, "After college, I want to go to OCS. And after that, I want to fly jets. I want to do exactly what you do, Daddy."

Zack beamed with pride, but Paula surprised them both by asking her daughter a question.

"What do you think happens to a woman who's captured in combat?"

"Women don't fly in combat," Shannon replied smartly.

"But they will by the time you come along," said Paula. "Zack, tell her what can happen in the Middle East when a woman is captured."

Zack made a little face. "Don't you think she's a little young for this subject?" he asked warningly.

"She's fourteen," said Paula. "Tell her or I will."

Zack took a deep breath. "We've seen a lot more of this since women have been allowed to serve in combat," he started tentatively. He struggled to come up with words that would soften the message, but Paula's intense eyes demanded more. "In the Middle East, it's not uncommon for our women combatants to be brutally gang-raped by their captors," he concluded.

Shannon considered the warning soberly. Then she said with total conviction, "I know war can get ugly. I've read books. But this is what I want to do. I've known it forever. I know I will be good at it. I know I can do good for others."

From that day forward, her resolve to fly jets only sharpened. Then her mother died, and everything got put on hold.

To invest once again in this dream seemed almost crazy. There were a million ways it could blow up in her face. And the penalties for getting caught were harsh. But if the rehab leader was right, and this was between her and her own conscience, why not have a dream?

Doing the math, she knew she would have to complete her rehab within six months if she wanted to make it into FRS before the Navy retired her father. There could be no more relapses. There wasn't time for that. She knew her biggest obstacle in applying for Officer Candidate School was her name. Applying as a Mayo would be tantamount to appearing naked on a Rose Parade float. She had no doubt that her father would fulfill his promise to bar her from jet training.

Finally, she settled on a daring plan. There was a fellow addict who owed her a big favor. His name was Enrique Castellano, and he was gay. They slipped away together into the city one day and got married. The next day, she applied to OCS as Shannon Castellano.

There were glaring flaws in the plan. To anyone paying attention, her social security number would connect the dots back to her father. And the comprehensive background check that the National Security Agency would eventually conduct to qualify her for top-secret clearance would leave no ambiguities about her past. But for now, she just had to stay under the radar until she came face to face with her father in jet school. She was not worried that the Navy would find Enrique Castellano. He had been an itinerant druggie most of his life, and his parents had wasted a fortune trying to find him.

Six months after entering rehab, Shannon received notice of her acceptance into OCS. In an emotional fireside ceremony, she announced her news, albeit in code. "I've been accepted to the Police Academy," she announced. "I'll be saying goodbye to you at the end of the month."

When that day arrived, Monkey and the entire family took turns embracing her and wishing her well. Shannon was moved. But once again, she had to say goodbye to family without knowing when another dose might come.

On the flight back to Virginia, she divided her dangerous plan into "phases." Phase One had required staying clean and graduating from rehab. Phase Two, which would consume the next eighteen months, included surviving three difficult Navy schools: thirteen weeks of Officer Candidate School, eight months of Primary Flight, and seven of Advanced Flight. Phase Three, if she could make it that far, would bring her face to face with her father at FRS, where she would need to prove to him her worth over a year's syllabus.

Phase Four, the ultimate phase, was harder to define. She wanted a full rebirth. She wanted to make her mark on the world like her successful parents, and she wanted the kind of love and family she had experienced before the world crashed in on her. That phase felt a universe away.

Arriving back in Virginia Beach, she liberated her Harley from storage. She was deeply tanned from her hours of picking oranges and in the best shape of her life. When she arrived at the gates of the Naval Officer Candidate School in Newport, Rhode Island, she took a big breath to steady her nerves. This was the leaping-off point. Once she crossed this line, she was committing a felony that could send her to prison. The Marine Corporal at the gate took her in suspiciously until she showed him her orders in the name of Shannon Castellano. Then he snapped to attention like a toy soldier, and she crossed the threshold.

Thirteen weeks of OCS went by in a blur. The pace was relentless. It was basic training combined with officer training. Navy chief petty officers conducted the training instead of the tough Marine drill sergeants of her father's era. They barked orders like their Marine counterparts, but they did not inspire the kind of fear that her father described when he recounted his thirteen weeks under the merciless tutelage of Gunnery Sergeant Emil Foley.

Every day, Shannon and her fellow candidates were drilled in arcane subjects like celestial navigation and aerodynamics and were indoctrinated into a strict code of honor that would guide them as officers. Lies of any kind, even a minor half-truth, were not tolerated. It was against the Code. *And there she was, concealing her giant lie.* Not one day went by without her wrestling with her conscience over that one.

In her vigilance to remain sober, and in a yearning for love and family, she attended a Narcotics Anonymous meeting every week, choosing venues an hour away from base to avoid her worlds colliding. She knew her classmates whispered and joked about her aloofness and mysterious ways, but she didn't care. She had a plan. She graduated first in her class in OCS. Then it was on to Basic Flight.

In Corpus Christi, Texas, she found herself struggling with sobriety for the first time. When she was introduced to her first jet, the T-6 Texan, the rush reminded her too much of the high she had gotten from "chasing the dragon" on opioids, a process whereby one ignited a line of crushed opioids on a sheet of tinfoil with a lighter and inhaled the smoke with a glass straw. She shared her concerns with her fellow recovering addicts in her Friday night meetings, always reverting to code, and always as "Chelsea."

Her central issue was this: *Do I have the right to this dream if it means risking the lives of others?*

Advanced Flight in Kingsville, Texas, put her behind the controls of the more powerful jet trainer, the T-45C Goshawk. Immediately, she stopped sleeping through the night and her day-mares returned with savage vengeance. She started attending two NA meetings a week and finally settled into a rhythm, allowing the rush of the Goshawk to become routine.

She graduated from Advanced Flight second in her class to Annapolis hotshot Taylor Daniels. Their high scores assured them both of their "pipeline" of choice: jets. Shannon knew she could have gotten the top spot, but she had taken her foot off the pedal at the halfway point to avoid the attention that might expose her secret. On graduation night, their class went to a famous pilot bar to celebrate, but Shannon, as always, went her separate way. She treated herself to an ice cream cone and was in bed before ten.

Phase Two was over. On to phase three. Her father.

FIVE

CHIN PATROL

FLEET REPLACEMENT SQUADRON
October 2010

"Instructors, escort the students to their classroom," commanded Zack. Before Shannon could join the flow, he barked, "Lieutenant Junior Grade Castellano, my office now." He angrily strode up a long flight of metal stairs into his office and slammed the door after him.

The class shared looks. They all knew about Captain Mayo's wife's tragic death and his missing daughter. Now they buzzed excitedly that they had witnessed a father and daughter reunion that had not gone well.

Shannon was stunned by her father's anger. She had climbed the Khumbu Icefall of Mount Everest to be here. The ride down was unthinkable. As her classmates filed out, she noticed Taylor Daniels grinning her way. Knowing their fathers' history, she suspected that his interest in her would only quicken now that he knew she was Zack Mayo's daughter. A glance up at her father's closed door reminded her that it could be a moot point. She had lived day by day in the hope that, when he saw her in the flesh, he would welcome her. Now she realized that her actions had taken a severe toll on him, and she had no idea what he was going to do or say.

With each tentative step up the stairwell, she felt her balance deserting her. There was a dryness in her mouth that reminded her of the night he'd picked her up from jail. She paused at his closed door and took a deep breath. *Here we go.* She knocked, and they were suddenly face to face, two people with the same proud chins. Paula had dubbed them "The Chin Patrol."

As Zack closed the door behind them, he felt a cold prickling along his spine as though some part of him believed she could be an impostor or a ghost. He was overjoyed that she was alive, but he felt like the butt of a cruel joke. That she had been alive all this time and not made contact was unthinkable. How do you tabulate the hours of pain that come with slowly giving up on the life of a beloved child?

"What the hell, Shannie? You fall off the face of the earth for two years . . . no word . . . nothing." The betrayal in his voice was hard for her to hear.

"I had no choice," she replied softly, her eyes clear and persuasive. "You would have pulled the plug if you found out."

He had no quick retort because he knew it was true.

"Getting clean was harder than I thought," she continued. "Much harder." Her eyes tried to tell him the whole story, but how was that possible? How could she explain her journey? She was still trying to make sense of it herself. "I found a rehab place in Mexico. No names, no records. You pay for your treatment by working your butt off." She held up her hands to show him old callouses from picking oranges.

"Who the fuck is Castellano?" he asked irritably.

"My husband," she answered. She couldn't resist a crooked smile. "Enrique is a gay guy I met in rehab. I plan to change my name back when I can pin him down long enough to sign the divorce papers."

"Very clever," acknowledged her father. He had been a master schemer at her age. His uniform scam in OCS was only one example. He'd been a hustler of some kind all his life. Even under the distinguished mantel of a naval officer, and a hero to boot, he sometimes found himself reverting to form, shrewdly bargaining with mechanics and dentists and scrutinizing every restaurant tab with hawk-nosed suspicion.

"What did you tell the Navy about your drug use?" he asked pointedly.

"Nothing, of course," she said, her eyes flashing defensively. "How could I?"

Zack's face was cold. Since his chaotic youth on the streets of Olongapo, when he broke every rule known to man, he had lived his life by playing by the rules. He was an officer and a gentleman. It was a blanket he had wrapped himself in for the last thirty-five years of his life.

There can be no secret in your heart.

"Not disclosing your drug history is a crime, Shannon," he stated flatly. "If I don't tell command what I know, I'll be complicit."

"If you tell them, they'll lock me up," she countered, "and my life might as well be over."

"You should have thought of that before you got hooked on drugs," snarled her father. "You're a Navy girl. You knew the rules. Now you expect me to break the law for you after what you've done?"

"Yes," she insisted, her jaw protruding. "You owe me."

The air seemed to find its way out of the room.

"I owe you?" he sputtered. "I owe you?" His jaw joined hers in a duel.

"After Mom died, I carried us," she challenged. "Now I need you to let me do this."

Zack wasn't sure how to respond. He knew he had not been in top form in the year following Paula's death, but he resented the idea that his teenage daughter had carried him. "We both had a rough year," he countered lamely.

"I need this," she persisted. "Please give me a chance to show you who I really am."

Zack's heart went out to her. The last time she had lowered her guard to seek his help, he had sent her running. The courage and hard work that it had taken for her to be standing here was impressive. "Shannie, Shannie, I see what you've done, and I'm very proud of you for it, but there's no way the Navy won't find out, now that they know our connection."

"Why do they need to find out?" she challenged. "Those girls all have marriages and careers to protect. You're the only other person who knows about that bust." She recognized her own duplicity in the moment. She had resented his always bailing her out, and now she was asking for him to do exactly that.

"That may be so," said Zack, "but the Navy's rules about drug addiction are there for a reason. Even the AA guys will tell you that addicts are always in recovery."

She said nothing. She knew what was coming next.

"What if that happens in an eighty-million-dollar airplane?"

His words dug right at her most central fear. Shannon had considered this question from every angle and had not come up with an answer. *Once an addict, always an addict.*

"I've been clean and sober for two years," she boasted. "I swear I will never touch alcohol or drugs again."

The dam broke for Zack. "Do you have any idea what you did to me with this little end-around? Every day and night, I waited for the phone to ring and to find out you were dead. After your mom, how do you think that felt?"

Shannon's eyes glowed a cobalt blue. "Do you think it was a joyride for me? I couldn't contact a soul. I had to create this whole other identity. I couldn't trust anyone. I was alone, totally alone."

"Alone," said Zack. The word filled the room. It defined the two people in it. They stood there, facing each other with those Mayo chins. They were the same person. They had always been the same person. "When you set your shoulders like that, you remind me so much of her," he mused sadly.

"Now you love her for her strength?" Shannon wore a mocking smile. "You were so threatened."

"That's not true," Zack argued. "I loved your mom's strength."

"Be honest, sir," she countered sharply. "You loved that pretty, unworldly girl you carried out of that factory. Then you couldn't keep up with the woman she became. Don't try that bullshit with me."

"Whoa. Hold on. Why am I the bad guy here?" he demanded. "I came home from fighting a war to find out the only person I loved in life was hooked on drugs."

"I tried to stay strong," she said earnestly. "I tried so hard. Finally, I ran out of energy."

A grisly image assaulted Zack's brain with a suddenness that made him dizzy. He had deleted the photo from his phone, but the picture of that lump of chewed human flesh traveled with him wherever he went. "Were you anywhere near that boat fire?" he asked with an intensity that made her want to take a step backward.

"Yes," she admitted. "I jumped out and swam to shore. There was a miscount. No one knows I was on that boat."

Zack's heart felt like it might implode. His words were barely audible. "I thought it was you," he croaked hoarsely.

"What?"

"This . . . this thing they found."

"My God," was all she could say. She could vividly recall the agonized scream as she struggled to swim to shore.

Zack's tone softened. "Honey, I'd give anything to see you fly the FA/18, but if you die trying, how could I live with that? How could I face Mom?"

"I'm not going to die," she countered, hoping she sounded stronger than she felt. "I'm an even better pilot than you."

Zack felt a smile tease his lips. This was the old Shannon. This was the girl he had raised to go toe-to-toe with any man or woman. He had poured his life into this person, all his knowledge and experience, all his tricks and wiles. He would give anything to have their dream back.

With her father's hesitation, Shannon saw an opening. "I'll make you a deal," she began her pitch. "If there's even the slightest hint that I haven't recovered, you won't have to kick me out; I'll quit on the spot."

"How do I know you're a woman of your word?" he asked. "The last time didn't inspire a lot of confidence."

Shannon faced him squarely. "I went through a lot to get here, sir. A lot. I'm not a little girl anymore. I had to grow up." She lowered her voice to a whisper. This was the important part, and she had to make him understand. "I know I'm asking you to break the law, but I know I'm a great pilot, and I can do a lot of good for our country, like you did."

"Now you're blowing smoke up my ass?" he chided. Then he frowned. "Are you aware of what you're asking from me? I could lose my pension. I could serve time, and so could you."

"I know what I'm asking," she said with no hitch in her delivery.

Zack could feel his heart dialoguing with his military mind like drunks at a bar. If he acquiesced, they would both be breaking the law. But what his daughter had achieved to get here was monumental. And in a nagging way, it was true; he owed her. He had failed her that day she ran away on her Harley. "The slightest hint and you walk?" he asked. "No arguments?"

"No arguments," she answered evenly. She held her breath in anticipation of what he was about to say.

"Okay, we'll give it a try," he said evenly.

Shannon let out a breath she had been holding for too long. "Thank you, Captain," she sighed gratefully. She wanted to throw her arms around her father's neck and cry. But he wasn't through.

"I won't lie to you, Lieutenant," he continued. "My goal is to show you this is a mistake before you ever get behind the controls. Do you understand? This could be over fast, Shannie."

Shannon was stung by his words. The warmth she had felt drained out of her. He had already made up his mind that she was unfixable. This was just a face-saving ploy. She thrust out her chin defiantly. "I'll show you," she vowed.

"I hope you do," he replied. "There's nothing I want more."

Shannon dismissed his effort with a little smirk before saluting in preparation for leaving. "By your leave, Captain," she intoned dutifully.

"Wait," he exhaled. "I've missed you." His voice was choked with emotion.

Shannon met his intense gaze. "I've missed you, too," she replied with equal emotion. For a moment, the love they had known long ago returned like an old friend.

"Can I buy you dinner tonight?" he asked hopefully. "Maybe that little Thai place you and Mom and I used to go to?" He felt like a teenage boy trying to make his first date.

Shannon missed her father in the deepest of ways. She had dreamed of coming home, of starting over. But now that she was here, she wondered if a new beginning was even possible. On her way to report at the base, she had driven by the family home and seen a family playing tetherball in the front yard. When she asked someone in admin where her father was living, she was informed that he was renting a cottage at "The Ranch," an infamous enclave of aging pilots who partied with much younger beach girls. It made her sad to think of her father as another old dude chasing his youth.

Suddenly, it was glaringly obvious to Shannon why she felt so distant from her father. It had been almost a decade since her mother's death. She was a woman now, not a child. Dinner with a stranger held no appeal.

"That's sweet," she said diplomatically. "But after all that's happened, I wouldn't know what to talk about. Would you?" She did not mean it as an insult, but she felt like she hardly knew this man.

Zack felt her pull away and had no idea how to bring back that warmth. He awkwardly mumbled, "In case it still matters to you, I love you. I will always love you."

Shannon was moved. Those kind hazel eyes, that thick head of military-cut white hair, that easy grin, this was her dad. But it was so much more complicated than that.

"I love you, too. But I'm still trying to figure things out," she replied.

Zack nodded understandingly. "I'm still sorting things out myself," he mumbled. "Maybe if we actually talk about it for once, we can work it out together." When she failed to reply, the seconds that followed were like temple gongs. "Can I, at least, give you a hug?" he asked with deep frustration and longing.

She didn't know what to say. She wanted that hug, and she feared it. It had been such a lonely journey, and it was far from over. If she let her guard down now, would she be able to get it back?

Zack didn't wait for an okay. He closed the distance between them and put his arms around her. Shannon hesitated a moment, then put her head on his chest. She could smell his distinctive cologne. Acqua di Gio. Zack would have held that embrace forever, but Shannon suddenly pulled away and saluted smartly. "By your leave, sir."

"Carry on," he muttered reluctantly. Shannon quickly walked out. Zack closed his door and sat down slowly in his weathered chair. He felt tears of supreme joy fill his eyes. His favorite person in the world was alive.

Maybe I can still turn this around.

SIX
★ ★ ★
THE FISHERY KID

THE VIRGINIA BEACH FISHERY
That Same Day

Twenty-nine-year-old Dylan Harmony looked up with boyish awe as four FA/18s flew overhead in formation. Growing up near NAS Oceana, many people put fighter pilots on a higher level than rock stars, and Dylan was one of them. One of the planes suddenly left the formation to soar heavenward.

"Wow!" he exclaimed like a fan at a football game. "That's a 'Missing Man.' See the one leaving the formation? They're honoring a pilot who died," he explained.

"I know," chirped his best friend and sort-of-sister, Nickie Jordan, also twenty-nine. In many ways, she understood the military world better than him. Her parents had been Marine Infantry.

Dylan Harmony had sensitive sea-green eyes set into an intellectual but still rugged face. Nickie was an elf. A blithe spirit. There was nothing they wouldn't do for each other. They called each other silly names and sometimes double-dated. They were bros. When Nickie's parents had died a year apart in Afghanistan when she was twelve, Dylan had convinced his mother and older brother to take her in. Today they were part of a shift of thirty men and women in red slickers and hip boots eating lunch in the outdoor patio of the monolithic fishery that was one of the largest employers in the area.

"Check it out, Bro-diddly," said Nickie, pushing the current edition of *Stars and Stripes* in front of Dylan. Under a byline "Largest Number of Women in FRS History" were four photos. She pointed out a woman with blond hair and Asian features. It was Sidney Lee. "Meet my future wife," piped Nickie.

"Here we go again," laughed Dylan. Nickie was always coming up with a new scheme to escape her hopeless life as a fishery worker. "How do you know she's gay?"

"I've got superpowers," joked Nickie. Nickie had known her sexual proclivity since she was old enough to walk. But a serious relationship with someone of the same sex had mysteriously eluded her. She had a habit of always going after the ones who were out of reach, socially and monetarily.

An annoyingly loud buzzer split the air like a fire alarm, and the workers rose and bussed their trays, then trudged back inside the doors of the fishery like an army of the dead. This was a job you did because it paid well. But they all hated it, and each person had developed his or her own way to handle an eight-hour shift.

Dylan and Nickie's job, as part of the pit crew, was to grab a thrashing tuna as it descended from one of four chutes and plunge a sharp spike through its brain. Dylan's brother had worked here when they killed the fish with baseball bats. This new method was regarded as more humane. As Dylan worked, Mozart's "Sonata Number Seventeen in C Major" pumped into his ears from water-resistant ear pods. Loud classical music was his way to get through the day. He had learned the trick from his older brother. Nickie's solution was to listen to her favorite dance tracks and do her job to the beat.

As the hours passed, the workers began to look more and more frequently at an overhead clock. Nickie suddenly splashed water at Dylan. "Swallow fish guts, Bro-ster-ino," she shouted playfully. Dylan took out his ear pods and put them in one of his pockets like precious gems before splashing her back.

"You swallow fish guts, Nick-O-Ramus." Their fight ignited other water fights around the floor, tired workers seizing the opportunity to blow off steam from their gruesome tasks. The big fish cascaded down the chutes and swam around in a euphoria of temporary reprieve.

A man in a suit and tie emerged from a bank of offices on the catwalk above, and the workers sprang back to their tasks. Their foreman raised a bullhorn to his lips.

"Union Reps Harmony and Jordan, management wants to see you," he announced before returning to his office. Dylan and Nickie climbed out of the pit. After removing their outerwear and hanging them on hooks, they started up a stairwell in jeans and T-shirts. The workers cheered their union reps, and Dylan and Nickie joined their hands overhead like prizefighters.

As the newly elected reps, Dylan and Nickie had a unique amount of power. For someone who had only completed high school, Nickie's bargaining skills were as shrewd as any lawyer. Dylan had been an avid reader all his life and could speak with the precision of a college graduate.

It was dark when they left the fishery and trudged slowly to their separate vehicles in the fishery parking lot. "I can't take it anymore, Bro-diddly," announced Nickie. "I'm seeing fish eyeballs in my sleep." Then she brightened. "But this Friday night, all that changes."

"What happens then?" asked Dylan.

"That's when I meet my wife," she said. "One of the candidates in the new class at fleet has a band. They're playing this Friday night at Molly's." She turned pleading eyes on Dylan. "Please come with. I always do better when I got my wingman."

"I have my Friday meeting," he reminded her.

"Come after," she persisted. "Please. I know this is going to be my lucky year. And who knows? You might fly out of here like me on the wings of a naval aviator."

Dylan laughed. "You are incurable. I'll try to stop by, but you know I hate to be around drinkers."

"That's my bro." She put her arms around his neck and kissed his cheek. Then she mounted a bright yellow motor scooter and rat-a-tat-tatted out of the lot. Dylan got in his black 2005 Ford pickup and followed her out.

Dylan stopped at an Italian restaurant and picked up a takeout order of chicken parmesan. Driving home, he passed the YMCA and saw Nickie welcoming a group of local children to a dance class. She had changed into a lime green leotard and looked like a gecko with a pixie cut. Nickie was a world-class, self-taught dancer. She led her charge in a wild shake-your-bootie dance. Dylan had championed the idea of Nickie taking her skills to New York City. He had gone so far as giving her a bus ticket as a present. But after losing her parents, she was terrified of change. He knew her wild scheme to marry a Naval aviator was doomed, like all her dreams, because of this fear.

It was 7 p.m. when the fishery kid got home. Dylan lived alone in a tiny studio apartment with a slight view of the bay. Nickie had a place in the same building on the ground floor. From the collection of classical albums that he'd inherited from his brother, he chose the one he depended on to lighten his mood. Richard Wagner's "The Ride of the Valkyries" surged like galloping steeds from state-of-the-art speakers, another "gift" from Stevie. Then he walked out onto his balcony and took in his slice of the harbor.

A night trawler passed, seagulls swirling lazily in its bright navigational beacons. Dylan had not said anything when Nickie brought it up, but the prospect of turning thirty and still working in the fishery weighed heavily on his thoughts tonight.

Dylan's life had not been easy. His father, a peacock of a man, ran out on the family when Dylan was twelve. He had never been much of a father to the boy, but Dylan had worshipped him anyway and had never stopped trying to encourage his love. As was his nature, Dylan took his father's sudden departure personally. That same year, Nickie lost both of her parents to war, and Dylan convinced his mother and brother to take his friend into their home. This brought some needed levity back into his life, but it was short-lived. His mother never recovered from her husband's desertion. When Dylan was fifteen, she had to go into a nursing home. This put the burden on three teenagers to put in long hours at the fishery to pay the mortgage on their house and the cost of that nursing home.

Dylan experienced one shining moment in high school. He had written a short story for an English class about life in a fishery that won first place in a school contest. His teacher had submitted it to *The New Yorker* for their annual contest, and Dylan won second place. The prize came with a paid trip to New York to receive his award, and there he met Celeste Stein, a literary agent in her midfifties.

Ms. Stein praised his ability to write complex local characters. She called him "The Master of the Metaphor." She encouraged him to send her his work, but it had been over a year since he'd sent anything to her. He had fallen into the old rut. He felt trapped and helpless to do anything about it.

He wanted a beer. Fuck that. How about a line?

Dylan blamed his lack of writing in the past year on his sobriety. It had always been easier to write when he was a little lubed or stoned or both. Lately, he had not found much to stimulate his imagination. Life was settling into the same old pattern. He worked his horrible job, and he listened to his restorative music. His efforts to make a relationship work with a woman had been disappointing. The girls he met in high school were all working class, like him, but lacked his inner nature and sensitivity. In his city-college classes, he met a more curious breed of women, but this also introduced him to drugs. After an unfortunate incident with a fellow druggie nearly took his life, his dating life had been on hold for a year. It had also been his first full year of sobriety since his early teens. When he felt like being social, he went out to eat or saw a movie with Nickie.

Dylan sometimes wondered if he felt things that no one else felt. This carried over into his writing. He could write from the eyes of a woman as easily as he could those of a man. This didn't mean he was in any way ambivalent in that matter. He just had more antennae than most people. It was what Ms. Stein had picked up on in that early short story.

Dylan knew that Nickie was right. It was time to take drastic action. That didn't mean trying to fly out on the wings of a naval aviator. His one and only shot was his writing. After he finished his takeout, he sat down at his laptop and created a new Word document. Then he stared at the shimmering-white screen and thought of cocaine.

SEVEN
★★★
A FRIEND AND A MENTOR

FRS

End of Week One

Class had ended at 1600 hours, and already Shannon had seen enough to know that FRS made her previous schools look like summer camp. The pace in the classroom was relentless. If your mind wandered for even a moment, you could lose the thread of the assignment and have to start over. Her eyes hurt. Her back ached from being a crab crouched over a computer. The sanctuary of her Bachelor Officers Quarters apartment was a welcome respite at the end of the day.

She had made the choice to live on base, reasoning that most of the class would be renting apartments in town, and this would give her the isolation she needed to protect her secret. If you don't make friends, you don't have to watch what you say.

As she showered, she directed the spray onto the painful knot that started between her shoulders and reached down her spine like an eagle's claw. She told herself to be happy that her father had given her this tiny window of hope. It could have easily gone the other way. But the realization that he was determined to fail her was daunting. Her journey getting to this stage of her plan had been hard enough. She had prayed that, when he saw that she was alive, he would welcome her home. Now she was in a war of wills with a man whom she regarded as the most unbeatable opponent she had ever faced.

After learning that she had been selected to OCS, she had been haunted by an idea that was so crazy as to be laughable, but it wouldn't leave her alone. Growing up, her father had told her again and again that he was the last person in the world who should have been anointed an officer and a gentleman. He was a street rat, a pimp, a scam artist. He had succeeded in his impossible quest because of a mentor, the fearsome Foley. Her father had used Foley's name like a dreaded boogeyman. *If you don't brush your teeth, I'm sending you to Foley.*

Combined with the vivid stories of his mentor's powers of intimidation, she had elevated the man to mythical status in her mind. The realization of how impossible the mission she had chosen weighed on her more and more every day. She knew she needed a mentor. Maybe Foley could work his same miracle on her.

Using the computer in Monkey Millstein's office, she began a search and found an article in *Stars and Stripes* reporting that Emil Foley was discharged from the Marine Corps twenty-five years ago at the age of fifty-eight after losing his legs in a training accident. In another article, she learned that, shortly after his discharge, he had gone off the end of a pier in an apparent suicide attempt and had to be rescued. There had been no record of his whereabouts in the last ten years. By the time she reached FRS, she had given up on trying to find him.

As she got out of the shower, the door into the room opened suddenly, and one of her classmates appeared, a heavy duffel on one shoulder, mail, and the base newspaper in one hand. Sidney blushed as she saw Shannon's naked body. "I'm sorry," she blurted. "I should have knocked."

"What can I do for you?" asked Shannon guardedly, wrapping herself in a towel.

Sidney produced a nervous smile. "I guess we're bunkmates."

Shannon's brow knitted. "There must be a mistake. Admin assured me I'd have this room to myself. Bad allergies." She coughed to make her case, then shrugged helplessly. She had used this ploy with generally good results before.

Sidney looked hurt. She turned around to leave, but Shannon felt a sudden change of heart. She was sick of being a loner. After advanced flight, she had vowed to be happier. It was part of her plan to love herself more. Now that she had gotten into FRS, she could take some chances. *Make a friend.* If it didn't work out, she'd ask for a room by herself or rent a place in town.

"No worries," she said warmly. "Come in."

Sidney brightened. "You sure?" Her almond eyes with their light blue corneas seemed enormous behind her thick spectacles. She lowered her duffel onto the unclaimed bed and tossed the mail and newspaper beside it. "I hope you're not allergic to me," she said, smiling in a clever way that told Shannon she hadn't bought the allergy line.

Shannon laughed. At least her bunkmate had a sense of humor. That was a start.

"Cool tattoo," observed Sidney, looking at Shannon's neck. "What does it mean?"

Shannon blushed. She didn't like explaining her ink. "I was angry about something at the time," she said, hoping to cut it off there.

"Are those someone's initials?" persisted the other girl.

"Yeah," said Shannon, without offering more. She put on gym shorts and a tee and sat at her desk to study, hoping by her posture that Sidney would get the message. She had agreed to be roommates, nothing more, but Sidney was relentless.

"Your father didn't look happy to see you in the class," she observed.

Shannon bit her lip. "We have our differences," she confessed, and left it at that. She was starting to regret her invitation to be bunkmates.

"I know what that's like," Sidney proclaimed, not missing a beat. "I haven't spoken to my dad in a year. That's when . . . " She trailed off before completing the sentence, " I came out."

She removed a framed photo from her duffel and put it on her bedside table. Shannon glanced at it perfunctorily. Posed outside their Bremerton home, her father and her four brothers wore blue naval officer uniforms and Sidney a Timberland coat. Her father was Chinese, and the brothers all revealed a mix of two different races like Sidney.

"Where's your mom?" asked Shannon. She immediately wished she could take back her question. It would surely inspire a similar question. Her mother's tragic death had made headlines. As Shannon Castellano, she had dodged this problem, but now at FRS, her identity was known.

"We never talk to her," Sidney informed her. "It's a family rule."

"That's pretty harsh, isn't it?" said Shannon.

"My dad is punishing her," explained Sidney. "My mom cheated on him. She left him for a woman." She explained that her father was a Navy captain who commanded a submarine. Her three brothers were all lieutenant commanders in the surface Navy. Her mother was a landscape designer and was Swedish, hence the blond hair and blue eyes.

Then the dreaded question came. "I heard about your mom. That must have been tough."

Shannon cleared her throat. "Sidney, forgive me, but I never talk about my mom, and I really need to study."

"Oh, of course," stammered Sidney, clearly wounded. Time passed awkwardly. Shannon could feel a question coming out of her bunkmate for a minute before it came. "I can ask them to reassign me, if you want," offered Sidney. "I know how some people feel about . . . about people like me."

"Jesus, Sidney," Shannon interrupted, waving a hand as though clearing the air. "I'm just not a very social person."

Sidney accepted that and happily returned to her unpacking. "It's still so new to me," she resumed. "I know it's supposed to be 'don't ask, don't tell,' but I don't really know any gay people. My only experience was this girl at OCS, and she won't talk to me now." Then she caught herself. "Sorry." She made a comical zipped-up face.

Pulling a case of toiletries from her duffel, Sidney started toward the bathroom. In her hurry, she accidentally knocked the mail she had brought off her bed and onto the floor. The base newspaper landed at Shannon's feet. As she picked it up, her body froze.

"Oh my God," she muttered, dumbstruck. She was staring at an ad for a martial arts gym that had just opened in Chic's Beach. "FOLEY'S FITNESS—MARTIAL ARTS—SELF-DEFENSE—SPECIAL RATES FOR MILITARY."

Shannon couldn't believe her good fortune. *How many Foleys could there be who knew martial arts?* She bolted from her chair and pulled on sweats. She was out the door before Sidney emerged from the bathroom and found her gone.

Thirty minutes later, Shannon's lean body shone with perspiration as she toyed with her male instructor, Ramon, in one of three rings in the old boxing gym that had been transformed, with little coin, into a fitness center. Peppering the Latino's chest with front kicks, she forced him to retreat. She knew she could take the thirty-year-old down any time she wanted, but it had to be when Foley was watching, and he had not looked at her once since she'd arrived.

After less than an hour, she was having second thoughts about coming here. The fearsome Foley of her imaginings was now an eighty-seven-year-old torso in a motorized chair. He was a sour old curmudgeon on top of it. She wondered if he was questioning his decision to open this old gym at the same time as they were opening the state-of-the-art Star Fitness Center just down the street. She and a teenage boy hitting the speed bag were the only paying customers in the cavernous old building at this hour in the evening.

Shannon executed a sudden crescent kick, sending her much larger opponent reeling to the canvas. Foley spoke for the first time. Apparently, he had been watching her all along.

"Nice crescent," he said with a scowl. "Who taught you these moves?"

"My father," she replied.

"Unconventional," he observed. "More like street moves."

"That's how he learned," she replied. "He grew up in the Philippines."

Ramon was back on his feet, and he and Shannon were circling again. Sweeping one of her opponent's legs wide with a foot, she grabbed his shoulders and brought a knee up hard into his stomach, sending him to the floor gasping for air.

Foley frowned. "Take a break, Ramon."

"Yes, sir," replied the short, muscular Latino. He climbed out of the ring, giving his boss a withering look before walking outside to get some air. Shannon climbed down from the ring. As she removed her gloves, she saw Foley watching her shrewdly.

"I've only seen that Muay Thai takedown a couple of times," he said. "Once from a kid in Afghanistan and one time . . . a long time ago . . ."

"In Officer Candidate School," she interjected, thrusting out her hand. "Shannon Mayo. My father's Zack Mayo." For the first time, she detected a hint of a smile from the old man's lips.

"Mayonnaise," he said, massaging the name with a sense of history. Even in retirement, he still managed to keep up to speed with military news, and he had followed his old student's rise to military celebrity-hood with a mentor's pride.

"Is he still running that jet school across the bay?" he asked.

"This is his last class. And I'm in it," she replied, making a little face that said *We don't exactly see eye to eye.* She waited for Foley to say something, but he seemed to have lost interest in her. He motored over to the boy hitting the speed bag and demonstrated a better technique. His legs may have deserted him, but his hands were still weapons. Shannon clapped and Foley scowled.

"What do you want from me?" he asked suspiciously.

Shannon was taken aback. "I've been looking for you since I started this little adventure," she began lamely. "Then, lo and behold, you're right here in my own backyard."

The old man's eyes turned fierce. "What do you expect from me?" he demanded as if she'd come here to ask him for money. "Do I look like I can help people now?" He had spoken so loudly that the boy hitting the speed bag looked at them cautiously before resuming his workout.

"This is the battle of my life, Gunny," she said openly. "I can come in on Saturdays, teach, clean up . . ." She knew she sounded desperate, but despite first impressions, her instincts were telling her she needed this man if she was to stand a chance with her impossible quest.

Foley seemed to regret his hostile tone. "I can't help you," he said more civilly. "I only knew your father for thirteen weeks, and that was more than thirty-five years ago."

"He said you made him a man," she persisted. "I was hoping you could do that for me." She threw in the crooked grin that had always worked for her in the past.

Foley's weathered face twisted like he'd bitten into a jalapeño. "In the infinite wisdom of the United States Marine Corps, I've been out of that business for twenty-five years," he spat. "I'm sorry, but you came to the wrong place." He motored away, an angry and lonely old man.

Shannon had a sudden inspiration. "Gunny?" she called. Foley turned slowly in his motorized chair. She took his photo with her phone, waved, and walked out.

Foley stared after her. Feeling a tightening in his chest, he fumbled in his wheelchair pocket for his vial of pills and washed back two tablets with water from a sports bottle. The sudden appearance of this girl was unexpectedly disturbing to him. Zack Mayo was different from any other officer candidate he had encountered in his long tenure at that school. He was a younger version of himself, a reminder of all the unanswered questions he'd had about his own youth. When they parted company, the hardened warrior had felt a sense of loss that he could not explain to himself. He realized finally that he had come to think of Zack in some ways as a son. He made a promise to himself that, if his daughter showed up again, he would have Ramon ask her to leave.

EIGHT
★ ★ ★
AN OFFICER AND A GENTLEMAN

FRS

Wednesday Night of Week One

Zack and Perryman sat at the long and stately officer's club oak bar in their khaki uniforms, drinking Angel's Envy bourbon, neat, at cocktail hour prices. Officers and their guests sat at the bar or around the formally appointed room that opened onto an expansive outdoor patio. This was "Officer Country," its the old-world decorum punctuated by the oil portraits of officers in uniform dating back to John Paul Jones.

"Some friend," mumbled Zack sourly. "How long did you know about this?" He was still trying to process Shannon's surprise appearance after two years on the missing list. It was Wednesday of week one, but this was the first chance the two friends had had to compare notes.

"Whoa," protested Perryman, throwing up both of his large hands like a shield. "I was as shocked as you." He explained how he had missed seeing Shannon in the TCTS building during the dogfight and so had been shocked a few minutes later to see her with the new class receiving their issue of uniforms. He wisely decided to let the father and daughter reunion happen without his help, but later that day, he had approached her on the parade ground and emotionally welcomed her home.

"I'm glad you're giving her a chance, Zack," said his best friend. "You know I felt you were too hard on her after that graduation stunt." Perryman was the only one Zack had confided in about Shannon's descent into addiction.

"You never lost someone to drugs," Zack responded hollowly. "It's the most insidious illness there is. I watched my mother unravel one thread at a time."

"Shannon isn't your mother, Zack," replied Perryman. "She's a modern girl, strong like Paula. And it's complicated between you two."

Zack fixed sharp eyes on Perryman. "Meaning?"

Perryman searched for the right words. "With Paula focused on her career, you and Shannie were as thick as thieves. Then Paula died, and that was over. Don't you ever ask yourself about that?"

"We both took her death hard," reasoned Zack. "I was a reminder of her mother, I guess. She turned to gaming because it gave her a safe place to go." He shook his head in frustration. "I swear I don't know her anymore, Louis. This girl isn't my Shannie. She's got this street edge. She's angry, defensive. There's something . . . wild about her."

Perryman smiled. "Sounds like someone I met awhile back. My money says she turns it around like you did."

Perryman's words brought a nostalgic smile from Zack. "I had a lot of luck," he mused. "Paula, Sid, Casey, you guys."

"Aren't you leaving somebody out?" asked Perryman with a twinkle in his gray eyes. When Zack didn't reply, he provided another clue. "Guess who just took over the old boxing gym on the boardwalk?"

"Foley's here?" he replied, astonished.

"What's left of him after that training accident," said Perryman. "One day, you, Emiliano and I should drop in on him for old time's sake."

"Or not," said Zack with a rueful grin. "I still have nightmares about that guy."

The two old friends spontaneously launched into a routine they had enjoyed over the years. When Della-Serra was in the group, it got even more hilarious.

"Are you eyeballing me, boy?" bellowed Zack in his best Foley voice.

Perryman answered with equal menace, "I'm going to yank your eyes out of their sockets and skull-fuck you!"

A group of officer wives at a nearby table exchanged disapproving looks, but since Zack and Perryman outranked everyone, no one said a word.

Conversation shifted to a familiar topic, retirement. "I just can't wrap my head around it, big guy," Zack said in words barely above a whisper. "I never thought it would be like this."

Perryman nodded empathetically. They were both warriors at heart, professional soldiers, and it was coming to an end. How would they fill that void? The tall Texan had been so wedded to the Navy that he had sacrificed family in its service. His wife had decided to become a country western singer at forty. After a judge ruled that he could not claim a stable residence, she moved to Nashville with their two sons. Their friend Della-Serra lost his son and his marriage because of his own grandiose dreams to be a frogman. When his son drowned in hell week at BUD/S, his wife of twenty-five years divorced him. Military life contained many stories like this.

"Maybe Shannie will help you figure out the next move, boss," offered Perryman in his honey-soft drawl. "Wouldn't it be fitting if you turned out to be the one with grandbabies on your lap?"

Zack chuckled cynically. He could not see himself with grandbabies. He could not see himself working for the airlines. He could not see the future at all.

Zack swam in the ocean in front of his beach cottage, his strokes relentless, like a man fighting, not only age, but memory. He was not shocked by Shannon's end-around. She had surprised him every day of his life. She had never been an easy child. There was a wildness about her, an insatiable hunger for adventure and attention that frightened her parents. Neither Zack nor Paula could understand what was driving their only child. But it was in plain sight. She was doing everything in her power to fit in with first one, then two, superstar parents.

Returning to his cottage after his swim, Zack experienced the empty feeling he always felt when he walked into his new digs. Selling the old house and moving to the Ranch had been a bad idea. He was not a player like Della-Serra, or even a once-in-awhile-er like Perryman. As a big star in this world, and still maintaining a youthful body, he could probably sweet-talk younger girls into his bed, but he knew what would happen if he tried. He had already put that myth to rest. The Paula filter would shoot that down in a very embarrassing manner.

He had concluded on his first night of residence that this beach cottage was not a home. "Home" was a subject he had ruminated on often throughout his lifetime. His boyhood with his mother had not been a home. For fourteen years, he had waited for the inevitable to happen, and finally it did. She swallowed a bottle of pills while he was at school. She left no note. She just checked out. When no one from his mother's family would take him in, Zack went to live in a state home for boys while the authorities attempted to locate his father. If you wanted to see human cruelty under a microscope, this was your chance. Born into a world of abuse, these boys were capable of every adult atrocity imaginable, and some that transcended adult imagination.

Luckily Zack was not there long before he was sent to live with his sailor father, Byron Mayo, an eternal child-man in his midthirties stationed in the "armpit of the Orient," Olongapo, the Philippines. For Byron, having Zack live with him was just another scam. The Navy paid him a substantial allowance for a dependent. No one said anything about being a dad.

Zack's mind drifted back to the day he arrived in the Philippines. He would never forget that cacophony of car horns or the smell of bodies in the heat. Jeepneys swarmed the streets like multi-colored beetles. Vendors sold monkey meat.

"Zack? Is that you?" asked the boyish sailor on the opposite side of a metal fence as fourteen-year-old Zack got off the flight in Manila. Behind him was a poster advertising *The Godfather*.

Young Zack had only seen his father once, when he had visited—out of the blue when the boy was five—to bang his mother. He had looked like a teenager then, and he still looked like he would get carded in a bar. He sported deep dimples on both cheeks and a shock of reddish hair cut to regulation while still forming a Superman curl in front. It was not hard to see why his mother had fallen so hard.

"Yes, sir," said Zack warily, unsure what to call him.

"You look even more like your mom now that you're almost all grown up," observed Byron. "Welcome to the PI," he added expansively, as though welcoming a child to his first trip to Disneyland.

"They tried to find you for a year," said Zack accusingly.

"I was out at sea," replied Byron. "But I'm here now."

"Mom said you promised to come back for us," said the boy bitterly. "When you didn't come, she took those pills."

Byron pouted. "If you came all this way to blame me for your mother being a coward, maybe you should go back to that state home."

"I'm not going back there," vowed the fourteen-year-old. "You gotta take me in. It's the law."

"Tough little shit, aren't you?" commented Byron good-naturedly. "You'll need that here."

Unknown, of course, by the Navy, Byron ran a modest prostitution business, consisting of two teenage Filipino prostitutes named Tiki and Maria. They were waiting when Byron and Zack walked into their small apartment in the redlight district of Olongapo, the city that supported the Navy forces stationed in Subic Bay.

"Say hello to your sisters," said Byron. "That's Tiki. She's the oldest. And that's Maria."

"Welcome home, Zacky Boy," said Tiki and Maria at the same time. As Zack would soon learn, they often replied as one. At nineteen, Tiki was the oldest and the prettier of the two, taller and more curvaceous. Maria was eighteen, with large liquid eyes, narrow hips, and teacup breasts. They wore Fruit of the Loom underwear from the PX, and the boy stared at their fit young bodies with obvious appreciation. The girls embraced him and kissed him on the cheek.

"The girls work as hostesses," explained Byron. "Today's their day off." Zack was no child. He knew what that word meant. Byron gestured to a cot inside an open closet. "That's where you'll sleep," he said. "Make yourself at home."

Zack walked into his cramped new quarters and opened his suitcase on his small bed. He bumped his head trying to turn around.

"Are you hungry?" asked his father.

"I'm starving, Byron," said the boy.

His father put up a hand in friendly warning. "My name is Byron-san," he corrected. "Ladies, give your brother some of your famous pork adobo," he instructed imperially, relishing his role as boy-king of the household. "Then you'd better get some sleep, Zack. You start school tomorrow on base."

Zack found the pork adobo amazing and ate two helpings. Against all instincts, he allowed a touch of hope to enter his pinched heart. This was a big improvement over the state home. And his "sisters" were little hotties, not much older than himself.

Byron awakened him the next morning. "Good morning, sport. There's food on the table."

"Good morning, Zacky Boy," heralded the girls from the kitchen where they were cooking eggs and bacon.

As he wolfed down his breakfast, his father fixed him with shrewd eyes that contradicted his boyish face. "I didn't want to get into this last night with you so tired after your trip," he began, "but we got rules here, right, ladies?"

"Yes, Byron-san," they piped together.

"We're a family," he began expansively. "Everybody pulls their weight in this household. Nobody gets a free ride."

Zack chastised himself for his soft thinking. In life there was always a catch. "I ain't selling myself to nobody," he declared in his tough guy voice. "The Navy pays you for keeping me," he reminded his father.

"Your brother's a pisser, ain't he, ladies?" commented Byron. "Nobody's talking about you selling yourself, sport. But if you want walking-around money, and every boy your age needs walking-around money, you gotta work for it."

"What kind of work?" asked Zack warily.

"You like girlie pictures?" asked his father with a comically lurid arch of a brow.

"I suppose," replied Zack. Boys in the state home had passed around nudie magazines.

"What do you think of these?" asked Byron. He dumped a dozen eight-by-ten still photos from a manilla envelope onto the breakfast table. Byron was an amateur photographer with a lurid imagination. In addition to pimping out the two girls, he did a brisk trade in pornography.

Zack almost gagged. This wasn't some airbrushed centerfold. This was raw fare. He was staring at graphic closeups of his sisters having sex with each other or pleasuring Byron who wore a Zorro mask to hide his face.

"That's disgusting," said Zack.

Byron laughed good-naturedly. "I think they're very artistic, don't you, girls?"

"Very artistic, Byron-san," the girls giggled.

"I ain't selling those," insisted young Zack. "You can't make me."

"Nobody makes anybody do anything in this house," soothed Byron. "That's your call, sport. No workie, no eatie, no beddie-by, right, girls?"

"Right, Byron-san," they chorused in their childish way. The girls showed no fear of Byron. They competed for his attention like rival daughters. Zack would soon learn that his father was true to his word. He never hit anybody or forced them to do anything. He was a jolly, sophomoric soul, a post-adolescent Peter Pan.

Zack was welcomed into ninth grade by a kind middle-aged male teacher. It was a good school, considered on a par with private schools stateside, and he found himself immediately behind the curve. But he was a born salesman and, by the end of the day, had sold all his photos, enabling him to make a deal with a fellow student to do his homework.

That night, as he bedded down in his tiny closet, Byron shook him roughly. "Don't get too comfortable, Sport. The girls have to work."

Zack glanced at his sisters. They were wearing their working clothes and were applying their makeup. "Where will I go?" he asked fearfully. On his way to school and back, he had seen a host of street toughs; one was a giant with terrifying tattoos.

"You'll figure it out," said Byron dismissively. "I was younger than you when I had to do it. It'll make you a man."

It was swelteringly hot during the days, but at night, the cold wind off the water whistled through the streets and alleys of Olongapo, pushing the temperature to near freezing. Seeing that seven-foot giant with the afro that added another foot to his height making his rounds with his two lieutenants, Zack hid in the shadows of an alley. He didn't dare close his eyes. There was a black cat that was hiding out, too, and they made eye contact as the night wore on.

Luckily, it was a slow night for his sisters, and he saw a light go on in their window at two in the morning, signaling that he could come home. His body was so cold and cramped that climbing the outside stairwell to the fifth floor was difficult. He immediately jumped into the shower and stayed under the hot spray until Byron came in from roaming the bars and kicked him out.

When Byron was out at sea, Zack's "sisters" took great pleasure in teaching the boy, only a few years their junior, how to pleasure a woman. They played mind games with him to teach him not to finish before his lover.

"Count backward from a hundred, Zacky Boy."

"Think of your mama in heaven, Zacky Boy."

He was a kid in a candy store, but it was not a home.

Zack's first real glimpse into what "home" might look like occurred two months after his arrival in the Philippines. To avoid a run-in with the giant and his boys, he always stayed off the main streets. But one afternoon, they were waiting for him outside his apartment building.

"Give me your money, Big Spendah," ordered the giant. By now, Zack knew his name was Crisanto. "Time to pay the tax man," he sang.

"I don't have any money," replied Zack.

"Liar," snarled the giant. In addition to his intimidating tattoos and height, he had a fake diamond in his navel. "We know about your dirty pictures."

"I don't do that anymore," lied Zack. "Look, I don't have any money." He pulled out his pockets to show that they were empty.

Crisanto exchanged a quick look with his lieutenants. Then he made a screeching sound, like a cat in a fight, and unleashed a sweeping outside crescent kick that nearly tore Zack's jaw off.

"Yaaaa!" cried Zack in pain as he crashed onto the cobblestones, his mouth bleeding. Crisanto's men yanked off his shoes and found the money hidden in one of them. Laughing, the trio sauntered off.

That was when "The Officer in White" entered Zack's life. Zack never knew his name, but the man became a mythic figure in his memories. Tall, handsome, dressed all in white, the officer picked him up off the street, cleaned the blood off his face with a snow-white handkerchief, and gave him money for food.

"I've seen you on the base," observed the officer. "You're a Navy kid." Then his brow creased. "What are you doing in this part of town?"

Zack knew he had to be careful. The Navy wouldn't be happy to learn that Byron's residence was in the redlight district.

"I got lost," lied Zack.

At that moment, four fighter jets swooped low overhead, the shrill blast of noise causing every head on the busy Filipino street to look up. Zack's eyes grew as large as goggles. "What are those?" he asked.

"Tomcats," replied the officer. "And those are my boys flying them. You could do that someday."

"Really?" asked Zack incredulously. With only a drug-addicted mother for parental leadership, he had not harbored many dreams in his young life and none as lofty as this.

"But you'll have to stay in school," his mentor warned. "And stay clear of this neighborhood. Get your college degree. You can't be an officer without it." He met the boy's eyes intensely. "Think you can do that?"

"Yes, sir," answered Zack. He watched the officer in white stride off through the neon world. Zack never saw him again, but he dreamed about him often.

For the first time in his life, Zack had a goal. He was determined to finish high school with college-worthy grades. One day in the base library, he asked the librarian, a short, enlisted sailor with a jet-black toupee, if he could suggest any books about flying jets. He checked out two books. One was the biography of Chuck Yeager, and the other was a slender book of poems about flight. One poem moved him the most. He liked it so much he copied it and carried the paper around with him until it frayed into pieces. Entitled "High Flight," it was written by John Gillespie Magee, Jr. in 1941.

> *Oh! I have slipped the surly bonds of earth,*
> *And danced the skies on laughter-silvered wings;*
> *Sunward I've climbed, and joined the tumbling mirth*
> *Of sun-split clouds— and done a hundred things*
> *You have not dreamed of—Wheeled and soared and swung*
> *High in the sunlit silence. Hov'ring there*
> *I've chased the shouting wind along, and flung*
> *My eager craft through footless halls of air . . .*
> *Up, up the long, delirious, burning blue*
> *I've topped the wind-swept heights with easy grace*
> *Where never lark or even eagle flew—*
> *And, while with silent lifting mind I've trod*
> *The high untrespassed sanctity of space*
> *Put out my hand and touched the face of God.*

Over the years, Byron was many things but never a father. He was a man-child, a raunchy big brother. On Zack's sixteenth birthday, he insisted the boy accompany him on his rounds. "To see how a man enjoys himself." He got the boy drunk. He bought him a lap dance. He insisted Zack watch as he had sex with one of his regulars. It was a weird relationship for the boy to navigate. Byron was not a dad, but he wasn't a bad man either. He was an insatiable satyr, squeezing pleasure out of every second of his life with total disdain for the consequences. Women adored him. Men welcomed him rowdily. He was the life of the party, a raconteur overflowing with tales from his world travels. It made the boy wonder about his father's past, but Byron-san never talked about that.

One day Zack was cleaning up his father's room and came across an old theater pamphlet advertising an Italian family who billed themselves

"The Mayo Brothers." Heralding from Naples, Italy, they performed in a traveling circus, touring the Borscht Belt. In one picture, a boy of nine was being levitated by a magician. He had a mop of reddish-brown hair and cute dimples. Was it his father?

"Who are these people, Byron-san?" he asked his father, holding out the pamphlet. Byron snatched it from him so suddenly it made the boy freeze.

"Don't go sniffing around my things," ordered his father. He offered no explanation for what Zack had seen or why he had reacted so emotionally.

Zack graduated from the American School at eighteen. Despite his dream, he found his big plan in jeopardy. His grades were decent but hardly in the league to attract a college scholarship. He had saved up enough money for plane fare to the States, but Byron had filched his stash to pay a gambling debt.

One night, the local man who was in charge of pimping Tiki and Maria was sick, so Zack had to take over the job. He had been filling in like this since he was sixteen, so he had the dance down to a science.

"Oy, oy, Big Spendah, short time, long time, ten dollah," he crooned to the passing sailors from the Seventh Fleet, Tiki on his left arm and Maria on his right. Now twenty-three and twenty-two, the girls had given their youth to their job, and a desperation was creeping into their features. It was harder and harder to get their old prices for their services.

Further complicating his life, Zack had developed romantic feelings for Maria, the younger of the girls, and she for him.

"You and I get married someday, Zacky Boy," she would giggle in his ear as they made love. Maria had been born into a poor family in Luzon. At sixteen, she came to Manila and got a job right away as a dancer. Then she found out what that really meant. She was the only one Zack told about the officer in white or his dream to fly jets. As their closeness grew, it became harder and harder for him to sell her on the street. Afterward, they would cry in each other's arms.

Suddenly, Crisanto and his henchmen appeared in their path. Zack had managed to avoid them since the tall young man with the afro had nearly killed him with those kicks. In the meantime, Zack had mastered kicks like those and some Muay Thai moves that could kill a man, but he remained wary of this man and his lieutenants. Now in their midtwenties, they had graduated from street toughs to seasoned criminals who wore suits, but no shirts, the better to display their collections of gold chains. They carried weapons and worked for the biggest crime boss in Subic Bay.

"Lookee-lookee what we got here," whistled Crisanto. "Our old friend who sells dirty pictures." He bowed to Tiki and Maria. "Afternoon, ladies. If you play your cards right, this could be your lucky day." He reached out both hands and gently twisted Maria's nipples like he was tuning a radio. Zack felt his stomach tighten into a fist.

"Leave them alone," he ordered. "Go home, girls. Go!" The girls ran off. Zack spread his legs a little to center himself. "Don't fuck with me, Crisanto. This is my turf."

Crisanto laughed and pulled a 9mm Sig Sauer from his pocket, pointing it at Zack's forehead. He had graduated from street fighting. He had a more direct way of making his point now.

Zack was ready. He yanked a tear gas cannister from his pocket and sprayed it into Crisanto's eyes before turning it on the other two. The three men screamed and stumbled backward. Zack's street fighting skills were a thing of wonder. He executed a roundhouse crescent kick that sent the giant's gun flying. Then Zack followed with a side kick that caught Crisanto on the neck and sent him to the cobblestones. With crisp kicks and snapping punches, he sent the other two men to the ground. Then Crisanto sprang up from the ground, his eyes clearing from the spray. His afro spiked menacingly into the sky.

"You fucking little shit," he spat. "You're going to die today."

Zack ran into the busy street, and the three followed. Drivers slammed on their breaks to avoid hitting them.

Crisanto caught Zack by the arm, but he spun around like a cat. Grabbing Crisanto's ears, he pulled down hard as he brought his own forehead up fast to meet his attacker's skull at a point just above the start of his nose.

"Fuck!" grunted Crisanto, his eyes going back into his skull as he crashed to the ground. Rifling through Crisanto's pockets, Zack found the equivalent of two thousand dollars in pesos. He pocketed the money and ran.

That next day, he gave half the money to his sisters and said goodbye. He and Maria cried in each other's arms. "Promise me you'll go home to Luzon," he urged her passionately. "Don't wait too long. Crisanto will be coming around again soon." Maria tearfully nodded her assent.

"*Mahal kita*, Zacky Boy," she said. The words meant "I love you."

"*Mahal kita*, Maria," said Zack. He used some of his money to purchase an airline ticket and boarded a flight to New York City. The movie that played on the flight was *Easy Rider*, and he identified passionately with the new era the film was dramatizing. As he landed in New York, he saw that many young men wore their hair shoulder-length. Girls wore miniskirts. A few shunned bras.

From 1969 to 1975, Zack cobbled together the degree he needed to apply to Officer Candidate School. He was dangerously handsome, a walk on the wild side for the rich college girls he encountered in his classes. He paid for his tiny East Village apartment by working clever pyramid schemes he had learned from street hustlers in the Philippines. He partied at all the hot nightclubs. Pot was everywhere, along with everything else, but he wouldn't go there. On the streets, he had seen the results of drug use in painful closeup.

He was out of step with the new world in other ways. While his classmates argued passionately against the war in Vietnam, as a military brat he hewed to the government's party line. Socially, he found the era of "free love" an easy fit. He never saw a girl more than once. He had no friends. He counted on no one. Growing up the way he had, he saw all women as whores of one stamp or another and all men as bullies and predators.

As he neared graduation in the spring of 1975, he applied for officer candidate school. He made it clear that his goal was jets. On the day the Vietnam War officially ended, he received a letter informing him that he had been accepted. His joy could not have been more profound. But he had no one to share it with. This was his fate, and he accepted it, but his heart still ached for family.

At his modest graduation, he was shocked when a long-haired young man in bellbottoms and a tie-dyed shirt was suddenly in his face. At first Zack mistook him for a classmate. And then he spoke.

"A college graduate. Who would have figured?" said the man in a boyish voice. "That's a ticket to print money."

Zack was stunned. He knew that voice. He knew that red hair and those dimples. His father had to be in his midforties, but he looked no older than most of Zack's fellow graduates.

"Hi, Byron-san," he managed, deeply confused by his feelings. This man had been no father, but his presence was warming to Zack today. All his classmates had family and friends. He had craved Byron's love as a boy, and he still craved it. "How did you find out about this?" he asked.

"I live here now. I saw your name in an announcement," explained Byron before adding, "In case you're wondering, the Navy and I didn't see eye-to-eye on a few matters."

"Where are Tiki and Maria?" asked Zack. He had hoped the money he gave them had bought their freedom.

"They work for Crisanto and his boys now," said Byron. This saddened Zack. Byron slung an arm around his son's shoulders. "This is your lucky day, and you're about to find out why, but first we're going to party." He crooked his finger in the direction of two young women in their thirties in hippy attire who appeared high on coke.

"Say hello to my son, ladies. Him and me are going to be business partners."

The girls pressed their bodies into the handsome young man and murmured their congratulations. Byron rewarded them by pulling out a gram of cocaine and a tiny spoon and giving them each a pop. "This is all on me, champ," roared the handsome huckster, his dimples framing his boyish smile.

"Thanks, Byron-san, but I have other plans," said Zack coolly.

Byron stared at him hurt. "What could be more important than a father and son reunion?" he implored.

Zack didn't know how to reply. He had spent his teenage years hoping for his father to give him the time of day. He had never stopped wishing for family in whatever form it might take. He wanted to stop this charade in its tracks, send Byron-san and his girls packing. But he didn't. He allowed himself to fall, once again, under his father's spell.

The following morning, Zack heard his father throwing up in the bathroom. The girls lay in a naked tangle beside him on the bed. Orgying with your own father might seem off-putting to most people, but this was Byron's twisted concept of fatherly love. Cursing himself for his weakness, Zack handed his father a towel with a weariness that suggested he had a lot of experience with his father's morning-afters.

"Wait until you hear my plan," began Byron. "You're gonna shit your pants. What would you say if I told you I know how to parlay this bogus degree of yours into a fucking empire?"

"My degree wasn't some scam, Byron," Zack replied, bristling. "Finishing college was the hardest thing I ever did in my life." He did not mention that he had been forced to buy a passing grade from one of his professors. "And I already have a plan for the next few years," he concluded.

"What kind of plan?" asked his father skeptically. "I was hoping we could get a little place together again. Get to know each other as men."

Zack cleared his throat. It was time to set Byron straight. "Get ready for this one, man. It's gonna blow you away," he began. "I'm going into the Navy."

"You? The Navy?" scoffed Byron. "Why on earth would you do something stupid like that?"

"I've been accepted to Officer Candidate School," Zack informed him proudly. "I report next Monday to this school in Port Townsend, Washington."

"You? An officer?" challenged his father. "Officers are the most uptight assholes in the universe. And they don't get paid diddly-squat."

"I want to fly jets," said Zack.

"Jets? That's like saying you want to run for president," ridiculed

Byron. "They'll see through a little con artist like you before you walk in the door."

Zack feared that Byron was right. He knew his education hardly matched most of his fellow candidates. "I hope you're wrong," he said. An awkwardness descended like a curtain between them. "I need to start packing," announced Zack suddenly. "Take care of yourself, Byron-san." On some weird instinct, he opened his arms to embrace his father.

"Don't get all girlie with me," growled the boy-man. "When you fuck this up, like you fuck up everything in your life, don't come around begging me to take you back in."

"I won't," said Zack.

Byron shot a glance at the bimbos in Zack's bed. "I hope you know this cost me a small fortune," he said. Zack dug three hundreds from his wallet and gave it to him.

The next morning, Zack took off on his Triumph motorcycle for the opposite coast. It was September 18, 1975, the day Patty Hearst was arrested for armed robbery. At the age of twenty-five, his life was about to take a dramatic turn. The Officer in White's promise would come true. The Navy would be a home. The Officer Corps would become his family. Here, at last, was order and continuity for a chaotic soul.

The only problem was that, by now, he had become so skilled at being a loner that he could not have been a worse fit for a program designed to teach the blessings of teamwork. In jeopardy of being kicked out because of his scores in Aerodynamics and Celestial Navigation, he sought out the smartest kid in the class and, in his streetwise way, set about turning him into a friend.

Many positive things would happen for Zack during those seminal thirteen weeks. The smart kid would become a true friend, Zack's first since before his mother's death. Near the end of the curriculum, when that friend took his own life, Zack nearly renounced everything good about his new life. Once again, someone he had relied on had just checked out. It was starting to feel like a pattern. Open your heart to someone and they reward you by killing themselves.

He survived, in large measure, because of the love of a girl who worked in the local paper bag factory. Paula Pokrifki surprised him a week after their first encounter at an officer's club dance, by refusing to allow him to treat her like a prostitute or common one-night stand. Her brutally honest brand of love healed him in ways he hadn't thought possible.

On the day he became an officer and a gentleman, he repaid Paula's unshakeable love by carrying her out of the paper bag factory where she worked and into the bright light of a new life. This was a fairy tale ending, proof that love could lift you up where you belonged. Of course, the trouble with happy endings was that they were endings, not beginnings. The road going forward would be its own story.

NINE

★★★

A NEW COMMANDING OFFICER

OCEANA BEACH, VIRGINIA
1989 to 2001

Four years after Shannon's birth, Zack was home from deployment, watching news of the Tiananmen Square protests on TV, when Paula came home crying after her monthly luncheon at the Officer's Club with the officer wives from Zack's squadron. For fourteen years, she had suffered their catty jealousies and pompous ways. Eileen Britton, the buxom wife of the commanding officer of the squadron, had gone out of her way to make Paula feel small. You didn't have to look far to know why. Her husband ogled Paula every time he saw her.

"She talks like she's a character in *Gone with the Wind*," Paula had lamented tearfully to her husband, shifting into an imitation of the older woman. "Where did you say you went to college, Paula? Was it Radcliff? Or Smith?"

"What did you tell them?" asked Zack. All the officer corps and their wives were college graduates. The wives unofficially carried the ranks of their husbands and acted accordingly. At thirty-nine, Zack was a lieutenant commander, which put thirty-six-year-old Paula in some middle ground. She had cleverly skirted her feelings of insecurity for fourteen years, but today she had been cranky from caring for a sick four-year-old, and the truth just came out.

"College, ma'am?" she replied flippantly. "I didn't even graduate high school."

"Dear God," mumbled Zack, amused. "You have to be more careful than that."

"I'm sick of being careful," she said. "I just want to be me."

Zack held her tightly. Coming off the streets like he had, he had his own issues with the pompous and judgmental side of life as a Naval officer. "I hate that elite shit, too," he confided. "But we have to play their game." They were working-class heroes. They had snuck in the back door. Just having this between them gave them courage to play the game.

The next day, Paula enrolled in a class at Virginia Beach City College, where she completed her high school degree in record time. Zack found a high school graduation gown in a used-clothing store and made her wear it to dinner in celebration. Shannon was five. Zack toasted his wife's accomplishments, bragging in a loud voice to waiters and other diners, "My wife just graduated from high school."

"I wish he were here," Paula whispered suddenly. Zack knew she was talking about her real father. She had never met him, but she carried his picture in her wallet. Her mother, Esther, had supplied his name and informed her curious daughter that he was a Navy pilot, but Paula had never worked up the courage to try to contact him.

One day, Zack called BUPERS, the Bureau of Navy Personnel, and asked about Tom Hollingsworth. Zack learned that he had enjoyed a ten-year career flying reconnaissance flights for the Navy and had retired to fly for Delta. Zack tracked down a phone number and gave Paula the news. "I've found him, sweetheart."

Paula took one look at the number and threw it in the trash. "If he wanted to be in my life, he would have done it before now," she told her husband.

For the next five years, Paula juggled motherhood and her online classes. In 1995, the year that O. J. Simpson was acquitted of the murders of Nicole Brown Simpson and Ronald Goldman, Paula welcomed Zack home from overseas with exciting news. "Guess what you're looking at?" she teased. Waving a certificate in the air, she announced, "A college graduate."

"That's wonderful, baby," replied Zack. He snapped his fingers. "I have a great idea. Maybe you can help over at the base school. I heard they need help."

Paula felt her throat tighten. She was forty-two years old, and she had done the impossible. The factory girl was a college grad. And her husband had no concept of what that meant at all.

A month later, Shannon was harvesting tomatoes with her mother in their backyard when Paula's cell phone rang. Zack was working nearby to erect a basketball hoop. When she finally ended the call, Zack walked up and asked, "Who called?"

"The CEO of one of the companies I wrote to," she replied.

"Wrote to about what?" he asked.

"About working for them one day," she said. Then her face burst with pride. "They loved my letter and want to meet me in person."

Zack shook his head. "It's not the right time for you to go to work," he announced. "The Middle East is heating up. And Shannie needs you at the rudder, don't you, baby?"

Shannon had enjoyed her mother's full attention for ten years. Paula was a disciplinarian, and they often butted heads, but they had forged a strong mother-daughter bond to help endure Zack's long absences. "Why do you want to work, Mommy? Don't you want to have fun with me?"

Paula bit her tongue and didn't reply. While many women were claiming their right to work like men, the military was a throwback to an earlier era.

The next morning, she got a call from her stepfather in Port Townsend, informing her of her mother's death. Esther was only sixty-five, but she'd had a hard life. Paula had been close to her mother growing up, but their paths had diverged after Paula became the wife of a naval officer. Paula never traveled back home, and Esther visited just once a year at

Christmas. As she put the receiver down, Paula felt a strong sense of loss over her mother's passing. Then she saw an opening.

"I have some sad news," she announced that night at dinner. Her eyes found Shannon. "Your grandmother Esther died last night."

Shannon's eyes welled up. "Oh, no . . ." she said sadly. Her grandmother had visited every Christmas of her life, and the child loved the older woman for her odd mix of religion and off-color humor. Starved for family, it hurt to lose what little she had.

"I have to go to the funeral," announced Paula. "I could use some company." She knew that Zack was scheduled to fly for the coming week, so she was unsurprised when he bowed out.

"Why don't you take Shannie with you?" he suggested. "Show her where this all started."

"Can I go, Mommy?" implored the lanky ten-year-old with the ponytail. "Please?"

"Let's do it," said Paula. Shannon flew into her arms, and the two danced around the dining room.

The next day, as they waited for their flight to take off, Paula turned to her daughter with a conspiratorial smile. "Can I let you in on a little secret?"

"Does that mean I can't tell Daddy?" asked Shannon.

"Just for now. Then we'll tell him later," said Paula. "Our flight stops in Atlanta for a few hours. I have a meeting there."

"A meeting for what?"

"It's too soon to explain all that," said Paula. "Mommy just needs to do this."

They took a cab into the city and got off downtown in front of a tall, imposing office building. While Shannon read magazines in the waiting room, her mother spoke with a man in an expansive corner office on the top floor. As they returned to the airport to complete their trip, Paula made no mention of her meeting, but Shannon could feel a new energy radiating from her.

———

The factory belched a green-gray smoke into the Washington sky as Shannon followed her mother into the front office where she asked the manager for permission to show her daughter where she had worked when she met Zack. He was a florid-faced man in his midfifties with eyebrows that pushed together like dueling worms. He had been hired when Paula worked there.

"Sorry about your mom," said the man with genuine sincerity. "Bless her heart. That was a God-fearing woman."

"That was Mom," said Paula.

As they entered the factory, Shannon's eyes widened upon seeing a gray beehive of workers on assembly lines turning out paper bags. Compared to the elite world of Navy Officers, this was like entering the world of Oliver Twist.

"Are you okay, Shannie?" asked her mother.

"I'm fine, Mommy. Are you okay?" Her mother's pallor worried her.

"I'm fine," said Paula. "Just so many memories."

"Did Daddy really march in here in his dress whites and carry you out of here?" asked Shannon.

"Oh, yeah," answered her mother, recalling the moment. She pointed to a young woman listening to music on her ear pods. She wore a jaunty foreman's cap. "See that girl? That was my station. Your father walked in from back there." She pointed to a doorway at the rear of the factory. "I didn't see him at first. I was listening to my music like that girl. Then he kissed me on the back of my neck. I turned, and he was so handsome in his uniform, like a dream come true."

"I don't want a man to do that for me," said Shannon, her chin emphasizing her point.

"You say that now, but having someone love you that much is nothing to sniff at," said her mother. "And I never saw it as someone saving me. It was a trade-off. We saved each other."

Paula's gaze shifted suddenly, and her face underwent a transformation. Shannon saw that she was staring at an overweight woman working on the line not far from the girl with the ear pods. The woman saw her mom and grinned in recognition.

"Who's that woman, Mommy?" Shannon asked.

"An old friend," said Paula. "I've told you about Lynette." A moment later, the woman took a break and rushed up to hug Paula.

"Look at you," chortled Lynette. "Just look at you. And who is this young lady?"

"Shannon, this is my friend, Lynette," offered Paula. "We grew up together. We were best friends." Lynette hugged the child warmly.

"I'm sorry about your mom," said Lynette. "I was planning on coming to the service tomorrow, but Craig's in the hospital. Another motorcycle accident."

"I'm sorry," said Paula.

"Were you hurt, too, Aunt Lynette?" asked Shannon, eyeing a bruise on Lynette's chin.

"Aunt Lynette had a little accident on the job, sweetheart," said Paula tactfully. "It happens a lot on the line."

"Accident hell," corrected Lynette. "Be careful when you pick a man, Shannon," she advised. "Pick one you can beat up on." Lynette laughed like she'd just told the greatest joke.

Driving to their motel a short time later, Shannon said, "Mommy, how could you work in a place like that?"

"I didn't have a choice," said Paula. "I didn't have your options."

"Your friend looks really old," observed Shannon. "Like she could be your mother."

Paula nodded thoughtfully. "Working in that place takes its toll," she began. "And Lynette made some bad decisions in her life."

"What kind of bad decisions?"

"She tried to trick a friend of your father's into marrying her."

They drove past the gates of the naval base that had been shut down years ago. "That's where daddy was in training to be an officer," reported her mother. "It's been closed for a while. Sometimes, I'd park my truck right over there and watch him and his class run in full gear."

A few minutes later, they passed a beachfront motel that still bore the name "The Tides Inn." "Your father and I stayed there most weekends," she said. "We had our favorite room overlooking the water."

"Did you love Daddy right away?" asked Shannon.

"No. He scared me at first," replied her mother. "Your father was from another planet. He'd experienced things that had made him hard. I had to file off the rough edges before I could see who he really was."

"Who was that?" inquired Shannon.

"An abused boy who needed a lot of love," said Paula.

As they drove past the last unit of oceanfront cottages, Shannon noticed her mother tense up. "What's wrong, Mommy?"

"That was where your dad's friend took his life when Aunt Lynette wouldn't marry him," said Paula. "I'll never forget that moment as long as I live."

"Why does someone take their own life, Mommy?" asked the child.

Paula clenched her jaw. "I believe it's a very violent act that's meant to hurt as many people as possible." Then she changed the subject. "Would you like to see where Mommy grew up?"

A moment later, they entered a blue-collar world of dirt driveways and pickup trucks. Paula pointed out a simple one-story home on a hill overlooking a track of similar homes. "That's it. My stepfather still lives there," she said.

Shannon was stunned to see how humble her mother's world was compared to their life now. "Why didn't you take me here before?" she asked.

"Good question," replied Paula. "I suppose I was a little ashamed."

"But why now, Mommy?"

Paula thought for a moment before replying. "Mommy has a big decision to make when we get home, and you're a big part of it."

"What kind of decision?"

"About Mommy's future," said Paula.

Esther Pokrifki's funeral was the next day at the Saint Mary Star of the Sea Catholic Church in the center of Port Townsend. Aunt Bunny, Esther's older sister, met them outside when they arrived. She was a scarecrow in her late sixties with a shrill, sarcastic tongue. "If it ain't my famous niece," she heralded dramatically. "About time you paid your poor relations a visit."

"Aunt Bunny, this is my daughter, Shannon." Bunny embraced Shannon tightly. The gaunt woman reeked of cigarette smoke.

"Honey, your mommy is famous around here. The one that got the prize." Then she bitterly added, "May they all crash and burn." Paula laughed. Aunt Bunny often cursed the flight candidates she had chased without success.

Paula and Shannon took their places in a family group at the front of the church where Paula's stepfather, a hulking presence bathed in shadow, greeted them without warmth. The priest praised Esther as a God-fearing woman who had done much for the church and the community. Paula's stepfather said a few words about how it had taken a death in the family to drag him to church. Then it was Paula's turn to speak.

"I want to thank my mother for the most important decision of my life," she told the gathering. "When I was a young woman, she advised me to choose character over fear. Now I have the man of my dreams and a beautiful daughter." She almost stopped there, then went on to add, "And a shot at making a difference in the world. Thanks, Mom."

Shannon saw a man standing inside the church's entrance, staring alternately at her mother and her. He was a handsome, patrician presence removed from the working-class people in the church. When he saw the child looking at him, he awkwardly glanced away. When Paula returned to her seat, Shannon asked, "Who's that man, Mommy?" Paula looked over her shoulder and paled.

"My God," she exhaled. And immediately her daughter knew who the man was. This older gentleman bore little resemblance to the young ensign in the black and white photo she carried in her wallet, but his eyes gave their ancestry away. Nobody but Shannon had eyes that blue. As the priest began a closing prayer, the man hurried out.

"Stay here with your aunt Bunny," Paula instructed. She rushed toward the exit.

Shannon had no intention of being excluded from such a moment.

She darted out before her aunt could react. Then she hid behind a truck as her mother caught up to the man near his waiting taxi.

"I know you. I have your picture," Paula began haltingly. "You're Tom Hollingsworth."

"And you're Paula," he replied.

"Your daughter," she reminded him.

He looked uncomfortable. "You may find this hard to believe, but before today, I had no idea you existed."

Shannon saw her mother's cheek twitch slightly. "Mom said she told you about me."

"Your mother told me she was pregnant. I never knew that she had a child," he replied. "You're a pretty woman, Paula," he said in a respectful way. "I liked the way you spoke just now."

Shannon saw her mother blush proudly. "I just finished college. It was the hardest thing I ever did."

"Good for you," gushed Tom Hollingsworth. "I'm proud of you for that."

"Thank you," said Paula gratefully. Shannon remembered her father's lackluster response to her mother's news. For a second, it looked to her like they might hug, but it didn't happen. In the awkwardness, she decided it was time to make her presence known.

"Hi," she announced, popping suddenly into view.

Paula was surprised. "How long have you been hiding there?" she asked.

"The whole time," said Shannon. Then she looked up at the man. "You're my grandfather."

"Yes, I am," he said. "What's your name?"

"Shannon," she replied.

"You're a pretty girl like your mother, Shannon," he said awkwardly. He was clearly struggling with the enormity of having both a daughter and a granddaughter. "Where's your husband?" he asked Paula.

"At work," she replied. "He's a Navy pilot like you were. You fly for the airlines now, right?"

"For another few years before they retire me," said her father.

"Do you have a family?" asked Shannon. She held her breath. The prospect that she had brothers or sisters she didn't know about was enticing. She had craved family all her life.

"No," he answered, remorse in his bluer than blue eyes. "I never married. Never really came close," he concluded.

"Why?" inquired Paula with great curiosity.

A deep pain shaped Tom Hollingsworth's mouth. "I made a bad mistake," he began haltingly. "I loved your mother more than I knew at the time. I never got over losing her."

Paula shook her head incredulously. "If you loved her so much, why didn't you come back for her?"

"I wanted to. Oh, God, how I wanted to," he confessed in a rush. "I knew after a month in flight school that I'd made a big mistake. Then I read she married some local man."

"My stepdad," confirmed Paula with a bitter look on her face.

Tom Hollingsworth looked tired. "This is a lot for me to take in, all in one day," he offered quietly.

"Me, too," said Paula. Shannon watched as they exchanged phone numbers and made promises to stay in touch.

As they drove to the airport to catch their flight home, Shannon asked, "When do I get to see my grandfather again?"

"That might be awhile off," answered Paula vaguely.

"Why? I like him," said the child.

"Sometimes you can't reverse time," said her mother remorsefully.

———

The following night, Shannon could feel tension in her mother as the family watched the trial of O. J. Simpson on television. As they sat down for dinner, Paula said, "I've got news. That company in Atlanta offered me a job."

"What company in Atlanta?" asked Zack, nearly choking on a mouthful of spaghetti.

"On our trip west, Shannie and I stopped in Atlanta where I met the CEO."

"Why didn't you tell me about this little stopover?" he asked, clearly offended.

"Because I knew you'd say no," she replied. Zack said nothing because she was right. "The starting salary is sixty-five thousand," Paula boasted, "with all kinds of perks and ways to make even more."

This time, Zack was more attentive. "Sixty-five thousand?" As a Navy commander, he earned a paltry $27,000 a year. As a pilot, his flight pay brought his take home to roughly $40,000 a year.

"That's right," she replied. "I'd be a fundraiser for one of the largest children's cancer charities in the country. It would require some travel. We'd need to work out a different plan for Shannie."

"We have a plan, and it's working very well," insisted Zack.

"Not for me," replied his wife. "I need this, Zack, especially after going home and seeing all that. I need to feel like I have my own value, besides being a mom."

For the first time in her life, Shannon felt a fissure in her family, and it was terrifying. She had been the center of her mother's life since birth. As was her habit, she searched her memory for something she had done wrong. The week before their trip, her mother had caught her smoking cigarettes with a girlfriend. *That had to be it.*

"I'm sorry, Mommy," she began emotionally. "I won't smoke cigarettes ever again."

"This isn't about you, darling," said Paula. "This is all me. I meant what I said in that church. I want to make a difference in this world."

Zack drummed his fingers loudly on the table. "I thought I made it clear, when this subject came up the first time, that this is the wrong time to make such a change."

This time, Shannon was surprised to see her mother not back down. "We have a deal, Zack, remember? Ten years. Then it was my turn. We shook on that twenty years ago. After this trip, I see it so clearly. I'm forty-two years old. If I don't take this opportunity, it'll never come back. I'm taking this job, Zack."

Things unraveled rapidly. Her mother accepted the job. Fortunately, she was not asked to travel right away. Her father moved into a guest bedroom. Her parents tried counseling. Matters of custody were discussed. The house they lived in on base was technically her father's residence, so her mother would have to move. Since Shannon was going to school on the base, it was in her best interest to remain under her father's roof. At a court-mandated meeting with the middle-aged male social worker assigned to give the child counsel, Shannon broke down sobbing.

"Don't leave us, Mommy," she cried. "You and Daddy can both work. I'll be fine." Her sobbing grew convulsive, and both parents rushed to her side at the same time.

"Don't cry, baby. Nobody's leaving you," soothed Paula. "When your father's away, you'll stay with me."

"But you'll be away, too," wailed the child. "Who will take care of me?" Her sobbing became hysterical.

Zack saw the effect Shannon's tears were having on Paula. She looked like she was going to cry as well. He felt an outpouring of love for his wife. She had dutifully lived in his shadow for twenty years. She had more than waited her turn.

"I'll do it," he announced suddenly. "I want to do it." Zack felt the social worker's eyes go to him in surprise.

"Do you mean it?" asked a stunned Paula.

"If I make a deal, I keep it," said Zack. "I'll request instructor duty. I'll be a stay-at-home dad." He looked surprised by his own words.

"Oh, Zack," gasped Paula.

Shannon watched her parents embrace and kiss. She had seen the photo of them kissing the day he carried her out of that factory, and this kiss reminded her of that. The following day, Zack lived up to his word. Requesting shore duty, he became an instructor at fleet replacement and turned his back on war for the first time in his life.

During the following six years, Paula would do more for children's cancer fundraising than all but a few in the field. And Zack would become arguably the best stay-at-home dad in history. They were the poster family for the new era.

With her parents' roles swapped, Shannon saw their relationship enter a new chapter. It wasn't long before her mother was making four times what her father earned. In her new role as a successful working woman, Paula conducted a total makeover on her rough-edged husband. She challenged him to read more than detective novels. She took the family to museums and concerts. She confronted Zack on his racism and homophobia. She corrected both his and Shannon's grammar.

Paula rose up the ranks rapidly. She was a natural fundraiser. She was devoted to the young cancer survivors she was building hospitals to accommodate. Watching her mother encourage these children gave Shannon a new respect for her. But there were times she felt jealous. Of course, she added that to her list of failings.

Taking over as the main parent, Zack tried being a hardliner like Paula. *I am the adult, and you are the child.* Shannon rejected it from the start. "Don't treat me like Mom does. I'm not a baby," she would snap. Finally, he settled into a compromise plan, deftly toggling between father and friend.

Shannon was delighted to have a new commanding officer, one that she could wrap around her fingers. If her mother had struggled to curb her wildness, it flourished under her father. At twelve, she gutted the toilet in the Christian Science Reading Room with a cherry bomb. She faced serious charges, but her father bailed her out. That same year, he bought her first bra and became the great explainer when she began her period when her mom was away. At thirteen, she stole a fistful of comic books from a pharmacy, and Dad did his thing.

As a high school freshman, Shannon had the stick-thin body of a pre-pubescent girl. A year later, at fifteen, that all changed. Her hormones began attacking like a colony of red ants. Her emotions became volatile, her dreams crazy and coded. The faces that popped into her head ranged from a hot senior with a turquoise Ford Thunderbird, to her social studies teacher, to a bag boy at the local market.

One day, she found herself with that hot senior in his car. Rickie Martin's "Livin' La Vida Loca" pulsed from his surround speakers. He kissed her on the lips. Then he caressed her breasts. He was determined to go further, but she drew a line. Afterward, her confusion about the incident wouldn't abate. She felt a tug of war within herself that she couldn't explain. She was both drawn to the promise of physicality and repelled by it. Her father had been "the great explainer," but after turning fifteen, she felt awkward talking to him about sex. It was a time when she needed her mother. But Paula was never there, and when she was, she was always on the phone.

Luckily, her aunt Casey came to town for their regular lunch dates. They had been enjoying these occasions since Shannon was eight. Casey wore a blue uniform with captain stripes. She had moved up rapidly in the Navy hierarchy after a distinguished decade as a fighter pilot and was widely expected to be selected for admiral.

"Can I ask you something?" blurted the fifteen-year-old after they had ordered their salads. "It's sort of personal."

Casey smiled sagely. "I've been wondering when this dialogue would come. It's a weird time, isn't it, kid?"

"Yeah, really weird," sighed Shannon profoundly. It felt so good to be having this talk.

"Are you using birth control?" Casey asked.

"No. I haven't done anything yet," confessed Shannon.

"Have you talked about this with your mom?"

Shannon shook her head. "She's been really busy."

"I'll make an appointment with the doctor for you," said Casey.

"That's great, Aunt Casey, but that's not what's bothering me."

"What is it then?" asked the older woman. She relished these moments when she could play mom with her surrogate daughter.

Shannon sucked in a breath of air. "Boys don't turn me on," she confessed.

Casey nodded soberly. "Do girls?" she asked directly. "If they do, that's fine."

"It isn't girls," Shannon rushed to explain. "It's me. There's something wrong with me."

Casey reached across the table and put a hand on Shannon's. "What is it, sweetheart? You can tell me, and it won't go any farther."

"Last week, I let a boy touch me," confessed Shannon, her eyes flicking to the part of her anatomy she was referring to. "He wanted a lot more, but I wouldn't let him. It was scary."

"Scary how?" asked her aunt.

"He was breathing like an animal," said Shannon. "His hands were so clumsy. His body smelled."

Casey laughed. She had had her own struggles with sexuality, partly thanks to an overbearing father. "I remember thinking the same thing at your age," confided Casey. "How do they always manage to smell like they just farted? I finally concluded it was because they had just farted."

They shared a laugh. Then Shannon frowned. "There must be something wrong with me. All my friends are doing things. One has already gone all the way."

"There's nothing wrong with you," Casey assured her. "You have a full life with your tennis and your adventures with your father. When you're ready for sex, it'll be there waiting."

Shannon nodded doubtfully. "I hope you're right." She couldn't explain her feelings, even to her aunt. She was straddling an awkward line. Being a grown man's best friend was complicated. Preferring her father's company over people her own age felt suspect. She was the anomaly. While her friends were in competition over how much they hated their parents, she glowed with tales of adventures with her dad that they could only imagine.

Zack was, in most ways, very astute about human nature, but his upbringing had given him a significant blind spot. Cruelly plunged from innocence into jungle warfare at fourteen, he had been robbed of his adolescence and had no reference points to help him understand his daughter at this awkward turn in the road.

At a Christmas party during her sophomore year, she ran into that handsome senior again. He was now in college, but he still had his Thunderbird. She noticed right away that he had discovered cologne. This time, he went inside her bra again. Then, he stroked her thigh until he had a finger only millimeters from her privates.

"Stop," she ordered firmly.

He laughed. "And what if I don't want to?" That was the year her father had begun her lessons in self-defense. As he moved his finger closer, she grabbed his hand with both of hers and bent it backward using a street move she had learned from her father until she heard the brittle snapping of bones.

"Jesus Christ!" he wailed. "You broke it!"

Word of this incident traveled through the school fast. After that, boys steered clear of her. When she turned sixteen, her father gave her the Harley 350 and the flamed helmet, and she began to confront her sexual confusion with speed. She took the bike out to a salt flat to test its limits, and her own. On the day she topped out at 119 mph, she discovered that she had had an orgasm.

When Zack learned of her secret speed runs, he voiced hurt that she had not included him in the adventure. "I like to do some things on my own," she told him. This was his first signal that times were changing.

In June of 2001, the Mayo family went to Rehoboth Beach to celebrate. Paula had single-handedly funded a ten-million-dollar children's cancer hospital in Las Vegas and had been featured on the cover of a national magazine. They had an oceanfront suite at the Hotel Bethany Beach and indulged obscenely on room service all week.

Watching her father and mother steal kisses after a year of long separations made Shannon happy on one hand and jealous on another. It confused her to see her mother as some kind of rival for her father's love. But there was something very right about the picture before her eyes. It liberated her in ways that were unexpected.

While her parents took their *siestas*, she wandered the quaint beach town on her own and introduced herself to some young people. One night, she flirted with a boy walking his dog on the beach.

On their last night, they ate at the Henlopen City Oyster House. Her mother and father went through one bottle of champagne and ordered another. Shannon could tell they were both tipsy. She could not remember seeing them this way since her mother had gone to work.

"I want to propose a toast," said Paula suddenly. "To the core three," she said, touching her champagne glass to Zack's, then Shannon's Shirley Temple. Tears formed in her eyes. "I want more of this," she said with great longing. "I've missed it so much more than I knew."

After dinner, they stumbled onto a street fair where Zack used his clickety-click skill to throw a ping pong ball into a goldfish bowl, winning his two women the biggest prizes on display. Then he kissed his wife with passion and high-fived with his daughter.

In Shannon's eyes, this made sense. Being her father's running mate this past year that Paula had been gone so much had become a mixed blessing. Some days, her father's grand adventures were in conflict with spontaneous teenage get-togethers. When they returned from their holiday, Shannon felt a new peace in the home. For the first time in her life, she looked forward to being what she was, an adolescent.

TEN

SOBER PALS

FRS

End of Week One

Shannon and her fellow students were hovered over their laptops, as they'd been for the last five days. She glanced at her bunkmate at the desk beside her, and they exchanged smiles. They had continued to warm to each other during the week, even though Sidney did almost all the talking. Shannon had come to think of her roommate as a female Candide, a wide-eyed innocent trying to navigate a hostile world.

A buzzer brought groans of relief, and a moment later, Zack strode in with Perryman and their team of instructors. "Enjoying the pace, children?" he inquired, his eyes scrutinizing their faces one by one, assessing the winners and losers from week one, looking for early cracks in their armor. "We double it next week," he continued. "Crawl, walk, run." He turned to the tall officer beside him. "Captain Perryman?"

Perryman cleared his throat. "We got a directive this morning from SECNAV. The top student from this class will go to Lemoore, California, to learn to fly the F-35 Joint Strike Fighter, the super plane of the future."

The students erupted with excitement. The Strike Fighter was all the talk in military circles, the next generation of fighter jet that would eventually replace the FA/18.

Zack cast Taylor a knowing look. "Lieutenant Daniels, this must be your father's brainchild. I assume it's a coincidence you happen to be in this class?"

"A baffling mystery, sir," answered the JFK lookalike with his annoying smirk.

Shannon muttered under her breath, "Too bad you won't get the slot."

Everyone in the room heard her, including Zack. He had to smile. This was pure Shannon. His little competitor.

"And why's that?" asked Taylor, running a hand through his military-cut auburn hair.

"Because it's mine," Shannon replied, meeting his eyes with steely resolve.

"I beat you in advanced," he jousted. "Why should it be any different here?" He was flirting with her, and Zack could see it. Clearly his daughter wasn't buying any of it.

"I was just laying back in advanced," she advised. "This is where the real action is."

"Back then, I didn't know you were Mayonnaise Mayo's kid," said Taylor. "That puts a new spin on this."

"Sorry to spoil your party, kids," interrupted Sidney, forging a macho face, "but that bad boy is mine." The class laughed. Sidney was becoming the class clown.

As Shannon was leaving with the others, she heard her father's commanding voice echo loudly in the room. "Lieutenant Castellano, as you were." Shannon watched the last of the class file out. All week she had studiously avoided being alone with her father. It was too hard to feel his eyes on her. She could never forget his face the day he had learned of her addiction. The disgust. The revulsion.

Zack got right to the point. "What's with you and that boy?"

"It's nothing," she assured him. "We've been shit-talking like that since primary." She didn't say that Taylor Daniels was fixated on getting into her pants. Every rejection only energized him more. Now that he knew she was Zack's daughter, she had seen a more intense glow in his eyes.

"Be careful," warned Zack. "If his father gets wind of our little experiment, you and I could be in some very deep shit."

"Don't worry," she replied. "I don't make friends."

Her words moved her father and gave him an opening. "When are we going to talk about what happened? It's killing me to have you here and not be able to talk to you."

"I don't know what it would accomplish," she replied flatly. "It's been almost ten years since Mom died. We aren't those two people anymore."

"Of course, we're not," he agreed. "How could we be? But there's still a powerful link between us. There always will be."

Shannon wanted to bridge the gap, too. But something very permanent had happened between them after Paula's death. Secrets had entered hearts and been left there to fester and grow larger than their hosts.

"They're throwing me a party at the Ranch tomorrow night," her father awkwardly announced. "It's the big six-oh."

Shannon felt torn. "I'm sorry. I already have plans." She was lying. She had no plans for Saturday night. "By your leave," she said, saluting.

Zack hesitated to return the salute that would free her to go. "Is this how it's going to be?" he asked quietly. "Aren't we even going to try?"

"Where would we begin?" she asked. "Until I win back your respect, nothing else matters." Without waiting for his salute, she marched away.

As she left maintenance, she found Taylor Daniels waiting for her. "I wanted to invite you to my show tonight," he said, holding out a flyer. Shannon had heard he and his band were playing at a boardwalk club that night. The entire class was going. She rejected the flyer with a wave of her hand.

"I'm sorry. I have other plans." She turned in the direction of the BOQ, but he was her shadow.

"Whoa, hold on," he offered good-naturedly. "It's always like this with you. Just because our fathers have a little issue doesn't mean we have to."

She stopped and faced him. "This isn't about them. It's you," she said unflinchingly.

"Me?" he grinned cockily. "How do you know what I'm all about if you don't spend any time with me? I'm not my father at all. In fact, I've dedicated my life to not being him."

"I don't trust you," she said flatly.

"Those are funny words coming from you," he replied. "The mysterious Shannon Castellano, a.k.a. Mayo. She makes no friends. She disappears usually about this time at the end of the week on some clandestine mission. Where does she go?"

"My life is none of your business," said Shannon forcefully.

"Maybe one of these days, I'll follow you," he warned, arching a brow.

She wasn't amused. "Do it and I'll break your arm."

"Oh, we've got a tough girl here," he teased.

"If you only knew," she warned before marching away.

Taylor laughed and called after her, "This just gets better and better." Shannon flipped him the bird.

Three hours later, Shannon's Harley roared past a sign that read NEWPORT NEWS 44 MILES. Seeing a car in her rearview, she tensed until it drove past. She had played this cloak and dagger game through OCS, Primary and Advanced, ever fearful that the Navy would discover her secret. After Taylor Daniels' warning, she was being especially watchful tonight.

She had discovered "the program" at the rehab in Mexico, and it was her lifeline. She needed it like others might need a church or a confessional. She relied on it to keep sober and sane. To ensure that she kept her worlds separate, she attended meetings at least an hour's drive away from her training facility, always keeping her real name secret. In this other world, she was always "Chelsea," her chosen handle as a gamer.

Tonight, she had driven an hour to Newport News for a 7 p.m. Narcotics Anonymous meeting at the local YMCA. Making sure no one was watching her from the street, she entered late. From the door, she scanned the faces of the attendees, hoping not to recognize anyone.

A young man was addressing the group. It was the fishery worker, Dylan Harmony. In contrast to his fishery attire, he wore jeans and a dress shirt. "Those of you who know me, know that I drive an hour from Virginia Beach to avoid the usual suspects," he said. "It seems to be working. If all goes well, I'll get my one-year cake in two weeks." The men and women in the room applauded. From a seat in the back, Shannon clapped dutifully. As Dylan resumed his seat in the front row, their eyes caught briefly.

The group leader, a woman in her forties with long gray hair worn in thick braids, took the microphone and reverted to mandatories. "I forgot to ask earlier. Do we have any visitors or newcomers? We ask this not to embarrass you but to get to know you better."

Shannon raised her hand. "Hi. I'm Chelsea, and I'm a drug addict and an alcoholic."

The room of addicts replied as one. "Hi, Chelsea." Shannon found a little smile. These were her people. This was her home. She ascended the stage.

"I just got here from Texas," she began in a strong and eager voice. "I've been on the road and couldn't find a meeting, so I really need this." Her openness was refreshing, and the faces of her fellow addicts told her they welcomed her into their family.

"I came here to train for a dangerous job," she resumed in code. "The only issue is I left out one small detail from my résumé." This made the whole room erupt in laughter. Shannon grinned. She loved sharing. The embrace of her fellow addicts was what now passed for home.

"The kicker is, my boss knows about my past," she resumed. "And he happens to be my father." The addicts went crazy for that one. She was on a roll.

Dylan adjusted his chair to see her better, and their eyes caught again, this time a little longer.

"I've been clean and sober for two years, but he thinks my addiction will resurface in a moment of crisis," she said. "And to be honest, I worry he might be right." This confession brought another round of applause, more enthusiastic than the last.

After the meeting, Dylan ran up to her as she mounted her Harley. "Chelsea? Chelsea?" he called. Shannon didn't react. Dylan positioned himself in front of her. "Earth to Chelsea. What's the hurry?"

Helmet in hand, Shannon blushed and stammered, "I'm sorry. I didn't hear you." She recalled their brief eye contact during the meeting. She had felt a disturbing chemistry, and she recognized it again now.

"I'm not 'thirteenth stepping' you," Dylan hurried to reassure her. It was against rules to use the program to hit on someone. But everyone did it all the time. "I enjoyed your share," he said honestly, thrusting out a hand. "Dylan Harmony."

Shannon didn't take his hand. "I don't mean to be rude, Dylan, but I don't go to meetings because I want to make friends." This was her standard comeback when guys pulled this at a meeting, as they often did. Everyone broke the thirteenth-step rule.

"Me either," said Dylan. "It was what you said about recovery," he explained. "I've been thinking about that a lot lately. I don't want this to be a life sentence. I want to believe I can beat this and beat it for good."

Shannon stared into his ocean eyes. He had nailed it. This was the central question of her existence. She could not, in good conscience, go forward with her dream to fly the FA/18 or perhaps the F-35 Joint Strike Fighter, unless she was a thousand percent sure she was fully recovered, and not just on some endless rat's wheel called "recovery."

"Well, you know what they say?" she offered in a sing-song voice. They both piped up with the words that addicts always say after the Serenity Prayer.

"It works if you work it," they chorused, then added in the same singsong way, "and it's working right now." They shared a relaxed grin, and their eyes touched shyly.

"Well, see you next week," she said. "Stay clean."

"You, too," replied Dylan. *Ask for her number. Ask for her number.* But he didn't.

Shannon put on her flamed helmet and accelerated out of the lot. As she gathered speed on the highway to the base, a smile worked its way onto her lips and into her eyes. It had been over two years since she had had sex with anyone. But she had felt those stirrings in the company of this handsome and soft-spoken young man. Then as quickly as those thoughts had entered her mind, she banished them. By the time she was back inside the city limits of Virginia Beach, she had resolved to start looking for another meeting.

On his ride back to Virginia Beach in his pickup, Dylan could feel his heart still beating urgently from their encounter. He wondered why he felt this way after such a short time in her company. Chemistry would explain a lot of it. He was blown away by her physicality. He couldn't stop staring into those unusually blue eyes. He sensed that she was someone, besides Nickie, who might get the real him.

But a half-hour into his drive home, his high spirits had given way to depression. Dylan had experienced mood swings like this all his life. It came with his sensitive nature. The more he replayed their exchange, the clearer he saw that he had overplayed his hand. He knew that, if their shoes were reversed, he'd be looking for another meeting.

Since the late sixties, Molly's had been the hip Virginia Beach nightclub. Shannon parked in an area for motorcycles and walked into the loud world. It had been a sudden decision after a tiring hour on the road and totally out of character for her. She never partied with her classmates, but she decided to make a brief appearance tonight. Everyone would be there, and it might soften her image. Mainly she wanted to see how her naive bunkmate was faring.

The nightclub was sardined on a Friday night with tourists, locals from the sportfishing world and fisheries, and military personnel, enlisted and officer, in civilian attire. Taylor Daniels and his band were performing. In contrast to his Navy persona, he was a white hip-hop artist in the style of Macklemore. His three bandmates were edgy hip-hop types, civilians.

"THE BELT, THE BELT," he wailed in his powerful falsetto.

The band joined the chorus. "snap-crack! DON'T LET HIM SEE YOU CRY! snap-crack! STARE HIM IN THE EYE!" The words were delivered with such a raw edge that Shannon wondered if he was singing about himself. Taylor saw her and beckoned her to join their classmates at the front. Shannon waved back but went in search of Sidney instead.

She found her in a remote corner of the club, playing a video game. She wore an Eddie Bauer shirt, Dockers, and of course, her clunky glasses. "Shannon. I didn't expect to see you," exclaimed the taller girl.

"How's dickhead's band?" asked Shannon. This was her first taste of the flip side of Taylor Daniels. At the lip of the stage, their classmates seemed stunned by this raw and sensitive side to the cocky Annapolis graduate.

"He's really good," said Sidney. "It's like he's a whole different person. Can I buy you a beer?"

"I don't drink," said Shannon.

Sidney was surprised. With her edgy haircut and tattoo, she figured Shannon to be a hip lady. Realizing it was none of her business, she said, "See that girl at the end of the bar? She's been looking over here since I walked in."

Shannon took in a girl with a pixie face, torn jeans, and a tight cowboy shirt. It was the fishery worker, Nickie Jordan, and she cleaned up well.

"Cute," said Shannon. "What's stopping you?"

"Everything is so new to me," Sidney admitted. "I don't know the rules."

"You mean like who goes first?" asked Shannon, amused. "Does that really matter anymore?"

At that moment, Dylan pulled into Molly's lot. He loathed being around drinkers, but he had promised Nickie that he'd make an appearance.

"There you are," chirped Nickie happily as he joined her at the bar. "I don't understand why you drive an hour away when there are a million meetings here in VB."

"You know why," answered Dylan. "And I see more than a few here tonight."

Nickie didn't share Dylan's vulnerability to drugs and alcohol. Getting high only made her dance better. "Why the long face?" she asked intuitively. She was an expert at reading his moods. Dylan was the most sensitive man on the planet, while Nickie hid her feelings behind a tough-girl façade and a quirky sense of humor.

"It's nothing," he said unconvincingly. "There was a girl there. She was . . . different. I think I scared her away." Then he asked, "Your 'wife' show up?"

"She's right over there," said Nickie turning around, only to discover that Sidney was no longer there. "At least, she was. I hope she didn't leave." Unseen by Nickie, Shannon was leading Sidney their way.

As Nickie looked for Sidney, Dylan turned to the bartender and ordered a coke. With his back turned, he didn't see Nickie brighten as the two girls walked up to her.

"Sorry to bother you," began Shannon. "But my friend wanted to meet you." It had taken a lot of persuasion to get Sidney to act, and she stood there awkwardly, exhibiting zero confidence. With his back to them, Shannon had no awareness of Dylan. Busy paying for his coke, Dylan was similarly unaware.

"Hi," piped Nickie happily. "I was hoping to say hello."

Sidney stared at Nickie with unmasked desire, but no words came out.

"Say something, Sidney," said Shannon, taking over.

"Hi," said Sidney nervously.

"Hi to you," chimed Nickie. "You're tall. I like tall girls." She put out her hand. "Nickie Jordan."

"Sidney Lee," replied Sidney, offering a firm handshake. Shannon wanted to laugh. Sidney was like some virginal boy, winging it move to move, with absolutely no clue about how social forces worked.

"Now that we've accomplished that," said Shannon, "I've got to get back to the base."

Just then Dylan turned suddenly, coke in hand, and his eyes collided with Shannon's like meteors. It was a moment out of time. It made no sense whatsoever, but there they were.

Shannon thought fast. "We've met before, right? Help me remember where it was," she stammered, pulling him away from Sidney and Nickie.

Nickie stared after them, a curious grin on her face. "Well, well. My bro is keeping secrets," she observed dryly.

"Is he your brother?" asked Sidney.

"Not by blood, but yeah," said Nickie. "His family took me in after my folks were killed overseas. They were Marines."

"I'm sorry," said Sidney. She could see past Nickie's upbeat façade that the loss still impacted her strongly. Emboldened by her progress so far, she decided to take the lead. "Want to dance?"

"I was afraid you were never going to ask," answered Nickie with a toss of her head.

"I have to warn you," said Sidney, "I'm not a great dancer."

Nickie laughed. "You're in luck. I am."

When they were away from the crowd, Shannon fixed Dylan with sharp eyes. "Who are you? Why are you following me?"

"I'm not following you," he assured her. "I'm as surprised as you. I live only a few blocks from here. I go to that meeting to avoid old 'friends.'"

Shannon relaxed slightly. It was an odd coincidence but totally logical that they had both gone to that far off meeting for a reason. And Molly's was the hot club. "Look, Dylan, if the Navy found out about NA . . ." she began, but he held up a hand.

"Relax," he said. "It's Narcotics Anonymous. Emphasis on anonymous." His voice was calm, his eyes kind and direct. "So, that dangerous job you were talking about is jet school?" he asked, amused.

"Yep," she answered with her trademark grin.

Dylan's eyes grew large as he put the pieces together. "Oh, my God, your father is Mayonnaise Mayo?"

"You've heard of him?" She knew it was not unusual for people from this area to know about Zack Mayo.

"Like every kid in VB, I had a poster of him on my wall," recounted Dylan. Then a thought intruded. "Who's Chelsea?" he inquired.

"That was my name as a gamer," she answered. "I use it for meetings."

"Gamer?" he repeated, confused.

"*World of Warcraft*," she explained. "We competed online. People around the world bet on us."

"Do you have a real name?" he asked with an easy smile.

"It's Shannon," she replied, then hurried to steer things back to less personal terrain. "I meant what I said earlier. I don't have time for a social life. Too much depends on succeeding here."

"That's funny," he replied in his unthreatening manner. "I'm getting a whole different message." His eyes seemed to be laughing at her.

Shannon blushed and looked away. Dylan had one card to play, so he played it. "I forgot to ask if you had a sponsor?"

The question caught Shannon off guard. It was recommended in the program that everyone have a "sponsor," a leader and friend who could guide you in hard times. It was suggested that it be the same sex, although exceptions were made.

"I just got to this area. I don't have one."

"That's what I figured," he said. "Hard to trust a recovering drug addict with a secret like yours."

"Exactly," she allowed. This was a smart man, she decided. *Maybe a little too smart. And maybe a little too good-looking.*

Dylan saw his opening. "I know it's supposed to be the same sex, but if you ever need someone . . ." He penned his number on an old business card and handed it to her.

Shannon laughed. "Now that's definitely 'Thirteenth Stepping.'" She pocketed the card absently. "Who's your sponsor?"

Dylan laughed grimly. "He relapsed a couple of weeks ago. The guy before him lasted a month. You want the job?"

"We can be sober pals, if that's what you want, but it stops there," she said firmly.

"Sober pals. Got it," he said agreeably. "But I'm still getting those mixed signals."

"Shut up," said Shannon, blushing slightly before hurrying out.

As her Harley gathered speed and the December wind assaulted her face, Shannon wondered how long their deal would last once he figured out that she would never sleep with him.

Returning to his apartment, Dylan eagerly opened his laptop. The empty white screen stared back challengingly. Suddenly his fingers started to move on the keyboard, and soon they were flying. He began a short story where he attempted to make sense of what had happened that night, when he had met the woman of his dreams twice, first as a fellow drug addict, then as a student in jet school.

He titled it "Sober Pals."

ELEVEN
★★★
FAMILY

OCEANA BEACH

Saturday of Week One

The disk jockey was a geeky kid, barely twenty, a little belly under his white tunic. His eyes grew enormous as this fit and beautiful young woman walked in on a Saturday morning wearing blue and gold shorts and a T-shirt and showing lots of tanned skin.

"How can I help you?" he asked, turning down the volume of the speakers in the control room so they could talk.

"I want to record an ad," said Shannon. After her abortive first encounter with Emil Foley the previous Monday night, Shannon had considered giving up her plan. How could such a decrepit and bitter old man be of any good to her? But as this brain-crunching week came to a merciful finish, she decided to go all out to win the curmudgeon's respect and mentorship.

He saved my father. Maybe he can save me.

Minutes later, the DJ was in stitches as she played the role of hot surfer chick. "Be part of a new kind of mixed martial arts gym run by a Marine Corps hero," she gushed breathlessly. "Get your ass kicked by a living legend," she purred. "Foley's Fitness. Special rates for military."

The young sailor applauded and asked for her number, which she declined, citing Navy regulations against officers fraternizing with enlisted men. "Sorry. You're cute," she said, planting a kiss on his cheek. The disk jockey aired the ad while she was still there and promised to run it often. For the next two hours, Shannon drove around the city, putting up fliers featuring the photo of Foley's menacing scowl that she had taken on her first visit.

At noon, she walked into Foley's Fitness and was pleased to see that the place, if not exactly humming with activity, was doing much better than on her previous visit. She counted eight customers. Foley held a heavy bag for a young man with a buzz cut, while Ramon was conducting a self-defense class for three women in one of the boxing rings.

"Hi!" she offered brightly. "I see business is picking up."

"What do you want from me?" Foley snapped gruffly. "I said I can't help you." He had heard her radio ad when he was shaving that morning. It had made him laugh. When he picked up a coffee at his neighborhood coffee shop, he saw one of her fliers, posted irreverently in front of the shiny new Star Fitness Club.

Shannon had rehearsed what to say. She knew she had scared him away the first time. "All I want is a place to hang out on Saturdays," she began. "I can man the desk, teach, clean up. You don't have to pay me."

Foley's brows knitted suspiciously. "Why would you do that?"

"You're the only family I have, that I can talk to anyway," she replied.

"Family?" he questioned. From the way it came out, she sensed it was not a word he used much.

"When I was bad growing up, my father would threaten to send me to you," she said, before adding with a warm grin. "Doesn't that make us kin?"

Fear danced in the old man's lonely eyes. A vein in his forehead grew larger. "I don't want family," he snapped. "Or friends," he continued. "I got my hands full taking care of myself." Five teenagers entered at that moment, and Foley looked uncertain.

"Take care of those customers, Gunny. I got this guy," she offered. Without waiting for his response, she stepped between him and the bag and took over. The buzzcut guy grinned, endorsing the change.

That day she taught a class. She manned the desk. She took on the gargantuan task of unpacking boxes from Foley's prior residence and putting the contents into storage cabinets. It wasn't the ass-kicking she had imagined, but it was service, as they call it in AA, and it made her feel good.

As she was putting some files in a drawer, an X-ray of a man's chest fell to the floor. A doctor had drawn a circle with a Sharpie around the heart. Before she could put it back in its folder, a stern voice stopped her.

"I'll take that." Shannon spun around guiltily. Foley held out his hand, and she gave him the X-ray.

"I'm sorry," she stammered. "I didn't look at it," she lied.

Foley scowled and motored away without another word. This is what he had been afraid of, another dose of unwanted human involvement like he'd experienced with her father. Opening his heart to relationships was the most difficult challenge of his life. This was why he had allowed it to happen so rarely. In his condition, he could not take such a risk now.

The retired DI's upbringing had been nightmarish. Growing up in the gangster underbelly of Atlanta, he was the classic case of a ghetto kid who was given the choice by a judge to serve out a term of three years for petty theft or join the military for the same amount of time. He chose the Marines and never looked back, trading eighteen years with no discernible order for an absolute straight jacket of rules and supervision. He had been retired for twenty-five years, but he still lived by those rules.

Foley had been a handsome young man with a tall, athletic physique, and women wanted his companionship, but his abuse as a boy had made him innately suspicious of both men and women. His father, a drunk and a compulsive gambler, had beaten him often. When Foley was ten, he was forced to watch as his father was executed mob-style in the basement of their home for failing to pay a gambling debt. The look his father had given him in the second before his brains spilled from his skull was seared into Foley's soul.

His mother, a renowned beauty in her youth, was sent to prison for leaving her brood of six children in a hot car while she got high on heroin. Two of Foley's siblings had died in that car, and he had barely survived a severe case of dehydration. He was sent to live in one foster home after the next. It never worked out. Before long, he was in a gang. He held up a store and landed in jail. That's when the judge gave him the choice.

One of the perks of military life was the ubiquitous availability of prostitutes around most bases in the world. Foley found this a safe choice. It kept things more honest. You got what you paid for, and it eliminated tearful goodbyes. If this suggested a man living outside the realm of emotions, it would be an insufficient portrait of this complex man.

In every port of call, he "adopted" street children that he did his best to mentor and set on a new course. He bought them food and shopped at the PX for clothes they desperately needed. They were his "family," and he never forgot any of them.

There was one street kid who stood out the most in his mind, a Cambodian boy named Somchai who he encountered one night while sitting at a bar in Kailua, Hawaii. The boy, a peanut-sized six-year-old with a wild shock of black hair and eyes that could have been drawn by Keane, had crawled onto the stool next to him. The bartender knew the boy and brought him a plate of french fries.

As Somchai hungrily wolfed down his fries, Foley asked him about his life. The boy told him that he and his mother had arrived recently from Cambodia, and that his mother worked in the Thai restaurant next door, bussing dishes.

"What's your name?" inquired Foley.

"Lucky," said the boy. It was the American name he had chosen for himself.

Later, when Foley left the bar, he saw the boy enter a ramshackle cardboard world of packing boxes in the alley behind the Thai restaurant. Somebody had written with a Sharpie, "LUCKY'S HOME." Foley would later learn that this was where the boy stayed until his mother's shift ended at 11 p.m., and they walked together to their tiny studio apartment in the poorer section of town.

Foley was stationed in nearby Kaneohe and returned to that bar in Kailua often to engage the boy in conversation and encourage him to persevere. Lucky was an amazing boy. At six he wandered the streets alone, talking to all the homeless, all the crazies. He knew everybody, and everybody knew him. People affectionately called him "The Mayor of Kailua." Foley and Lucky stayed in touch over the years, through letters and the occasional call.

When Foley lost his legs and the Corps turned its back on him, it destroyed him. Then, just days later, he received a letter informing him that Lucky had been killed in an automobile accident involving a drunk driver. It was too much. Strapping himself into his wheelchair, he drove off the end of a pier in Pensacola. Two young men from a motorcycle gang pulled him out before he could drown. Letting that boy into his heart had nearly killed him. He couldn't survive another hit like that.

Foley motored back to Shannon. "Miss Mayo, I've taken advantage of you enough," he began. "Since I have no way to help you in return, I must ask you to collect your things." He left before she could reply.

Mad at herself for examining his personal records, Shannon collected her belongings without changing out of her gym clothes. As she was about to leave, a large man of indeterminate race entered. He wore gold chains, a gaudy black Puma warmup suit, and sported a bleached stripe of hair that ran fore-and-aft on his shaved cranium. A posse of four large bodybuilders filed into the gym behind him. Trevor Dominion wrinkled his nose dramatically as though the place smelled.

"Can I help you?" Foley asked the hulk of a man. He knew he was the featured martial arts trainer at the new Star Fitness gym.

"Just came to see what kind of place you got here," said his visitor in a surprisingly high voice. The large man's eyes fell disparagingly on Ramon, who quickly looked away. "Not much from what I see. You wanna fight me again, Ramon?"

"No, sir," said Ramon.

"Some high-octane gym you got here, old man," scoffed the retired fighter. "You won't like what I say on Facebook."

Foley scowled. He couldn't afford a thumbs down on social media.

Shannon saw her opening. "I'll fight you," she said in a sharp tone that shocked everyone in the room.

Trevor Dominion looked at her and laughed so heartily his gold chains tinkled like chimes on his muscular chest. "A girl?" he asked. "Do you know who I am, honey?"

"No," she replied. She knew from the looks Ramon was giving her that she was being foolhardy, but the moment had taken on an oversized importance to her.

Foley felt guilty. He knew she was doing this to impress him. "Don't be stupid, Shannon," he advised. "I don't want to see you get hurt."

"That's Trevor Dominion," warned Ramon. "He fought in the UFC."

Shannon's street fighting skills included her wise mouth. It was another trick she had learned from her dad. Talk the talk, then walk the walk. "When? A century ago? I'm not afraid of this clown." She fixed the large man with her warrior face.

"Who are you calling a clown, mosquito?" challenged the retired fighter, igniting laughter from his cronies.

"You want to do this or just posture for your friends?" taunted Shannon.

Trevor laughed and climbed into the ring. "This is going to be fun," he chuckled. Shannon joined him, a five-seven female David against a six-four Goliath.

"Watch out for the quick takedown," shouted Ramon. "That's his thing."

Dominion snapped a barrage of jabs that she easily ducked or side-stepped. Dancing, circling, she was careful to stay out of reach of a sudden takedown. Then one of his jabs clipped her chin. It was not a solid blow, but it staggered her, and she saw her opponent grin confidently.

"Got your attention, mosquito?" he asked.

What the hell are you doing? thought Shannon. Her only experience as a street fighter had come from fending off men or women who had tried to take advantage of her sexually in a drugged state. Since joining the Navy, she had squared off with MMA fighters and knew their weaknesses in response to a street fighter's tricks. But this was a big man who had been a feared warrior in his time.

Foley motored past Ramon to get a closer look at the action. Watching Shannon circle her opponent like a cat, compact, ready to pounce, he recalled images of her father at her age. Foley had never faced a fighter with Zack Mayo's skills and tricks. It had taken a dirty trick to beat his student in that old blimp hangar. If Mayo's daughter possessed any semblance of her father's skills, she might stand a remote chance of not embarrassing herself.

In the pitch of battle, Shannon recalled how difficult it had been to learn her father's sometimes shockingly brutal street tricks. Consistent with his swimming instruction, he was a relentless taskmaster. "You're turning sixteen. You're pretty. That makes you a target."

"Dad, you always get so over-dramatic," she had complained. "People aren't as bad as you make them out to be." At fifteen, she was becoming a woman physically, but she still saw the world through the eyes of a child.

"You're right. They're much worse," he grunted menacingly. "It's a jungle out there. You're just another part of the food chain. Now get back on that mat and stop me." It became a weekly event. He took her through endless scenarios of encounters she might face, inspired by events he had lived or witnessed on the streets.

"There's two of them, big men, and just you," he would propose. "Which one do you go for first?"

"The biggest one," she answered confidently. "Send a message."

"Send it where?" he demanded.

"Where he lives," she would answer.

"And if he's got the family jewels under lock and key?"

"The magic spot," she would declare, pointing to a place on her forehead just above her eyes.

"Bingo!" he announced. "That's my girl." This was the move he had used to defeat Crisanto and his boys. It had to be executed perfectly. She came away from these sessions bruised and bloodied, but her father had given her the tools to never fear any attacker, male or female. Trevor Dominion was another matter.

Shannon deftly eluded her towering opponent, slowly tiring him. She was a mosquito, and she was stinging him with kicks and jabs. She leapt in the air and executed a spinning crescent kick that clipped Trevor Dominion's jaw, stunning him enough to make his eyes widen. Everyone in the old gym, including the retired fighter's posse, saw that kick and knew that this was no joke. This girl could fight.

"Fucking mosquito," snarled Trevor. "Now you're pissing me off." He lunged for her, but in another move she had learned from her father, she grabbed his ears and brought his head down with both hands to meet her rising knee.

"Fucking bitch!" he screamed. Now Trevor was spitting blood, and he wasn't laughing. He charged behind a barrage of sidekicks, forcing her to retreat. For the first time, Shannon looked uncertain. Trevor caught her with a spinning crescent kick that sent her caroming off the ropes and crashing onto the mat. She turned over quickly, but she knew she was in serious trouble.

"And the mosquito went splat," said Dominion in his high voice. He leaped in the air to make the pin, a giant manta ray filling the universe.

Shannon's eyes entered a primal place. She knew her timing had to be perfect, her aim precise. She reached up and grabbed his gold chain as he descended and used it like a halter to guide his head to the perfect point of impact with her forehead.

Trevor's eyes crossed. Shannon winced. She had been slightly off target, but her pain was minimal. Deflecting his falling weight with her forearms, she was on him like a leopard, pinning him. The move was redundant. It would take another forty seconds for Trevor's cadre to revive him and get him on his feet.

Shannon raised her arms in triumph and did a little victory dance over her fallen foe. Ramon had recorded the fight with his phone, and that victory dance was the capper. It was hilarious. She squatted and grunted, her tongue hanging down over her lower lip, her eyes bulging ferociously. She had learned this Māori war dance or *haka* at the age of six when her father had performed it after beating her at backgammon. "I won, I won!" he had crowed before launching into that crazy celebration of victory while Shannon had cried uncontrollably in her mother's arms. After that, she never cried when she lost, and there were no penalties for "excessive celebration."

When she climbed down from the ring, Foley motored up to meet her, pure awe in his weathered eyes. "My Lord," he mumbled reverently.

"Does that mean I can stay?" she asked with her crooked grin.

TWELVE
★★★
BIRTHDAY BOY

THE RANCH
That Evening
The Saturday birthday bash was in full swing, but the birthday boy was all alone in his cottage. He had a lot on his mind today, and he'd had his fill of small talk earlier when the first wave of girls arrived.

The Ranch, a collection of loosely connected cottages in Chic's Beach, had been an institution since the opening of Naval Air Station Oceana, Virginia, in 1950. Unmarried active duty and retired pilots held court here for the local beach girls. Since the rent was staggeringly high for someone on military pay, the age of the men skewed older.

Della-Serra had been the first to move there. Despite his age, he was regarded as one of the premier players. Then he talked Perryman into it. Together they pestered Zack to join them, believing it would help him come back to life. The plan hadn't worked. After Paula's death, Zack had had no luck with bachelor life. Every day that he woke up in his cramped beach digs, he missed his family home.

Della-Serra poked a head in Zack's back door. "There you are. Everyone's asking where the birthday boy is." He knew Zack had been struggling all day. They had done a shopping run at the PX together that morning, and Zack had been so lost in thought that Della-Serra couldn't find him for close to an hour, finally stumbling across him in the furniture section where Zack was sitting in a La-Z-Boy chair, watching a lava lamp spew its colors on a wall.

Zack gave him a rueful smile. "I went around earlier, asking every girl if she had heard of Ho Chi Minh," he recounted. "One was sure he played second base for the Dodgers."

Della-Serra chuckled, but it was no joke. Time marched on ruthlessly, especially for warriors like them.

"Did you invite Shannie?" asked his friend casually.

"Yeah," answered Zack. "She's busy." His shoulders sagged. "I don't know what to do to get through to her," he confided. "I thought, now that she's come back, things would change." He had never told Della-Serra about the drugs. The party line was that she had simply run away after graduating from college. But he knew that Della-Serra understood his pain. He had lost his own son and his marriage.

"This is killing you, isn't it, boss?" asked the Latino sympathetically.

"Yeah," admitted Zack. "It's not exactly how I imagined turning sixty would feel." As he said the words, he recalled his father's death.

It was 1996, the year after the changing of the guard. Shannon was eleven, and Zack was forty-six. The family had recently moved into the Moorish home that Paula's income had allowed them to purchase after all the years of living in government housing on base. In the new normal, father and daughter were alone and engaged in one of their swimming races in the backyard pool. As always, it was close until the end. Then Zack edged her out by an inch.

"Don't do it," warned Shannon, knowing what would come next. Zack made his Māori face. "Stop it, Daddy!" she laughed. Then she twisted her face into her version of that war mask. They both roared.

They were not alone in the moment. A man was watching them intensely from a backyard gate. Shannon noticed him first. "Daddy, what's that man doing?"

He was a cadaver in an ancient tracksuit with sparse hair and the face of an apple carving. His stomach protruded like it might be hiding cancer. He looked ninety, but he was only sixty-five.

"Stay here," Zack told her. Dripping water from the pool, he walked to the gate. Halfway there, his eyes widened in surprise. The transformation was shocking. The once ageless playboy looked like he might not have long to live.

"How's it hanging, Byron-san?" Zack offered cautiously.

"If you expect me to salute you, forget it," said his father. "'America's Favorite Son'? With a name like that, you must get all the pussy in the world."

"I'm happily married," announced Zack.

"That your kid?" asked his father.

"Yeah, that's your granddaughter, Shannon."

"Shannon? Nice name," remarked Byron. He waved to Shannon, and she waved back. Then his crafty eyes scoped out the grounds. "Sweet little pad. I know you didn't buy this on the Navy's money."

"My wife is a successful businesswoman," Zack informed him, then wished he hadn't. He knew how his father's mind worked.

"That's my boy," applauded Byron. "Use that cock for more than a doorstop."

Zack shifted his weight anxiously. It was hard to reconcile this ruin of a man with his memories. "What can I do for you, Byron-san?"

Byron Mayo took a moment to gather his courage. "You can give me a place to die," he announced. Then he just stood there with a challenging smirk on his face.

"Why can't you go to the veteran's hospital?" asked Zack.

"They threw me out of there," admitted Byron. "I got nowhere else to go."

Zack heard the words he had once coughed up to Foley when the DI was pressuring him to drop on request from Officer Candidate School. It was a theme in his life. He had nowhere to go at fourteen when he was forced into that state home. Byron had taken him in, even though he had ulterior motives for doing so. He knew he should ask Paula, but there was no doubt she would urge him to take the high road. Finally, he nodded.

"Welcome home, Byron," he said. The smile of gratitude that

sprouted on the dying man's face was moving to his son. Sadly, Byron would be in the ground before Paula returned home two weeks later.

Shannon would be the greatest beneficiary of her grandfather's surprise appearance. Tom Hollingsworth, her mother's father, had failed to reappear after that funeral a year earlier, and Shannon's hunger for family was greater than ever. In the coming days, the eleven-year-old would besiege her grandfather with questions, and he would regale her with stories he never told his son.

"My family came here from Italy when I was nine," he told her one morning at breakfast. Zack looked up from his paper, surprised. He had never heard any of this. His father went on, "We worked for a two-bit traveling circus that performed in the Borscht Belt. My dad and mother were jugglers. My uncle walked the high wire. My aunt did tricks with a dog we called Tubby Teagarden."

"Tubby Teagarden? What kind of a name is that for a dog?" asked Shannon with a laugh.

"All the animals in our traveling circus had funny names like that," her grandfather told her. "We had a parrot we called Rudy Vallee who could whistle the National Anthem." Byron had an older sister who swallowed fire, a cousin who was a contortionist, an uncle who was in the *Guinness Book of Records* for juggling the most ping-pong balls with his mouth.

Zack shook his head in quiet disbelief. *Why didn't he tell me these things?*

One day, Byron asked Shannon to bring him five oranges from their tree, and he juggled them perfectly. "Will you teach me?" she asked.

"Happy to do it," he replied.

Zack remembered that flier he had discovered as a boy. He knew now that the boy being levitated was his father.

One night, Shannon asked Byron-san where his family was now. It took the old man awhile to answer. "All dead," he replied in a pained whisper. "Our bus plunged over a cliff outside Fallsburg when I was your age," he told Shannon. "I was the only one who survived. The circus kept me on to clean the animal cages. When I was old enough, I joined the Navy."

Now Zack understood why his father hadn't shared his past with him.

Losing his family in that tragic way had blindsided the eleven-year-old boy, and he was still living its tragedy at thirty-five when Zack had come to live with him. Fate had transformed Byron into this eternal child-man who would do anything to forget his loss. Rampant hedonism had brought him to this turn of the road.

The day Byron died, Shannon was at school. The old man lay in bed, his head sunk deeply into a pillow. He seemed to know his time was short because he got right to the point when Zack entered his room to check on him. "Thanks for not turning me away," he said. "If I had been betting on it, I would have lost."

"It's been good for Shannon to have you here," said Zack.

"And you?" asked Byron.

Zack pondered the question. "It's been nice to see this version of you," he said at last. "I just wish you could have been a father to me when I needed it."

"I did my best," protested Byron. "I thought we had a lot of fun."

"I needed a father," countered Zack. "You wanted a buddy to carouse with."

"Isn't that what you're doing with Shannie?" charged Byron before erupting into a coughing jag.

Zack felt his face grow hot. "Shannon and I are good friends. But I know my role as her father."

"Of course, you do," said his father sarcastically. "I forgot that America's Favorite Son's turds don't stink."

Zack wanted to unload a lifetime of resentment, but he knew he was dealing with a dying man. "You're right. I'm not perfect," he said at last. "Growing up with you as a father made sure of that. It took a stranger to teach me to be a man."

"Too bad he didn't finish the job," said Byron.

"What does that mean?" demanded Zack testily. "Look at my life. Look at this home. Look at my family. What do you have? You're a penniless old man who nobody gives a shit about because all you ever cared about is yourself."

"At least I don't hide my head in the sand," said his father.

Zack felt his anger surge. "What does that mean?"

"This little deal you got with your wife can't last long," predicted Byron smugly.

"You've been a guest in this house for less than two weeks. What do you know about my wife and me?"

"I'm not stupid," snapped his father. "Shannie told me how much her mother's been gone. It's only a matter of time before monkeys want out of the cage."

"Not everyone's like you," replied Zack. "Some of us have taken the time to build character, integrity." Even as he said the words, he knew that Byron had accurately sensed the undercurrent of their lives. People weren't meant to be apart so much.

Byron wasn't through. "Your daughter is the one I worry about."

"Shannon's the happiest kid I know," argued Zack.

"She's pulling the wool over your eyes," said Byron.

"What did she tell you?" stammered Zack.

"It's nothing she said," answered Byron. "It's just what an old man sees." In his short stay, he had seen the longing in the child's eyes when her mother called home. He also witnessed how dependent she was on her father. Instead of staying after school to play with friends, she rushed home in anticipation of their adventure of the day.

One day she read an essay to her grandfather she had written for one of her classes that spelled it out clearly. Entitled "Living with Heroes," it was a child's passionate recollection of growing up as the daughter of a military hero and then having a mother who was being heralded as a superstar, too.

"How do I measure up? Good question. I've been wondering that since I was born. My father is not just a hero. He's America's Favorite Son. My mom is not just a hero. She's the first woman to raise enough money for an entire children's hospital, and she did it in her first year on the job. Then there's me. How did I slip through the cracks? I'm the most average person in the world."

Byron had also witnessed his son's loneliness for his wife and his corresponding eagerness for Shannon to arrive home from school. He would come back from his duties as an instructor at midday and start planning their afternoon activity. They wouldn't be back until late, always eager to share their adventure with Byron-san over dinner.

"You've built a card castle, just like me, Zacky boy," he warned. "Don't blink or you might wake up, like I did, with nothing." His dimples deepened, and his eyes glittered in some final whisper of youth. A short time later, he died.

Zack was jolted out of his reverie by a sharp knocking at the front door of his beach cottage. Perryman poked his head in. "Everybody's asking for you, boss," he announced in his gravelly drawl. "Time to do the cake thing." He shared a look with Della-Serra. They had made a pact to get Zack through this day and night. They were encouraged that he had yet to mix himself a birthday cocktail.

Minutes later, Zack was on the beach, blowing out the candles on his cake. His pilot buddies and the beach girls they were hosting had formed a rowdy circle around him and were singing, "Happy Birthday, dear Mayonnaise, Happy Birthday to you." When he had extinguished the last of his sixty candles, they applauded.

He looked around the circle. Decades spanned his age and the youngest ones there. In his secret heart, he felt every one of his sixty years. The sound of an approaching motorcycle made Zack's heart race. He knew that motor. Shannon appeared on the road above, and their eyes came together across the distance.

After her win over Trevor Dominion, Shannon had felt an outpouring of gratitude to her father for his tutelage. What could it hurt to wish him a happy birthday? But seeing him surrounded by girls half his age made her stomach turn. She was ready to drive away when he ran up a grassy embankment from the beach.

"Wait! Don't go!" he shouted breathlessly. "I was hoping you'd come."

"It looks like you're busy," said Shannon.

"Not too busy for you," he insisted. "Come join us. It would mean a lot to me."

"I don't like parties," she said. "I was hoping we could be alone."

"Of course!" agreed her father. "We can go to my place. I've been looking forward to a chance to have a little talk."

Shannon suddenly felt a wave of fatigue wash over her. She was starting to feel the blows she'd taken in the fight earlier. "Maybe another time," she said. "I've had a big day."

Zack searched for a way to extend the moment. "I'm proud of your scores from last week," he offered.

"Thank you," she replied. It was nice to hear his encouragement.

"I see you've made a friend in the class," he commented, remembering her pronouncement about not making friends.

"What friend?" she asked dismissively.

"I understand you and Lt. Lee are living together at the BOQ."

"This is a trial run," she replied. "The jury's still out." She looked around, anxious to escape his questions.

"Anything on the dating front?" he asked lamely. There was so much he didn't know. He knew she couldn't still be a virgin. After learning of her drug use, dark visions about her sexual experiences had kept him up at night. Given his boyhood, his imagination in those matters knew no limits.

"Nope, not even remotely," replied Shannon. "I'm not looking for it either."

"Can I ask why?" he inquired with fatherly concern. He was hungry to know anything about her.

"Boys have never been my strong suit," she explained curtly. Her gaze shifted to the young women on the sand, some in bathing suits so small as to be redundant. "I see you're holding your own," she remarked cattily.

Zack was not a man who divulged his feelings easily. But he knew he had to start somewhere. "There's a lot about me that might surprise you," he said. "I've tried to move on after Mom, but I just can't do it." He collected himself before pressing on. "Have you been able to move on, sweetheart?"

Shannon seemed unprepared for the question. She had asked it of herself so many times without getting an answer that she had willed it to go away. "I can never forget that day," she said simply.

The look that passed between them was soul-wrenching.

"It was like watching the world come to an end," he concurred at last. "All the good just stopped." When she didn't speak, he decided to press his case more aggressively. "Come to my place now, Shannie. Let's go right at it like we always did. Let's take that first step."

Shannon felt like her brain was on fire. *Go right at it? How could she?* She'd kept it from herself for ten years. She had dodged looking at it in multiple ways. She shook her head. "I'm not ready. I may never be ready." She abruptly started her engine and accelerated into the night.

Zack suddenly felt old. He had no more party in him. As he was about to start back down the slope, he saw a familiar figure step out of a taxi. In her dress whites, she stood out against the beach-clad partyers below like a deity from a mythical planet. Her hair was almost completely gray now, but she still wore it in the same short bob she had favored as a young woman. "Happy Birthday," heralded Casey Seegar.

Zack took her in appreciatively. There was always a slight reset between them after not seeing each other in a while. The last time had been his trip to Washington for his award two years earlier. To his eyes, she hadn't aged a day. And her shoulder boards now bore the lofty rank of vice admiral.

"You made it," he said. "Your office said it was a 'negatory.'"

"My office doesn't always know my secret mind," said the highest-ranking woman in the armed services. "Was that Shannon you were talking to when I drove up?"

"Yeah," he sighed defeatedly.

Casey cocked her head. "What's going on, Zack? I thought, when she showed up, things would change for you guys."

Zack knew that Shannon had often confided in her "aunt" growing up. He wondered if Casey knew anything about Shannon's struggle with drugs. That would make her complicit in their felony. "What has she told you?" he inquired vaguely.

"We've only spoken once since she got back from her trip," said Casey. "I blame myself for that. My work has been backbreaking. I was hoping to take some extra time to see her here, but I have to return for meetings."

"What did she tell you about the past few years?" he asked in a casual tone.

"She told me about her trip around Mexico and her failed marriage." Zack was relieved. Their secret was intact. Then Casey added, "She said you told her she doesn't belong here. Why would you tell her something like that?"

Zack searched for words that might explain his feelings without exposing any details about their secret. "There's a lot you don't know that I'm not at liberty to tell you," he said. "These past few years, Shannon's been struggling with her mom's death in ways that make me question if she can handle a plane this unforgiving."

"Her scores in basic and advanced were off the charts," replied Casey.

"As you know, the Super Hornet is a whole other animal," he countered. "She'll get her chance to prove herself, but I have to trust my instincts."

Casey seemed troubled. "I know the two of you have been through a lot," she began. "I may not know the details, but I'm not blind. I've seen the changes in you both. But this is an important chance for you both to move forward. It's what Paula would want."

Zack nodded. "I want that with all my heart, Case. But as her father, protecting her life is my first priority. I've tried to reach out. I begged her just now to come to my place and hash this out, but she won't do it."

Casey squared her shoulders. She had the gesture down to a science. It sent a signal that she was not a person you could bully. "Can I ask you a question?" she began, with no intention of stopping. "Do you believe in your daughter?"

Zack heard an edge in her measured tone he hadn't detected before. He remembered that Casey had grown up under a tyrant father who had wanted a son and gotten a girl instead. But this was the first time he'd seen her show such unguarded emotion.

"My situation with Shannie is different from you and your father, Case," he insisted.

"You're wrong. It's the same. I know she's had some struggles, but your daughter is going to be a great fighter pilot and a great human being like her parents."

"I hope you're right," Zack said. "But if you knew the full story, I'm not sure you'd say that." He was afraid he'd already said too much.

"It's about belief, Zack," persisted Casey. "Either you have it or you don't. One day you'll thank me for this birthday present." She kissed him on the cheek, then hurried to her waiting taxi, which quickly drove away.

Zack went directly to his cottage and crawled into bed, but music and laughter from the party attacked his ears, making it impossible to sleep. The world was young, and he was old. Byron's dying words grated in his brain. *You've built a card castle, just like me, Zacky boy. Don't blink or you might wake up, like I did, with nothing.* Zack found himself wondering if he'd make it as far as Byron and whether anyone would take him in to die.

THIRTEEN
★★★
THE CHELSEA YEAR

FRS
Friday of Week Two
Multiple screens circled Shannon's simulator chair, and six projectors provided her with a 360-degree simulated world. During the past week, they had learned to take off, land, and fly in formation. In week two, they would graduate to bombing and strafing, and to Basic Fighter Maneuvering, a.k.a. dogfighting.

At the end of week one, Shannon was again the frontrunner in the class, just ahead of Taylor Daniels. For her, simulator training was like slipping back into a familiar pair of socks. She had developed her skills to a fine point following her mother's death playing countless hours of *World of Warcraft* online against fellow competitors around the world.

Gaming had been a natural choice for Shannon. She had grown up as a toddler on video games, and she was uniquely good at playing them. In *World of Warcraft*, everybody had a pseudonym, and hers was Chelsea, a name she had chosen randomly after reading about the daughter of an Arkansas governor with presidential ambitions. She labeled the loneliest year of her life, "The Chelsea Year."

As the formidable, take-no-prisoners "Chelsea," her mind escaped her body, and she entered a realm where only waging war and winning mattered. It was her first taste of the drug that had hooked her father at such a young age: the adrenaline rush of survival. With a refrigerator full of Red Bull, she could take on the world all night and day. While she was gaming, she never thought about her mother's death or her role in it.

After 9/11, she witnessed her father enter a war zone of his own. When she left for school in the morning, he would be planted rigidly in front of their living room TV, arm-chairing the nation's war on terrorism. When she returned, it seemed he hadn't moved.

After Zack's old squadron was sent to Afghanistan in the first wave, Shannon woke up to find her father watching the news. Illuminated by the ghostly glow of the TV, he hissed through contorted lips, "Fuckers! Bastards! Kill them all! Kill them all!" The sight was terrifying to the young girl.

Halfway through her Chelsea year, she noticed that her father had started adding a second cocktail to his nightly regimen. This caused no alarm at first. He never got tipsy. But when he was carted off in the custody of the Oceana Beach police after celebrating her seventeenth birthday at the O Club, she was certain she had lost both her mother and her father. After that incident, she doubled down on her gaming.

The Chelsea year came to an end one morning when the phone rang while they were eating breakfast. Zack answered it and listened quietly. A moment later, he put the receiver down. His daughter saw a smile spread slowly across his lips. "Who was that?" she asked between mouthfuls of cereal.

"The White House," replied her father. "The president wants to see me."

"Why?" asked Shannon, suddenly on full alert.

"His secretary didn't say," he replied. "Do you want to come with me? It would do us both good to get out of this place for a few days."

"Will I get to meet the president?" she asked.

"I don't see why not," he said, happy to see some animation from her.

They flew to Washington that afternoon and took a suite at the Watergate Hotel. The next morning, they were picked up by a limousine and taken to the White House. Zack had met George W. Bush several years before and found the man to be down-to-earth. There was a bowl of gaily wrapped candies on his desk, and the trim president offered Shannon her pick before turning his attention to Zack.

"I'm a big fan of yours, Captain," drawled GW. "I know you and your daughter are still in mourning, but the country is in a crisis, and I need your help." His eyes found Shannon. "I'm glad your daughter is here with you, Captain. What I'm about to ask of you will require sacrifice on her part, too."

"How can I help, sir?" asked Zack.

Shannon was keenly aware of how alert her father had become.

"The past year has been hard for this country," said the nation's leader. "America needs her favorite son. Captain, I'm begging you to take over your old squadron."

Shannon's eyes turned fearfully toward her father. She had sensed something like this might happen. Zack met her gaze and smiled supportively. "That's very flattering, Mr. President. But my daughter needs me right now."

Shannon was relieved by his firm declaration. Lately, her Chelsea mantle had begun to feel like a crown of thorns. She was achingly lonely. She needed the normalcy of a home again. But it wasn't as simple as that. First, she still had no idea why she had turned off the faucet of family love after her mother's death. And second, she understood she was the offspring of royalty, and she had a responsibility to her country. The President of the United States was hanging onto what she would say next. A freshly minted seventeen, this was the headiest moment of her life. She had been a skilled actress all her life, so she slipped into that role now.

"I'll be fine," she reported confidently. "My father got me ready for this, Mr. President," she boasted. "Since I turned ten, my life has been a boot camp." The president and her father laughed.

"Is there family to look out for you?" asked the president.

"My aunt Bunny will watch after me," volunteered Shannon. Since Esther's death, her sister had become their Christmas visitor. She was a colorful, foul-mouthed old scarecrow, but she had impressed Zack by being strict yet loving with Shannon during her stays.

Shannon raised a palm to high-five her father. "Go get 'em, Daddy."

In the taxi headed back to their hotel, Zack said, "I can still tell them no, sweetheart. My first priority is you. I just want us to be close again like before Mom died."

Shannon wanted that closeness again, too, but she couldn't go there for reasons that were unclear even to her. "It's only for a year," she said. "It's what Mommy would have wanted."

A month later, Shannon waved goodbye to her father as he boarded a military transport to join his old squadron in the Middle East. Returning home, she felt lonelier than she'd ever felt in her life. When Aunt Bunny went outside to smoke a cigarette, Shannon beelined for her laptop to lose herself in some online battle, but her hands were shaking in her urgency and the slim laptop slipped from her grip and fell on the hardwood floor, shattering the screen and rendering the device useless. She broke down sobbing. She had not cried once during the Chelsea Year, but today, the dam broke.

During the night, she wrestled with what to do. Gaming had gotten her through the worst year of her life, but it had taken its toll. Normally an active person, she was so out of shape that simply riding her bike to and from school exhausted her. The next morning, she embarked on a brave new path. She had been the proverbial B student, but she was determined to finish her junior year with As and lead her tennis team to a state title. She did it. Her senior year, she ran for student body president and won. Her achievements would earn her a coveted full scholarship to the University of Virginia.

On a carrier in the Middle East, Zack celebrated her accomplishments with anyone who would listen. This was welcome proof that he had been right to trust in her maturity. The first year, he returned often to check on her, but she always seemed to have her life together, something he could not say about himself. On these visits, he did everything he could to bring back the old warmth, but she was always busy with her tennis or her friends. At the end of the year, he asked her if she wanted him to come home, and she assured him she was doing great. He made the same offer a year later with the same result.

In college, Shannon continued her superstar ways for three years.

Then, at the end of her junior year, she tore her rotator in a tennis match. The doctors gave her a prescription for a year's supply of OxyContin, and everything changed. It felt good to take her foot off the pedal. She had been a gamer, then an overachiever. Now she had found a new way to escape the pain of her mother's death.

Changes came furiously. On drugs, daddy's girl was suddenly in free fall. The more casual the hookup, the better. It was a severe departure for the protected girl whose idea of love was to be swept off her feet, like her mother had been by her father. Driven by emotions held in check too long, she embarked on a journey of self-debasement. This was not making love. This was the opposite.

Eighteen months of addiction and drug-fueled sex took its toll. When she finally quit drugs, it was only logical that she would quit sex, too. She saw them as the same thing. The prospect of ever finding someone she could love in a truly romantic way was off the table.

All week, she had replayed her run-in with Dylan Harmony in her mind which had sent ripples of foreboding through her. His eyes, his smile, his laugh, they were like granules of crushed opioids laid out in a teasing line that seemed to stretch to the horizon and beyond. It couldn't be clearer to Shannon. *If I start something with this recovering addict, I'll go right back to drugs. I know it. And I'll do the same to him* As the first week of simulators came to an end, she had not had the time to find another meeting, so she began looking for another out.

"Who wants to make a hundred bucks for taking over my watch tonight?" announced Taylor Daniels as the class assembled at the end of the week. Every weekend, one member of the class was required to stand watch. He waved a bill in the air.

"I'll do it," said Shannon, grasping the note. *Problem solved.* She thought of calling Dylan and offering some explanation but decided against it. It was simpler to find a new meeting.

Shannon would pay a price for her decision to take Taylor's watch. Missing her Friday NA meeting and her Saturday stint at Foley's robbed her of her source of family and left her ill-prepared for the week that followed. The first week of simulators had been a trip into a familiar closet, fun to try on old clothes, but the second week, with its emphasis on combat skills, jettisoned her with a vengeance into the numbing loneliness of the Chelsea Year.

In college, she had tried to describe the Chelsea Year in a creative writing assignment: "One day, I had the perfect life. The next, I was serving a life sentence for murder. As part of my sentence, I had to say goodbye to my father and all my friends. Someone as evil as I am doesn't deserve love. My world, once so boundless, was now a ten-foot by ten-foot cell in which my daily survival depended on my ability to win imaginary wars against imaginary enemies. From Russia to China, I became a feared warrior. I took no prisoners. Opponents called me ruthless. Despite my feminine pseudonym, most thought I was a man and up there in years. No one knew I was a teenage girl."

At 1600 hours on Friday, the end of three weeks of training, Shannon stepped free of her simulator cage on unsteady legs and joined the flow of classmates leaving the building. Despite grappling with a replay of the Chelsea Year last week, she was, once again, first in her class, ahead of Taylor Daniels. Next, they would begin preparing for their first flight with an instructor. Her eyes swept over her classmates. They were only three weeks in, but the cracks were starting to show. As they emerged into the sunlight, loud slapping sprang off the tarmac.

A Sikorsky S-76C helicopter descended, the words DEPARTMENT OF THE NAVY emblazoned on its sides. Topper Daniels jumped out like the self-appointed savior of the planet. His dyed-red hair had thinned since the medal ceremony in DC, and the transplant plugs were even more visible in the harsh sunlight.

Zack had a warrior's second sense. He knew this visit did not bode well. Looking on with her classmates a short distance away, Shannon could feel her father's tension.

"Good morning, sir," said Zack, saluting smartly. "Command informed me that you'd be visiting today."

"Good morning, Captain," purred SECNAV in his breathless southern way. His eyes found Shannon. "Is that pretty young lady your daughter? I'd like a word with her if I may."

Zack beckoned to Shannon, and she marched over and saluted. "Shannon, our boss, Topper Daniels, Secretary of the Navy," said her father.

"Congratulations, Lieutenant," said SECNAV, rising on his toes to reach her height. "Your scores in simulators are the highest ever recorded by a woman. Any secrets you want to share?"

Shannon felt an intensity in his eyes that she'd noticed in a lot of drug addicts, but she knew from her father's stories that this man's "drug of choice" wasn't ingestible. "Play a lot of video games," she replied with an easy grin.

"Keep it up and the Strike Fighter is yours," promised SECNAV.

Shannon and her father exchanged a look. His steel hard eyes said *Be careful.*

"The smart money is all on your son," Shannon demurred. "An honor to meet you, Mr. Secretary. By your leave, sir." Saluting, she returned to her class, where the instructors had begun their debriefing.

Zack faced his old nemesis without offering a smile. "How can I help you, sir?" he intoned civilly. "We have a very busy schedule today."

"We go back a long way, Captain," began Topper. "I felt I owed you the respect to talk to you about this matter privately."

"Go on," grunted Zack warily.

"In their efforts to clear your daughter to fly the FA/18, the NSA couldn't find a record of her whereabouts between graduating from college and entering OCS six months later. She claims to have been vacationing in Mexico, where she met her husband."

Zack could feel his hands forming fists at his sides. "I assure you my daughter has nothing to hide," he said testily.

"That's what you said when you came up for admiral," said Topper, clearly enjoying the moment.

Zack felt his bad hip tighten. He wanted to put a fist through the shorter man's face. "I had a rough patch after my wife died," he conceded. "But it didn't warrant passing me over, especially given my war record."

"Come on, Captain. Our nation's 'Favorite Son' gets a DUI and is cited for child endangerment. If you didn't have friends in high places, you'd be selling used cars right now." Zack knew he was referring to Casey Seegar.

Shannon could not hear what they were saying, but she sensed that she was the topic. Noticing that Taylor was watching her, she looked away.

"I'm not proud of my behavior," Zack responded candidly. "But that isn't what this is all about, is it, sir?" He had gone this far. Why not go all the way? In less than a year, he would be retiring.

"What are you suggesting, Captain?" replied Topper through pursed lips.

"I barely knew you at OCS," said Zack. "But you've made me some kind of target all of my career. Now you're making my daughter one as well?"

"I'm only doing my duty," said SECNAV righteously.

"Are you sure it's not more personal than that?" Zack knew he was taking a big chance by poking the bear, but his patience with this man had run its course.

Topper's face reddened, and the words that left his lips dripped with bile. "You laughed at me when that animal nearly killed me," he hissed. Zack knew he was referring to an incident in OCS when Foley had pinned Topper to the mat in a martial arts class and called him out for not fighting for his life. It was laughable that Topper had held onto this brief insult for so long.

"Foley was right to do that to you," said Zack. "You'd been wussing out like that in every drill."

"I was not wussing out," snapped Topper. "I was struggling with a sinus condition. I nearly drowned in the Dunker because of it."

"You panicked just like you did in that martial arts drill," Zack reminded him. "There was no discussion about being sick."

"I came to you the night before and asked you to help me," charged the shorter man. "I told you about my condition. Or have you forgotten about that?"

Zack searched his memory. That was thirty-five years ago. He remembered seeing Topper in the showers that night. Zack had been alone under the spray when he suddenly looked over and saw Topper standing in the doorway. His stare had been so disconcerting that Zack didn't hear anything about his sinus condition or his need for help with the Dunker. He just knew he wanted to get out of there and out of Topper's sight.

"I'm sorry if I offended you in some way," said Zack sincerely. "I just remember the occasion being awkward for both of us."

Topper became redder under his artificial tan. "Are you suggesting that I was inappropriate in some way?"

"No," Zack insisted. "It was a long time ago. I barely remember any of it." Now it was coming into sharper focus for Zack. He was dealing with a man who had personalized their brief encounter as a symbol for his own confusion and denial. That he was still wrestling with critical choices like this so late in midlife made Zack feel empathy for his enemy.

Topper immediately threw cold water on that warmth. He was finally getting his chance to vent emotions that had been trapped inside for too long. "For decades, I've watched you take all the bows, Mayo. My own family held you up to me as the hero I was supposed to be. Every accolade, every honorarium for 'America's Favorite Son' was another knife in my side. But it's my turn now. My son will win the F-35. And I will make him president of this country." He snapped his fingers, and his two aides scurried back to flank Topper as he strutted toward their helicopter.

Shannon glanced at Taylor. It moved her to see the look in his eyes as he watched his father fly away without a personal word to him. "What are you looking at?" he demanded. Clearly, he knew she had seen inside his fortress.

"Nothing," Shannon assured him with an easy smile. Then she made a little face and spoke one word that she felt said it all. "Fathers."

Taylor smiled empathetically.

"Lieutenant Castellano, I'd like a word with you," barked Zack. Shannon gave Taylor a look that said, *See what I mean?*

"He's onto us, Shannie. I can feel it," said Zack. "And he's got an army out there turning over every leaf to build a case."

"I know," said Shannon. She could see that her father was deeply shaken. Maybe it was fully dawning on him, the risks he was taking by giving her this chance. "I'm sorry I put you in this position," she offered sincerely. "Tell me to quit and I'll do it." She had not meant to say those words aloud, and now she had to hold her breath and wait to see how he replied.

Zack met her eyes, surprised by her brave offer. After his talk with Casey at his birthday party, he had resolved to believe in his daughter. "Fuck that bastard," he announced. "I promised you'd get your shot, and you'll get it."

Shannon felt an old warmth make a welcome reappearance. "Thanks," she said. "I won't let you down."

Zack felt his eyes mist. She had lowered her guard at last. This was his long-lost daughter. His fellow traveler. Hope returned that he had a chance to fix this. "I've missed you so much," he whispered emotionally.

"I've missed you, too," she said with equal warmth. The silence after her words lengthened. Finally, Zack opened his arms to her. Shannon considered going to him, then her features hardened again. This was much more complicated than a simple hug could fix.

She saluted and marched out before he could say something.

FOURTEEN

★★★

THE BULLY DUCK

NARCOTICS ANONYMOUS MEETING
End of Week Three

It was raining hard as Dylan drove to Newport News. He got to the meeting early and put his phone on the seat beside him to save it. After her failure to show last week, he kept his expectations low. But tonight was a big milestone for him. At the end of the meeting, he would receive his one-year cake, and it would be the cherry on the cake if his sober pal showed up. The previous Monday, he had taken solace in Nickie's news that Shannon had drawn the watch. Then he had been forced to listen patiently as his "sister" recounted the sexual adventures of her first weekend with Sidney, detail by graphic detail.

Dylan was grateful for his writing. His nightly session with his laptop had kept her alive in his life for two weeks. He often fell asleep only to wake up a few hours later with renewed energy. What a heroine he had found to write about. Had any other addict in history set their sights on flying jet planes? As her character came to life on the page, she took over his dreams. Tonight, sitting in that meeting, hoping for her to show, he knew that he had fallen in love for the first time in his life.

The minutes passed. Speakers droned on, and he began to give up hope. Then Shannon burst in out of the rain, and his heart did the same dance as when he first saw her two weeks earlier. He gestured that there was a seat beside him, but she avoided his gaze and sat near the door, looking like she might bolt at a moment's notice.

Dylan watched her curiously as the meeting unfolded. Every time someone came in late, she grew tense, staring out into the stormy night as though expecting some terrible surprise. At the break, he saw her dart out suddenly into the storm.

"Hey, slow down," he shouted, jogging after her with an umbrella. The downpour was even heavier than before. Shannon seemed unaware of his presence, her eyes flinching as headlights found her. "Why are you leaving early?" he demanded in a hurt tone when she reached her motorcycle.

"I have to get back to the base," she lied.

"I get my one-year cake at the end of the meeting," he said. "As my sponsor, I was hoping you'd be there." He knew he was laying it on a little thick, but he was desperate.

Shannon didn't seem to hear him. Another vehicle approached, and she spun away from the glare of its headlights, looking like a wild thing. "What's the matter?" he demanded. "You've been acting like a rabbit in the headlights all night."

"I think I'm being followed," she said.

"Followed? By whom?"

"The Navy, the NSA, the FBI, the CIA," she replied, her eyes riveted on another passing car.

"Is this a joke?" he asked.

"The Secretary of the Navy has it in for my father," replied Shannon. "Now he's going after me."

Dylan shook his head incredulously. "The Adventures of Shannon Mayo, Fighter Pilot. Tune in next week for our next thrilling episode."

"Don't make fun of me, Dylan," she snapped. "I've given up everything to fly this plane. If that son of a bitch finds out about my past, I'm finished." Another car passed slowly, and he saw her fingernails claw at her wet leather pants, leaving marks.

"I wasn't making fun of you," he assured her. "I'm in awe of you.

Nickie showed me a video on YouTube where you whipped some big guy's butt."

"Now you're stalking me on the internet?" she asked with only mild annoyance.

"I'm not stalking anybody," he replied, hurt. "I thought we were friends."

Shannon softened. "I'm sorry, Dylan. We are friends. I was looking forward to seeing you. I'm just not myself tonight."

Dylan brightened suddenly with an idea. "Let's get out of this weather," he said. "I know a little place not far from here. Great food." He hurried to add, "It's not a date."

Shannon was literally starving. A week of RAG was so overwhelming, both physically and mentally, that she entered every weekend famished. "What about your cake?" she asked.

"I'll come back for it later," he said. "Why don't you ride with me in my truck. It won't be so wet."

Shannon shook her head. She always gave herself an exit plan. "I'll follow you. I can't stay long."

A short time later, they sat in a Korean barbeque restaurant, cooking strips of steak on a burner in their table. The rain continued to fall outside their window, and Shannon stared like a person transfixed at a colony of ducks that had gathered in a pool of rainwater. As she watched, a brown gander the size of an over-inflated football put a fat, webbed foot on a smaller spotted bird and held its head underwater. In her troubled frame of mind, that bully duck was the symbol of her own battle to keep her head above water. Life was that duck, always putting its fat, webbed foot on her neck.

"Stop him," she heard herself say in a voice that didn't sound like her own.

Dylan immediately walked out into the downpour and shooed the bully bird away. When he returned, he was drenched and had to dry himself off with several napkins. Shannon seemed to have forgotten the brown duck. Instead, she was staring at a man with a newspaper who occasionally peered in her direction.

"How about a thank you?" suggested Dylan. His question drew a blank face. "The duck," he reminded her, but her eyes were on that man.

"He's been staring at me since he walked in," she said. Dylan noted that, despite her fear, she was eating like a starving person. She couldn't cook the strips of steak fast enough.

"Maybe it's because you're staring at him," Dylan suggested.

Shannon shook her head and sighed. "You're probably right."

"Our worlds are so different," observed Dylan in a soft voice. "I'm pinching myself to be sitting here with someone who's accomplished what you have."

Shannon stared at him, looking for the mean brown duck. She saw it in everyone. Since she started taking drugs, life had no soft tones for her anymore. Drugs had taught her that everyone wanted something, and that love and fellowship were fictions for the weak to cling to.

"I still don't know what you do for a living," she asked. "All Sidney would tell me is that you and Nickie work together."

"I work at VB Fishery," he said, lowering his eyes.

Shannon had not expected this. His speech and appearance suggested a lot of other options. Office manager. Insurance salesman. Coffee broker. "You're a 'fishery kid'?" she blurted.

"You know that term, huh?" he said with a little smirk. "Yeah, I'm a fishery kid. If that's too low on the old totem pole, trust me, I get it."

"You kidding? My mom worked in a paper bag factory," Shannon replied with pride in her voice. "When the Navy officer wives put her down, she went back to school and became an executive fundraiser for a national charity."

"Go, Mom," said Dylan. Then he added, "I read somewhere that she died in a fire. Was that why you got into drugs?"

"No," she answered quickly. "Drugs came later. I did a lot of other dances first."

"But why drugs?" he persisted.

Shannon had no answer. She had been trying to explain this to herself forever. "I just ran out of steam trying to be strong," she said flatly. "What about you?"

"It was a bunch of things," replied Dylan. "My dad ran off with some hottie he met online. Mom went into a home. Then I lost Stevie."

"Who's Stevie?"

"My brother. My hero. He drowned," Dylan reported sadly. "That's when I started doing Red Bull and rum, and long lines of cocaine. It took about a year before I lost the house that had been in our family forever."

He felt her hand settle on his and willed it to stay there. It did. They sat there pensively for a long moment before Dylan resumed. "You and I are such opposites in the way we dealt with getting clean," he observed. "You became a daredevil, and I became a coward."

"Aren't you being a little rough on yourself?" she asked, finally taking her hand away. "I'm sure you have your brave side."

"I do own a boat, with the biggest motors in the harbor," he bragged. "It was Stevie's. When he was alive, we would take it out in open water and race through high surf as fast as we could go, Bach or Beethoven or Mozart at full volume. It was such a high."

"No dreams of your own?" she asked softly.

"Dreams?" he repeated. It wasn't a question he got a lot. "Last month Nickie and I got elected union reps. That could lead to moving up into management," he offered with little emotion.

"I meant big dreams," she clarified.

Dylan shrugged self-deprecatingly. "I've been writing since I was a kid. I won a national award in high school." He told her about Celeste Stein. "She still reads my work and makes suggestions."

"Have you written anything lately?" she inquired.

He thought about lying. What would she say if she knew he'd been writing feverishly about her since they met? *Stalker. Pervert.* "I started writing again the night we met," he admitted.

Shannon's lips curled suspiciously. "What are you writing about?"

"It's about a character like you, a jet school like FRS," he replied. "It's all fiction."

Shannon felt threatened. She was harboring a dangerous secret that she could not allow to surface, even in some random manner. "Why am I just learning about this now?" she asked with no effort to conceal her annoyance.

"You didn't show up to the meeting last week," he reminded her. "I was going to tell you then. If you don't want me to do it, I'll stop."

"What's your story?" she asked, her curiosity checking in.

"It's a love story," he announced.

Shannon snorted with amusement.

"About a daughter and her father," he resumed. "It's all made up."

"Are you in this story?" she asked with a half-smile.

"No," he answered. "I'm nothing in all this. Just the storyteller."

Shannon felt divided. She was flattered by his interest, but this was an enormous step after two years living in the shadows to protect her secret. Too many things could go wrong. "I can't let you do this, Dylan. I'm sorry. It's just too risky."

Dylan nodded disappointedly. He had considered the possibility that she would feel too threatened. But the threat of having to stop this journey was terrifying. For the first time in over a year, he was writing, and it was the best work he'd ever done. He had only one hope to turn her around. It was honesty.

"I respect your feelings," he began. "But I want you to consider what this story could mean to a lot of people who need to start believing in themselves again."

"Aren't you being a little dramatic?" she suggested.

"Not at all," he insisted. "What you're doing is the very definition of a hero's journey. If you pull it off, so many people will get strength from it."

Shannon hadn't seen her mission in this broader light. The fact that he saw it that way was intoxicating. Her father had been a hero, her mother, too. This imaginary version of herself belonged up there in their league, a heady first in her mind. "I'm no hero," she answered modestly. "I'm just trying to make sense of my life."

"What if I promise to show you everything I write before I show it to anyone else?" he asked. "Anything you want out, out it goes on the spot."

"How do I know I can trust you?" she asked.

"Don't you already know that?" he asked unflinchingly.

Shannon knew he was right. She had made that leap of faith at Molly's. Additionally, this was a very insightful man. She wondered what he might discover about her in the process of his writing.

"There can't be any slip-ups, Dylan," she insisted. "You can't say anything about drugs or anything about my father that could jeopardize his career."

"I understand," he assured her. A silence fell between them. The rain pattered against their window. Dylan gently took her hand, leaned across the table, and kissed her on the lips.

Shannon pulled away like she'd been burned. It had been two years since she had allowed anyone to kiss her. His touch could not have been briefer, but his lips had sent shock waves through her body.

"I wish you hadn't done that," she said.

"What're you afraid of, Shannon?" he asked. It was the kindest voice Shannon had ever heard.

"Do you want the truth or some bullshit answer?" she asked.

"Go for it," he urged.

"I'm not into sex. I never have been," she said with finality. It felt good to have the truth on the table.

Dylan's eyes twinkled mischievously. "Whatever you say, but I'm getting a different message." She blushed and looked away. "Drugs steal the life out of everything," observed Dylan, as though reading her thoughts. "Once you trade the search for the miraculous for cheap thrills, there's no going back."

She stared at him, moved by the wisdom of his words. "I hope you're wrong."

"You know what they say?" he asked in that sing-song way. When she didn't chime in with an AA saying of her own, he provided one. "We're only as sick as our secrets."

That brought a crooked smile from Shannon. This was her favorite AA saying. It defined her perfectly, perhaps too perfectly.

Dylan chose his next words carefully. Before now, he had been in the same social rush to judgment as everyone else. Casual hook-ups.

One-night stands. But he was desperate for something better. "Shannon, I think you and I are good for each other," he began. "I think it's more than friendship, but call it whatever you want. If you want slow, then slow is how we go."

"Thanks," she intoned gratefully. In her climb out of the dungeon of her past, "slow" was all she could handle.

On their way out, the rain had abated, and the bully duck was nowhere to be seen.

FIFTEEN

FIRST FLIGHT WITH AN INSTRUCTOR

THE WORKING AREA

Three Weeks Later

Dylan's hands were shaking at the helm of his brother's boat. It was taking all the courage he could muster not to turn back. Nickie sat beside him in a warm hoodie that made her look like an elfin Yoda. He had said nothing to her about his intentions and watched her eyes widen as they neared the mouth of the harbor and began to encounter large waves.

"What's gotten into you, Bro-Derek?" asked Nickie, confused. "We haven't gone out of the harbor since Stevie was alive."

"Today's their first flight with an instructor," he shouted over the clamor of surf and wind. "I have to see this." As they cleared a jetty and entered open waters, Dylan sucked in a deep breath of air and tightened his grip on the controls. He was so scared he could feel his face tighten into a mask, but he was more alive now than he had been since Stevie died.

"Breathe that air," he commanded. "Just breathe that air."

Nickie laughed. This was Stevie's famous battle cry. He had bellowed it every time they entered open water. Dylan activated a boom box and Mozart's *The Marriage of Figaro* blasted louder than the slap of the waves against the prow of their boat. Another infusion of pure Steven Harmony.

Nickie scrunched up her nose. "I get nervous when you're fired up like this," she chirped. "It usually means you're about to fall off the wagon."

Dylan laughed. Since he'd met Shannon, he woke up every morning with a sense of purpose, and usually something else a little more physical. He wasn't falling off the wagon. He was falling in love for the first time in his life.

After that attempted kiss at the Korean restaurant, it was imperative that the next move come from her. But Shannon offered no encouragement in that regard. The three Fridays following that night, they had dined at different restaurants in Newport News. He came with pages of questions, and she would answer each one patiently. She showed him videos on her phone that she found on Google to illustrate the various stages of the syllabus. She explained that there was a lot she couldn't tell him because of security issues. Last Friday she brought model airplanes to teach him the basics of dogfighting.

In the weeks since SECNAV's appearance, Shannon had slipped to second place in the race for the F-35, but she hoped to regain her lead with a good showing in her first fight with an instructor.

True to his promise, Dylan was careful to fictionalize anything that might put her secret in peril. He changed all the names and invented a fictional flight school and a fictional father and daughter whose deep love had been shattered by tragic events, forcing them to wage the battle of their lives to find their way home. Instead of drugs, his fictional Shannon's secret was that she had been arrested as a teenager for nearly killing a young man who had tried to rape her and had not reported it on her application to jet school.

He reassured himself every time he sat down at his laptop that he was writing fiction, but he knew he wasn't. He was doing everything in his power as a writer to put himself inside this unique young woman's head. This duplicity weighed on him today as he cut his engines, focused his powerful field glasses on the sky, and braced himself for what new discoveries would come his way. He was glad Nickie had joined in the adventure. He doubted his courage without her.

His research told him that "the first flight with an instructor" was the first major test in the syllabus. This was the moment when theory became reality. To have any hope of flying the plane alone, she would have to survive today.

Zack, Perryman, and their team of instructors marched out of maintenance and walked toward the assembled class on the shimmering tarmac like gunslingers in a spaghetti western.

"Big day, ladies and gentlemen," announced Zack. "But before we let you fly our eighty-million-dollar airplane, we've got a little surprise."

Perryman and the other instructors started shouting, "Drug test! Drug test! Report to the infirmary on the double!"

Shannon felt her father's eyes on her. *Did he really think she'd be that dumb?* As she hurried to the infirmary with the rest of the class, she noticed Taylor Daniels saunter casually in another direction. She knew what he was doing. His band were all stoners. His song lyrics were laden with pot references. After two years in the Navy, she knew all the clever ways people faked a drug test.

She was waiting with the rest of the class outside the infirmary as Taylor walked out last, grinning smugly. Shannon gave him a look, and he winked back. She wondered what the gesture meant. Had his father learned something about her drug history? It was probably as simple as one druggie knowing another druggie.

A short time later, with all drug tests reporting negative, Shannon inserted her legs into tight holes and strapped in. It seemed to her a miracle that a human body could fit into so small a space. She was shocked when her father slipped into the back seat. Without radio connection in their shared cockpit, they were forced to shout to hear one another.

"I thought Lieutenant Commander Kelly was my assigned instructor today," yelled Shannon.

"Change of plans," Zack shouted back. "I know your tricks. You could con one of the young ones with those baby blues."

Shannon felt blindsided. "Isn't this against regulations?"

"Fuck regulations. This is how it is," came her father's reply. He didn't tell her that he had gone to his superior, the rear admiral in charge of the base, to over-ride Perryman's decision barring him from being her instructor. It had created a rare coolness between the two old friends.

Since his encounter with Casey at his birthday bash, Zack had been doing his best to believe in his daughter. His decision to step in as her instructor today was not a departure from this. He prayed that this flight would dispel his lingering reservations and he could stop being an adversary in her eyes.

"Turn on the fucking battery so we can talk like civilized people." he barked irritably. He intended to use every trick he had ever learned to expose a student's weakness. If she got through this gauntlet, he vowed to be her biggest fan going forward.

Shannon threw a switch and lifted her oxygen mask to talk. "Battery on, sir."

"About time," he groused. "I was holding my breath back there at the infirmary."

"I told you. You don't have to worry about *me*," she announced with an emphasis on the last word.

"Oh, really? Someone in the class cheated on that test?"

Shannon was not about to throw Taylor under the bus. "I'm no snitch," she replied coolly. "Can we do this please? I've only looked forward to this all my life."

"I was enjoying our conversation," Zack answered grudgingly. "First one since my birthday." Grabbing the manual, he started at the top. "Ejection arm in place?"

"Ejection arm in place," she replied after making sure it was.

He went down the list. "Ejection seat pin in place? Initiate ICS check. Fire warning test A." Shannon depressed the test switch, and they heard the recorded voice of "Bitchin' Betty."

"Engine fire right. Engine fire right," bitched Betty. "Engine fire left. Engine fire left," the recorded voice droned on. "APU fire. APU fire. Bleed air left. Bleed air left. Bleed air right. Bleed air right."

"Don't forget your plane captain, Lieutenant," warned Zack, and

Shannon waved three fingers in the direction of a figure in orange coordinating activity on the ground.

"Ready to start APU, sir," she said.

"About time," complained Zack. "This is the slowest start I've ever seen."

Shannon discreetly flipped him off, but Zack glimpsed the gesture in her rearview.

"I saw that," he announced smugly.

Shannon felt her ire rise like a thermometer under a match. She couldn't let him provoke her. Sometimes, in her Chelsea Year, she ran into players who tried that mental whammy approach, but her father had it down to a science. He had used it time and again to beat her at their games. He had done it to the star student from the last class the day she arrived. It was one of his street tricks.

Pulling the engine crank switch, Shannon started the right engine, labeled "Engine Number Two," which was the main engine, with all the hydraulics. When she had the necessary RPMs, she introduced fuel into the combustion chamber. "Engine two, good start," she reported.

"Don't tell me. Tell your plane captain," Zack corrected disparagingly.

Shannon waved a finger, and the plane captain signed back. When she had the RPMs, she pushed the left throttle and engine one started. She held up her forefinger, and the captain signed back from the tarmac.

"Ready for system check," she announced.

"Begin control wipeout," Zack ordered. Shannon tested her stick. It easily moved forward and back, but her left and right movements were hampered. She tried again. The stick only moved an inch or so. She was stymied.

"I have binding controls, sir," she reported, her eyes scouring the complicated cockpit for answers.

Zack laughed. He was pressing his thighs on his controls, hampering her left and right movement. "It's my fucking legs, dummy," he laughed.

"*Anak ng puta!*" Shannon swore back in Tagalog. The words translated to "Son of a bitch!"

"*Tangina!*" Zack responded. It meant "Stupid piece of shit!" He moved his legs, freeing the controls. "That was fun," he exclaimed. "You still remember those words, huh?"

"Every single one, 'Big Spendah,'" she bragged, using her foot pedals to steer the plane toward its takeoff position.

Shannon accidentally pressed one pedal too hard, and the plane began to swerve. "Great," complained Zack. "You're going to kill us before we even get in the air."

Shannon quickly corrected her error, settled into the ground speed, and throttled through a barrier. The sudden surge of the afterburner pushed her back into her seat and took her breath away. She watched the nose of her plane rise into the sky like a shimmering silver phallus. The power was awesome.

"It's . . . fucking . . . amazing . . ." she stammered. "Oh, my God . . . oh, my God . . ."

Zack felt that dry cough come out of nowhere. Studying her features in the rearview, he knew that what he was witnessing was not new. Shannon had evidenced an addictive nature from earliest childhood. To both her father and mother, her passion for life felt almost manic at times. The Chelsea Year stood out in his mind, but he could cite a dozen other examples of her take-no-prisoners assault on life.

"Begin G-Warm," he commanded gruffly.

Shannon banked hard to the right. As the g's mounted, her face became rubbery. Her eyes were pinpoints. "Oh, shit . . . oh, shit . . ." she crooned.

Zack hunched forward suddenly, his restraints biting into his chest as he prepared himself to take over. This was what he feared might happen when his daughter encountered the power of the Super Hornet for the first time. The force was nothing short of transcendental. The next few seconds would be critical.

Far below, on the water, Dylan and Nickie watched the skies with binoculars as the four FA/18s performed G-Warms high above. "How do you know who's who?" asked Nickie. "You can't see diddly with these."

Dylan's eyebrows bunched as he scrutinized the four planes doing their aerial tricks high above. His research had taught him that every pilot had their own style, based on their level of acuity and their personal habits. It was a signature you couldn't fake. "If I had to make a guess, I'd say that's Shannon," he announced, pointing to the plane making the most precise turns.

Nickie indicated the jet furthest to the left. "I bet that one's Sidney." Dylan laughed as he saw the muscular turns of that plane. Dylan knew that, while his courtship of Shannon was in slow motion, if it was moving at all, the opposite was true for Nickie and Sidney. His "sister" may have started her courtship of the Navy pilot with an agenda, but she returned after every date more in love than the time before. Her graphic replays of their adventurous lovemaking kept Dylan in stitches.

High above, Shannon's face was ecstatic. The power was so much more than she had imagined. "Oh, God . . . oh, God . . . oh, God . . . " she moaned. She was not ready for what happened next.

Zack suddenly threw his throttles to idle and pulled a lever, loudly retracting their landing gear into the underbelly. "Why did you do that?" she demanded in disbelief. This meant her flight was over, and she had failed the drill. Because of their deal, Shannon knew this failure would draw more than a reprimand.

"That landing gear is only rated for two hundred fifty knots," Zack reminded her sourly. "You could shear it off while you're tripping out."

"I wasn't tripping out," she protested. "I was about to retract them when you did it." She knew that this was a lie. She had completely forgotten about her landing gear. She had been on the trip of her life.

"Your eyes were pinned like a junkie's," he persisted.

Shannon had no retort. She had to admit that she had been totally unprepared for the breath-stealing rush of the afterburner, or the skull-collapsing feeling from pulling seven times the force of gravity in a tight turn. The terrifying truth was that she had felt as high as she'd ever been on drugs. She found the two sensations disquietingly similar. Both were like out-of-body travel.

Zack was heartbroken. He had wanted so desperately to get past this hurdle, but his role as a protective father was the only option left to him now. He knew his decision would kill all hope for a reconciliation in the immediate future. It might preclude them ever reuniting. But he had to do what was right. He had to be a man. He never stopped faulting himself for not keeping Paula from leaving on that fateful trip.

"We have a deal," he said with finality. "Fly us home."

Far below, Dylan lowered his field glasses, concerned. "Oh, shit. Oh, shit," he muttered.

Nickie watched him with sisterly warmth. This was a new one. Her bro was in love.

———

Perryman looked up from paperwork as Zack entered his office, still in his flight suit, Shannon behind him, still in hers. "Scratch Lieutenant Mayo off the roster, Captain," Zack announced. "She's withdrawing from the class."

Perryman turned his eyes on Shannon. "Lieutenant Mayo, is that true?"

"No, sir," she replied. Upon landing, she had learned that three others in the class had made the same mistake, and all received their first "Signal of Difficulty." You had to accumulate three to get kicked out. "I wasn't prepared for the power, but I will be next time."

Zack felt his face grow hot. "We have a deal," he reminded her. "I can't pass her, Louis," he declared. "In two weeks, she'll be alone in that plane. I saw her face. I know that look. She will kill herself. I'm sure of it."

Perryman's eyes flashed with resentment. "This is why I insisted you assign another instructor. Then you went behind my back to get your way." He turned his kind gray eyes on Shannon. He was her "uncle." After losing his wife and sons because he had given more to the Navy than he had to them, Shannon was his only real touch with family. Knowing about her drug use, he had feared for her life when she went missing, but he had never given up hope that she was alive.

"I just got a little carried away, sir," she said, knowing she was not being entirely truthful. "It won't happen again."

"I'm giving you a Signal of Difficulty, Lieutenant," announced Perryman. "Two more and you're out."

Shannon was deeply relieved to be held to the same standards as her classmates. Her father was glaring at Perryman. She saluted quickly and walked out, but their voices followed her down the corridor.

"If she dies, it's on you, Louis!" bellowed her father.

"She's not going to die," shouted Perryman. "Not from drugs anyway. She's the best pilot I've seen since I first saw you fly."

After her abortive first flight with an instructor, Shannon tried to focus on her classwork, but she had seen something in herself that morning that frightened her. She needed her sponsor, whether he was a real one or not. It was Monday. There was no way she could wait until their Friday meeting.

She went to the infirmary and complained of a stomachache. Without changing out of her khaki working uniform, she left the base on her Harley. As she parked near the entrance to the monolithic Virginia Beach Fishery, there was a pungent odor in the air that was both sweet and sticky. Her stomach recoiled, but she pushed past the feeling. She needed to see her sober pal.

She walked into the cavernous enclosure and remembered coming here with her third-grade class. In that era, the workers had killed the large fish by hitting them with baseball bats. Her eyes swept over the men and women in red slickers, killing the large tuna with spikes that glinted in the bright indoor lights. Disappointed not to find Dylan, she turned to go. Then she saw Dylan and Nickie appear on the catwalk above with three executives in suits. He waved, obviously surprised to see her.

As Dylan left the fishery, he saw from Shannon's deflated demeanor as she lounged against her motorcycle that she had come to him in his role as her sponsor.

"Shouldn't you be in class?" he asked. He knew from his research that the curriculum for FRS moved lightning-fast, and she was missing important training that would be hard to complete later.

"I had a bad morning," she sighed.

"I know," he said. "Nickie and I were out there on my boat."

Shannon stared at him, remembering his words at dinner three weeks ago. "I thought you didn't do that."

"It was a nice day. I needed to do some research for my book," he replied lamely.

"Don't get over your head with this," she warned.

"Me? You're the one playing hooky to hang with your sober pal," he reminded her.

She glanced in the direction of the fishery. "I hope I'm not getting you into any trouble."

Dylan assured her that, as union rep, he could take as long a break as he wanted. She had his ear.

"I really lost it today," she confessed in a rush. "My father was right. I totally forgot about my landing gear. I was in a whole other world."

"What other world?" he asked. These were the nuggets he mined every time he was with her. The guideposts to the character he was basing on her.

"In advanced, when I got my first jet, the Goshawk, I had to go to two meetings a week to stay on planet Earth," she explained. "This is a hundred times the plane."

"So, add another meeting to your schedule," he quipped. "Or get a real sponsor."

"That's not funny, Dylan," she remarked. "If I lost it like that my first time up, what about when I'm flying solo?"

"What are you afraid will happen?" he asked.

"I don't know," she ventured tentatively. "Maybe I'll lose it completely and shoot out there like Icarus flying into the sun. I did it with drugs. Oh, boy, did I do it with drugs."

"It's not the same thing," he insisted. "You'll learn to control the rush."

"But what if I can't? What if I kill someone?" This fear had trailed her every day of her flight training. It was the subject of most of her "sharings" in NA meetings, although she always couched it in code.

"Shannon, you made one little mistake this morning," he offered in a soft voice. "Otherwise, you were poetry up there."

Shannon felt a smile fight its way onto her face. "Thanks, 'sponsor'," she said. She suddenly leaned close and planted a kiss on the side of his mouth.

Dylan was stunned by the feelings that the simple gesture stirred in him. It was not a romantic kiss, but it was more than a statement of gratitude. He considered returning the gesture, innocent as it was, but thought better of it. He didn't want to tip the scales the wrong way.

As Shannon got back on her bike and drove away, Dylan produced a rueful smile. This was taking more perseverance than he had anticipated, but the upside was more than he could have imagined. If a kiss like this could have such power, what would it feel like if their lips actually touched?

Turning on the highway, Shannon accelerated to a breathtaking speed. The smell of the fishery dissipated into normal harbor smells. Her lips could still feel the slight prickle of his afternoon stubble. Her pulse was loud in her ears. Her sudden show of affection was a personal milestone. A burst of laughter came from a forgotten place.

The search for the miraculous was still alive and well in her heart.

SIXTEEN
SURROGATES

OCEANA BEACH

May 3, 2011

It was Zack's first hot shower of the day. He remained in that tiled enclosure until the water ran cold. He never wanted to come out. It should have been a day of celebration. Last night, the Navy Seals had killed Osama bin Laden in Pakistan. Instead of bringing a welcome conclusion to that saga, the news only opened up old wounds for Zack. The list of friends he had lost in the war on terrorism was a long one. If they had killed a thousand bin Ladens, it wouldn't have been enough.

He had nowhere to be today. He thought of going to the base gym. Maybe a good workout would clear his head. Then he remembered that he had scheduled a session with his Navy therapist at noon. After Shannon had miraculously shown up, he had abruptly discontinued his sessions with Eric Mann, but after three and a half months of failure to bridge their differences, he had scheduled a return to therapy.

Wearing one of his garish Hawaiian shirts, Mann welcomed Zack into his office at the base infirmary. "Good afternoon, Captain. I smell soap. Did you just get out of the shower?"

"Guilty as charged," replied Zack, taking his seat on the familiar leather couch.

"I thought that would taper off after your daughter showed up," offered Eric. "How's that going?"

Zack's posture told the therapist a lot. He sat askew to favor his bad hip. There was a grayness to his complexion that spoke of lack of sleep. "Doc, my daughter is going to die if I don't find a way to stop her," he declared at last. "But I don't have the balls to do what's right. I'm the same weak shit I was the day I let my wife go to Atlanta."

"Still hung up on that manliness concept, I see," observed the therapist wisely.

Zack scowled. He knew it was true. All his life, the tenets of manliness had been his grail. *The strong survive. Don't share your feelings. That makes you a girl.* The boys in the foster home survived by jungle rules. So did the children on the streets of Olongapo. For his father Byron, being a man's man was a creed. Then flying jets in war became his testament of manhood.

"You and I are just very different people," insisted Zack.

Eric smiled benignly. "Captain Mayo, you couldn't be more wrong." Then he zeroed in on his message. "This problem between you and your daughter is especially complicated because of gender," he explained. "And gender seems to be your blind side."

Zack looked away, but the therapist was not through.

"When your wife began a career, your daughter built her life around you, and you built yours around her," said Eric. "But when your wife died, your relationship with your daughter died with it." He paused to draw Zack's fullest attention. "Explain that to me, Captain Mayo."

Zack shook his head. There it was again, the question with no answer. "I can't," he said. "You'd have to ask her. Things changed right away after we lost her mother. Shannie withdrew into herself totally. I tried everything to reach out to her. I'm still trying. It should be the other way around. She should be chasing my forgiveness."

"Get off your high horse, Captain," said Eric. "When are you going to start seeing your role in this?"

Zack sank back on the sofa, shaken by the rebuke. "I was a good father," he insisted. "I gave up serving my country for six years to teach a teenage girl to be strong. I never abandoned our family like my daughter did. And I'm not abandoning it now." Zack was starting to wish he hadn't made a return to therapy. Before Paula, he would have been the first to scoff at head-shrinkers.

"Your parenting was exemplary," injected Eric. "Nobody's arguing that point. But you're ignoring the role of gender. Read your Freud," he suggested. "The better the job the parent does, the more confusing it can be to a growing mind."

Leaving the base, Zack felt worse than he had before his session. Passing the Beach Cinema Alehouse, the marquee advertised the film *Bridesmaids*. A block later, he saw a line waiting to get into Foley's Fitness. Every time he had driven by over the last few weeks, it seemed that business had improved. He never watched YouTube or consulted social media, so he knew nothing about Shannon's fight with Trevor Dominion. Deciding it was now or never, he found an empty space in the parking lot between the old gym and Nudies, a strip club next door.

Peering through the large front windows, he saw a crowd surrounding a ring where a demonstration was taking place. A young woman in a Navy-issued blue-and-gold T-shirt and shorts was helping an infirm, elderly man into the ring. To Zack's shock, it was Shannon. He stayed at the window to watch.

Ramon's video of her fight and her victory dance had drawn a lot of hits on YouTube, and Shannon tried to offer some new demonstration every week to extend their outreach. Today's clientele was the largest to date. Her opponent in the ring this time was a thin septuagenarian with sparse white hair whose body shook with a nervous disorder. She raised his hand like a boxing announcer introducing a combatant.

"Ladies and gentlemen, meet Fred," she intoned in her surfer-girl voice. She had decided to carry that persona into the gym. It energized business. She was the hot surfer girl who had taken down Trevor Dominion. Prospective patrons came in every day wanting to meet her. She was amused when people asked for her autograph. Shannon saw Foley watching her from the front desk where a line of patrons was waiting to get in. He flashed her a thumbs up. She felt a new appreciation in his rheumy eyes today.

Outside, Zack took in their relationship with unmasked jealousy.

"We're trying something new today," resumed Shannon in character. "Fred has Parkinson's. He brought along some friends from his support group." She led the applause for the six men and four women with Parkinson's in Fred's rooting section.

Zack watched from outside as though seeing a stranger. His daughter was no longer a child by any stretch of the imagination. She was an adult with enviable skills and a passion to do good like her mother. Her warmth toward this frail, afflicted man reminded him of Paula touring one of her cancer clinics for kids.

"Go on, Fred. Hit me with your best shot," Shannon challenged her elderly opponent, striking a pugilistic stance. Her eyes were warm and supportive. She did not see her father watching from outside.

Fred had the posture of a praying mantis. His control over his own body was marginal, but he was a jolly soul and game-on to be Shannon's guinea pig. "I'll sure try, Shannon," he said, assuming a boxing stance to match hers. His knees and elbows shook. He tried to punch her and stumbled, forcing Shannon to catch him and help him stay upright.

"You can do this, Fred," she said with conviction. "Just get into the rhythm. Move your feet like we talked about. It's all in the rhythm. Shuffle, shuffle, jab, jab . . . shuffle, shuffle, jab, jab." Fred did his best to imitate her movements. "That's it," she encouraged. "Get into a groove."

After his early struggles, Fred's focus grew. Finally, his feet and his hands locked into a rhythm, and his punches started landing with regularity on Shannon's gloves. They were pitty-pat punches, but nobody cared. He was doing it.

"Oh, boy . . . oh, boy . . ." giggled Fred. "This is fun!"

Foley wore a smile that could define smiles. This was his dream. After all the years since being terminated from the Marine Corps, here was an opportunity to give to the community, to be more than another bitter old man. And it didn't hurt that his cash drawer was full. Even his poor health had not been an issue in a long time. Shannon was a lucky penny.

Zack watched from outside with amazement. There was so much he didn't know about his daughter, so many chapters to fill in. Would she ever allow him back into her life?

As she parried her patient's feeble punches, Shannon addressed the crowd. "Boxing tricks the left brain and right brain into reconnecting the old neural highway," she said. "And the effect lasts for hours." She allowed Fred to finish with a flurry. He even pulled off a version of the "Ali Shuffle" to resounding applause.

"That's enough for your first time, Fred," she said. "Good job." Fred climbed down from the ring with near-total dexterity.

As Zack watched, Shannon got out of the ring and went over to Foley where she planted a kiss on his bald head. The old man looked up at her with warmth and gratitude. Zack frowned. Clearly, this was not her first visit. They had formed a familial bond. What an odd twist of fate. He had been replaced by the most impactful man in his life. Zack turned suddenly and walked away.

As he started to get in his Corvette, Katy Perry's "Firework" assaulted his ears. He took in its source, the gaudy old strip club next to the gym. "Nudies Gentlemen's Club. Since 1961." He hadn't been in a strip club since his days in the Philippines. As an officer, it didn't feel right.

But like a lost soul, he found his feet taking him inside.

Shannon finished sweeping the floor and put the wide broom in a closet. Foley looked up from his desk where he was going through receipts. Tonight, he felt like a proud father. This girl was pure magic.

"I'm going to start paying you for your time," he announced in a business-like voice that resonated with gratitude.

Shannon knew she should feel flattered by his offer, but she wasn't here for money. She needed him to understand it and see it the way she did. This was about family.

"Thanks," she said, "but I like it this way."

"I feel I'm taking advantage of you," he persisted. "It's not right." He held out an envelope to her. "There's two hundred dollars in here. If business keeps up, you'll get that every week."

Shannon waved a hand dismissively. "I don't want your money," she insisted. "Coming here is a holiday after what I go through all week." She studied him with warm eyes as he put the envelope in a drawer. He seemed genuinely confused.

"Gunny, did you ever have family outside the Corps?" she asked softly.

Foley seemed to mull over the word "family" as though it belonged to a foreign language.

"No," he admitted. "The Marine Corps was my family. It never seemed right to start a real family after what I'd seen as a boy."

"Why did you single out my father like you did?" she asked. It was a question she had pondered since she heard her first Foley story at the age of five.

"I never ran into anyone like your father," he told her. "I knew my own upbringing didn't make me officer material, so there was no way I was going to let him make it. It was personal to me."

"What went wrong?" she asked.

"It was like seeing myself twenty years younger," he recalled. "For the first time, I realized a white boy might have had just as shitty a time of it growing up as me."

Shannon struggled to make sense of his confession. "If he was unworthy, why did you graduate him?"

Foley thought a long moment before he spoke.

"He changed," he recounted. "He made a friend, a troubled boy who looked up to him like a god. Then he met a local factory girl."

"My mom," supplied Shannon. She felt compelled to add, "I've made some friends. My roommate's a real character. And I met a boy. It's not romantic, if that's what you're thinking."

"Why not?" asked Foley, amused by her speedy clarification and flattered by her openness.

"Sex isn't my thing," she said candidly.

"Oh? Why not?" he asked.

Shannon knew this was a dialogue she had wanted to have with her father, but she was having it with this man instead. "I associate drugs with sex," she explained. "I started both at the same time, and I quit both at the same time. I figure, if I start one back up, I'll start the other."

"What does that have to do with your new friend?" inquired Foley. "Does he want you to do drugs?"

"No. The opposite. He takes my sobriety as seriously as his own," she answered.

"Is he pushing himself on you sexually?" asked her surrogate father, because that was what he had become, and they both knew it.

"No, he never pushes," she explained. "We have an understanding."

"Then what are you afraid of? That, under the right circumstances, you might like it?" Foley's rheumy eyes glowed with a special energy. He was warming to his role.

"It's just not a big deal to me, that's all," she reiterated. She was sorry now that the subject had come up. Her feelings about sex were complicated and talking about it only made it worse. "Flight school is all I have the energy for," she concluded.

Foley nodded. Sex was too personal a matter for some surrogate to venture opinions about. He would have to wait for her to bring the subject up again.

Eager to change the subject, Shannon said, "When I was unpacking, I found this." She reached into a box and pulled out a gnarly swagger stick covered with old notches. Over time the wood had darkened into a rich caramel color.

Foley took it from her and felt its weight in his hands. It was as though he'd been reunited with a best friend. He took in the notches as if putting a face to each one. Then he tucked his old symbol of power and sovereignty into one of the side pockets of his wheelchair. "Thank you," he said. "I was wondering where I put that old thing."

When Shannon left Foley's gym and straddled her Harley in the lot, she didn't see her father's black Corvette parked a few rows away.

Accelerating onto the street, she sucked in the night air with a sense of accomplishment. She was slowly letting life back in.

The girl working the pole in front of Zack was a petite Filipina, maybe twenty-one. The club was about half-full on a Saturday night. Zack drained his second Angel's Envy neat. He was not drunk yet, but he was feeling the buzz. At first, he had felt out of place among the younger, mostly blue-collar patrons, but that second drink had filed off the edges. Watching the girl work the pole, he flashed back to his early days on the streets of Olongapo, pimping out his sisters when the regular pimp failed to show. Then his thoughts turned to little Maria.

The girl undulating on the pole in front of him looked nothing like Maria or Tiki, but she shared their sad eyes. The ringsiders waved their dollar bills and called out to the dancer in profane ways. "How much for a blow job, honey?" shouted a dockworker in a wife-beater.

Suddenly, Zack put down his empty glass, climbed onstage and started dancing with the girl. He still had some boyish moves, and the dancer laughed and applauded. The words came out of his mouth as if it was yesterday when he last sold his sisters.

"Oy, oy, Big Spendah, short time, long time, ten dollah," he serenaded.

The young dancer found the handsome, white-haired man amusing. Zack sang out, "*Mahal kita*, Maria," which translated to "I love you, Maria." Hearing her own language made the girl laugh and flirt even more. Men in the audience began to complain, and a bouncer in a muscle shirt came over and told Zack he couldn't be up on the stage.

"Well, *excusez-moi*," slurred Zack. As he was climbing down, he stumbled and fell on his face.

Someone shouted, "Get that drunk out of here."

Zack snarled back in Tagalog, *"Tangina mo, gago!"* The words meant "Suck my cock!" The crowd only grew angrier.

Just then, a motorized wheelchair appeared beside Zack and a familiar voice spoke through the din of voices and music. "Come on, Captain. Time to go."

Zack looked up, and the sight of his old mentor brought an incredulous expression to his face. "You . . ." he stammered. "What're you doing here?"

Foley often came next door to unwind after work. It was what passed at his age for a social life. "Same thing as you," he said. "But I'm not embarrassing myself. Let's go, Captain."

Strong hands gripped Zack under the armpits and helped him to his feet. Foley may have lost his legs, but he was very strong in the upper body. Zack brushed himself off. *Who did this retired enlisted man think he was talking to?* But his head was swimming from the drinks. And he urgently needed some air.

Outside, Zack turned to confront his old mentor, marshaling as much sobriety as he could manage. "Thanks, Gunny. I owe you one. I've wanted to stop by your gym."

"So, I've noticed," said Foley sarcastically. He had seen Zack drive by on several occasions without stopping. "What are you afraid of, Mayonnaise? That an old man with no legs might still have something to teach you?"

Zack had no ready answer. This diminished Foley was irreconcilable with the towering figure from the past. "I thought about you a lot over the years, Gunny. I was sorry to hear the Corps retired you after your injury."

"Everything comes to an end," mused the older man. Then his flinty eyes bore into Zack. "Aren't you retiring soon yourself?"

"Yep," replied Zack with forced jollity. "Can't wait to hit the links." There was so much that Zack wanted to say, but his tongue felt thick in his mouth. "Well, thanks again. Let's grab a beer sometime," he said, turning to go.

"Stop, Captain," ordered Foley. "You're not going anywhere. You're coming with me."

Zack wasn't sure he had heard correctly. "Thanks, Sergeant, but I'm a big boy. I know how to hail a cab."

Foley pulled his old swagger stick from his wheelchair pocket and held it up into the flashing neon lights of the strip club's marque.

Zack stared at the familiar object like he was seeing Moses' staff. He wanted to ask the obvious, but he couldn't get a word to leave his tongue.

"Same one," said Foley, reading Zack's mind. "Now move it, Mayonnaise. I may be in a wheelchair, but in your condition, I could put a big hurt on you, and you know it."

"I had two lousy drinks," insisted Zack. "That's nothing."

"Maybe it was nothing when you were fifty. But right now, you are legally drunk and in danger of hurting yourself and bringing shame to the armed services. Move it," he ordered. To make his point, he prodded Zack hard in the chest with his swagger stick.

"Hey! That hurt!" complained Zack, stumbling back slightly.

"Then don't make me do it again," said Foley. He was enjoying himself. Thanks to this man's daughter, he was coming back to life. Foley opened a gate to his back property with a key.

"I'm not going in there," declared Zack.

"Yes, you are." Foley pushed Zack hard with his stick, sending him sprawling backward through the gate and onto a courtyard lawn.

"Hey!" cried Zack. As he struggled to get up, Foley locked the gate. "You can't do that!" protested Zack just before a cold blast of water hit him. Foley was holding a garden hose. The pressure was powerful. Immediately Zack felt transported back in time to when this had happened before, thirty-five years ago.

"What're you doing? Stop! That's freezing!" he complained.

"You make me sick," snarled Foley, fully in command of his DI persona again. "How soon before you have to fly with students? Five hours?"

"Something like that," Zack managed.

"What about 'twelve hours from bottle to throttle'?" challenged his old DI. Originally, the saying had been "eight" hours bottle to throttle, but as jet airplanes became more complex, recovery time got longer.

"I bounce back fast," sputtered Zack. He made a lunge for the hose and fell in the mud.

Foley continued to hose him off in a merciless assault of freezing water.

"Stop!" cried Zack, holding up his hands to block the spray. "No more! Stop!"

Foley finally turned off the faucet. "Take off your clothes," he commanded.

"What?" Zack stammered, shivering in the night air.

"So, I can wash them," snapped Foley irritably. Zack stripped off his clothes, and Foley tossed him a towel. Zack looked at his old mentor in confusion.

"Why are you doing this?" he asked. Zack had never understood why Foley had taken on the role that he had in his life. It was critical that he know this now.

"It certainly isn't for you," Foley explained coldly. "Your daughter and I are friends. Didn't she say anything?"

"No," admitted Zack. "Today was the first I knew about any of this."

Foley heard the jealousy in the other man's tone. "Get some sleep, Captain. Reveille is at 0600." Foley opened the door to his guest quarters and gestured for Zack to enter. Gathering up Zack's wet clothes, he threw them into a washer.

Zack heard Foley lock the door behind him. Looking around, he found the room spartan to the extreme. The bathroom was so small he had trouble turning around in it. He found the military cot as welcoming as a bed of nails. But in a matter of seconds, he was asleep.

He was awakened by a loud recording of a bugle playing "Reveille." The sound was so jolting he reasoned that the speaker had to be right outside his window. He tried the door and found it unlocked. It was still dark, but a hint of morning sun came from the east. He saw his street clothes laundered and on hangars. He opened a paper bag and removed a coffee and a muffin.

As he was leaving, he looked for Foley to thank him and found him in his bedroom above the gym, sitting in his wheelchair, a Bible in his large hands, his lips moving in silent prayer. There was a bottle of pills on a bedside table. Zack stared gratefully at his old mentor for several seconds before he tiptoed out.

When Zack reported for the day's exercise on the tarmac, Perryman cornered him. "Where the hell did you curl up last night? Emiliano and I were worried."

"Get ready for this one, big guy. He did it to me again."

"Who are we talking about?" asked Perryman.

"Foley," said Zack. "I swear it was like time had stood still."

"You slept at Foley's?" asked the taller man incredulously. "Why?"

"Because he made me," admitted Zack. "It was quite a night."

Perryman added it up in his mind. Their old drill instructor must have intervened because of Zack's drinking. He took in his boss appraisingly. "You're up first," he reminded Zack. "The dash four."

Zack felt surprisingly rested after his night at Foley's. But he had taken an important message away from his experiences the night before. "I think I'll step down today, Big Guy."

SEVENTEEN

FIRST SOLOS

THE WORKING AREA
June 2011

Dylan was alone in his boat, fifteen miles offshore in the Navy's "Working Area." A month had passed since Shannon's near-kiss in the fishery parking lot. His hopes for a repeat performance, or better, had faded over time. She religiously attended their meetings and patiently answered all his questions over dinner. But intimacy was clearly off the table.

The previous Friday, they changed it up and went to a public park to eat fried chicken that Dylan picked up after their meeting. The moon was full. The nearby playground was empty. "Why is it so hard for you to trust me?" he asked suddenly.

Shannon gnawed on a drumstick. "I had some bad experiences," she allowed.

"Any specific one stand out?"

"Why? You want some juicy tidbits for your book?" She often challenged him like this. His preoccupation with her sometimes frightened her.

"I'm just trying to be a friend," he said softly. "I went through some experiences on drugs I wouldn't want to repeat."

"Do you want the truth or some sanitized version?" she inquired.

She had never told anybody about this. But this man was different. She could tell him anything.

"Whatever version you want to tell me," said Dylan.

"I was the ripe old age of twenty-one when I had sex for the first time," she began. "Before that, I was a daddy's girl. An athlete. An overachiever. Overnight, I was hooking up with strangers. I didn't care who it was, what they looked like, how young, or old, what sex, anything." She paused briefly to assess his reaction.

"Sounds familiar," he said supportively.

"It wasn't making love," she explained. "It was the opposite. Two weeks before that boat fire, this guy put me in the hospital. It was my own fault. I kept screaming at him to be rougher." She shuddered at the memory. "When I decided to get clean, I decided to give sex a breather, too."

Dylan nodded sympathetically. He knew that self-punishment was standard fare for addicts. "My thing was cutting myself," he volunteered at last. "Some time I'll show you the scars."

"That's awful," she said. She had met other "cutters" in her drug days.

"I told myself it felt good," he explained. "It proved I was alive. Then one day, I went too far. Nickie found me just in time."

Shannon reached over and put a hand on his. Their eyes touched. There was nothing sexual about it, but week by week, they were letting down their guards more. Physical intimacy remained elusive, but at least now, they both knew why.

Over the weeks, Dylan continued to meet or surpass his three-pages-a-day writing quota. It was the easiest writing he'd ever done. Shannon Mayo was the worthiest of heroines. Her battle for her own soul was pure Tolstoy. But he was experiencing a growing conflict of conscience. He had promised that his story would be fictional, yet the real story he was living was too exciting, and the lines were blurring more and more.

From reading Zack's biography, Dylan knew the origin of Zack's famous mantra: "There can be no secret in your heart if you want to fly my plane." It had started with the death of his OCS pal, Sid Worley, but had grown into a theme of Zack's leadership. Addressing the graduating class at the Naval Academy in 1995, he explained that secrets of the heart got their name for a reason. They were secrets to their own victims.

"They arrive unbidden like termites and go to work tearing down your house," he had lectured that day. "They accrue over time like plaque. It's quantum. Secrets beget secrets. They create an alternate you, one that is your mortal enemy, out to destroy you."

Dylan suspected that Shannon suffered from secrets of the heart. It was the only thing that could explain her dichotomy. And from what he knew about her father, he was probably a violator of his own cardinal rule as well. Their conflict was too great to belong to one person alone.

Applying this yardstick to himself, Dylan asked, what were his termites? There was a reason why he had relapsed regularly over the years. In his NA meetings, he had learned that his fatal flaw was that he had never formed his own character. Instead, he had worshipped a succession of heroes. His father was the first one, and he had abandoned Dylan. Stevie was his replacement, and he abandoned Dylan, too. Stevie found his little brother's hero worship exhausting. "Stop shadowing me, dude," he had barked at Dylan one day after one of their boating adventures. "Get a fucking life." Dylan took the rebuke badly. *Get a life? What does that mean? What's supposed to fill the bottle called life?*

Now he was leaching off the life force of Shannon Mayo, Fighter Pilot. *What happens when she pulls the plug?* When his father disappeared, Dylan started drinking to excess. When Stevie drowned, Dylan gave himself over to drugs and lost the family home. With Nickie's help, he had clawed his way back. He had his old job back at the fishery, and he was a union rep. He had his one-year cake. But that bottle still felt unfilled.

A whining sound grew louder, pulling him back into the present, and Dylan grabbed his powerful Swarovski EL binoculars, another of Stevie's legacies. Four FA/18s began G-Warms 30,000 feet above his head. After six weeks of watching the students fly with instructors, he had learned the styles of every pilot in the class. It was easy to pick out Shannon. Watching her, he was always reminded of how he felt listening to Igor Stravinsky, one of his favorite composers from Stevie's collection.

Okay, okay, thought Dylan. *Steady as she goes, One Four.* He had watched endless videos online and learned all the lingo. He studied each component of the cockpit and knew what everything was called and what it did. He even researched video games that offered a window into "Dogfighting."

Coming out of her G-Warm, Shannon executed a "Squirrel Cage," starting with a full loop. Then, she went into a "half-Cuban eight" that she seamlessly turned into an "Immelmann" half-loop. Exiting at the top of the loop, she finished with a "Split S," leaving her flying upside down.

"Oh, fuck... oh, fuck... oh, fuck..." she gasped. She had hoped that, by the time she reached "first solos," she would have gotten used to the explosive power of the afterburners, but she found herself, once again, in borderline territory.

Far below in his boat, Dylan was alarmed. *Stay in control. Walk that line. You can do it.*

In maintenance, Zack watched his daughter's conflicted features on a monitor. Since his stay at Foley's, he had assigned other instructors to Shannon's training. He had been encouraged when she passed her subsequent three flights with an instructor without making a mistake. He was secretly proud that she had remained a close second to Taylor Daniels in their race for the strike fighter. But this first solo flight had stoked his old worries.

Perryman was suddenly in Zack's ear, his gray eyes pinched with concern. "Captain, we've detected a storm from the north." Zack wasn't surprised. Storms were common at this time of year, and you didn't waste Uncle Sam's money on a gamble the storm might not hit you.

"Bring them in," he ordered. As Perryman radioed the pilots to return to base, Shannon was beginning another aileron roll. She heard the order but decided to finish her roll before acting on it.

"Yeah, baby... yeah... oh, shit..." she exhaled.

Dylan saw three planes start for land while Shannon completed her aileron roll. "Snap out of it!" he shouted. "Come on, come on!" Just then the wind picked up and waves doubled in size. Old fears surged through Dylan like clogged sewage.

Shannon heard her father's stern voice over the radio. "Roman One

Four, what the hell's going on? Do you copy?" His tone jolted her senses just as it had when she was his teenage protégé in the passenger seat of a rented plane. She quickly shut off her afterburners.

"Roman One Four, heading home," she radioed back. Starting her turn, she saw lightning slash close by her window like a cosmic announcement. And just like that, she was in one of her day-mares. Flames licked at her from every direction. She was burning alive.

"No!" she shouted, wrenching her brain out of her dream. Feeling strong winds buffet her plane like a leaf, she knew she had made a huge mistake. "Roman One Four, encountering extreme weather," she reported, struggling to stabilize her controls.

Dylan lost sight of Shannon in the darkening sky. *Oh, shit*, he thought. *Don't get caught in it.* Suddenly, a wave smacked the starboard side of his boat, and its spray drenched him. *What am I doing out here? This is where Stevie died.* Gunning his powerful engines, he started in the direction of land.

In maintenance, Zack was furious. "Those few seconds you were out-of-body traveling put you in the eye of it," he shouted. "Get lower!"

"It's worse below! I have to go up!" she stammered. Shannon prided herself on her instincts. Her father had taught her never to doubt her first impulse. *Never change an answer in an exam. Never doubt yourself.*

"Shut up and do what I say," he commanded.

Shannon swallowed hard. She descended, and the storm shook her plane like a rag toy in a terrier's mouth. She felt sick. She struggled to breathe.

"It's worse! I have to go up!" she pleaded.

"Get lower!" he ordered.

Shannon was frozen. She had gone on her own instincts since her mother's death. She trusted no one.

"I have to go up! I'm going up!" she insisted.

"Get lower! That's an order!" Shannon could not remember a time when he sounded more authoritative. Terrified, she did as she was told and descended. And suddenly she was below the storm, the ocean sparkling like a magic carpet below. Her father had done it again. He had saved her.

"Thank God . . ." she whispered, crossing herself as her mother had taught her to do.

In maintenance, Zack and Perryman exchanged a look of profound relief. Zack had been certain his daughter would defy his leadership out of sheer perversity. His stomach was still in his throat, but at least, she was alive. That was all that really mattered.

"Get your ass home, One Four," he instructed icily. "I think we both know what this means."

Shannon turned for Oceana. She was shaking so hard from her brush with death that her turn was erratic at best. She knew she could not rely on her Uncle Perryman to bail her out this time. Of the four pilots attempting their first solos, she was the only one who was negligent enough to get caught in that storm. To compound matters, her instinct to go up, instead of down, would have surely gotten her killed.

Her sense of defeat was overwhelming. Her impossible dream was over. Then, her eyes seized on an object in the shimmering sea below. Dylan's boat raced along the water five hundred yards below her, turning right and left in wide arcs to get her attention. Shannon broke into a smile. Her heart thumped giddily in her ears. After her brush with death, a strange mood overtook her. If this was her last time at the controls of an FA/18, then . . .

"What the fuck!" she announced, not realizing she had broadcast her intentions over the common frequency.

Dylan was in a state of euphoria after surviving the sudden change in weather. Instead of succumbing to panic, he had navigated expertly out of danger. Even Stevie would have applauded his seamanship. Exhilarated, he began making those wide turns to attract Shannon's attention.

Then he heard a high-pitched sound building. He turned and saw her coming, a missile off his starboard stern. He braced himself. She was flying so low he wondered if he needed to duck. The shrill noise became unbearable, and the force of her flyover sent a rush through his system like a train blasting through a mountain tunnel. His knees became spider webs. He braced a hand on the gunwale to avoid falling over the side. He crooned from a deep place, "Oh, baby . . . oh, baby . . ."

Inside her cockpit, Shannon felt the exhilaration of reclaiming life after almost losing it. "Oh, yeah . . . oh, yeah . . ." She gasped. Her body was feverish inside her flight suit. Steam obscured her face guard.

In maintenance, Zack's mouth was agape. "What did she just do?" he stammered.

Perryman wore a cryptic smile. "She just buzzed some guy's boat," he rumbled, pointing to a monitor where Dylan's ecstatic face was on display.

"Well, I'll be goddamned," Zack muttered in amazement.

Perryman studied him wisely and didn't say a word. Since his stay at Foley's, there had been a new humility about Zack. He seemed to be searching for answers, instead of blindly asserting his will on an unruly universe.

Zack was waiting as Shannon descended her ladder to the tarmac. "What the hell? You nearly killed yourself, then you pull a stunt like that?" His jaw protruded pugnaciously.

"I wanted to feel alive," she countered, her chin sending back the same message. "The old you would have understood." She braced herself to get the boot.

"Face it, Shannie, you nearly died just now because of your illness," he asserted. "When are you going to recognize this yourself and do the right thing? Why make me the enemy? I'm only trying to protect you."

"I made some mistakes," she admitted. "But not because of my illness. I'm still learning how to fly this plane."

"Sweetheart, I'm your father," he began reasonably. "I know you better than anyone in the world. You've always had this wildness in you. You scared your mother and me every step of the way growing up. Always taking everything to an extreme. Then you turn your life over to drugs. Surely, you can see a pattern in this."

"You were wild growing up," she argued defiantly. "You bragged to me about all the chances you would take in the air. You were arrested for being drunk. You almost killed that boy from the last class. All my classmates talk about is whether you've got all your marbles." Then she concluded with an edge of sarcasm, "Surely, you can see a pattern in this."

Zack had no answer. Everything she had said was true.

"You can kick me out if you want to, but don't expect me to quit," asserted Shannon defiantly.

Zack didn't like his options. Unless this decision came from her, he would lose her forever. Then he seized on a whisper of hope. Maybe the boy in the boat was his answer. "Whose boat was that?" he inquired offhandedly.

"My sponsor," she said.

Zack knew that sponsors were generally of the same sex, but he didn't point that out. "There's a Fourth of July party in two weeks at the O Club," he said. "Bring him." He abruptly marched away, leaving her slack-jawed that he had not kicked her out. She wanted to feel relieved, but her instincts told her that her father's invitation was a trap.

EIGHTEEN
★ ★ ★
FIREWORKS

FRS

July 4, 2011

Shannon stood before her bathroom mirror in crisp dress whites, nervously checking out her appearance. It was the halfway point in the syllabus. She had the room to herself because Sidney, as usual, was camped out at Nickie's for the weekend. A knock at her door surprised her. When she opened it, she broke into a wide smile. Vice Admiral Casey Seegar was standing in the hallway, also in dress whites.

"Aunt Casey," exclaimed Shannon, rushing into her arms. "I heard you were coming." The two women embraced emotionally. They had not seen each other since before Shannon's disappearance.

"I've wanted to check in since you arrived at Fleet, but these past six months have been crazy for me," said her self-appointed aunt.

"Come in," said Shannon, remembering her manners. Casey entered and looked around.

"Not much has changed since I lived in one of these," she observed.

"Congratulations are in order," said Shannon. "The most powerful woman in the military."

"I'm still playing catch-up with your mom," offered Casey warmly. "And you're not doing so shabbily. Second in the class."

Shannon shrugged modestly. "By next week, I could be history if my father has his way."

"I'm sorry to hear that," said Casey. "I was hoping things would change after he and I spoke." Then she smiled suddenly. "I hear you've got a date for the big gala tonight."

"He's just a friend," insisted Shannon quickly.

"Does he smell?" her aunt joked.

Shannon laughed, recalling their conversation when she was fourteen. "No. But it's not romantic or anything close. We're just good friends."

The older woman took the time to appraise Shannon with her wise eyes. "You're a woman now. A very pretty one. Still on the fence about sex?" she asked.

Shannon laughed. "I'm not a virgin, if that's what you mean. I just don't love it like I'm supposed to. It's been years if you want the truth."

Casey had struggled all her life over her relationships with men. "I'm the wrong person to give any advice on that subject," she allowed. "My father wasn't a great model for me to follow. He died without ever letting me know him even in the most basic of ways."

"Did you love him?" asked Shannon.

"In some ways too much," admitted Casey. "It blinded me for a long time to what was going on. Without realizing it, I was letting him swallow my personality with his."

Shannon wondered if this was true about her and her dad. He was such an all-encompassing force that she simply lost herself in his magic. Then a question sprang from Shannon's lips that she had wanted to ask for a long time. "Are you in love with my dad?"

Casey blushed. "You come right out with it, don't you? Your mom was like that." She paused a moment and then said, "Yes, I am. I think he knows it, too. But your father will always love only one woman, and we know who that is."

"You can't know that for sure," said Shannon.

"But I do," said Casey unequivocally. Then she decided to go further in her role as mother appointed substitute. "Your father implied there were things he couldn't tell me about your life after your mom died. I need to know what that was."

Shannon looked at her, alarmed. "I can't talk about that stuff."

Casey squared her shoulders in that signature way. "Shannon, I'm begging you to tell me. I swear it will not go beyond us. But I need to know my role in this."

Shannon respected this woman more than anyone in her life. And she trusted her. "It was pretty bad," she offered in warning. "I broke the law. If the Navy knew about this, I would go to jail."

"How did you break the law?"

Shannon bit her lip. "I got strung out on opioids. I sold drugs to pay for my own."

Casey nodded soberly. She had imagined something as bad as that, but hearing it was still shocking. She understood suddenly that she had crossed a major ethical line in her life. "Thanks for your honesty," she said. "Your father doesn't need to know we had this talk."

Shannon nodded gratefully. Casey left, and Shannon felt a wave of relief wash over her. She was finally shedding her secrets, and the world hadn't gone up in smoke.

Shannon arrived at the Officers Club to find it filled with officers in dress summer whites and civilian guests in colorful summer wear. Tables were draped in white linen and appointed with pewter cutlery. A Navy band played "Anchors Aweigh," and a banner proclaimed: HAPPY 4TH! After six months of training, Shannon's class was at the halfway point in the syllabus, and their parents and families had joined them for the occasion.

Searching for her father, she saw Sidney at a table with her family, all in dress whites. Her father, a captain, was a slender, hatchet-faced man, fully Chinese in origin, but her three brothers, all commanders, were of mixed race like her. Sidney appeared tense in her chair. Shannon knew that this was a momentous family reunion. Their first since

Sidney had come out, and her bunkmate was beginning to question her decision to include Nickie in the mix.

Then Shannon saw Taylor Daniels wave to her from a table where he sat with his mother, who at fifty-five was a stunning reminder of the film ingenue she had been in her youth. His father, a penguin in a tux, worked the room nearby. Shannon waved back. Since SECNAV's appearance the day they finished simulators, she and Taylor had become friends. One day after class, he was especially talkative and open. He told her that his mother had given up a major acting career to be his father's arm candy and drank like a fish to compensate. He confided that he had been in conflict all his life between his music and his desire to please his father.

Shannon had asked, "How much of what you say in your songs is true?"

"All of it," he replied. "My songs are the best part of me."

"Did your father hit you with a belt?"

"Oh, yeah," he sighed.

"Does he still do that to you?" she asked, horrified by the prospect.

"No. That stopped. But he keeps that belt in plain view when I visit." He seemed lost in those memories because his lip twisted bitterly. "His father hit him like that, so he thinks it's cool."

In the spirit of their openness, she asked, "Do you know why he's gone after my father like he has?"

Taylor laughed. "Your father's not the only one on his shit list. He's at war with every man he meets."

"Any idea why?" she persisted.

"My mother said something once," Taylor recounted. "She said he has personal issues she wasn't at liberty to discuss. She said he doesn't acknowledge his true self, or he's fighting it, so it comes out in other ways, cruel ways."

Their exchange took a sudden turn. "I want to clear something up," he began, in a tone that suggested he had wanted to do this for some time. "I know you know I cheated on that drug test."

"That's your business," she assured him. But he wasn't through.

"I need you to understand this about me, Shannon," he persisted passionately. "I'd never go into the cockpit high. I'd never risk your life or anyone else's. That's just for my music."

"I appreciate that," she said. Remembering the collusive wink that he'd given her that day, she wondered if he expected a similar reassurance from her. But he didn't. Whatever mission his father was on to unearth her drug past, he was not a part of it.

Shannon pulled herself back in the moment as she saw her father seated alone at a table for three. In the late afternoon light, he looked strikingly older. The lines on his face were more profound than she remembered. His piercing hazel eyes seemed to have settled deeper into his skull. In some way, she would always see her father as that swashbuckling hero he had been in her teens, so seeing him like this now was especially disturbing.

"Hi," she heralded brightly before taking an empty chair. She didn't try to hug him or kiss him. This weighed on Zack.

"Where's your friend?" he asked impatiently. "It's about to start." Determined to make this a sober occasion, he was nursing a beer.

"He'll be here," she assured him.

"He'd better be," said her father. "They make you prepay for these things."

Shannon was secretly amused. Her father's penny-pinching had often been a source of amusement for her mother who notoriously over-tipped.

Applause drew their attention to a stage as Topper Daniels strutted up to a mic, Vice Admiral Casey Seegar at his side. She towered over him. Seeing Zack and Shannon at their table, she waved.

SECNAV adjusted the mic down several inches. "Happy Fourth, everybody," he began in his high-pitched Alabama accent. "Everywhere I go in the capitol, people ask about the F-35 Joint Strike Fighter, the super plane of the future. I'd like to introduce the person overseeing the program, the highest-ranking woman in the armed forces, Vice Admiral Casey Seegar."

Applause erupted as Casey took the microphone and adjusted it to its original height. She was a popular figure in military circles, a hero to young women in the ranks. "The rules of engagement change every day," she began. "So, the Navy is always looking into the future." A distant roar grew louder, and she pointed in its direction. "Behold the future of naval aviation. The first plane that can actually disappear."

An F-35 Strike Fighter soared above like something from a space odyssey. Triangular and small compared to the FA/18, it was built for stealth. After a series of aileron rolls, it went into afterburner and appeared to vanish. It was a trick accomplished by the unique metal coating on the plane and the plane's jaw-dropping torque. Everyone on the patio cheered.

Zack moodily joined the applause. His career was winding down. He had flown fast planes either in war or in training for three and a half decades, and in six months, it would all be over. What would be left? A few friendships. Too many memories. A daughter who didn't want anything to do with him. The image of his father at the gate haunted him.

Shannon was clapping enthusiastically. "Wow, this is a game-changer."

"I could beat it blindfolded," boasted Zack grouchily. He had broken down a few weeks back and started looking over the job offers from the major airlines, but the thought of becoming some "old guy hero," shaking hands for a living, had turned his stomach. He remembered seeing Joe Louis, the great heavyweight champion, glad-handing fans in a Vegas casino to pay off debts. He had given the old champion a dollar and received a look that would dog his dreams forever.

"You miss the point, sir," Shannon explained in a patient tone. "Dogfights and smart bombs are the past. With the Strike Fighter, we can penetrate the enemy's defenses without them having a clue we're there."

Zack cleared his throat. He hadn't arranged this moment for a lecture on the future of naval aviation. "What does this 'sponsor' do for a living?" he inquired casually.

"He works at VB Fishery," she replied. She saw no reason to embellish Dylan's credentials. She wasn't auditioning a future husband. He was her friend; that was all.

"So, if you have a sponsor, then you go to meetings?" he inquired casually.

Shannon had nothing to hide. This was how she remained sober.

It was how she stayed sane. "I go every week," she admitted. "I always drive a long distance away to be sure no one knows."

Zack nodded. He admired her for being straightforward. "A Fishery Kid, huh? I thought you'd set your sights a little higher."

"You didn't with Mom," she noted sarcastically.

"Your mother was a force of nature," he said, his eyes misting. "There was no holding her back."

"Then why did you try?" Shannon asked pointedly.

Zack thought for a moment. "I wanted to freeze time," he said. "Two kids in a factory doorway, starting a new life. But your mom had her own ideas."

Dylan and Nickie showed their IDs at the guard gate. Nickie's card identified her as a military dependent. She came to the base often to shop at the PX and visit her parents' graves. As Dylan drove onto the base, Nickie pulled out a joint and lit up.

"What're you doing, Nick-orette?" snapped Dylan. "This is a Navy base."

"I burn here all the time," said Nickie, taking a big hit. "My mom and dad are buried right over there." She pointed to a wide lawn dotted with crosses.

"I know that," replied Dylan. He had attended both funerals, and he often accompanied Nickie on her PX runs. Grabbing the joint, he stubbed it out in his ashtray and tossed it.

"Hey, I need that," chirped Nickie. "I'm really nervous. She's seeing her father and brothers for the first time since she told them she came out. They're all bigshot Navy officers. What if they don't like me?"

Dylan held his tongue. Nickie had not chosen her outfit to blend in with conservatives. Her hippy dress, silver sneakers, and jaunty foreman's cap screamed "Take me or leave me."

"You think you're nervous?" Dylan offered. "After one little kiss on the cheek in six months, suddenly it's 'Meet Daddy.'"

"Aren't you leaving out something a little more relevant than a kiss on the cheek?" Nickie knew about Shannon's dramatic fly over.

Dylan blushed. "Yeah, there was that," he admitted sheepishly, the memory of it surging back in physical ways as if it were happening again.

Captain Perryman, Captain Della-Serra, and Vice Admiral Seegar were talking with Zack and Shannon at their table as Dylan walked up. "Sorry I'm late," he offered sincerely.

Shannon studiously avoided touching Dylan's hand or giving him even a chaste hug. "Dad, this is my friend, Dylan," she began. "Dylan, this is my Uncle Perryman. He was best man at my parents' wedding. And this is Uncle Emiliano. He made balloon animals at all my birthdays. And this is my aunt Casey. She was my mom's best friend."

Dylan shook their hands, leaving Zack for last. He found her father a formidably handsome and fit man for his age. "You're a hero of mine, Captain Mayo," he said.

"Buttering me up, huh?" Zack commented with an arched brow.

"No, sir," insisted Dylan. "I had a poster of you hanging over my bed growing up."

Casey said, "We'll leave you to get to know each other," and led the other men away, giving Shannon a secret wink.

As the trio took their seats, an awkwardness threatened to descend. Then, Zack smiled warmly at his guest. "Would you like a cocktail, 'Friend' Dylan?"

"No, thanks, sir. I don't drink."

"Now I remember," Zack replied cheerfully. "You're in the program together."

"Not so loud, sir," hissed Shannon, her eyes sweeping the faces of those within hearing range. At that moment, she saw Nickie rush up to Sidney's table in her hippy garb. The men stood up as one, a wall of frowns. Sidney cast Shannon a worried look.

Waiters and waitresses descended on Zack's table with prime rib, baked potatoes, and wedge salads. "I hear you're a Fishery Kid," he said brightly.

"For now," said Dylan, meeting the older man's eyes unflinchingly. "Your daughter's encouraging me to set my sights a little higher."

"Dylan's a writer," Shannon injected. "He's won awards."

Zack nodded vaguely. This was a military maneuver. Small talk was not a part of it. "I hear you're her sponsor," he said in a cagey tone.

"That's an inside joke between us," Dylan explained candidly. "But we both try to be a good influence on each other." The looks they exchanged confirmed this.

"Has she told you how I feel about her flying the FA/18?" asked Zack.

"Captain, please," interrupted Shannon. "This was supposed to be a relaxed get-together." She began to twist the napkin in her lap with both hands.

"What choice do I have?" Zack replied testily. "You've been back for six months. I can count the minutes we've had together on one hand. After that little incident in the storm, I'm seriously worried about your life. Yes, your life. I was hoping that your sponsor or friend would help us talk about this."

Dylan felt honored. "I'd be happy to help, if I can," he volunteered. Then he felt her kick him under the table, and he knew he'd been suckered into an unwinnable position.

Zack launched into his planned speech. "A few years back, I went to AA meetings for a few months, so I know a little about the program."

Shannon's eyes sharpened like needles. "He got a DUI with me in the car," she interjected. "They charged him with child endangerment and locked him up in jail." She wasn't sure why she said all this. She had forgotten this incident from halfway into the Chelsea Year until she heard SECNAV bring it up on his visit.

Zack acted like he hadn't heard a word she'd said. He had his battle plan, and he was keeping to it. "Dylan, you and I know that drugs and alcohol are not the same thing," he began in a reasonable tone. "Aside from a single incident when I was grieving Shannon's mother, I've never had any trouble with my drinking." He frowned as he remembered his forced stay at Foley's.

Shannon turned to Dylan, distressed. "See why I can't talk to him? He's Mr. Perfect, and I'm a worthless piece of shit." Her fingers twisted the napkin like she was trying to shred it. Although she was starving, she hadn't touched her food.

"I never said I was perfect," Zack countered, doing his best to keep his voice down. "But I didn't violate your trust like you did mine."

"How did I violate your trust?" she challenged.

"We were close," he recalled longingly. "We had to be, with your mother gone so much that last year. But when she died, you slammed the door on me like a stranger."

Shannon wanted to disappear. What her father was charging was true. She had pulled away from their closeness. Knowing why was another thing. "It was the hardest year of my life," she said at last. "I did what I had to do to survive." Then she went on the attack. "And you went off to war like I didn't matter at all to you."

"You insisted I go," Zack reminded her. "You acted like you had the world by the tail. You were very convincing."

"You were America's Favorite Son. How could I tell the President of the United States no? I thought it would be only a year. How did I know you wouldn't come home for five years?"

"Be fair," he contested. "In the beginning, I came home so often I got reprimanded for it. At the end of that tour, I asked if you needed me to come home. And the answer was always the same. 'I don't need you, Daddy.'"

Dylan concentrated on his prime rib and let their words record themselves in his brain.

Night had fallen, and suddenly fireworks exploded in the sky. The explosion of sound and light worked its evil magic on Shannon. "No!" she cried out suddenly. She was on that Atlanta rooftop engulfed in flames. Another round of fireworks made her eyes grow even larger. "No. No," she cried out, lost in that alternate world.

"What is it, Shannie?" demanded her father, worried.

"Shannon, are you all right?" asked Dylan.

"No, I'm not all right," she exploded. Bolting to her feet, Shannon hurried away from the table, her sudden exit drawing curious looks around the room.

As Dylan rose to go after her, Zack looked up helplessly. His big plan had backfired.

"You heard it all yourself," he grumbled. "She holds the answer to this whole ugly mess, but she's too willful and self-centered to do anything about it."

Dylan knew that he was overstepping his bounds. He had just met this man tonight. His knowledge of Zack's struggle to reclaim his daughter was, at best, second hand. But he couldn't remain silent. "Forgive me for speaking my mind, sir, but this is too complicated to be one person's problem." Not waiting for a reply, he hurried after Shannon.

NINETEEN
✯✯✯
WALLS TO CLIMB

That Same Night

When Dylan caught up to Shannon, he could see that she was trembling. "Here," he said, removing his suit jacket and putting it around her shoulders.

"I'm sorry," she said in a rush. "I should have known it was a trap."

"It's all good," he replied. "I like your father. I think he liked me, too."

"He put you down," she reminded him. "He was rude."

"He was just testing me," countered the fishery kid. "You don't know how lucky you are. I'd give anything to have a father like that." Then his tone changed. "What happened to you back there? Was it the fireworks or something he said?"

"I don't want to talk about it," she insisted. She had never told anybody about her day-mares.

"Suit yourself, but you seem pretty shaken," he persisted.

Shannon looked at him. This earnest young man was slowly gaining her trust. "You know how my mother died," she began. Dylan nodded. "The littlest thing can set it off. I have no control over it. I'm her. I'm burning alive on that rooftop. It's crazy."

"How often does this happen?" he asked.

"More often lately," she admitted. "Sometimes it happens when I'm flying."

"That's not good," he said.

Shannon suddenly wished she had not opened up. "Now you probably think I'm even more of a whack-job than before."

"The opposite," he assured her. "I'm seeing how strong you are."

"I'm not strong," she snapped irritably. "That's all you. You need a hero, so you settled on a pretender like me."

Dylan was hurt. Her insights could be frighteningly on the money. Mister Empty Bottle. He shook his head. "That's the old me you're talking about. I've changed since we met."

Shannon softened suddenly. "I'm sorry," she said. "I'm just angry about tonight. Maybe I shouldn't be with anyone right now."

"But you didn't eat a bite," he reminded her. "You must be starving. How about I cook up something at my place?"

"Your place?" she stammered.

"I thought, when you asked me to come today, that we'd, at least, get some time alone," he said in his earnest way. "Shannon, we've been doing this dance for six months. When have I ever made you do something you didn't want to do?"

Shannon was exhausted and hungry. "These are the days when I miss drugs the most," she said, hoping it sounded like a joke. The truth was that all she could think of when those fireworks started going off was getting high. Anything not to relive those painful days when her perfect family disintegrated before her eyes. She cursed her addiction for its lingering hold on her. Maybe a few minutes at Dylan's would help her reset her clock.

"Okay, I'll follow you," she agreed. "But I can't stay long."

Dylan broke into a wide smile. "Where have I heard that before?"

"Shut up," she replied, her mood lifting.

―――

Dylan led Shannon into his small apartment and selected one of his brother's classical albums. Beethoven's "Moonlight Sonata" soon purred out of his state-of-the-art speakers. Shannon took in his writing desk and laptop, as well as his queen-size bed and the abstract line drawing of a nude woman hanging above it.

"The bachelor in his lair," she observed nervously. "You must do well with this setup."

"You're the first person I've brought here besides Nickie," he said. He opened his refrigerator to take stock. "I've got some chicken. I can make a salad," he suggested. When he got no reply, he turned around and a smile formed. Shannon had curled up like a cat on his bed, and her eyes were closed. "You still with me?" he asked softly. When he got no reply, he spread a comforter over her and went to work at his laptop.

In no time at all, he had met his quota of three pages, but he kept going. The drama he had witnessed at the officer's club had been a windfall. For the first time, he felt like he was getting a true handle on his characters. There was another component to his enthusiasm, Originally relegated to the role of the narrator, the fishery kid was finding his place on the stage.

An hour later, Shannon awakened and saw Dylan asleep at his desk beside his glowing laptop. She got out of bed with the intention of leaving; then her curiosity got the best of her. Peering over his sleeping form, she read the last page he had written.

"Clearly, her mother's death was a greater turning point in her life than he'd imagined. It marked not only the death of a beloved mom but the death of a family. Why? Did she blame her father for her mother's death? Did she blame herself?"

Shannon felt violated. She wanted to shake Dylan awake and tell him how she felt. Instead, she scrolled to the beginning of the manuscript and started reading. He had changed all the names and created a fictional jet school, but he was not writing a work of fiction.

An early passage read: "She is the perfect Gemini. There are two of her. One is a superhero who can do the impossible. The other is riddled with self-doubt. These two 'hers' have existed side by side in a difficult truce, but in the crucible of this school, she will have to decide which of her identities will rule her future."

With a shaking hand, she scrolled to another entry. "Now that he knew about her experience with rough sex, it dawned on the fishery kid that he had misread her signals from the start. This was a platonic relationship on her end, while he wanted so much more. To avoid what was sure to be a devastating heartbreak, he should be honest with her about his true feelings and cut her free. But that was impossible. He had never been so vested in another person. By writing about her, had he taken his empty bottle mentality to a new level? Or was this something different? It dawned on him suddenly. For the first time in his life, he was putting the needs of a woman before his own needs."

Then she came to this one: "For six months, he had courted a woman with all his soul and had only received one almost-kiss. Then that flyover changed everything. He had never experienced anything like it. To call it sexual would be a gross understatement. He had never made love to a woman and felt what he had that day."

Shannon felt dizzy. A drop of perspiration fell from her neck onto his arm. Dylan murmured something, changed the position of his arms, then was still again. She suddenly saw the scars. They lined up neatly on the underside of both of his arms. Thin white lines carefully carved by a sharp razor.

She read on. "He knew that, when they ultimately had sex, it would be nothing short of transcendental. He had concluded that, despite their sexual history, they were both technically virgins."

Shannon stopped reading, overwhelmed by conflicting waves of emotion. She was at a crossroads, and she knew that what she did next would come with life-altering consequences. She hit the key for "Select All," and the manuscript became a muted color. Her finger found the delete key and hovered over it. One little touch and it would all be gone. Then she would be out that door, and she would never come back.

Dylan made another little noise in his sleep, startling her. His features in repose caught the soft glow off the laptop screen, and she took him in warmly. He really was a beautiful man. Seconds passed. She removed her finger and, with that hand, started unbuttoning her uniform.

Dylan awakened to a naked Shannon pulling off his T-shirt where he sat. "What's going on?" he asked dreamily.

Shannon had no words to express her sudden passion. She was in a space and time that she had only touched in her fantasies. She helped him up from his chair and led him to the bed. Then she gave in fully and gratefully to her romantic passions for the first time in her life. That flyover had been only a taste. He had nailed it. This was nothing short of otherworldly.

When Dylan awakened a few hours later, she was gone. He saw his open laptop and his heart skipped a beat. Cursing himself for not telling her what he was writing, he bolted out of bed. She had left an entry in red below his last words.

"GOOD JOB. KEEP IT UP. YOU ARE A GREAT WRITER!"

The Fourth of July gala at the O Club was winding down as midnight approached. Zack sat numbly at his table alone, pondering the disaster of the night. Casey walked up, concerned. "Everything all right with you and Shannie?" she asked.

"We fought," admitted Zack.

She offered a kind smile. "Want to take a walk?"

A full moon made the parade ground look like it was covered in a patina of blue ice. They strolled side by side, a lifetime of memories in each step. They had both dedicated their lives to protecting their country. They were heroes. And yet so much was missing in both their lives. As they approached the obstacle course, they stopped as they saw it at the same time—the dreaded wall. Their shared crucible thirty-five years ago rose into the night sky like a mythic hurdle even gods feared.

Casey whistled softly. "Up until I had to face that challenge, I was exactly what Foley called me: some Sugar Britches who was trying to win her father's love."

"It was a big turning point for me, too," admitted Zack. "I was a selfish punk. You taught me what it meant to be an officer."

Casey's eyes darkened. Her visit earlier with Shannon troubled her in deep ways. "Zack, did we make a mistake?"

"Mistake?" He appeared confused.

"Since your birthday party, I've thought a lot about our time at the lake," she offered.

"And?" he asked with some trepidation.

"Remember our little deal?" she coaxed.

He stared back blankly. "What deal?"

"You know," she replied. "You have to know."

Zack was baffled. "Honestly, See-gar, I don't have a clue what you're talking about."

Casey squared her shoulders in her trademark way. "Zack, I couldn't live with it if I knew I'd set a family tragedy in motion."

Zack was stunned by her words. "What would make you think that?"

"I know about the opioids," she said.

"Shannon told you?" he stammered.

"I forced her," admitted Casey.

Zack didn't know how to respond. Casey had put her career on the line for him and his daughter. They were co-conspirators in a felony.

"Don't worry," she assured him. "I have no intention of saying anything. But I need to know my role in this."

"Your role?" he asked, confused. "You're not making any sense."

"The whole song and dance with the president. Don't you remember that?"

Zack felt his words catch in his throat. "You set that all up?" he asked in disbelief.

"I assumed you knew," she said.

Zack was in full denial. "I walked into that office without any idea he'd ask me to deploy. I turned him down, but Shannie wouldn't have it."

"You're rewriting history, Zack," said Casey in her direct way. It was not hard to see why she was the top woman in the military. She had a backbone of Midwestern steel.

"Paula had only been gone six months when I took that trip," he reasoned. "By the time I got that call from the White House, I was back on my feet."

What happened next was totally out of the blue. Casey slapped him hard. The sound was as loud as a bullet in the night air. "What was that for?" he cried, raising a hand to feel the heat from his cheek.

"Goddamn you, Zack," she declared. "How dare you do that to me? I promised Paula I'd watch over Shannie like a mother. Then I send her into the nightmare of drugs?" She turned to go, but he caught her arm.

"Don't go," he begged. "Shannon wasn't a child when she got into drugs. She was a twenty-two-year-old senior in college."

"You're lying to yourself, Zack," charged Casey. "Your daughter wasn't fine after Paula died. She was a total mess. She blamed herself for everything. Gaming was a desperate cry for help, just like the drugs. She still isn't okay. I could see it in her face when I visited her room earlier. I'm worried about her. Not in the way that you are. I know she's a great pilot. It's her heart as a woman that concerns me."

"What is that supposed to mean?" Zack asked in a lost voice.

"You figure it out," she said dismissively. "Don't call me or try to see me until you've fixed this," she commanded before marching off.

That night as he tried to sleep, Zack's mind took a turn down an old road riddled with sinkholes. In 2001, his world had been shaken by three disturbing events in rapid succession: his wife's horrendous death on August 9, his daughter's subsequent retreat into her own world, and three weeks later, 9/11. To his credit, Zack held it together for six months. He was a shell of himself, but he made sure he was there if his daughter needed him. It was not his fault that she never did.

One night, he took her to dinner at the O Club. He did not drink any more than usual. A cocktail. A glass of wine. Driving home, a blast of red light flooded the car, and they heard that distinctive siren. To his recollection, he walked the line perfectly, touched his nose, touched his toes. Then the policeman brought out a breathalyzer. Zack stared at it a second too long, and they snapped on the cuffs.

Zack was furious. "Don't you know who I am?" he bellowed. The two young police officers were new to the area, and both shook their heads in the negative. They asked where they could take his daughter for the night, and Zack gave them Perryman's address and number. He was desperate to go to Shannon and reassure her that it would be ok, but they dragged him to a squad car. Zack would always remember the look on his daughter's face.

At the police station, he tested a point below the line on his first test, then exactly on the line on his second effort and was charged with a DUI and the more serious charge of "Child Endangerment." The next morning, when he was released from police custody, he drove to Perryman's house to collect his daughter. His friend met him at the door.

"You really freaked her out, boss," said Perryman. "She was up all night. After losing her mom, she thought she was losing you, too."

"It was all a mistake," Zack insisted. "Those young cops had a quota to fill. You know I can hold my drinks."

Shannon was emotionless on the drive home. He swore he would never put her through that again. Immediately, he moderated his drinking and tried to be more present in the home, but now Shannon was in full hibernation as Chelsea. When he tried to lure her out on one of their old adventures, she only rolled her eyes like he was being juvenile.

A month after his arrest, Zack received notification that his first bid for admiral had been rejected. He was not surprised that SECNAV had been the deciding thumbs down. His DUI and the charge of child endangerment was cited as the reason. Perryman and Della-Serra were turned down as well. Their only crimes were falling on SECNAV's shit list as young men at OCS and their friendship with Zack.

This rejection was a bitter pill for Zack. Since his early years as a pilot, his achievements had made him the talk of the Navy. If anybody had been a shoo-in for "the club," it was him. It was hard to accept that his one little slip-up warranted such a damning rejection.

He sank into a debilitating depression. To his embarrassment, his daughter had it far more together than he did. She had her gaming friends around the world. He could hear her excited voice on the other side of her door. She kept their house neat. She cooked TV dinners for them. She kept up her grades in school. She maintained a cheery disposition while he had days when he couldn't get out of bed.

Zack knew that, if he didn't do something soon, he would probably make another mistake like the DUI. Secretly, he craved an infusion of his own personal drug. He knew from experience that he would die without it. And he knew exactly where to make a score.

"Congratulations," he began the call. "How about I fly up to DC tomorrow and take you out for a celebratory dinner?"

Casey said, "I have a better idea. Why don't you visit me at the lake?"

A few days later, the two old friends were in a boat on a lake in the mountains outside the capitol, fishing. Zack had flown up that morning to Casey Seegar's vacation lodge in Cunningham Falls to congratulate her for making it into the admiral's club. After a day on the water, Zack felt better than he had in a long time. Maybe this was all he had needed. A relaxed day with an old friend. Maybe he wouldn't ask the favor he'd come here to request.

"Oh, look, I got another one," exclaimed Casey, reeling in a large lake bass to add to her collection of three that were swimming in the confines of a cooler.

"That's not fair," he complained. "You've caught all the fish."

Seegar laughed. "What can I say? I'm a fish-catching machine." Their eyes caught for a moment.

"You've had an incredible career, See-gar," praised Zack expansively. "I'm betting on you to set a new high for women in the Armed Services."

Casey laughed. "Now I know you came here for a favor." Her eyes softened. "I owe my success to you, Mayo," she volunteered with a raw sincerity.

"No, you don't," he said. "You got over that wall on your own."

"Did I?" she asked in a way that suggested she had searched her soul about that moment and still carried doubts.

"I was there. You made it on your own." He was about to say more when he felt a fish take his bait. "Oh, yeah!" he bellowed. "It's a big one!" It took all his strength to reel in his fish, which was smaller than her four.

Casey watched him with warm eyes. "You haven't said anything about Shannie," she said.

"She's doing a hell of a lot better than I am, Case," replied Zack. "It's kind of amazing how she hit the ground running."

"Your daughter's a unique young woman, like her mother," commented Casey. Then she grinned wistfully. "You know, I've always envied you for your family life. I wanted kids. I think I would have been a good mom. So much for those thoughts. I'm an old woman now."

"You're still a stunning woman, See-gar." He meant it. In his memory, she would always be that girl he'd embraced in celebration atop the wall as Foley and their classmates looked on in surprise. "I'm struggling, Case," he said suddenly.

Hearing the urgency in his tone, Casey placed her pole into a rusty holder and put a gentle hand on his shoulder. "What can I do for you, my friend? Just name it."

Zack met her gaze and immediately felt like the conman he'd been in his youth. He felt guilty for coming here with a motive. Motives were the precursors of secrets. "It can wait," he said suddenly. "Let's have some fun before I get all serious."

"Your call," she replied. "I hope you'll spend the night. I'd love to show you our waterfall in the morning."

Zack didn't answer right away. He could read between the lines. Six months had passed since Paula's death, and Casey had religiously respected his time of mourning. He had not made love to anyone but Paula since they met twenty-five years ago. Now with Paula gone and Shannon missing in action with her gaming, he had been stripped of family again, and he was lonely, the kind of lonely he had known as a boy on nights that passed without any signal from Tiki and Maria that it was okay to come home.

"I know you're still grieving," Casey said as though reading his thoughts. "I'm happy to be your friend, Zack. In whatever form that takes." Zack didn't reply. Casey saw a desperation in him today that reminded her of the Zack Mayo she'd met in OCS, before life as a naval officer and a wife like Paula softened his edges.

He suddenly leaned in and kissed her on the lips. Casey was stunned. They stared at each other a long time. Then she returned the kiss. "You don't have to do this to get that favor," she joked. It had been years since she had slept with anyone, but she had gone into Victoria's Secret on her way out of Washington in anticipation of his visit.

They returned to the house and showered separately. Then Zack heard a soft knock on his door. Casey stood in the doorway in a lavender peignoir. They kissed as they'd kissed in the boat earlier that day. But this time Zack's mind played a cruel trick on him. He was certain that it was Paula he was kissing.

His heart soared like it had when he had first seen her at that Officers' Club formal. He kissed Paula's mouth as he'd done so many times. He licked the little mole on her throat. He removed her peignoir. He lifted her naked body in his strong arms and slowly lowered her onto the bed. That was when Casey turned on a bedside light and studied his features in the glow.

"What's going on, Zack?" she asked evenly.

"What do you mean?" He looked at her and the image of Paula evaporated like the fantasy it was, and with it his ardor.

"Are you here with me?" she asked, feeling the change in him and knowing the answer.

"Of course," he insisted, but they both knew the evening would not be sexual.

He put his hands over his eyes. Sounds squeezed out of his throat like canaries fleeing a doomed mine. He could not share such feelings with anybody but her.

"Poor Mayonnaise," she whispered.

"I'm going crazy," he confessed. "I don't know what to do. I can't talk to Louis or Emiliano about this stuff. I don't know who I am anymore, Case. I feel a lot like I did before I met Paula."

"Now I see what this is about," said Casey, her brow knitting as the pieces came together. He was here to ask her to send him to war. "Who would look after Shannie?" she asked directly.

"Her aunt Bunny has offered to do it," he said. "She's a tough cookie. A real drill instructor." He was pleading his case like a small-town lawyer. "Shannie's strong, Case. Paula made her strong in one way, and I made her strong in another. She'll be fine on her own."

Casey studied him thoughtfully, as though seeing him for the first time. Then she kissed him on the top of his thick head of gray hair and walked out of his room.

Zack sat there without moving. He did not know it, but this was the moment when the secrets crawled unbeckoned into his heart and began to propagate.

TWENTY

★ ★ ★

CLICKETY-CLICK

FRS

August 1, 2011 — Strike Phase

Zack watched from an observation tower half a mile from the target area as four FA/18s "Circled the Wagon" against an azure sky. Since his abortive attempt at the Fourth of July gala to mend fences, he had made no further effort to connect with Shannon. They had fallen into a pattern of barely acknowledging each other when they passed in the corridors or on the parade ground. Perryman reported that he'd seen her leaving a movie with Dylan and that she looked happy. Della-Serra had seen them shopping together at the PX. On Saturdays, Zack often saw her motorcycle parked in front of Foley's Fitness. She was regaining her hold on life, while he felt the opposite.

Casey's words the night of the OCS party assaulted his conscience relentlessly. If she was right and he'd gone into GW's office that day with any knowledge that he had orchestrated the moment, he would have to own all of it, and it was a staggering list. Had he sent his daughter into drugs to service some personal demon? Had he destroyed what remained of their precious family and blamed it on her? Had he ever been a true hero? Or was he just another conman like his father?

It was Friday of Week 38, the culmination of the bombing phase of "Strike," and today was "Live Day" when they would be dropping live bombs for the first time. An electronic board showed Taylor Daniels first and Shannon Castellano second; Sidney was back in the pack as always. Since her boasts when the strike fighter challenge was announced, she had never been in the race. Zack and the other instructors had noticed that she came out of every drill more shaken than any of her classmates.

LCDR Lance Kelly was flying in Zack's "dash one" lead plane. The ruggedly handsome veteran Top Gun and father of three, swooped down on a target shaped like a skeleton key, the bullseye a lake at its top. "Roman One, one in," he announced, pushing the "pickle." "Roman One, one away," he exhaled as the bomb under his right wing fell. Rolling up on a wing, he watched as it landed four yards wide of the lake.

Zack scowled. "Kelly, I put you in my seat, and you embarrass me with that sloppy hit? You owe me a beer."

Flying in the dash two spot, Taylor dropped his bomb, and it landed inside Kelly's but missed the lake. His name shot to the top of the leaderboard.

At that moment, Perryman drove up in a Jeep and joined Zack on the tower. "Good morning, boss," said the tall Texan in his rumbling voice. "I thought you were supposed to be flying the dash one spot today."

"I decided to bench myself, big guy," replied Zack easily.

Perryman was not surprised. Zack had been stepping down a lot since his night at Foley's. An aura of defeat had formed around him like a body bag, and none of his friends' efforts to snap him out of it had been successful.

Flying the dash two spot high above, Shannon knew that this was a make-it-or-break-it day. After nine months, Taylor Daniels had built a sizeable lead, and he could sew it up today with a win. That she was still even marginally in contention she accredited to Dylan. In the month since they had first made love, they had settled into a routine that they each looked forward to more with each weekend.

Their second weekend together, she took him to Foley's gym and gave him a black eye teaching him a Muay Thai move.

"You need more muscle," Foley had barked in Dylan's ear that day. "Where have you been all your life, at a library?"

After that, Dylan started coming in several times a week to pump iron and hit the bags. One Saturday, when Shannon was looking on, Foley interrupted Dylan's pathetic efforts at hitting the heavy bag. "Whoa, stop right there," he had ordered. "Haven't you ever been in a fight?"

"Nope," admitted the fishery kid. "My brother was the fighter in our family."

Foley instructed him on how to form a fist and deliver a punch with a little turn of the wrist at the right moment. Afterward, Shannon watched Dylan take his attack on the bag to a new level. When they returned to his apartment, he made love to her with a new confidence.

Shannon looked forward to their adventurous voyages out of the harbor on his boat. With classical music pumping from Dylan's boom box, the thrill of speed on the water would transport her into that "thin place" where life and fantasy became one. The best part was that someone she could trust was in control, allowing her to relax and enjoy the pull of the wind on her face.

This past Saturday, when Shannon and Foley were alone and cleaning up, Foley had remarked, "You seem happier since you started hanging out with that boy."

"I am," she admitted.

"And did you go back to drugs, too?" he asked facetiously, remembering their earlier discussion about giving up sex and drugs at the same time.

"Never even think about it," she boasted, suddenly realizing that her dreams of relapsing and her day-mares had taken a holiday.

"Any future plans?" asked Foley. He had quizzed Dylan like a father about his intentions, and the earnest young man had been very candid about his love for Shannon.

"No plans," she insisted. "We both like it that way. He has his novel to finish. And he knows I need to work things out with my father before anything more can happen between us. With only a few months left in the syllabus, that isn't going to happen."

Foley frowned. "You said this boy makes you happy . . ."

"He does," she confirmed, that glow like a beacon for all to see.

"What about that little matter we discussed?"

Shannon blushed. Sex was still a subject she found difficult to talk about. "Our sex is . . . well, amazing," she confided. "Everything about us as a couple is good. We have the same dopey sense of humor. We like the same bad movies. We can talk about anything."

"Sounds like something you wouldn't want to give up," said Foley pointedly. Something in his tone made her stop and take in the man in the chair in a new way.

"Did you ever feel like that about someone, Gunny?" she asked.

Foley faced her with sad eyes. "No," he said. "I never let a woman in. Never even came close."

"Why?" she inquired.

"It was my sick way of paying back my mother for what she did," he reasoned. Then he got back on point. "Habits become who we are," he lectured. "Make a habit of running away, and you might end up doing that the rest of your life."

Shannon just nodded. She had been in some form of flight since her mother's death.

Dylan had been very sweet when they said goodbye Sunday afternoon so that she could rest up for Monday's drill. All weekend she had been in a negative place, and by late Sunday, nothing had changed. "Break a leg tomorrow, or whatever they say," he whispered encouragingly.

"You can spare me the pep talk. I already know what's going to happen tomorrow. I say sayonara to the strike fighter."

Dylan was surprised. At her darkest, she had never sounded this defeated. "Since when do you give up like this?"

"It's a matter of numbers," she groused. "Taylor's the better pilot. Everyone knows it. I've been kidding myself that I'm in his league." Dylan took her in his arms and kissed her on the forehead.

"You're better than you think you are," he assured her lovingly. Then when that one fell on deaf ears, he said the words he had held in reserve for this moment.

"Don't forget, we're going to win," he intoned.

Shannon looked at him, moved. Those were the magic words. How many times over the years had she watched her parents resolve their problems with that simple phrase.

"Thanks for that," she said. She kissed him and allowed her lips to linger on his for several seconds. He was right. Giving up was not an option. *I can still turn this around.*

"Roman One Three, in," she announced, descending on her target and pulling out of her dive. She reported, "Roman One Three, one away." She frowned. Her hit was disappointingly outside Kelly's.

"Thirty feet at ten o'clock," announced the range master. "Good enough for second."

Standing nearby, Zack and Perryman shared a look. The stakes today were the highest they'd been since the start of the syllabus. Despite Zack's lingering reservations about his daughter's recovery, he still harbored dreams that she would win the strike fighter.

Taylor made his approach on the target. Pushing the pickle, he said, "Roman One Two, one away." He watched his bomb hit just inside the lip of the lake. "Yeah, baby. Beat that, Mayo."

"Best hit of the day, Daniels," twanged the range director over the common frequency. "Keep this up and the F-35 is yours. Lieutenant Mayo, you'll need a miracle to turn this around."

In her cockpit, Shannon scoured her brain for that miracle. Images of a backyard dart-throwing contest between her and her father flickered to life like an old family video. It was 1998, and Britney Spears sang and danced silently on a neglected TV. Shannon remained stick-thin at thirteen. At forty-eight, her father's thick, military-cut hair was all gray. As had become the new normal since her mother had taken the job with the charity, father and daughter were alone and engaged in one of their ferocious competitions. Darts. The lead had changed hands for over an hour.

"Mom called earlier. She has a dinner meeting," Zack informed his daughter between throws. Then he added with a sigh, "I wish she'd hang out here more."

Shannon could hear the loneliness in her father's voice. She knew that, as much as he loved the perks of having a powerhouse wife, he missed the old days when he didn't have to share her with the world. Shannon loved her mom totally and aspired to be like her, successfully juggling career and family. But she was her daddy's best friend, his sidekick, and she felt his pain as if it were her own.

"Give her a break, Daddy," she advised. "Mommy was a factory girl. She has a lot to prove." She flashed a flirty smile that she was trying out for the first time. "And I'm a better cook."

"That's for sure," Zack agreed. "And a much better dancer." They had won contests around the state dancing together. Their specialty was the Lindy Hop, and their signature move was "the Pretzel." It took incredible timing and teamwork. By contrast, Paula was a famously clumsy dancer and her own best imitator.

Then his daughter asked, "Daddy, are you jealous that Mommy is around all those handsome young men she works with?" Zack glanced at her, amused. Lately, their conversations had become more mature and open. "I trust your mom," he replied without reservation. "I just miss her being around like before."

"I miss her, too," said Shannon. Then she cocked a wise brow. "I see the way women look at you."

"You're imagining things," he assured her.

"No, I'm not," she insisted. "Aunt Casey's in love with you. All the women in fleet replacement treat you like a rock star."

Zack grinned. "What are you suggesting?" he chided good-naturedly. "That I would do that to Mom?"

"Would you?" she asked with brazen curiosity.

"Never," he answered definitively. It was true. He had had many opportunities over the years to be a philanderer like his father. Overseas on long tours of duty, he had been tempted often. But ultimately his love for his wife kept him true. This turned out to be good karma. After Paula went to work, she became as great a target for infidelity as he had ever been. A year after Paula had started her job, his jealousies had come to a head, and he accused her of sleeping with a coworker. Paula had laughed at the absurdity and assured him that he had nothing to fear as long as she had nothing to fear. Paula made things simple like that.

"We have an understanding," he explained to Shannon. "To make a relationship of any kind work, you must have trust. And trust comes from trusting yourself first." Then he glanced at the target on the wall. "Go on. It's your turn," he said, handing her a dart.

Shannon's throw caught the edge of the center circle. "Bullseye," she exclaimed. "Beat that, Big Spendah."

"I'll do my best," replied Zack. He faced the target, and his eyes narrowed with concentration. "Clickety-Click," he said in a sing-song way. The words were his magic mantra when he needed to do the impossible.

His dart hit the very center of the bullseye.

"Daddy, how do you do that?" exclaimed his daughter. She knew that growing up on the mean streets of Olongapo, he had mastered a million tricks, and this was just one of them.

"Just lucky," maintained Zack.

"No, it's more than that," she persisted. "You get into this place. I see it in your eyes."

With a mischievous glint, Zack found a plastic schoolhouse in a bucket of old toys and put it on top of a picket fence just above a knothole the size of a silver dollar. "We ran into this all the time," he began. "Terrorist cell imbedded under a kindergarten or hospital. No one wanted the job, but I knew a trick. I could slow down time."

"You're making this up," she accused him, laughing.

"No boo-shee you, Big Spendah," he replied in his street hustler voice. "Slow down da time thingy, you like Superman guy, do magic thingy." This was part of his act, the street character he had been as a boy growing up.

"*Tarantado!*" swore Shannon. It was Tagalog for "Bastard!"

"*Tangina mo, mamatay ka na!*" answered her father. The words meant "Eat shit and die!" They cracked up, laughing. Then he proceeded with his story.

"In the PI, there were some bad dudes I had to watch out for—older, better fighters. So, I taught myself this trick. Slow it all down, see it at half-speed, and there it is, your opponent's weakness."

"But how do you do it?" Shannon pressed.

"You pull a switch in your head," he replied matter-of-factly.

"Yeah, right," she answered.

"I know it sounds crazy, but it works," he assured her. "Look how people get well when you give them a placebo. The mind is a sucker for tricks. You see yourself pull that switch. You say the words the same way. And weird shit happens." He faced the target and said the magic words, "Clickety-Click." As Shannon watched, the dart flew from his fingers, narrowly missed the schoolhouse, pierced the knothole in the fence, and stuck with a soft thud in a neighbor's tree.

"I have the best daddy in the whole world," proclaimed Shannon, hugging him tightly. The top of her head came up to his Adam's apple. A year earlier, her ear had been against his chest. Zack beamed happily. Nobody was pinning any medals on his chest lately, but this was better than winning a war.

The present rushed back suddenly as Shannon dove on the target and uttered the magic words in the prescribed way, "Clickety-Click." To her surprise, time seemed to slow measurably. The lake grew huge. In what seemed like slow motion, her live bomb left its bay and pierced the surface of the lake at its very center, kicking up a spray that washed the underbelly of her craft.

On the tower, Zack and Perryman exchanged astonished looks. "On the money, One Three," announced the range master. "Best hit of the day. Now we got a race."

In his cockpit, Taylor appeared shaken. Even the best instructors had never laid down such a perfect hit.

"Way to go, One Three," Zack bellowed into his radio. He knew what he'd just witnessed was on a level he could have barely touched when he was her age. He certainly couldn't do it now. In the excitement of the moment, he wanted to believe that she was free of her addiction and they could pull off their miracle. In such a scenario, he could pass the torch, and his life would still have meaning.

In her cockpit, Shannon heard the pride in her father's voice. It was turning around for them, but why did she still feel so unsettled? Wasn't this the goal, to win back his respect? Then it hit her. She would need to win back her own respect before any of it mattered, and she didn't have the first clue how to do that.

After long and languorous lovemaking at Dylan's apartment that started in the shower and finished on the soft blue lounge on his plant-shielded balcony, Shannon suggested a hike in the mountains around the Cape Henry Memorial.

After her breakthrough day in strike the previous Monday, there was a lightness to her step as she gathered wildflowers on a cloudless Sunday morning. Dylan photographed her adoringly with his phone. "Someone's in a better mood this weekend," he observed.

"I feel amazing," she said. "For the first time, I feel like I might have a real chance."

With the sun peaking in the sky, Dylan took off his T-shirt to get some color, and Shannon interrupted her search for wildflowers to stare at him. His workouts were paying off.

"What are you looking at?" he asked with a grin.

She blushed and looked away. She was starting to feel things for this man that she had not anticipated. After Foley had brought it up, she had been dreading the day when she would be forced to say goodbye.

Dylan knew the syllabus was winding down. They would finish the Strafing phase of Strike in the coming week. Next would come BFM (Basic Flight Maneuvering) or "dogfighting." And finally, "Night Quals." In three months, Shannon could be gone from his life, perhaps, forever.

"So, if you get the strike fighter, where will they send you?" he asked.

"Lemoore, California," she replied. "If I don't get it, I'll be assigned to a squadron somewhere else like Hawaii, Japan, or the Middle East."

"Exciting," he said.

"What are your plans?"

"Finish my book. Show it to my friend in New York," he replied. "I've promised myself that one way or the other, I'll quit the fishery.

That probably means waiting tables or tending bar in New York City until I make a sale."

"Good for you," she said. She could feel a new strength in him that went along with his toned physique.

"Anything new with your dad?" asked Dylan. Since their meeting at the Officer's Club, he had thought about her father often. Beyond his desire to render a fuller character of the patriarch in his book, Dylan wanted to prove himself worthy to this man.

"A trick I learned from him gave me the win in bombing," she said with a touch of wonder in her voice. "He had a million tricks like that. He was the best father in the world."

Dylan looked surprised. She had credited her father with teaching her how to fight, but this praise was something more. "You never talk about him like this," he remarked. "The picture in my mind is the absentee father always off fighting some war."

"That was only true when I was little," she clarified. "And even then, he was my bigger-than-life dad, always showing up after a long tour of duty to shower me with presents and carry me around on his shoulders. In eighth grade, he came into my classroom in his dress whites and carried me out in his arms."

"What happened after your dad took over as your main parent?"

"It was like a fairy tale," she enthused. "As an instructor, he was finished with work by noon. When I came home from school, he'd be waiting at the front door to announce our 'Adventure of the Day.'" Her face glowed as she spoke. "He taught me to ride a motorcycle. He taught me to fly a plane. We competed in dance contests and won a ton of prizes. We parachuted from planes. We bungee-jumped off cliffs in Mexico."

She was so caught up in her story that as she reached out to pluck more wildflowers, she encountered a thornbush instead. "*Aray! Putanginang 'yan!*" she cried, painfully extracting a thorn.

"Say again?" asked Dylan, amused.

"It's Tagalog," she explained. "My father taught me the worst swearwords he learned growing up in the Philippines."

"Give me another one," he encouraged.

"*Putangina mo!* Fuck you!"

"*PUTANGINA MO!*" Dylan shouted at the top of his lungs. Then his eyes brightened with a realization. "I get it now! I know why this is kicking your butt, his, too."

Shannon rubbed her arm to make the pain go away. "Do we have to talk about this now?"

"Hear me out," he urged. He knew he was taking a risk, pressing her about the elephant in the room, but time was running out. "You were thrown together because of a changing world. You were a bright and sensitive teenager who needed a strong figure in your life, and he was a man with a lot of time on his hands and a past he wanted to make up for."

She arched a brow. "What are you implying?"

"It was all good," he assured her. "What you and your father had was what every parent and kid dreams of having. But then, your mom dies, and that's over? Why?"

Shannon felt a surge of panic. On Independence Day, this question, and those fireworks, had provoked a day-mare. "I told you before. I didn't have the character to deal with her death. I was just trying to survive. So was my father. We did it separately. That's all. End of story."

Dylan put his hands on her shoulders. "Shannon, if that's all that happened, then why can't you guys come back together now?"

"I don't know," she shouted, pulling away from his grip. "Why are you grilling me like this? For your precious book?"

Dylan knew he had overplayed his hand. "I want to help you," he said openly. "It should be obvious to you by now that I love you." The words hung in the air, and he wished he could take them back.

Fear flashed in her eyes, and she shook her head defiantly. "Don't start that stuff, Dylan. I've never misled you about who I am or where this was going."

Dylan winced. For the past month, they had shared their lives like a married couple. He knew that the old him would have said nothing after one of her sudden pull-aways, but he was starting to own a role in his own narrative. "I have a right to my feelings," he insisted. "You don't have to share them. That's your call." Then he decided to go further.

"Fixing this thing with your father is your call, too, if you want. You just have to give up this . . . this thing . . . this secret."

Shannon had heard enough. "I should have my head examined for letting you write about me. I wish now that I'd hit that button."

Dylan froze in place. "What button?" Then he knew. "You were going to erase my book?" he stammered.

Shannon was in full retreat. Clearly, she was not ready to shine a flashlight into the vault where she kept her secrets. Maybe she never would be. "I need to get back to the base," she announced. "I fly tomorrow, and I need to get ready." There was a finality in her tone that sent chills through Dylan's body.

On their drive back to Virginia Beach, they were both quiet. Dylan noticed that her knee was pumping relentlessly. There was an angry look in her eyes that told him he'd gone too far. As they entered the city, they saw that the boardwalk was roped off. Lady Gaga's "Born This Way" blasted from speakers. Shannon suddenly snapped out of her trance.

"Look! A street fair!" she announced, a childlike wonder in her voice. "I want to go!"

Dylan was surprised by her sudden change of heart and her giddy tone. "You fly in the morning," he reminded her.

"It's still early," she argued. "Look! A Ferris wheel!" She was almost bouncing up and down in her seat in excitement. When Dylan found a parking space, she jumped out without waiting for him and disappeared into the crowd. Dylan felt his heart racing. He had a lot of personal experience in these matters. She was showing all the signs of a recovering addict on the verge of relapse. He wondered if he'd launched her onto this road by probing too relentlessly.

The last street fair Shannon had attended was on the Rehoboth Beach family holiday where the photo of the core three was taken. Shannon recalled her buoyant feelings from that trip and wanted to relive them. Sidney and Nickie were competing at darts as Shannon ran up. "Hi, guys," she announced.

Sidney spun around, surprised. "Shannon! I didn't expect to see you the night before a drill."

"I love street fairs," said Shannon exuberantly. She felt as lighthearted as she had that night in Rehoboth. For so much of her life, she had had her guard up to fend off attacks from the mean brown ducks, but tonight she felt weightless and omnipotent. It did not occur to her that this is exactly how she had felt on drugs. Bounding to an adjacent booth, she tossed down some money and started throwing baskets. *Swish. Swish. Swish.*

Dylan jogged up, and Sidney and Nickie gave him a questioning look about Shannon. She was an automaton, sinking baskets one after the other. He moved closer to her and asked, "What's going on?"

Shannon didn't pause in her attack on the basket. Swish. Swish. "I'm just having fun," she replied airily.

Dylan counted twelve throws without a miss. "You seem like you're almost high," he said.

Shannon didn't reply. She kept sinking those baskets.

Nickie's birdlike voice suddenly rang out from the next booth. "You did it! You did it!" she cried. Sidney had punctured a balloon, winning Nickie a big Oscar the Grouch. Nickie danced around with her prize in her arms. "I love him," she chirped. She threw her arms around Sidney's neck and kissed her on the lips. "I love you," she gushed.

"I love you, too," said Sidney huskily. Forgetting their public setting, she returned the kiss and lingered there longer than usual.

A nasal voice cut through the air like a truck horn in the middle of a funeral dirge. "Can't you ladies please do that in private?"

Shannon stopped throwing baskets. She recognized that voice from her drug days. She took in two large men roughly her age. They wore red "Beadalieu Brothers Sportfishing" caps.

"Is that you, Shannon?" asked Landon, the shorter and better-looking of the brothers. He had long dark hair tied back in a ponytail and a nose cratered down the middle like two halves of an apricot. His taller brother, Gabe, wore a tank top that left no doubt that he was a gym rat. He had lats like an armadillo.

Shannon felt her stomach shrivel. She knew these men from her party days.

Dylan knew them too. They were local toughs who Stevie had had to deal with. Their connection to Shannon surprised him. What could she have in common with the Beadalieu brothers? Then he knew the answer. *Drugs.*

"You look good, Shannon," said Gabe in a grating twang that matched his brother's. Shannon noted that both men's eyes were so shiny they had to be buzzed.

"A lot better than last time, I'd say," twanged Landon. The men shared a nasal laugh that sounded like dueling tubas.

Shannon was horrified. She had successfully kept her worlds apart for three years, and now they were crashing into each other like cymbals. She had partied with these men. She had bought drugs from them once. She thought fast. "Hi, guys. Still here in Paradise, I see." Taking Dylan's arm, she led him away, but Landon sprang into their path.

"What's the matter? Too busy for old friends?" His eyes were feverish.

"The lady is with me," said the fishery kid.

The Beadalieu brothers exchanged an amused look. "Harmony, I knew your faggot brother," said the bodybuilder, showing off unattended dental work. "It doesn't surprise me to see you hanging with the gay crowd."

"We can help you out again, little lady," whispered Landon, producing a tiny bottle of a white substance between his thumb and forefinger.

Shannon stared at it as if it were Kryptonite.

Landon and Gabe shared knowing grins.

Dylan, Sidney, and Nickie stared at Shannon as though seeing her for the first time.

Shannon spoke suddenly in a voice that startled everyone. "Enough," she warned. "You've got exactly two seconds to get out of my face."

"Or what, Dragon Lady?" challenged Landon.

"Or you lose your reproductive skills," hissed Shannon through clenched teeth.

The Beadalieu brothers honked their annoying laughs. Dylan realized that they had never witnessed her fighting skills.

"Bring it, sweet thang," encouraged Gabe.

Shannon's pretty features became as fierce as a gladiator's. "Yaaaaa!"

she cried, leaping in the air to deliver a sharp crescent kick to the larger brother's jaw. *Go for the big one first. Send a message.* The kick sent Gabe sprawling backward on the ground. He sat there, stunned.

"That was a stupid thing to do," growled Landon. He charged behind a barrage of jabs, but she was ready. Ducking his blows, she seized his T-shirt at the neckline, then brought a knee up into his groin as hard as she could. He screamed and sank to the ground, moaning.

"Look out!" shouted Dylan. Gabe had regained his feet and was in the process of unleashing a punch from outside her field of vision. The warning came a split-second late. His knuckles clipped her jaw, sending her to her knees beside his brother. Gabe put a foot on her throat to keep her from regaining her feet.

"Bitch!" he roared, putting his weight into that leg. "I oughta break your neck for that!"

"Stop!" commanded Dylan. Gabe spun around, and Dylan caught him with a crisp right cross on his mouth. Gabe went down hard and stayed there, his mouth dripping blood through his uneven teeth.

"Bro-ster-ino," applauded Nickie proudly. Dylan was shaking his hand in pain, but he felt good about what he had done.

"Everybody, hold it right there." A middle-aged female police officer had driven up on a motorcycle. She took in the Beadalieu brothers with familiar eyes before helping Shannon to her feet. "Are you okay, lady?" she asked.

"I'm fine," said Shannon, brushing herself off.

"Do you want to file charges against these men, ma'am?" asked the officer.

Shannon could see that the officer had the Beadalieu brothers pegged. Shannon remembered they were holding. One word from her and they would go down hard. But it would mean exposing her secret past to the Navy's scrutiny.

"No charges," said Shannon, allowing the two men to melt gratefully into the crowd.

The policewoman studied Shannon closely. "You know those two are drug dealers," she said evenly.

"I know," said Shannon. "Thanks for your help."

"Be careful," said the officer.

As she motored off, Shannon felt the eyes of her friends on her. She felt stupid for being so hopeful and unguarded. There was always a mean brown duck.

Dylan watched her carefully. "Are you all right?" he asked.

Shannon stared at him mutely. The collision of the past and present had taken a toll on her, even if the punch had barely hurt. "I'm fine," she insisted. "I need to get back to the base."

"I'll take you," said Sidney. "You should go to the infirmary so they can check you out."

"I'll go with you," offered Dylan.

Shannon turned to face them. "I'm fine," she insisted irritably. "I don't need anybody's help." Waving to a passing taxi, she was gone.

TWENTY-ONE

SECRETS OF THE HEART

FRS

The Following Day

When Sidney returned to the BOQ on Monday morning, she found Shannon at the vanity applying makeup to the bruise on her jaw. "How do you feel?" she asked with concern.

"Great," replied Shannon. "I slept like a baby last night."

"What did they say at the infirmary?" asked Sidney.

Shannon diverted her eyes "I decided not to go. Why give some overzealous intern the chance to roll me back?"

Sidney blinked behind her thick glasses. "You have to tell them," she insisted. "Or I will. I can't violate my oath."

Shannon chose her words surgically. "You and I swore an oath, too, as friends. Friends can have secrets. You have yours. I have mine."

Sidney felt uncomfortable. She was witnessing the street side of her bunkmate for the first time, and it sent chills through her. "Me? What secrets do I have?" she asked.

Shannon didn't like herself in this moment, but she was fighting for her life. "Flying scares the shit out of you. That's your secret."

"Flying scares everybody," said the taller girl defensively.

"It scares you more than the others," persisted Shannon. "I could squeeze a gallon of water out of your flight suit after every exercise. Your hands shake for hours after you've flown. At night I hear you moaning in your sleep like someone caught in a bad dream."

Sidney had no argument. It was all true.

Shannon stayed on track. She was doing her friend a favor. She did not see her actions as selfish. "We both know the real reason why you're here. And it has nothing to do with your love of flying."

"What is it?"

"To win back your father's love," said Shannon. "But nothing you do will change his mind. You could die, and it wouldn't change his mind."

Sidney felt dizzy. Everything Shannon said was true. Her father's oft-repeated dream was to have been a jet pilot. If she achieved that goal, surely he'd welcome her back into his heart. But there was a motive in Shannon's pitch that unsettled her.

"If I say no, will we still be friends?"

"Of course," said Shannon. "Do what feels right, but I swear to you on my mother's ashes that I'm totally fine. I'm just worried about you." Shannon felt like a street hustler. Her father had sold uniforms to his classmates at OCS so that they could pass inspection. Manipulating her friend in this moment was straight out of his playbook. Her grandfather's appearance in her life had confirmed that she was carny stock.

"If you're really okay, then fine, I won't say anything," conceded Sidney.

Shannon brightened triumphantly. "That's my roomie," she sang, hugging her friend tightly.

A short time later, Shannon was circling above the strafing target in the dash four spot. She was surprisingly upbeat, considering the events of the night before. She felt no effects from that glancing blow. If anything, she was more clearheaded than she could remember.

After her victory over Taylor Daniels in the bombing phase a week earlier, she felt confident that she could repeat the feat today. In this evolution, the pilots were required to descend onto a triangular target with a run-in line and unleash the fury of their Vulcan Cannons. Today, the magazines would be loaded for the first time.

"Roman One Four, in," she announced, beginning her descent. She could feel the g's rise. She was so confident she didn't bother to say the magic words. Her canons obliterated the run-up line and destroyed the target. She knew her name would shoot to the top of the leaderboard as it had the week before. She pulled out of her dive, her HUD climbing to six g's, turning her face elastic.

Suddenly she coughed and blood sprayed the inside of her visor. She knew right away what was happening. "No . . . no . . ." she whimpered. She coughed again, and now the blood was so thick she couldn't see.

Her plane began to go out of control.

"One Four, what's going on up there?" Zack barked into his radiophone. His answer was on the screen in front of him. Shannon's Super Hornet was falling out of the sky like a rock. Terror tightened his throat.

With the ground coming up fast, Shannon yanked off her visor. The pain was still intense, but at least now, she could see. On her HUD, an upward arrow flashed a warning, and the twangy voice of Bitchin' Betty screamed in her ears.

"PULL UP! PULL UP!" bitched Betty.

At the last instant, Shannon fought past the pain and pulled up, gratefully watching the nose of her plane leave brown earth and find blue sky.

"Thank God . . . thank God . . ." she mumbled. Tears flowed and her nose ran. The magnitude of her failure was staggering. She had nearly died and taken an $80 million plane with her because of a secret.

On the observation tower, Zack sucked in air with profound relief. Then he fixed Sidney with laser eyes. "Lieutenant Lee, what do you know about this?"

Sidney felt awful. The entire time Shannon had been in jeopardy she had held her breath, knowing she'd made a horrible mistake and praying she wouldn't have her friend's death on her conscience for the rest of her life. "There was a fight on the boardwalk," she blurted. "Shannon got hit, but it seemed like a nothing blow."

"You knew about this fight and didn't say something?" he half-shouted. "What kind of officer does that make you, Lieutenant?"

Then he decided to go further. He needed somewhere to unload his anger, and he had serious doubts about her motives for being here. "If I were you, I'd start asking myself a lot of questions," he concluded.

Sidney nodded, fighting tears. "Yes, sir," she said.

Zack was waiting on the tarmac when Shannon landed, his street instincts percolating various scenarios, none of them good. By itself, her failure to report her injury was not all that alarming. Pilots often hid minor injuries to avoid being rolled back. But learning that Shannon had been involved in a street fight made no sense, unless it was somehow connected to drugs.

Per protocol, a medical truck pulled up, and two attendants climbed the ladder to the cockpit with a litter, then passed Shannon down to two other medics. Protocol also dictated that no one engage the injured party in dialogue until the infirmary had evaluated their condition, so Zack's questions would have to wait. As they carried her past him, their eyes met awkwardly.

Shannon was taken directly to the emergency room of the infirmary where she was not allowed to move or speak until all manner of tests had been completed. She had just dozed off when she felt a needle enter her arm.

"What're you doing? What is that?" she demanded in a panic.

"It's morphine for your pain," said the young male nurse administering the shot.

"No! No!" she screamed, yanking the needle free so suddenly that she was bleeding profusely down her arm.

But it was too late. The drugs were coursing in her veins.

After almost three years of rigid sobriety, her body was ill-prepared for what happened next. She was so high that she thought she had transcended matter. She reached outer space, a comet trying to outrace time. Dark memories assaulted her. A friend's tortured features as she died from a fentanyl overdose. The boat fire and her desperate swim to shore. The cries of that shark victim. Her flight through the belltower. Her day-mares. The ocean rising up to claim her as Bitchin' Betty screamed in her ear. The sting of that needle. It played on a loop. She didn't sleep. She didn't eat. She rode the beast, hanging on for dear life.

Dylan was thrilled when Shannon arrived Friday night for their NA meeting and took the seat beside him. After learning about her concussion from Nickie, he had tried calling her every day, but the hospital wouldn't put him through. It had been six days since he'd seen her at the street fair and the physical changes were startling. She had lost weight, and there was a vacant, haunted, expression in her normally vivid eyes.

"Hi, stranger," he whispered softly, not wanting to disrespect the speaker. "How are you feeling?"

"I'm all right," she replied in a tone so void of warmth that it warned him of what was to come next. The woman who had been sharing stepped down, and Shannon volunteered to be next. She took the microphone and allowed herself a deep intake of air.

"I'll cut to the chase," she began. "I relapsed."

Dylan sat back in his chair in shock. Her fellow addicts sucked in a communal breath. A relapse brought a sorrow akin to hearing about a death.

"This will be my last meeting," she announced. "I'm quitting my job and leaving the state." Her eyes narrowed on Dylan. "I want to thank my unofficial sponsor. I'm sorry I let you down." She seemed to want to say more; instead she hurried off the stage and out the door. Dylan sprinted after her.

He threw up his hands as her Harley roared toward him. "Wait! We need to talk!"

Shannon screeched to a stop, her face distorted with self-loathing. "Forget about me, Dylan," she commanded. "I'm not who you think I am."

"Bullshit! You're the best person I've ever met!" he declared. "What happened in that hospital?"

"They gave me morphine. I was high for five days. It felt like I was in outer space. I want another bump right now. I want it, Dylan. I will always want it."

"I don't buy it," he snapped angrily. "You're not that girl anymore. You're strong, Shannon. It's sometimes scary how strong you are."

"Then I have to be strong enough to admit I can't beat this thing," she said emphatically. "I conned Sidney into lying for me. I was this close to killing myself. How could I live with myself if I killed one of my classmates or instructors?"

Dylan stammered, "What about us? Are you going to throw that away with everything else?"

She studied him with cold eyes. "There never was an us," she said. "That's you and your book."

"You don't mean that," he protested, panic in his tone. This was not Shannon, he decided. It was her secrets, taking over.

"Stop obsessing over me, Dylan. Get a life of your own." She gunned the bike around him and roared off into the night.

Dylan felt like his bowels had been yanked out of him by needle-nose plyers. *Get a life.* This was what Stevie had said. It was what his parents had each said in their own way. Now the woman of his dreams was passing the same judgment.

Driving home, he passed some of the bars he'd frequented in the past. He saw an old dealer buddy get out of his vintage silver Porsche 911 in front of a nightclub called Charley's Horse. It took all Dylan's willpower not to honk his horn.

When he got home, he tried to write, but he felt like he had the flu. He was sniffling and blowing his nose. His throat was inflamed. He was hot one minute and cold the next. He got in bed and covered up. He felt exactly like he had every time he had hit bottom with drugs, perhaps even worse. Then he realized why. He had fallen in love with two women, the real Shannon, and the character in his book. And he was paying an addict's price for it.

Foley was wrapping up his Friday night self-defense class with the aid of Ramon. Within the group of twelve were three nerdy young men and a similarly geeky young woman, all midtwenties, out of shape, and all wearing matching Navy-blue-and-gold warmups. As the class concluded, Foley asked them, "What squadron are you people with?"

One of the men replied, "U-CAV, Sergeant Foley. Drones."

"The future of naval aviation," added the plump, cherry-nosed young woman at the center of the group. Foley watched the four chest-bump, a jolly crew. *God help us*, he thought. Ramon left with the class. As Foley was preparing to lock up, Shannon walked in, dressed in her biker attire as before, looking pale and gaunt.

"Shannon," he exclaimed. "I thought tonight was your meeting."

"I left early," she said. "I came to say goodbye."

"Goodbye?" Foley felt like someone had kicked him in the stomach. This young woman had turned his life around. She had given him the only real taste of family he had known since his brief episode with her father thirty-five years before.

"I'm resigning my commission in the morning," she said. "My father was right. I'm an addict, and I always will be."

"Walk me through this," Foley implored. "Did you take drugs?"

"Oh, yeah," she replied. "The infirmary gave me opioids while I was unconscious."

"And you blame yourself for that?"

Shannon suddenly unleashed a side kick into a padded wall, and words spilled out in a torrent. "I got in a fight with some guys I did drugs with a long time ago and took a punch I should have reported to command. I almost died and destroyed a plane. I could have killed somebody."

"But you didn't," Foley pointed out. "That's the important thing."

"Thank God," she acknowledged. "But I can't take any chance it'll happen again."

"What does your friend Dylan think?" asked Foley.

"I ended it with Dylan," she answered hollowly. "He can do a lot better than me." She sank to the floor and put her face in her hands. Her body shook violently, but she contained the sound of her emotions at a personal cost.

Foley was moved in ways he wouldn't have thought possible a year earlier. In this time, he had let this young woman into his life in ways that eclipsed anything he'd experienced before, including his relationship with his father. He had watched her growth with personal pride, and he believed in her. This self-flagellation had shown its face before. He reasoned that growing up the child of superstar parents had taken its toll and becoming a victim of drugs hadn't helped. He felt miserably out of his paygrade as a surrogate.

"Don't make any decisions tonight," he advised soberly. "Get some sleep. I'll show you your quarters. Your father found it comfortable."

"My father slept here?" she asked in hushed surprise.

"Yes, he did. Reveille is at 0600."

Shannon settled onto that unforgiving bed without bothering to remove her clothes. She was relieved that Foley had insisted she stay. After her ordeal of the previous week and the events of tonight, her thoughts were frighteningly dark. A good night's sleep would restore order, but she knew it wouldn't change her mind.

TWENTY-TWO

★★★

REQUIEM FOR A HEAVYWEIGHT

FOLEY'S FITNESS
Later That Night

Two hours later, a loud moan pulled Shannon out of a half-sleep. When the sound was repeated a moment later, she stepped out into the courtyard. The moon was bright in the sky. She saw a door and found it unlocked.

Foley lay in bed in his quarters above the gym, moaning. His face and arms were slick with sweat. His large hands were splayed out on his chest like the branches of a tree.

"Gunny," she exclaimed in horror as she saw him. "What can I do?"

Foley pointed a shaking hand at his vial of pills that had fallen out of reach. Consulting the label, she tapped two tablets into her palm, poured a glass of water, and helped him wash them down.

"What is it?" she asked. "Your heart?"

Foley nodded. He was in a lot of pain, and the meds would take a little time to kick it.

Shannon dialed 911 on her cell. She asked for an ambulance and made sure they knew it was cardio. Then she called her father. She did it without thinking, and when he answered, she almost pressed the button to hang up.

"Is that you, Shannon?" he exclaimed. "I've been trying to reach you." He had received word earlier in the day that she had been released from the hospital. The doctor had informed him about the heavy dose of morphine that had been injected in her arm against her will. He warned Zack that his daughter was in a troubled frame of mind on her release.

"Dad, I need you," she implored. "I think Foley's dying."

Zack arrived before the ambulance. Shannon met him at the bedroom door. "Thank God you came," she said gratefully.

"What're you doing here at this hour?" he asked.

"I needed a place to regroup," she explained. "I understand I'm not the first."

Zack was surprised that they had both needed this sanctuary, but he pushed on.

"I spoke to your doctor. I know what happened," he said. "Are you okay?"

"Not really," she admitted.

Zack nodded thoughtfully. Then he approached Foley. "Gunny, can you hear me?" he asked. The older man's eyes opened slowly. "The ambulance is on its way," Zack assured him.

Foley looked at Shannon questioningly.

"I asked him to come," she whispered.

Foley's pain had subsided since taking his medicine. He struggled to sit upright, and his tired eyes focused on Zack. "I've been wanting a word with you, Mayonnaise." He cast Shannon a look that said he wanted to do this man-to-man.

"Of course," she replied. As she left them, she wondered if she had sought out this man so that this final moment could happen.

Zack knew he was about to get a lecture, so he rushed to fend it off. "Save your strength, Gunny," he advised. "You'll need it."

"Shut up!" snapped the older man in an explosion of energy that made Zack sit back in his chair. He was unprepared for the words that came out of his old mentor's lips. "I made a mistake," said Foley with deep regret. "I'm sorry I let them commission you."

His words knocked the air out of Zack, transporting him back to that night at OCS when he was on his hands and knees in the mud with Foley taunting him to drop on request.

"I think I've served my country pretty damn well, thank you, Sergeant," replied Zack defensively.

"I'm talking character," grunted Foley in much the same way he had said it to Zack back then. Then he said something odd. "I'm talking about what's wrong with me and you."

Zack wasn't sure he had heard correctly. "What do you mean?" he asked.

Foley's tired eyes revealed a psychological burden only understood by an abused child. Words Zack could have said himself came out of his mentor's lips. "You don't get lied to . . . over and over . . . by a druggie mother . . . who rewards you . . . by leaving you in a hot car while she parties."

Zack stared at the other man. Was Foley mocking him? A moment like that had happened to him with his mother. She had blanked out on her meds and left him in a department store. They had not been able to locate her until the next day.

Then Foley said, "You don't watch your own father get his brains blown out for not paying his debts and not come away with this thing we got. This . . . disease."

Zack was speechless. A week before he was due to graduate from high school at eighteen, he had come home from school to find his father on his knees, a Filipino gangster's gun to his head demanding a gambling debt be paid. "Pay him," screamed Byron. "I know you have the money." Zack gave the gangster the money he had put away for college. He suddenly knew why Foley had singled him out. They were fellow travelers on the road of abuse.

"That's where war comes in," Foley was saying. "Most addictive drug ever."

Zack knew right away where this was going. His dialogues with his Navy psychologist had prepared him for this discussion. "I didn't ask to be deployed," he argued righteously. "The president begged me to go." Since Seegar's words on the Fourth, he had clung tenaciously to his conviction that, if he had known Seegar had arranged his return to war, he never would have gone. He was an officer and a gentleman. He would never abandon his daughter to the horrors he had faced as a kid.

Foley shook his head. "That doesn't sound right. You hadn't flown in combat in six years. The military frowns on deploying a solo parent after the recent death of a spouse."

Zack glared back, shaken. "Are you calling me a liar?"

"You were a liar when I met you," said Foley. "You just polished up your act. But character generally finds its resting place."

Zack felt like he was in a time capsule. Hadn't this man said nearly those same words to him in his youth? "I've served my country unselfishly for half my life," he protested. "I have every honor they bestow in the Navy."

"You were passed over for admiral. I know about your DUI," said Foley. "You keep that on your mantle with the rest of your trophies?"

Zack's face reddened. "I had a weak moment. I'd lost someone I loved. That's probably not something you can wrap your head around."

Foley's eyes became bayonets. "Oh, I can wrap my head around it just fine," he grunted. He angrily tapped a spoon against his glass to summon Shannon. "I'm through with you, Mayonnaise. I've wasted enough time on you in my life."

"Wait, wait," choked Zack. "You're right. That shit doesn't go away." His voice was rich with pain. He had always wanted to share this part of his life with someone, but no one could understand who hadn't been there. Paula had been moved to tears on many occasions when he had shared details of his youth, but she could never fully grasp what his life had been like. No one could unless you were in the club.

Shannon slipped through the door quietly, then stopped, unnoticed, as she heard the emotional exchange. "You saved my life, Gunny," said her father humbly. "Everything good that happened to me—my marriage, my family, my career—I owe to you." Shannon had never seen her father so unguarded.

A warmth invaded Foley's dark features. In the final moments of his life, he was seeing the circle of life in closer focus. "Consider us even," he said. "I got all that back from your daughter."

Shannon felt a little sigh escape her throat. Hearing the sound, both

Zack and Foley looked over and saw her. "Shannon," exclaimed her father, suddenly aware that she had heard their exchange.

Foley permitted himself a tired smile. He had initiated an opening. Now it was up to them. He was shaken by another wave of pain and moaned harshly.

"Gunny, are you all right?" asked Shannon, alarmed.

"Sergeant, what can we do?" asked Zack.

Foley's eyes went from one to the other and the tiniest hint of a smile curled his lips. He had never married or fathered children. Adopting street kids had been his one taste of that elusive world, until he met these two. His gaze settled on Shannon at last.

"Is this what you meant by family?" he asked simply.

Shannon nodded. She put a hand on Foley's hand. Then Zack put his hand on hers. Father and daughter locked eyes solemnly. Then Foley's tired eyes closed, and his breathing stopped. Zack and Shannon didn't move. This man had been a father to both of them. His final act had been to bring them back together as family. This quiet, prayerful moment felt like a beginning.

An ambulance siren pierced the night and grew louder. As she heard the vehicle brake outside, Shannon's face tightened, and she removed her hand. "I can't watch this," she declared and bolted toward the door.

"Shannie, wait," cried Zack, confused. For a few seconds, they had been family again. "I thought, after what just happened, that we could talk. I have so much I need to say."

She turned at the door. "I don't want to talk," she cried. "I just want to die." He could hear her hurry down the stairs to the gym floor, and a moment later, he heard the report of her Harley like the scream of a house cat in the jaws of a coyote.

Shannon hit the highway at full throttle. She was in the greatest turmoil of her life. Nothing made sense. In the past week, she had suffered a concussion and come within a heartbeat of dying. She had spent five days jockeying for sanity in a hospital bed. She had quit NA and terminated her relationship with the first man to whom she had given her trust since her father. And now Foley was gone. He had been her father when she couldn't talk to her real father. In their exchanges, she had experienced the friendship of a truly great man.

One thing rattled her confidence. Why had Foley, a legendary judge of character, blamed her father for their falling out? How had she slithered under his radar? *Because I'm a fucking great actress,* she decided self-deprecatingly. This harsh self-evaluation wasn't new. She had felt like that as a child when people gushed so much about the color of her eyes. The power she had felt at so young an age was surreal. Since then, she had fooled a lot of people with that magic. Her parents. Her college friends. Monkey Millstein. Sidney. Foley. Dylan. God.

The evidence lined up in her mind like a prosecutor's dream case. *The pretty girl with the shallow heart. The attention seeker. The manipulator who had tried to drive a wedge between her parents. The demon child who wished for her mother's death so that she could have her father all to herself. The drug addict who had been willing to kill herself and her friends to punish her father for answering his call of duty. The deceitful girl who convinced her naive friend to share her lie.*

It was two in the morning when Shannon entered the boardwalk and began looking for a dealer. At that hour, dealers were everywhere, but none of their faces registered on her. *Have I been away that long?* Then she saw a skinny woman in her early forties pull up in an old Ford sedan with a pit bull beside her. Shannon had scored opioids from this woman before.

Shannon rushed out of the alley, fumbling in her backpack of memories for the woman's name. Then she saw her father's Corvette turn onto the boardwalk heading in her direction. *Oh, shit.* She rushed back into the alley and held her breath. The Corvette cruised past, her anxious father at the wheel, looking for her with feverish intensity. She felt powerless to do anything for the next two hours as she watched him canvas the area back and forth. When he finally drove away, it was four in the morning, and the dealer was gone.

Shannon was breathing like she'd just run a race. Life had served up another of its little miracles. It didn't mean she had stopped wanting to score. That annoying baby was still bawling loudly. But she had escaped the first real challenge. She told herself to build on that. She checked into a motel and fell into a sleep so deep that she imagined it was what death might feel like.

Shannon returned to the base at 1800 hours on Sunday night and found Sidney packing a duffel bag that sat on her bed. They had not seen each other for a week, and both women had changed physically in that time. While Sidney looked surprisingly relaxed, Shannon was tense and gaunt from her week's ordeal.

"Shannon!" exclaimed Sidney. "Thank God you're all right. I tried to see you at the infirmary, but they weren't letting in any visitors."

Shannon gestured to the open duffel. "What's up, roomie?"

"I quit," said Sidney with a little shrug. "You were right. I wasn't here for me," she said. "I gave up my wings. I'm being transferred to a desk job to finish my last nine months of duty."

Shannon was stupefied. "When did all this happen?'

"While you were in the hospital," she answered.

Shannon felt horrible. "Sidney, I said all those cruel things about you to get my way."

"But you were right about everything. That could have been me in that plane, instead of you. I could be dead. I'm grateful to you, Shannon."

"What about Nickie? Does she know?"

Sidney wiped the lenses of her glasses thoughtfully. "I asked her to come with me, but I don't think she's going to come. Living in Adak, Alaska, isn't exactly the plan she signed up for."

"But she loves you," said Shannon.

"Nickie's had a hard life," Sidney rationalized. "Without flight play, I can't give her what she needs."

Shannon pulled a duffel from the closet and put it on her bed. It was Sidney's turn to be surprised. "What are you doing?" she asked.

"I'm bailing before my father kicks me out," said Shannon. "I've already written my letter of resignation."

"He told you he's kicking you out?"

"He didn't have to. It's his duty." She took a moment to summon her courage before continuing. "There's a lot you don't know about me, Sidney," she confessed in a rush. "I lied about my past to get into this school. I was hooked on drugs for over a year. I sold drugs to pay for my own."

After the incident at the street fair, Sidney was not surprised. "I don't care," she declared. "That's ancient history. Everyone makes mistakes growing up."

"The Navy doesn't see it that way," said Shannon. She completed her packing and zipped up her duffel. Then she looked up to see Sidney watching her with concern from behind her sturdy specs.

"I hope you won't go back to drugs," whispered her bunkmate.

"I'm taking it a day at a time," replied Shannon honestly. She put her arms around Sidney and hugged her warmly. Her journey back had started with their bond. "Thanks for being my friend," she said. "You taught me so much."

Leaving Sidney, Shannon went to admin and, with a shaking hand, slipped her letter of resignation under her father's door.

TWENTY-THREE

HEAVY STONES TO CARRY

FRS

Monday Morning — The start of BFM

After Foley's harsh evaluation, Zack knew now that he had misread everything. He had violated his own sacred rule and allowed a secret to fester in his heart and obscure his better judgment. Thanks to his old mentor, he knew its name at last. Abuse. He should have seen through his daughter's act. He was the grownup. He was trained to read character and handle tragedy. Seeing the raw look in her eyes after Foley's death, he was certain that Shannon would go in search of a score and that he had to stop her. As soon as the paramedics drove away with Foley's body, Zack rushed out to search for her. Cruising the boardwalk, he had been shocked by the plethora of drug dealers and how young their buyers were. This was the cesspool that had claimed his daughter.

When he entered his office at 0600 on Monday morning, Zack found the envelope Shannon had slipped under his door. He opened it and was not surprised to learn that she was resigning her commission and dropping out of the class. She confessed her lies and exonerated him from any knowledge of her crimes.

He called both her cell and her landline at the BOQ, with no results. Panic flooded his mind. It was all coming to a head. His deceit was finally catching up with him. He had destroyed his daughter's life and his own for one pitiful reason: he couldn't come to terms with the past.

He went out onto the tarmac where the sun was yet to show its face. Navy mechanics were already pouring over the four FA/18s that would be employed in today's drill. The sky was a moody mix of night becoming day. He heard the bleating of a distant ambulance, and a dark image invaded his mind like it was yesterday.

The Port Townsend sky had been ominous that time, too, but it had been night, not predawn. He remembered finding his friend Sid in that motel bathroom, hanging from his own belt in the shower. The anger and betrayal Zack had felt at the time returned with a vengeance. The siren became deafening as the ambulance sped by on its way to the base hospital.

Don't be her. Please don't be her.

His one hope was that she would show up to say goodbye to the class. An hour later, when she didn't and Perryman was making the pairings for the day's dogfights, his darkest fantasies took over. Shannon had scored drugs. She could be dead.

The first pair had just gone out, and Perryman was about to call the second pairing when Shannon drove up on her motorcycle in her biker gear, a duffel bungeed to her back fender. His hopes soared like a hawk in liftoff. He had a final chance to turn this around. Leaving the class in Perryman's charge, he walked over to speak to her privately.

"Lieutenant, you know the rules against driving a vehicle onto the tarmac," he said with a grin, hoping to get things started on the right foot. In his youth, he had defied that rule on a regular basis, driving his Triumph 750 at high speeds down the runways.

"My resignation is in your office, sir," she said. "I came to say goodbye to the class." Zack knew he had to act fast. Foley had stopped him from resigning after Sid's death by challenging him to a fight in that musty, old blimp hangar. His testicles could still remember the schoolboy trick that had given Foley the win.

"I don't accept your resignation," he announced flatly. "Get into your flight gear. You and I are up next."

Shannon hadn't expected this. "I don't want to fight you," she said.

It was a lie. She had wanted to dogfight him forever. While other girls played their fantasy games with dolls and toys, she had fantasized about fighting her unbeatable father in any game or competition they engaged in, including one day the ultimate battlefield: aerial combat.

"Afraid you'll lose?" he asked.

Shannon shook her head. "No. I've watched you. You've lost a step. I'm pulling the plug before I hurt myself or someone else."

Zack studied his daughter. Her sapphire eyes revealed no hint of drugs. But he knew that beast could pounce at any time. However, he had made his decision to go to the mat for his daughter, and he would stick with it, even if it meant risking his life. "I'll take my chances," he replied.

His words confused her. "Why are you doing this, sir? I violated my oath. I nearly killed myself and destroyed an $80 million airplane. None of that would have happened if drugs weren't still a problem for me."

"Maybe," he conceded. "My guess is this runs a lot deeper than drugs. I'm hoping we can shake out the bigger picture today." He put his hands together. "Let's keep it simple. If I win, you stay and finish. If you win, you can do whatever you want."

Shannon stared back defiantly. She had been raised by her father on competition. Since he had made her cry at the age of six by performing his ridiculous Māori victory dance, she had always taken his challenges head-on. And when she won, which wasn't often, she rubbed it in his face, just like he'd done to her. This dogfight changed nothing. She remained determined to quit. But to go out with a win over her father would be a triumph she would savor forever.

"It's a deal," she announced defiantly.

Zack grinned. This was all he wanted. "Go change into your flight gear," he instructed.

———

A mile to the south on the sprawling military base, Nickie and Dylan sat cross-legged before the graves of Nickie's parents. Nickie had awakened Dylan with a text asking for a ride to the base, and they had arrived at eight in the morning. During the drive, Dylan had felt his friend's nervous energy but held his questions back for later.

Nickie reached out a hand and touched her mother's and father's headstones with affection before turning her pixie eyes on Dylan. "I got a big decision to make, Bro-Diddly," she warned. "Sidney quit Fleet. She's been assigned to some desk job in Alaska. Her flight leaves in a few hours. She wants me to come with."

"What are you going to do?" he asked, alarmed. He was still grappling with how he would survive losing Shannon. He had not contemplated having to carry on without his sidekick.

"Without flight pay, she won't be making shit," observed Nickie. "I'd have to work. God knows doing what." She paused and her eyes zeroed in on Dylan. "Then there's you. If I go, who's going to take care of you?"

"I'm fine," he argued unconvincingly. He took out a handkerchief and noisily blew his nose. The fever had subsided, but he was still going through withdrawal. So far he had avoided calling his old dealer.

"Yeah, yeah, but what happens when you figure out that Shannon's never coming back?" challenged Nickie. "And she's not."

"You don't know that for sure," protested Dylan.

"Yes, I do," said Nickie. "Because I live in the real world and not in a book I'm writing." She took his hand between hers. "I know you. And I remember what happened the last time."

Dylan looked away. The memory of hitting bottom was still searingly painful to him. The final time he had cut himself he had gone that deeply on purpose. Her name was Naomi. She was Japanese and had skin like white silk. She worked as a waitress and dealt on the side. She was the one who had introduced him to "cutting."

"It's a dance," she told him seductively. "Just you and God. You have to be as careful as a surgeon. I'll show you." She took a razor blade between her fingers. She pointed out a place on her inner thigh. "There's a vein here. Cut it and you're dead." As he held his breath, she sliced into her flesh just wide of the vein. The cut was only an inch long. There were thin scars beside it from the past. Dylan was surprised to see only a tiny line of blood bubble up. "Now you," she said, handing him the blade.

Dylan welcomed the feelings he experienced from cutting. On drugs, he was in a barrel going over Niagara Falls. Then, with one little slice, he was back in his body. *Hello, me. I know you're there because I can feel you.* The night he went too far, cutting had become something more. His life had become void of meaning. He had aimed for that vein.

"Don't talk to me about last times," he warned. Nickie looked away. Her last failed romance had put her in the hospital from an overdose of sleeping pills when her love interest, a college coed, had decided suddenly that she wanted to try the straight life. Dylan had found Nickie in time and rushed her to the base infirmary. That affair, hot and heavy as it had been, was nothing compared to what had gone on with Sidney. His sister had finally found someone who loved her fully.

He suddenly saw it clearly. If there ever had been a time to claim his own self, this was it. He faced his best friend with those earnest sea-colored eyes. "I'll be fine," he said. "Even if I never talk to Shannon again." He hoped he sounded more convincing than he felt. "But if you let Sidney go, I know it will kill you."

Nickie met his eyes, moved by his concern and by the new strength she saw in him. They had survived these hard years entirely because of each other. The idea of a life apart was difficult to imagine. "You're right, Bro-meister. I've never felt like this," she confessed. "I haven't loved anyone this much since my parents died. But how could I live with myself if I got some call that you've started hurting yourself again?"

"I'm not going back to drugs or any of that," Dylan assured her in a tone that rang with more confidence than before.

"I've heard those words before," she reminded him sarcastically.

"This time, I mean it," he insisted. As he went on, he felt his strength growing. "What Shannon does is out of my control. But I have a life now. I'm writing better than I've ever written. I can make it on my own. It will be hard to lose her, but my main job is not to lose me." He made a mental note to use those words in his book. Just as his character was taking shape in real life, his character in his novel was joining the heroic father and daughter at the heart of his story.

At that moment, a bus approached on the road above the cemetery.

Dylan put his hands on Nickie's slender shoulders with brotherly affection. "That bus goes right by your place," he said. "If you hurry, you can make that flight."

"Oh, my God, oh, my God," trilled Nickie as she made her decision. They hugged and went through their ridiculous handshake, then she ran for the bus. As it drove away, Dylan felt a longing for his "sister" that was physically painful. But his decision felt right. He resolved that, when he left the base, he would drive directly to the fishery and tender his resignation. Then he'd go to New York to finish his book.

———

Sidney's exotic eyes with their blue corneas swept anxiously right and left across the large air terminal. In anticipation of the frosty weather that she would soon have to adjust to in her new station in Alaska, she wore her winter dress blue uniform and carried a heavy Navy-issue dark-blue trench coat. She had gotten a big message when her new orders arrived. In the Navy, Adak, Alaska, was the legendary place they threatened to send you if you screwed up. The Navy was making it abundantly clear. Don't waste the government's money learning your heart. She heard the boarding announcement for her flight to Anchorage and grimaced. Time was running out.

Watching others line up, she pulled up a video on her phone that she'd shot of Nickie teaching dance to kids at the Virginia Beach Y. Nickie kept exhorting her young students to shake their booties, shaking hers in an outrageous way that made Sidney laugh every time she saw the clip. As the footage ended, Sidney felt a hand on her arm.

"Lieutenant Lee, we're closing the doors," advised the flight attendant.

"I'll be right there," Sidney assured her, her heart sinking. *This was it.* She had launched herself into space, and she was going to be all alone in Adak, Alaska.

And then she heard a bird-like voice pierce the din of the terminal. "I'm here! Don't go without me!" Sidney turned around to see Nickie approaching the gate at a full sprint. She wore a ridiculous fleece car-coat and Ugg boots in anticipation of the cold weather.

"You came," exclaimed Sidney happily.

"I love you," squealed Nickie.

"I love you, too," replied Sidney huskily. They embraced and kissed, then boarded their flight hand in hand.

The two Super Hornets took up position a mile and a half apart in the "Working Area," fifteen miles off the Virginia coastline. At 40,000 feet, the sky was a Michelangelo blue with clouds by John Constable.

"Before we do this, switch over to 'tech-freak' where only some bored sailor in Guam can hear us," commanded Zack.

"Okay, but I didn't come up here to talk," replied Shannon, shifting to the safe frequency.

Zack's hip tightened painfully. His throat was dry, but he held back a cough. This was going to be the hardest thing he'd ever tried to do. He had two peoples' lives to save today. His daughter's and his own. "Anything from that fishery kid?" he asked casually.

"That's over. Didn't you read my letter?"

"Never saw it," he lied. "For what it's worth, your mom forgave me when I melted down after my friend took his life. I'm sure the fishery kid will forgive you."

"That's not the problem," she explained. "He's been on my side from the beginning. I'm the one who can't forgive me."

"Why, baby?" he inquired softly. "What did you ever do that you can't forgive?"

"To start with, how about being born?" she quipped flippantly.

"You can't mean that," he replied. "You were a remarkable child. Smart. Athletic. Pretty. You ruled the world with those eyes."

Her reply dripped with sarcasm. "That's me, the face with nothing behind it."

"My God, Shannie, where is this all coming from?"

"Do you know what month this is?" she asked pointedly.

"Of course, I know," he answered soberly.

"Wouldn't it be fitting if I died in the same month as Mom?"

"Fitting?" he repeated, shaken. "Why would you say something like that, sweetheart?"

"You were there that last day," she snapped. "Only someone very evil would say things like that to their own mother."

Suddenly they were both time-traveling. It was August 8, 2001. They were in the living room, and Zack was teaching his daughter the fine art of dogfighting using teddy bears in each hand to illustrate his point. At fifty-one, Zack's gray hair was beginning to turn white. At sixteen, Shannon was still tall and slender, but she was becoming a pretty young woman with the athletic figure of a swimmer.

"What's the cardinal rule of dogfighting?" he challenged.

"Lose sight, you lose the fight," answered Shannon.

"Good girl," he said. He hid one of the teddy bears behind his back while the other searched hopelessly for it. "Where'd he go?" he queried in one of his character voices.

"That's not fair, Dad, you didn't say there was a giant to hide behind." With a laugh, she hugged him like she had throughout time, only now she was much taller, and as she attempted a daughterly kiss to his cheek, he turned unexpectedly, and their lips touched briefly.

"I'm sorry," she stammered, pulling away and blushing crimson. "I was trying to kiss your cheek and you turned."

"It's not a big deal, sweetheart," he reassured her. "You used to kiss me on the lips all the time when you were little." Then he looked at her, as though for the first time in a while. She had grown several inches in the past year and developed modest curves. An awkwardness fell between them.

At that moment, Paula joined them, pushing a travel suitcase as expertly as if it were an extension of her body. She sensed the tension in the room. "I miss something?" she asked.

"No," said Zack almost guiltily. "We were just playing some darts."

"Well, I'm off, guys," announced Paula brightly. "Big donors meeting at the children's hospital in Atlanta." Her husband and her daughter's faces fell.

"I don't remember you having a meeting," said Zack.

"It just came up. I couldn't get out of it," she explained. "I'll only be gone a few days."

"You told us you were quitting," said Shannon disappointedly.

Paula looked torn. A car honked outside, her airport ride. "I know what I said, but the company is making it very hard to leave," she confessed. "They want me to take over as CEO. The pay is ridiculous."

"How much?" asked Zack.

"A million dollars a year," said the ex-factory girl proudly. "With stock options and a signing bonus." Zack let out a prolonged whistle. Another honk from outside. "That's my taxi," announced Paula. "I have to go. We can talk about this when I get back." She wheeled her suitcase toward the door.

Shannon's chin jutted defiantly. "Don't worry about us, Mom. Dad and I will be fine." She pointedly started setting the table for just two.

Paula laughed. "He's mine, Baby Girl, and don't you ever forget it." She tickled Shannon playfully, but the teenager pulled away violently.

"I'm not a little girl anymore, Mom," she announced defiantly. Suddenly, it all came flooding out. "You're never here when I need you," she shouted. "I have to ask Aunt Casey the things I want to ask you. Dad needs you, too. You know who he talks to when he's sad? And he's sad a lot. Me." Then she said the words that she would never be able to forgive herself for uttering, "Why don't you just go away and stay away forever."

Time stopped. Her words hung in the air like a foul odor.

"That'll be enough of that!" commanded Zack.

Breaking into tears, Shannon ran into her bedroom and loudly slammed the door. Her parents exchanged a look.

"She didn't mean any of that," Zack assured his wife.

"Yes, she did," answered Paula, still smarting from the attack. "And so did you."

"We were both counting on having you back, Shannie especially," he said.

"I could do so much for the children as CEO, Zack," pleaded his wife. "With the money I'd make, Shannon could go to a private school. We could afford help. We could get a bigger house."

"This is more serious than you realize, honey. She's at a critical point in her life." Zack had not known how critical until just moments earlier.

"Why can't you deal with it?" challenged Paula. "You bought her first bra. You explained boys and dating."

"Because I'm part of her confusion," he offered candidly. "And I don't want to be."

"What are you saying?" asked Paula, alarmed.

Zack paused to gather his thoughts. That accidental kiss meant nothing, but the awkwardness that had ensued afterward was a tipoff that times were changing. Shannon had been trying out her flirting skills on him since she entered her teens. But lately this was happening more often. It was totally innocent. He had witnessed the daughters of friends practice their wiles on their fathers first.

"I wanted to be super dad," he explained. "Give her everything I didn't have as a kid. Maybe I did too good of a job of it."

Paula frowned. "What are you suggesting?"

"It's nothing bad. It's just how things have turned out," he said, pausing to marshal his thoughts. "We talk like you and I used to talk. No holds barred. Remember our card games? Our long walks? I do that with her now. That can be confusing to a young mind."

There was a more insistent honk from outside, and Paula went to the window and waved to her driver. "I hear you," she said. "I promise this will be my priority when I get home." She kissed Zack softly on the lips, then hurried out. Zack went to the window and watched the taxi drive away.

In her room, Shannon was regretting her outburst. Lately, her hormonal rollercoaster had been threatening to leave the rails. She had lashed out at her mother like that because she was desperate to have her counsel. Since the family trip to Rehoboth a month earlier, Shannon had begun to be friendly again with boys in her school. The story about her breaking a boy's hand was old news by now, and she had experienced some passes. But she was still struggling with her feelings about sex. Only yesterday, she had set a new record with her Harley on the salt flat, 121 miles per hour. She had it down to a science. She could achieve sexual release every time she teased the line between life and death.

She came out of her room and saw her father at the window, staring into the night. "I feel terrible, Dad."

"I'm not feeling so great myself," he murmured. "We were both pretty hard on her."

"Let's go to Atlanta and surprise her," suggested Shannon. "Can we? Please?"

"Start packing," he said.

Their military hop landed at NAS Atlanta in Marietta, Georgia, at 7 a.m.. Their goal was to surprise Paula before her big 8:30 a.m. meeting at the Children's Cancer Hospital. Rush hour through downtown Atlanta was a slog, so they stepped out of their cab a mile from their destination at 8:19 and tried to make better time on foot. They soon realized that they would be late for her meeting, so they stopped in a corner flower shop across from the children's hospital, and Zack bought a bouquet of two dozen red roses to present to Paula as she emerged from her meeting. They both wrote "I'm sorry" on a small card.

Zack checked his voicemails. There was one from Paula. "Hi, guys, it's me. You won't believe this. They gave me the key to the city. And you'll never guess who was there. Best day ever. Call you later." Zack triangulated her position at the time of her call with his GPS.

"She left the hospital," he reported. "She's just a couple blocks from here." As he spoke, a siren grew louder and louder and a fire truck roared past in the same direction they were walking.

When they rounded the corner, Shannon exclaimed, "Oh, God..." The twenty-five-story building in front of them was on fire. "What building is Mom in?" she shrieked.

Zack consulted his GPS and paled. "That one," he said, the words catching in his throat. As they got closer, they saw figures on a rooftop restaurant twenty-five floors above. Patrons were trapped. It was impossible to make out faces, but Shannon was certain she saw her mother.

As the flames reached the roofline, a desperate couple tried to jump onto an awning, but it collapsed under their weight, and they fell the remaining distance. Shannon stared at the carnage and started screaming at the top of her lungs. It was an unnatural sound. More animal than human.

"I'm sorry, Mommy! Forgive me, Mommy!" she wailed. Zack stared at her. It should have been the first red flag, but he was too caught up in his own horror to register hers.

For Shannon, her mother's death confirmed all the worst things she had ever felt about herself. The pretty face that hid a hollow soul. The weak link in a family of superheroes. The actress. Over the years, whenever she replayed the events of those two days, which she did incessantly, they took on a darker and darker meaning about her character. *What kind of demented creature wishes for her mother's death? What perverted girl plots to steal her father for herself?*

That night, they took adjoining rooms in a nearby hotel to await news from the police. After Zack got the call, he knocked on their connecting door. It opened, and the girl that stood there bore little resemblance to his daughter. She was as pale as a corpse, and her body was as rigid as one. Surprisingly, there was no evidence that she had cried.

"Mom's gone," he told her.

Shannon nodded numbly. That was ancient news. She had pronounced her mother dead at the scene. Zack was struggling with his own feelings. "We'll get through this, sweetheart," he assured her. "It's all right to cry." He opened his arms to console her. When she didn't move, he pulled her to him, but she remained rigid in his embrace. Zack began to sob uncontrollably, but Shannon remained a statue.

In the days that followed, Zack would learn more about his beloved's final day from two different sources. A donor who was at the hospital had seen her talking warmly with a nice-looking older man whose description matched Paula's father. The donor reported that they had left the hospital together. The only employee of the rooftop restaurant to survive the fire happened to be their waiter. He was on a cigarette break when the fire broke out.

"They asked me to take their photo," he told Zack on the phone. "They both kept saying it was the happiest day of their lives."

When Zack and Shannon returned from Atlanta, she disappeared into her room. Besides brief visits to the kitchen and bathroom, she stayed there from when she came home from school and then left for school the next morning. One night, Zack walked in and saw her cross-legged on her bed, playing a video game online. She wore a headset and spoke sharply to her opponent like a soldier in battle. She appeared to be on a better road than he was.

In the weeks and months that followed, she continued to put most of her afterschool energy into her gaming, but she also found time to keep their home tidy and to make microwave meals for them, further confirming that she was healing better than she was.

Now, a decade after Paula's death, Zack and Shannon's Super Hornets roared side by side toward the "Working Area" where they would square off in the air. The chin patrol was barely a memory, but Zack was determined to change that today. He knew this was more than an exercise. This was war. If Shannon was right and drugs still ruled her thinking, then she was a very real danger to him today, along with herself. Dogfights were fraught with enough risk without introducing a wild card.

"I need to get some things off my chest," he began.

"Don't you think it's a little late for that, Captain?" she challenged sourly.

"I pray to God it's not," he replied. "Since Foley died, I've done a lot of thinking. I could have saved us all this pain if I'd been a better father when your mom died."

Shannon wanted none of this. She only wanted to beat him and be done with it. "You don't need to do this, sir. I know what happened."

"I don't think you do," declared her father. "I think you're still judging yourself from the mindset of a child. What happened that day your mom left for Atlanta was totally normal."

"Wishing your own mother dead is normal?" she asked incredulously.

"Yes," he assured her. "You were becoming a woman. You needed your mom. So, you lashed out. It was a cry for help."

Shannon bit her lip to the point of nearly breaking skin. "It wasn't just me. I couldn't stand to see you sad. I thought, if she was gone for good, you'd be happy again."

Zack saw it with a clarity that made him forget to breathe. His therapist's words returned like cannon fire. *Read your Freud.* While he had been making up for his own abusive boyhood by showering his daughter with attention, she was developing the first crush of her life. He knew that every father and daughter experience something like this, but he was angry at himself for not seeing how this would impact his sensitive daughter when she saw her mother burn alive within hours of willing her death.

"I know why you turned against me after she died," he said. "You were punishing yourself for your feelings for me."

Shannon's face contorted with guilt. He had unearthed her secret. She had loved him too much. "You were my world," she blurted. "You were fun. You made me laugh. You were like some movie star who had picked me as his best friend."

"That's how I wanted you to feel," he said. "I wanted you to have everything I didn't have. I wanted to spoil you with love. I just carried the plan a little too far. If I had understood this the day your mother died, we could have worked through all this together."

"If I'm so perfect, why did I become a drug addict?" demanded Shannon as if this said all that was necessary about her character.

"That's on me, too, Shannie," he replied. "I never should have gone to war when you needed me."

Shannon felt her head spin wildly. "It wasn't your choice," she stammered. "The country needed you. President Bush himself—"

"That was bullshit," grunted Zack, his lips twisting sourly. "I called up a favor from your Aunt Casey. Over time I bought into my own lie. The truth is, I chose war over you, baby. I told myself that it was in your best interest, but Foley was right. I did that to feed some unhealed part of me."

Shannon took a moment to absorb the gravity of his confession. When she said those things to her mother, she was a kid crying out for help. That kiss on the lips was an accident, not some sick transgression. She'd had a schoolgirl crush on her dad, nothing more. Who could blame her? He was the most exciting person on the planet.

"Why did she have to die?" she asked tearfully.

"Nobody can answer that," he answered. "We don't get to choose how we die, only how we live. Your mom was looking for her father all her life. Thank God, she found him. And he found her. It's sad their story ended like it did, but your mother was true to herself every day of her life." He let that thought settle, then added, "Now we have to do the same."

Suddenly, Shannon felt like she was flying on her own power. If she could forgive herself for her mother's death, she could forgive herself for drugs and any moral lapses that went with it. If she could do all that, she could love herself without reservation for the first time in her life.

Tears gathered in Zack's eyes. Secrets are heavy stones to carry, abuse arguably the heaviest of all. But that was over. He had fought his last war, which had been against his secret self, and he had won. The taste of this victory was sweeter than any victory he had experienced in war.

"Are you ready to do this?" he injected into the silence, redirecting their focus to the battle to come. "I won't be pulling any punches," he warned. "If I'm wrong and you haven't recovered, we're going to find that out in the next few minutes."

Shannon felt an outpouring of love for her father for giving her this chance at redemption. In the next few minutes, she would need to prove, not only to him, but to herself that she had purged the demons that had driven her through most of her life.

"For the record, I won't be pulling any punches either," she informed him, her chin like the prow of a Viking ship.

TWENTY-FOUR

★ ★ ★

HIDE THE MAYO

THE WORKING AREA

A Dogfight

The two planes took up position a mile and a half apart. On Zack's command, they went to afterburner at the same time, closing at a combined speed of nearly a thousand miles-per-hour. As they passed, Zack said it first. "Fight's on."

"Fight's on," chimed Shannon.

Zack went on the attack right away, deftly somersaulting to put him directly behind her. "I've got tone," he announced cockily.

"Too late," she replied, releasing her counter-measure flares in time to spoil his lock.

"Nice move, One Two," he conceded. "See if you can follow this," he said, rocketing skyward. He saw her take the bait and grinned confidently. He felt good. This was like the old days when they had competed so intensely.

Shannon wanted to laugh as she chased his plane toward the sun. This was the same trick her father had used to outfox the best student from the last class on the day she arrived. Lead his opponent straight up, pulling as many g's as possible to scramble his younger opponent's mind, then pirouette into a lock. By now, she had mastered the mind-blowing speed.

"Haven't you come up with any new tricks in the last ten years?" she taunted.

"Watch this," he warned before executing a "barrel roll" over the top of her plane and appearing like a phantom behind her. "Trigger down," he announced.

She had to admit his move was brilliant, he still had the goods, but she was ready. "Not so fast, Big Spendah," she sang, executing a seven-and-a-half g break turn and rolling ninety degrees. Her body reacted to seven-and-a-half times the force of gravity, distorting her face like a bad face lift and burying her slender body into her seat like a fastball into a catcher's mitt.

And suddenly she was on his ass. "Trigger down," she announced, certain she had him this time, but Zack released his counter-measure flares so quickly that he broke her lock just as neatly as she had broken his, and he was quickly maneuvering for another attack.

"Nice try, One Two," he said. "But I know all your tricks because I taught them to you."

Shannon ransacked her memory for an exception to his words, unable to find one. Then she remembered the teddy bears. *The teddy bears.* A moment later, she saw a fluffy carpet of clouds. Slamming her throttles to idle, she extended her speed breaks and rolled inverted, executing a seven-and-a-half G pull toward those clouds.

Zack looked around. He had taken his eye off her for only a split second, and she was suddenly nowhere to be seen. "Where the hell are you?" he demanded.

"Behind the giant," Shannon replied cagily.

Unseen by him, her FA/18 cruised at minimum speed under that carpet of clouds.

Suddenly, she slammed her throttles into afterburner.

In his rearview, Zack saw her plane loom large behind him like a shark bearing down on a swimmer. "What the hell?" he gasped.

Shannon achieved a radar lock and fired her simulated cannon. "Trigger down," she crowed. "Pardon the expression, but I just 'rock-raped' you, Captain."

Zack was wide-eyed. No one had ever beaten him in a dogfight—not in war and not in training. His daughter had just annihilated him. Old West style. It hadn't even been close.

"Bravo! Bravo!" he cheered. "That move was so good it should have a name," he suggested expansively over the common frequency.

Watching the monitors with the rest of the class, Taylor had seen it from every angle. "How about 'Hide the Mayo?'" he offered respectfully.

Zack laughed at the suggestion. Then he addressed his daughter, "Where the hell did you come up with that one, Lieutenant?"

"Don't you remember? The teddy bears?" Shannon prodded.

Zack remembered now. It was the day Paula left for Atlanta. He shook his head proudly. The awe he felt for his daughter swelled in his chest. There was no lingering doubt that she had won her battle with drugs. She had just proved that she was everything he and Paula had dreamed of, and much more.

The two FA/18s touched tarmac a few seconds apart. As Zack and Shannon descended their ladders, they both saw a familiar helicopter drop menacingly out of the sky like an alien spaceship. Topper Daniels emerged wearing a bomber jacket, waving to the students and instructors like a short and pudgy General MacArthur making his promised return to the Philippines. The spring in his step and the happy focus of his tiny eyes were not encouraging.

Shannon watched as Taylor broke ranks with his classmates and jogged over to his father. From their talks, she knew he never stopped hoping that his father would show up simply to cheer him on.

Taylor saluted smartly. "Dad . . . sir . . . What're you doing here?"

"I have good news, Tay," drawled SECNAV. "The F-35 is yours."

"Dream on, Dad," said Taylor. "Shannon just beat her father. It was incredible. There's nobody alive who can fly like that."

Topper thrust a manilla envelope into his son's hands. "Read that," he ordered. "The NSA tracked down some gay guy she married in Mexico so she could come into the Navy under the radar. They found a college classmate who says she was hooked on drugs and sold it to pay her way. She nearly killed herself and three others in a small plane the day she graduated from college. Drugs were found, but her father covered it up. We nailed them, Tay. The girl might get off with a dishonorable, but America's Favorite Son should serve time."

Taylor looked like he might become sick to his stomach.

Topper turned away from his son and approached Zack and Shannon. "I hear I missed one hell of a dogfight," he began in his oily way, then his rodent eyes narrowed. "It is my duty to inform you that, when I return to the Pentagon, I will be filing charges against both of you for lying to the Navy."

Zack and Shannon shared a somber look. They had fought their way back to being a family again, only to be threatened with jailtime. And so, they were shocked when an unexpected advocate joined their cause.

"No, Dad, I can't let you do this," announced Taylor.

"She lied to the Navy," insisted Topper righteously.

"So did I," replied his son, his courage growing and his delivery with it. "I switched urine samples a few months ago. I did it all the time at the Academy."

Topper's face grew crimson. Spittle flew from his plump lips. "Why?"

"Because you taught me that no trick is too dirty if you end up on top. Winner takes all. The great American way." Taking a breath, Taylor resumed, "Except it was never meant to be so dog-eat-dog. There was supposed to be a decency to how we deal with each other."

Topper looked like every artery in his body was about to burst. At twenty-three, he had been all but disowned by his elite family when he bilged out of OCS, and it had taken Herculean measures to climb the civilian ranks to the office of Secretary of the Navy. Even then, his family, all heroes of naval aviation with lineage to John Paul Jones, hadn't welcomed him back into their fold. He remained a family joke. But he was set on putting a Daniels in the White House. Then watch his family squirm like roaches to get back in his favor.

"Just stick with our plan, Tay," hissed SECNAV.

"Or what?" challenged his son. Taylor saw his father's hands ball into fists at his sides. From a childhood of abuse, he knew what was coming next. As Topper tried to slap him, Taylor caught his wrist, and their eyes locked ferociously.

Shannon and Zack watched their exchange, knowing the outcome would determine their fate.

"No more," declared Taylor in a quiet voice that rang with power and confidence. "I'll give the Navy my best," he declared. "But then I'm going into my music full time."

"How dare you?" bellowed his father imperiously. "I dedicated my life to giving you the glory that should have been mine. Now you put a knife in my back like the rest of my family?"

"I'm not putting a knife in your back," insisted his son. "I don't understand you, but I love you, Dad. I just can't be you."

Topper knew how to play dirty. He'd built an empire on it. "I can put you in jail along with them for what you told me."

"Go ahead," threatened Taylor. "Then watch me bring down your world."

Topper stared up at his much-taller son, righteous fury slowly giving way to political reason. A spark of pride appeared in his eyes. *He had raised a strong son.* "Carry on," he grunted before marching toward the helicopter.

As his father flew away, Taylor turned to face Shannon and her father. He tore the document in his hands to shreds and tossed it like confetti in the air. Then he squared his shoulders and saluted Shannon. The gesture said it all. They still had Night Quals, but she had won their war.

Shannon returned the salute. As she and her father found themselves alone they exchanged relieved grins. Then Zack remembered the terms of their deal. If she won, she had the right to do anything she wanted, including quit. "Well? What's it going to be?" he asked. "Do we see this out together?"

Shannon faced him. There was no veil between them anymore. They were the fearless chin patrol. "I want to finish," she announced without reservation. "I want the Strike Fighter. I want to make a difference like you and Mom."

"That's my girl." They embraced heartily. Their dream had survived.

Their family had survived. "I wish your mom could see this," he whispered.

Shannon's emotions were too full to reduce to words, but she felt her mother's presence in the moment. She felt her complete and total forgiveness. By embracing her long-lost father on the final day of her life, Paula had sent her daughter a message across time and space to mend fences with her own father before it was too late. She knew her mother would applaud her choice of character. Shannon thanked her for blazing the way for her. If Paula hadn't made her brave journey, none of this would have happened.

Shannon knew that she had come a long, long way. She was locked into her sobriety. She had won the coveted F-35 Strike Fighter. She and her father were a family again. When the dust cleared, she planned to tell the Navy about her past. Shed every secret. It would put her fate in Topper Daniel's hands, but with her Aunt Casey's support, maybe she would survive that test.

Yet as far as she had come, there was another step she needed to take if she were to achieve her greatest dream, the unattainable phase four of her masterplan. However, she had already closed the door that led into that chamber. Dylan had known her so much better than she knew herself. He had loved her unconditionally. But she had broken their trust the night she had retreated into her secrets, instead of his embrace.

Zack was the first to see the figure standing at the chain-link fence guarding the tarmac. Then Shannon saw him, too, and a sigh escaped her lips. It was the fishery kid. How he happened to be on base was a mystery, but there he was. And now, after resolving her issues with her father, Shannon saw him in an entirely new light. With the glittering Atlantic spread out behind him, he seemed taller and more firmly planted on his own chosen road.

Dylan waved and she waved back. Leaving the cemetery, he had passed the airfield just as Shannon drove onto the tarmac to say goodbye to her classmates. *Keep driving. Don't even look over there.* But how could he not see how his story would turn out? Parking the truck, he planted himself outside that metal fence and held his breath until Shannon had made her decision to accept her father's challenge. Seeing their faces as they emerged from their cockpits, he knew that she had won their battle, and that they had resolved their issues. But it wasn't until seeing SECNAV's helicopter fly away, that he remembered to breathe.

"What are you waiting for?" asked Zack. Shannon broke into a wide smile.

Her feet flew under her. Even wrapped in her G-suit, she felt gloriously freed from the cement shoes of the past. She was no longer inferior to her famous parents. She was no longer strangled with guilt for a child's infatuation with a bigger-than-life father. She no longer blamed herself for the inflammatory words she had said to her mother on the eve of her death. She was no longer on the rat's wheel called recovery. She was beyond all that. She was a woman in love for the first time in her life.

Dylan saw her coming, and his heart started beating so hard he was afraid he might pass out. Out of habit, he cautioned himself not to read too much into anything. *Take it one second at a time.* Seeing a gate a short distance away that was guarded by a Marine, he ran toward it.

Shannon squeezed by the Marine and embraced Dylan so explosively that they almost fell over.

Their mouths came together in an awkward kiss. They laughed like high schoolers and tried again with more precision.

Dylan had not planned this, but it felt right in every way. His slow journey with this woman had taught him that love is supposed to come with some old-fashioned flourishes. Zack Mayo's biography gave him the perfect idea.

He suddenly lifted her in his arms.

"What are you doing?" exclaimed Shannon, laughing because she knew exactly what he was doing.

"It worked for your mom," he said, spinning her in his arms until the world became a blur to their eyes.

"I love you," she burst out joyfully. It had been a lifelong journey to love herself. Now she could finally love a man other than her father. Dylan had already declared his love on many occasions, so he felt no urgency to say it now. Spinning her in his arms like this was enough.

Their eyes said it all. The road ahead would not be easy. They would be on separate coasts and then, in all likelihood, separate continents.

Shannon would be risking her life in war. Dylan would be waiting tables until Celeste Stein sold his book. They had done the impossible by beating drugs and surviving the tests of the past year. But could they defeat the tests of time?

Their eyes contained the answer. If anyone could do it, they could. Theirs was no ordinary love. They had built their fortress brick by brick from the ground up.

Dylan stopped spinning her and brought his lips to hers. Shannon gave into that kiss without reservation. She had made it to phase four.

Watching them, Zack felt a sense of liberation greater than flight. He wasn't afraid of retirement anymore. He welcomed it. Sixty was still young if you kept yourself in shape. A second career? Not as some gladhander for the airlines. He would find a way to make an impact on the world in a whole new way, one far removed from war. Another shot at love? Maybe Casey would take his call now that he had "fixed it." Or maybe he would always be just a one-woman man.

Watching the lovers run hand in hand to their waiting truck and drive away, Zack Mayo was besieged with images of himself teaching an army of grandchildren his arsenal of tricks.

Check it out, Pokrifki. Just check it out.

THE END

ACKNOWLEDGMENTS
———— ★ ★ ★ ————

My ability to write a story about a young woman navigating this difficult modern age would not have been possible without my daughter, Shady Day Stewart, who introduced me to the magic of father and daughter love. Thanks to my sons, Dylan Stewart and Sean Stewart, whose own remarkable talents as writers challenge me on a daily basis not to fall behind my times.

Special thanks to American Indian Shaman Andrew Soliz who turned my life around when he blew the ashes of a dog into my face to help me forgive myself, something that needed to happen before I could ever achieve love in my life or do my best writing.

I want to deeply thank my friend and military advisor, Roman Solohub, for inspiring me to write a sequel to my movie *An Officer and a Gentleman* by sending me his own effort to do so in a box with a bottle of Angel's Envy bourbon and a Cuban cigar. To understand the unique challenge of flying the FA/18, Roman introduced me to ex–Top Gun, Lance Kelly, who inspired many of the action sequences of the book from his true-life experiences.

I will be eternally grateful to Martin Caan, my agent and manager over four decades and the man who sold the original film to Paramount. Marty saw the potential of this sequel in the earliest draft and spent five years reading and offering suggestions to the innumerable drafts that followed.

This book would never have been possible without the support and psychological insight offered by Dr. Eric Bellman whose wise counsel helped me understand the core issues in a father-daughter relationship.

My close friend and personal editor Camille Komine was with me from the start, helping me shape my story and providing invaluable insight into my central character's heroic struggle.

Thanks to my literary agent Matt Bialer for his very personal connection to my story and his diligence in finding the right publisher.

Thanks to Blackstone Publishing's Brendan Deneen, who was a big fan of my film and saw the potential of a sequel before anyone else in the publishing world.

In the final stages of writing this book, editor Jennifer Fisher challenged me to reach deeper into my characters and helped me navigate touchy subjects without sacrificing my own integrity.

Thanks to my Blackstone editor, Windy Goodloe, for her careful final pass. And to Blackstone's publicity director Sarah Bonamino, and marketing director Rachel Sanders, for their remarkable professionalism.

Finally, this list would be incomplete without the name of my friend Lou Gossett Jr., the first black man to win the Academy Award for best supporting actor for his role as drill instructor from hell, Sergeant Emil Foley. Lou's friendship over the years gave me invaluable insight into what the character of Sergeant Foley would be like in his later years. Sadly, Lou recently passed away.